A Place Like Jarrahlong

S. E. Jenkins

Published by FeedARead.com Publishing – Arts Council funded.

A CIP catalogue record for this title is available from the British Library.

This book is a work of fiction. Names, characters, businesses, organisations, places and events are either the product of the author's imagination or are used fictitiously. Any resemblance to actual persons, living or dead, events or locales is entirely coincidental.

For Tony, who keeps the laptop running;
for my family and friends, always supportive;
and for Kathy and Malcolm, with happy
memories of my stay at Wonganoo.

Author's Notes

During the twentieth century successive British Governments sent more than seven thousand boys and girls to orphanages and farm schools in Australia. In November 2009 Kevin Rudd on behalf of the Australian Government offered an apology for the physical and emotional abuse many of these child migrants received at the hands of their carers. Three months later, in February 2010, Gordon Brown, on behalf of the British Government, expressed regret for the "misguided" Child Migrant Programme and offered a formal apology to more than one hundred and thirty thousand children sent out to former colonies, including Australia, from the 1920s to 1970. In 1987 Margaret Humphreys, author of "Empty Cradles" published in 1994, founded the Child Migrants Trust which campaigns for children and their families sent to Australia under the Child Migrant scheme.

In October 1953 the British Government carried out two nuclear tests at Emu Field, part of the Woomera Rocket Range in South Australia. Despite efforts to evacuate all Aboriginals in the area there were families in the vicinity at the time of the testing who were exposed to the radioactive fallout. They report suffering from nausea, vomiting, fever, diarrhoea, rashes and general malaise. Some were temporarily blinded and others miscarried their unborn babies, and yet others developed cancers. Some children born in the months and years after these nuclear tests were found to have genetic abnormalities as were some children born to later generations. Military and civilian personnel exposed to radioactive fallout at this time were similarly affected.

PROLOGUE

[November 1951]

Jon Cadwallader's mind wasn't on chess; he stifled a yawn, blinked hard a couple of times and leaned back in his rattan chair. Over to the west the sun was sinking beyond the great jarrah trees, casting a familiar vermilion glow – that had been one of the first things to strike him about Australia, the magnificent sunsets.

Alice Macarthur looked up from the chessboard. 'Stan found his El Dorado, didn't he?'

Jon caught the penetrating look in her eyes and hesitated. It was almost a year since he'd discovered Stan Colley's gold reef, eleven months after he'd inherited Stan's mine and the mining rights to the whole of Yaringa valley, but, even so, her question had caught him off guard. 'What makes you think that, Alice?'

She nodded towards his hands. 'You don't get grazes like those working with Merinos and all that lanolin keeps hands soft as silk. Besides, why else would you choose to live in Stan's shack for so long?'

'Isn't having my own place enough?'

She drew on one of the cheroots she favoured; the end glowed as she inhaled the acrid smoke and waited.

He turned back to the chess, avoiding her gaze. Alice was as sharp as barbed wire and as tricky to handle; she'd probably known for ages, and had been waiting for him to tell her. He was surprised she hadn't asked before. But should he tell her the truth? She wasn't likely to break a confidence and she certainly knew how to keep her own counsel, she'd done it often enough with him.

'I wouldn't have found it except for Stan's last request.' He still had the letter he'd found in Stan's ironbark trunk outlining his last wish, and then it had taken him eleven months to get around to it, eleven months of guilt and disturbed nights when Stan turned up in

1

dreams nagging him about his failure to carry out his dying wish.

'And what was his last request?'

'To carve his name and dates deep in No Hope mine, in the lightning-strike cavern.'

Alice chuckled. 'That's Stan for you; so, is it a big reef?'

'Pretty big.'

'You told anyone?'

'No.' He hadn't even written and told Merle. He smiled at the thought of her, Merle McGhee with her long, auburn hair and green eyes, the woman he was going to marry just as soon as she'd qualified. He was saving the good news; he wanted to see the surprise and pleasure on her face when she learned he was wealthy and owned a station. She'd be a qualified doctor in a year. The timing was almost perfect, a few months to finish mining the gold and sell it and buy a place of his own.

Alice eyed him expectantly. 'You wouldn't want some tin-pot prospector jumping your claim, would you?'

'No,' he said, 'imagine the place; it'd look like Gilbert's Find over on Harrison Station. The land'd be ruined. I don't suppose you'd want an opencast mine next to your boundary either – all the noise and the muck – it'd upset the sheep.'

'I thought you hated mining?'

'I do. It scares the hell out of me.'

It had been his terror of confined spaces, his reluctance to re-enter the narrow passageways in No Hope that had led to the long delay in finding the reef in the first place, and in the year since then he'd only mined the gold in his spare time so no one suspected the truth about the mine. Except Alice had, damn her!

'So how do you do it?'

'Block my mind. I think about anything except mining.' He didn't tell her that he talked to himself when the panic threatened to kick in.

'What's the quality like?'

He pulled out a nugget from his trouser pocket and rolled it on the table.

She leaned across and picked it up in gnarled fingers and dropped it into the palm of her other hand, the gold gleaming in the light from the kerosene lamp she preferred to use in the evenings. 'It's a beaut. I'd say almost pure gold. How big is the reef?'

'About four inches deep in places with nuggets like that, the size of walnuts and bigger.'

'There much left to go at?'

'Plenty.'

Alice frowned. 'You turn up with a large amount of gold to sell and you'll have everyone watching you. Your secret will be out; Charlestown will be a boom town again and there'll be prospectors crawling all over the place.'

'I know, Alice, that's what's bothering me.'

'What would Stan have wanted?'

'It left alone.'

'Aye,' she said, 'I reckon he would – besides there's more than one way to invest in a place.'

'That's what I thought.'

'What do you plan to do when you've worked the seam dry?'

'Do you need to ask?'

'Buy a pastoral lease?'

'Yeah, a place like Jarrahlong, Alice.'

PART I

[May 1952 – January 1953]

CHAPTER 1

Jon stood at a crossroads in Kalgoorlie on a cool May morning and
took stock. The gold mining town was busy with local traffic and
people going about their daily business. He adjusted the haversack
on his shoulder and, ignoring his jittery belly, spat into the dust.
There was a lot at stake and if he got it wrong he'd live to regret it.

Six months back it had been Alice Macarthur's suggestion to sell
the gold in Kalgoorlie and in Leonora, a sizeable amount in each
place, but not enough to arouse suspicion if anyone noticed. Watch
out for blokes too interested in what you're doing, or not interested
enough, she'd said.

Stan Colley, the old fella who'd left him No Hope mine, had said
much the same thing. According to him men died because of gold,
he always reckoned it brought out the worst in them.

But there was more than gold at stake. If anyone got so much as a
sniff that Stan's valley wasn't as worked out as everyone thought
there'd be a stampede. Prospectors would be filing for mineral
leases on Alice's station and on Jindalee land next to Yaringa
Creek, and then all hope of saving the valley and its Dreaming
would be gone.

He hitched up his trousers, squared his shoulders and crossed the
wide main street. It was cooler still inside the jeweller's shop; an
ancient fan clanked its way unnecessarily through the chilly air.
Jon waited while the man in front of him was served.

'Not bad for a month's work,' said the bloke behind the counter.

'Aye, found a good patch, Connor, but dry-blowing's a killer on
the back, it's a young man's game if you ask me.'

Connor finished weighing the alluvial gold. 'Thirty pounds and
five shilling do you?'

'Aye, it'll have to do.' The prospector, a middle-aged bloke running to fat, picked up the notes and slipped the coins into his back pocket.

'Don't go spending it all on drink and fast women. There're plenty of whores on Hay Street able and willing to separate you from your hard won cash.'

'A man's got to have some relaxation,' said the prospector as he stuffed the notes into a battered wallet. 'Be seeing you next month, mate; let's hope gold prices are a bit higher by then.'

Connor turned to Jon as the bloke left the shop. 'Now then young fella me lad, what can I do for you? Found a mother-lode have you?'

Jon shook his head and took out a large, worn leather pouch stiff with age. He dropped it on the counter where it landed with a heavy thud. 'Just wondered if this is the real thing or fool's gold.'

'Don't you know the difference?'

'Reckon it looks right, but you never know.'

Connor tipped out the nuggets onto the counter and gave a long, low whistle. 'I haven't seen this quality in a while.' He picked up a sizeable nugget. 'Reckon it's as pure as it comes. This didn't come out of a creek bed, did it?'

'Wouldn't know, found it in a trunk I was left. What's gold selling for at the moment?'

Connor nodded in the direction of the board behind him. He weighed the gold. 'You've got a fair bit here all right and it looks pretty pure. I'll pay you top whack.' He counted out a large wodge of notes. 'I hope you're not going to do what matey's planning on doing.'

Jon grinned. 'Not likely.'

'You be careful,' said Connor, watching Jon fold the notes and stash them away, 'it's one hell of a lot of money you'll be having there.'

Out in Hannan Street Jon breathed more easily, there'd been no one around to see the deal. The problem would come later with future transactions, when word got round that a young fella was regularly bringing in large amounts of gold. Maybe he ought to find other places besides Kal and Leonora to sell it, spread it thin and hope no one talked.

Jon left Kalgoorlie at midday for Leonora. He'd been too wound up to eat earlier but now he was ravenous and he had no food with him, and no prospect of getting any until Broad Arrow or Menzies.

On the drive north he thought of Alice. Since he'd moved out of Jarrahlong into Stan's shack at Yaringa Creek they'd become closer. They still played chess regularly and over the years he'd known her he'd become a passably good player, certainly good enough to give her a run for her money. She enjoyed the challenge as much as he did and it was worth the hour's drive to Jarrahlong every Friday. They still had the same business arrangement except now he worked out of Yaringa Creek, the 'outstation' she called it, and she continued to pay him jackaroo rates, plus bonuses, for looking after the sheep over on the west side of the station, for maintaining the bores and helping with the big jobs, mustering for crutching, shearing and dipping the sheep, anything that required extra stockmen. She knew she could rely on him, not like that good-for-nothing relative of hers, Greg Morton, who spent all his spare time, and some, playing two-up. Greg had a problem; even Les Harper who ran the two-up ring in Charlestown reckoned he had. Les had warned Alice, and so had he, not that she listened to either of them.

Jon reached Leonora in the late afternoon and checked into the hotel where he and Stan had stayed not long before Stan's death. After a quick wash he went out for a short walk before dinner, heading for Tank Hill. The town hadn't changed since his last visit; the familiar landmarks were still the same but, according to Stan, it was nothing like the early days in 1903 when it was a fast-growing town of wood, tin and hessian shacks, brick built hotels and business establishments and the big rush was on.

He still missed Stan and his reminiscing about the old times. In the months they'd known each other he'd become fond of the old fella – he was the grandfather he'd never had and Stan had no family to speak of either. The friendship had suited them both, but he'd never expected the old man to leave him his mineral lease and all his other worldly goods. Who would have thought that a twenty-one-year-old fella like him, who'd been sent to Australia as an eight-year-old kid by the British Government, would end up owning a gold mine with No Hope's potential – it was incredible, he still couldn't believe it.

The sun sank below the horizon as he made his way back to the hotel and dinner. Belly rumbling, he stepped into the hotel lobby

9

and crossed the fancy mosaic floor into the saloon.

The Victorian hotel had been built on the back of the gold rush at the turn of the century. The bar, a huge affair, dominated the room and in front of it was a row of stools. The place was packed with men drinking away the dust from a day's work and catching up on the news. Most of them were from the gold mines operated by the big companies, but a couple he'd recognised from before, local blokes, a retired miner and the other, a lone prospector, in for an evening tipple and a bit of company.

Jon ordered a beer and checked the price of gold written up in chalk behind the bar. Along the counter men were arguing over government taxation and rising prices, the place was too busy to even consider flogging his gold, better to wait awhile; maybe tomorrow it'd be quieter.

His end of the bar was empty, just him and a middle-aged sot who'd had a skinful; the fella stank of booze and his filthy clothes were stiff with sweat. He sat hunched over an empty glass staring into the bottom of it and every now and again he waved an unsteady hand in the direction of the barman.

'Enoshther whisky,' he slurred for the third time.

The barman ignored him until he thumped his fist on the bar making the empty glass jump.

'I shed I'll have enoshther whisky.'

'You've had enough, Chips,' said the barman, removing the empty glass.

'I'ss sshalll be the shjuuudge,' slurred Chips.

The barman rang a bell next to the till and soon after a bloke appeared from a back room. 'Get him to his bunk, Sam, before he falls down.'

Sam came round to Chips's side of the bar. 'Come on, Chips, let's get you to bed.'

'Dinner,' Chips slurred, 'haven't had m'dinner.'

'I'll bring it up on a tray,' said Sam, 'silver service just how you like it.' He eased Chips off the stool and half leading, half supporting, guided Chips out of the bar.

'Another beer, mate?' asked the barman.

'Thanks,' said Jon. 'Who's that fella?'

'Chips Carpenter. The locals call him Chips Lasseter.'

Jon raised a questioning eyebrow.

'He's spent the last ten years or more searching for a gold reef he says he found in the outback.'

'And did he?'

'Your guess is as good as mine. I do know he's spent all his money searching for it. Now he lives on payouts from a family trust fund, he can only go looking once a quarter when the bank draft arrives. He clears his debt with us then spends the rest on flying his plane, quartering the bush, looking for his reef.'

Jon carried his beer into the dining room and tucked into a huge plateful of roast beef. The Lasseter story was legendary. Everyone in the gold mining community knew how, in 1908, the young Lasseter had been found in a bad way by an Afghan camel driver. He'd been clutching a bag of ore and telling of a great reef of gold he'd found in the MacDonnell Ranges. Thirty years later and after two attempts to find the reef again, Lasseter was dead, leaving cryptic letters to his wife indicating the location of his find.

Jon frowned as he finished off his meal. Chips wasn't searching for Lasseter's reef. He was in the wrong area for a start. The Mac-Donnell ranges were in the Northern Territory not Western Australia. Did that mean that Chips was searching for the gold reef in Paradise Canyon? He thought back to the time Curly had taken him there, when he'd found a wrecked plane with a box of gold nuggets hidden in the cockpit. Had Chips been flying it when it crashed? Was it Chips who had hacked the nuggets out of the reef in Curly's sacred cavern and stashed them in the wreckage for safe keeping?

Jon mulled it over as he sipped his beer. He'd only been back to Paradise Canyon once since then, when he'd returned Curly's tjuringa to the sacred Perentie cavern where the gold reef was. The tjuringa, a piece of carved mulga wood that Curly had entrusted into his safe keeping as he lay dying deep in the outback, was Curly's sacred title deed to the land. It showed the journeys of the ancestor in the Dreaming. Curly had known that he, Jon, would never betray the trust placed in him, or the location of the gold. And he wouldn't, but Chips would. One thing was certain, all the facts fitted. He finished his beer and ordered another.

If it was Chips's plane he hoped he never found it. The canyon was a sparkling jewel hidden in the middle of the eastern Ranges, a narrow gorge in the high plateau shaped like a question mark that was sacred to several Aboriginal tribes. According to Curly it lay on the junction of old tribal routes, like a crossroad in the desert, and even in the worst droughts food and water could always be found there. To them the Canyon was more precious than the gold it contained, but if the reef was ever rediscovered then the canyon and its Dreaming would become a wasteland just like the land at Gilbert's Find.

At breakfast, next morning, a cultured voice interrupted him. 'Mind if I join you, young man?'

Jon looked up. Chips Carpenter – sober this time; he nodded towards the empty chair even as Chips sat down.

'I'll have the same again,' Chips called, indicating Jon's breakfast to the barman, and then he turned back to Jon. 'I'm Giles Carpenter, but everyone calls me Chips.'

'Why Chips?'

'Carpenter...chip off the old block...take your pick...and you are?'

Jon hesitated, everyone in Charlestown knew him as Macarthur. 'Macarthur, Jon Macarthur.'

'With that accent, you're from Liverpool. I'm from London,' said Chips, extending a hand.

Jon shook it.

'And what brings you to Australia – same as everyone else here – gold?'

'No, I was sent out by the British Government when I was eight, to an orphanage inland from Perth.'

'Liked the place and stayed, is that it?'

'Something like that.' He didn't elaborate. He preferred not to think about those days, or of the Catholic Brothers who were supposed to care for them. A mental image of Stephen Hicks weeping in his bed and the memory of Father O'Brien's worn soutane rustling as the bastard crept out of the dormitory made him shudder. He shut his mind to the unwelcome recollection and concentrated on finishing breakfast, mopping up the last of his egg yolk with some bread.

'What do you do for a living?' asked Chips, coughing even as he spoke.

Jon wrinkled his nose, Chips's breath stank of grog, the fella must be pickled. 'Jackaroo, on a station out Charlestown way.'

'You're not into prospecting then?'

'No,' said Jon. 'I've got more sense.'

'Don't suppose you've come across a canyon with a wrecked plane, have you?'

'Not too many of those in these parts.'

'What? Wrecked planes or canyons?'

'Now there's a question,' said Jon. He studied the bloke sitting opposite him. His skin was badly mottled with patches of pigmented skin from too much exposure to the sun and his gimlet eyes were watchful even though he appeared unconcerned and relaxed about the topic of conversation. Jon guessed he was about fifty and slimmer than most, underweight even, too much booze and not enough food in his belly. Big problem for him though, selling gold in Leonora wasn't going to be an option, not with Chips breathing down his neck; he'd jump to the wrong conclusion. 'I've not explored that many, only the ones on the station and I haven't come across any wrecked planes. Why do you ask?'

Chips lit up a cigarette. 'Crashed one a while back.'

Jon leaned back in his seat and waited, glad that he'd finished breakfast – smoking was a filthy habit, he'd never really liked it when Mam smoked; she'd always smelt of tobacco too.

'Eleven years ago, to be exact,' said Chips.

'Must be a pretty special plane if you're still looking for it,' commented Jon.

'It isn't the plane, it's the canyon. There's a gold reef there.'

'Don't know why you're telling me. Who's to say I'm not going to go off and stake a claim myself if I ever find your plane.'

'It's not likely,' said Chips. 'For a starter you wouldn't find the reef, it's well hidden, and second, there's more than enough gold to satisfy me, you, and half a dozen others.'

Jon whistled. 'That big, eh?' He avoided the piercing eyes; the man was mad, obsessed…and desperate. Stan had told him often enough of how vast wealth turned men's minds, that the more they had the more they wanted. He couldn't see Chips wanting to share with anyone when it came down to it. That was what Lasseter's problem was. He didn't trust anyone with the co-ordinates and when he died the knowledge went with him.

Jon finished his tea. Chips would need to be damn lucky to find Paradise Canyon. The ironstone and sandstone ranges played havoc with compass bearings and the canyon was so narrow it was easily missed. Even from the air it would be difficult to spot. The route there was also pretty inhospitable and local Aboriginals wouldn't be keen on sharing its secrets. But Chips was right about one thing, the reef in Paradise Canyon was big in comparison to Stan's find at Yaringa Creek.

Jon watched him exhale a stream of smoke. 'How come you can't find the plane? Didn't you file a flight plan?'

'Not for the sort of flying I was doing, canyon hopping, looking for possible sites.'

'So, what happened?' He was curious to know how Chips had got out of the place alive.

Chips's eyes narrowed. 'You ask a lot of questions.'

'Just making conversation, anyway it was you who asked about a wrecked plane.'

Chips stared at him for a long moment, weighing him up, Jon guessed.

'I was trying to land on a plateau and ran out of runway,' he said, back to his easy-going self. 'The last I remember was hanging upside down still strapped into m'seat.' He leaned back as breakfast arrived. 'I was lucky to survive, I can tell you, the plane was matchwood.' He added salt and pepper to his fried egg.

Neither spoke while Chips ate and Jon wondered how much questioning he'd stand. 'Were you injured?' he asked when Chips had finished eating.

Chips shook his head. 'Concussion and bruising mainly, a few scratches, nothing serious.'

'How did you stumble on the gold?'

'Found it when I was searching for food…the reef's almost pure, with nuggets the size of golf balls.'

'A canyon should be easy enough to find,' said Jon.

'Yes, that's what I thought,' said Chips bitterly. 'But I reckon I spent the first eight years looking in the wrong ranges.'

Jon whistled long and low. 'You mean you don't know exactly where you crashed the plane?'

'No.'

'Didn't you take note of your route when you walked out?'

'I didn't exactly walk out. I think I was carried.'

'No wonder folk call you Chips Lasseter! So what do you reckon happened?'

'I was hacking away at one or two of those big nuggets I was telling you about and somehow a piece of rock above me got dislodged, at least that's my theory because when I was found I was wandering along a stretch of road on the edge of the Ranges, dried blood matted in my hair. I had no recollection of getting from the canyon to the road. Some say Abos found me and led me out then dumped me where they knew I'd be found.'

'Why do you think you were looking in the wrong area?'

'Because I've searched every gorge and canyon in those ranges by plane, and on foot, and found nothing, neither the plane wreckage, nor the gold reef. An old timer told me that Aborigines travel vast distances, he reckons my plane's lying in some canyon in another set of ranges.'

'And now you're searching around here?'

'That's right, and after this I'll move on to the north or maybe west, work m'way over the whole area unless I get lucky and someone like your good self comes across the wreckage.'

'Right,' said Jon, collecting his haversack. 'I'll keep a look out for it. What sort of plane is it?'

'Matchwood now.' Chips grinned. 'But it was an old Fokker.'

Jon smiled. 'Nice meeting you, Chips.'

He crossed to the bar and paid his bill conscious of Chips's eyes boring into his back. His earlier thought was right, there was no way he could sell his gold here, or anywhere else in the town. Chips would be on to it in no time and put two and two together and come up with six. It wasn't worth the risk. He'd have to think things through, find some other place to sell his gold.

CHAPTER 2

Edward Scally opened the fly screen door, 'After you, Alice.' He stood aside and ushered her into his bungalow then turned to Jon and nodded in the direction of the battered utility truck parked in the road. 'When are y'going to come to yer senses and sell Stan's lease? It'd bring in a bit and y'could buy yourself some decent transport. I don't know how Alice puts up with travelling in that old rattletrap.'

Jon laughed off the suggestion. 'It's not that bad and while it's still going it'll do me.'

Scally followed him into the kitchen and pulled out a chair for Alice to sit on as Rachel appeared from the back room.

'Hello, Alice, Jon, nice to see you both,' she said.

'Pull up a seat, Jon,' Scally indicated one by the dresser. 'Well then, Alice, what brings y'into town? I haven't seen y'since the last film show, a month back.'

'Business, I needed to arrange a bank draft for the new Merinos I'm buying in. You got the kettle on, Ed? I wouldn't say no to a cuppa.'

'It won't be a tick, the kettle's almost boiling,' said Rachel.

'Wool's selling well, I hear.' commented Scally.

'Could say that, and with the rainfall up these last few months we've had good grazing for a while now, you know we've gone for split shearing this year.'

'Aye, I had heard. Why is that, Alice?'

'Greg's keen, he reckons it's the easier option, anyway, we sheared half the mob last March, as usual, and we're doing the other half this spring, September probably.'

Jon scowled, he hadn't agreed with the decision, it wasn't as if Alice's mob was a particularly big one, shearing hadn't ever been

16

unmanageable and in his view it made lice control that much more difficult. A split shearing ultimately meant more work for everyone on the station and the divided mob would have to be kept apart for a while if there wasn't to be reinfestation of the treated sheep, but he kept his mouth shut. He didn't understand Alice. She didn't need to keep Greg sweet, but for some reason she wanted to. Greg might be Alice's great-nephew and her own flesh and blood but, even so, she was far too soft with him.

'I take it Cadge Coles was all right about it,' said Scally.

'Yes, he said he could fit it in.' Alice caught Rachel's eye as she made the tea. 'Where's that son of yours?'

'Joe? He's with Ty over on Harrison Station.'

'He's a bit young to go trapping dingoes, isn't he?'

'That's what I reckon,' muttered Scally, watching his daughter pouring water into the pot.

Rachel carried a laden tea tray over and set it on the table. 'It's only a short trip, three days at most. David Kenton thinks there's a dingo got pups out on the ridge so Ty's taken a ride over. He'll be back tomorrow; besides, Joe loves going with him.'

'And Ty doesn't mind Joe tagging along?' said Alice.

'No, Ty likes the company. Talking of family, how's Bindi doing, Alice? We haven't seen her for a while.'

'She's fine. Alistair is pleased with her progress, says she soaks up everything like a sponge.'

'You're looking well, Rachel,' said Jon.

She patted her swollen belly. 'Positively blooming, eh?'

He blushed, at least their relationship had improved since she and Ty Henderson had got together. He was glad she was settled, she was the sort marriage suited and she was a nice person, her sunny personality had reminded him of his sister, Kathy, when he'd first met her and now she and Ty were having a child of their own.

He looked at her speculatively as she poured the tea, had she told Ty that Berry Greenall was Joe's father? He brushed the thought aside; it wasn't his business, only hers, and Ty's, if she chose to tell him. Scally didn't know, of that he was certain, because he and Berry were still on speaking terms and Scally wasn't the sort to tolerate reprobates. He smiled, remembering Scally's furious accusation only a couple of hours after he'd arrived back in Charlestown following his trip to England, when Scally hauled him out to Alice's place, presented Rachel and her baby, called him a libertine and threatened him with Alice's shotgun if he didn't do the honourable thing. His brow furrowed, and now Berry had moved on to Val, the bastard!

'What're you scowling at?' asked Alice.

'Indigestion,' he lied.

'You shouldn't have wolfed down your breakfast,' she said drily.

Jon accepted a cup of tea from Rachel and forced a smile.

Alice turned her attention to Scally. 'You don't know how lucky you are, Ed, having your family around you. It's lucky Ty's the placid type, not many young fellas would be happy to move in with a miserable old so-and-so like you.'

'Works both ways, Alice. Ty knows I'll look after Rachel and Joe while he's away trapping dingos. In any case, I like the company.'

'And he's not an old so-and-so, Alice. Are you Dad? You're just an old softie.'

Jon noticed the slight flush under Scally's tan as he avoided Rachel's doting smile.

'Talking of offspring I've heard Val's got herself up the duff,' said Scally.

Shocked, Jon turned to look him, 'You mean pregnant?' Embarrassed he gulped down the hot tea, his mind racing. Why should he care what Val did? She wasn't his responsibility; she was old enough to make her own decisions. But he couldn't understand the woman, what was she thinking of, going with that, that…libertine!

'You heard anything, Alice?' asked Scally.

'Not much more than you; I picked it up in The Grand not half an hour ago.'

'Cadge told me, and he should know. He sez Berry's been shouting his mouth off. If you ask me he should make an honest woman of her,' said Scally.

'Maybe he's offered,' said Alice.

'Can't see it m'self. Berry's not the marrying type. I'm surprised he's hung around Val this long – how long is it now that she's been on the road with him?'

Alice's brow creased as she gave it some thought. 'Since just after Larry Simpson died.'

'Aye, reckon y're about right there, Alice.'

Jon kept out of the conversation; he hadn't understood at the time why Val had decided to go with Berry and Cadge and the rest of the shearers, travelling from station to station, doing the cooking. Not that she was a bad cook; she'd been good enough to get a job

18

working in the ship's galley when she'd sailed out of Southampton.

'She only went with Berry because Jon wasn't interested,' said Alice. She turned to Jon and tapped the table for emphasis. 'You're too wrapped up in that Merle woman back in Liverpool, that's your problem.'

He already knew Alice's feelings on the subject. She had never understood his ambivalence towards Val, not that he'd ever bothered to explain that he was like Stan had been, a one-woman man.

'Val and me are just mates,' he snapped, recalling the time he'd first met her and Merle – the time he'd returned to Liverpool to find his sister, but that was four years ago. Val Rayner had been working in a bakery then and Merle had been on the point of going to medical school.

'Seems to me you've got blinkers on,' commented Alice, pulling him out of this thoughts of Merle. 'Val's a good woman; you shouldn't ignore her like you do.'

'I don't ignore her.' It was next to impossible to ignore her. Ever since she'd arrived in Charlestown three years back she'd been in the thick of everything, flirting with anyone in trousers, befriending all the women in the district, organising fashion shows, buying in a hair-dryer and organising the occasional ladies' weekends in The Grand. Hair and nails in the morning, with luncheon organised by Connie, and followed by a fashion show in the afternoon, and then, in the evening, a dance or a film show when the women got to show off their finery and new hairdos and the men got an eyeful of the women done up like dogs' dinners. No, Val was all right, as a mate, but she wasn't Merle. He wished to God it had been Merle who had taken it into her head to emigrate and not Val.

He frowned. In Merle's last letter she'd once again written of her doubts about living in Australia, of it being too far from home, but at least she hadn't mentioned Paul Vincent, the chap who'd taken her to the Philharmonic a few times.

'Worst thing that ever happened,' said Alice.

'What?' asked Jon, jolted back to the present.

'Larry Simpson going and dying like he did. Who'd have thought that skinny fella had a heart problem. You know I suggested to Val that she should buy Larry's shop, I even offered to act as guarantor, but she wouldn't have it, said she didn't have enough savings behind her to put in an offer, she didn't want to be beholden to anyone.'

'No point anyway,' said Scally. 'Larry's brother wouldn't sell, reckoned it was a gold mine.'

'Well, he was right, it was when Larry died. You just think about what Val did for Simpson's.'

'That's right,' chipped in Rachel. 'She had a real eye for fashion; picked clothes in styles and colours she knew would sell.'

'And then there was the film club,' said Alice. 'Look how she chivvied Wes and Connie to get that reinstated. More social life meant more new clothes sold – men's, women's and children's. No, Fred Simpson was right, it was a gold mine.'

Scally finished his tea and put the empty cup back on the saucer. 'Yeah, well, he doesn't have Larry's business sense, does he?'

'You mean he didn't appreciate what he had in Val. Business dropped off the minute he sacked her, no one wanted the clothes he bought in – old fashioned, cheap stuff it was, even I wouldn't touch it,' said Alice, 'no wonder Berry wore her down.'

Scally rolled two cigarettes and offered one to Alice. 'You know she's living over Pilkington way?'

Alice looked at him sharply.

'According to the bush telegraph Berry rented Mike Smith's place soon after she got pregnant, said he couldn't do with her puking all over the place.'

'It's no joke being out on the road when you're pregnant,' said Alice, 'living in temporary accommodation, always on the move from one station to the next.'

Jon got up and went to sit outside. The three of them were at it like housewives chewing over the latest gossip.

He sat on the verandah step, elbows on knees, looking across to the main street while the others organised a bite to eat. To his mind Charlestown wasn't much of a place if you looked at it with a critical eye. The bitumen stopped at the edge of town and what there was was in a pretty poor state of repair. There was just the one intersection leading to Scally's bungalow and three others on one side of town, and the emergency strip, the racecourse, and the cemetery on the other. The main road led to Pilkington to the north-east, a place not much bigger than Charlestown; and, to the south-west, Willicubbin, a ghost town with only two families. Willicubbin and Cavanagh's Creek Station was all that lay between Charlestown and the main Perth-Kalgoorlie highway a hundred and fifty miles away. Charlestown was a crook place, but it was his sort of crook place and there was nothing crook about the locals, even the sick had the grace to die suddenly, like Larry Simpson. He finished his tea and leaned back against an upright post enjoying the shady spot, watching a pair of willie wagtails catching flies in the winter sun.

After lunch Jon sat in the utility truck mindlessly drumming his fingers on the steering wheel as he waited for Alice to say her goodbyes, knowing the minute she climbed into the cab he'd be in for an ear-bending, and he wasn't wrong.

Alice settled herself onto the passenger seat and rummaged in her handbag for her spectacles. 'Don't know why you never asked her to marry you?'

He didn't bother to ask who she was talking about. 'I keep telling you, Alice, Val's just a mate, and besides, she's not interested in me.'

'There's none—'

'So blind as those who will not see...I know...I know, but you've got it wrong. Val has her sights set on other things.'

'Like what?'

'A business. Soon as she's fed up with Berry she'll up sticks and go to Perth, get a job in a dress shop, or a hat shop, or something like that.'

'And what about the baby?'

'You don't know she's pregnant for definite.'

'No, I don't, and let's hope to God she isn't because I don't like the idea of her tied to that Berry,' said Alice.

Jon didn't reply. He didn't either, he couldn't stand the bloke, but he wasn't about to tell Alice that.

When Jon and Alice drove into the yard at Jarrahlong, Alistair Farlane and Bindi Henderson were sitting on the verandah making the most of the warm winter weather, a chessboard between them. Greg was slumped in a chair idly watching the game, a bottle of beer on the side.

'Did you manage to attend to your business?' asked Greg sarcastically as Alice flopped on to her favourite bamboo rocking chair.

'Yes, thanks, the new Merinos should be here just as soon as the bank draft clears.'

'If you'd told me I'd have driven you into town,' he said peevishly. 'It'd have made a change from minding the bloody sheep.'

'That's all right, Jon was going in anyway, didn't see the point in calling you away from the mob. So how are they? You still happy about having a spring clip as well as the autumn?'

'Yeah, as I see it there's no reason why we can't try it the once; if it doesn't work out we won't do it again.'

Alice picked up two bottles of beer from the crate at Greg's feet and passed one across to Jon. 'Yes, that's what I thought.' She looked across to Alistair and Bindi. 'How's the studying coming along?'

Bindi looked up and smiled at Alice and Jon suddenly realised Ty's half-sister wasn't a kid any more. She wasn't the skinny four-teen-year-old half-caste he'd caught watching him swimming na-ked in the green pool three years earlier. He felt his colour rising at the memory and concentrated on taking a swig from the bottle, letting the warm liquid wash away the dust in his throat.

'Alistair's a hard taskmaster, Alice. He said I had to get an A for my essay before he'd consider a game of chess.'

'I'd have thought you'd have been studying our game while I was gone, Alistair, working out a strategy for tonight,' jibed Alice.

Alistair half turned in his seat and solemnly peered at her over half-moon reading glasses. 'I think I can beat you in five moves, Alice. Indeed, I'm convinced of it.'

'You putting money on it?'

'You know I'm not a gambling man.'

Jon listened to the banter between them and disagreed. In one respect Alistair was right. He'd never asked to be taken to a game of two-up, but in Jon's book he was a gambler right enough. He had replied to an advert for a tutor that Alice had placed in an Eng-lish newspaper eighteen months back when she decided that some-one as bright as Bindi should have a good education and, four months later, Alistair arrived in Fremantle with three trunks full of books and enough artists' materials to last him years. If that didn't indicate a gambling frame of mind then nothing did – unless, of course, Alistair had something to hide.

Jon studied him as he returned to the chess. Alistair was in his early sixties and a Cambridge scholar. He'd told Alice he'd found it difficult to settle into academic life after serving in the army pay office during the war years. Was he telling the truth? On the face of it he was, but you could never tell with people and it wouldn't be the first time a fugitive had made it into the outback.

'Have you the measure of Alice's game yet, Alistair?' asked Jon.

'Just about.'

'She's a bad loser.'

Alice flashed him a withering look. 'Who says I'm a bad loser?'

'Stan.' Jon grinned, pleased to see that Alice had the grace to blush. He cast an eye at Greg to see if he'd noticed, but Greg was in another place, the empty bottles at his feet confirmation if it were needed.

He supposed it was no bad thing that Alice had another man about the place; at least Alistair's presence put a brake on the worst of Greg's excesses.

'I wouldn't say she's a bad loser,' said Alistair, 'anyone who is passionate about something hates losing.'

'That so,' said Alice dryly, lighting up a cheroot, 'it's a long time since anyone described me as passionate.'

Jon doubted that, not if what Stan had hinted at was anything to go by. Stan had never given up on Alice even though she'd refused to marry him two years after Jack's death.

He dragged his attention back to the game, and Alistair, studying the intensity on the man's face. He liked Alistair, not least because Greg couldn't abide the man. Jon guessed the feeling was mutual, although he'd never heard Alistair say a bad word about Greg.

'How's the metropolis?' asked Alistair, glancing in Jon's direction.

Jon roused himself from his thoughts. 'Much the same as ever. The constable's still on the warpath over the two-up.'

'I've never seen the game played.'

'You've never played two-up!' interrupted Greg. 'It's only the best bloody game in the State.'

'Would you like to go, Alistair?' asked Jon.

'Well, I suppose I'd quite like to have my horizons extended sometime should you not mind company next time you attend.'

Jon grinned. 'That's fixed then, not that I'm an expert.'

'No, he's dead right there,' muttered Greg.

Jon ignored the sarcasm. 'You can lose your shirt if you're not careful, Alistair.'

'You mean it's a mug's game?'

'Something like that.'

'And is Greg aware of your views on the subject?'

'Indeed *he* is,' snarled Greg, 'not that I agree with his assessment.'

23

Alice harrumphed, an explosion of air she reserved for those occasions when she thought the levity had gone far enough. 'Well, Jon, seeing as you are getting all considerate you might as well do something for me.'

'You fancy a trip to the two-up ring too, Alice?'

'Less of the cheek, young man! I want you to drive over to Pilkington and find Berry's place.'

'Why?'

'To check up on Val for me.'

'That Liverpudlian bird is more than capable of looking after herself, isn't she?' scowled Greg.

For once Jon was inclined to agree. 'It's none of our business, Alice. Besides, she's got Berry to look after her.'

'Not if he's away shearing, she hasn't,' said Alice.

'Val's tough as they come.'

'That may well be, but I still want you to call in on her. I want to know how she's coping out there on her own, how she's managing. It's not easy being isolated. It gets lonely. You can always bring her back here for a few weeks. She might be glad of the company. Besides, Rachel says the pregnancy isn't suiting her, she's being sick a lot.'

Greg laughed. 'Well! Well! Well! The bitch went and got herself in the pudding club.'

All four of them looked at Greg, shocked by the antipathy in his voice.

'What has she ever done to upset you?' asked Alice.

'Nothing.' Greg finished his beer and leaned down for another. 'Just can't stand mouthy women.'

'As I was saying,' said Alice pointedly, 'she might be glad of the company and I've a few things she might like.'

'Like what?' asked Jon.

'Books, baby clothes.'

'Baby clothes!'

'Aye, baby clothes, from when David was newborn.'

Alistair leaned back in his chair and when Jon saw a smile flicker across his face he knew he was beaten. The fastest way out of the situation was to do as Alice asked.

'I'll go tomorrow,' he said, and get it over with, he thought.

'Thanks,' said Alice. 'Now then, Alistair! Are we going to finish that game? Your move, I think.'

CHAPTER 3

Jon left at first light with Alice's brown paper parcel tied up with string and a basket containing a cast-iron pot full of mutton stew, a loaf of fresh bread wrapped in a napkin and assorted vegetables from the vegetable plot.

He decided to take the short cut across the sandhills on the west side of the station – still a good three hours' drive to Berry's place – trust Alice to take up do-gooding in her old age.

He changed down a gear and picked his way over the creek bed, his thoughts on last night's conversation. He hadn't realised just how much Greg Morton disliked Val. She wasn't that bad, true she was a bit in-your-face at times, but that was just the Liverpudlian way. The ute ground up the sandy bank on the other side. He'd never heard Val say a bad word about Greg, or anyone else come to that. He scowled; something must have happened for Greg to take against her, perhaps she'd given him the brush off.

The sandhills stretched ahead and following the old tracks concentrated his mind, but even so it wasn't long before the wheels were spinning, chewing into soft ground. The short cut was a mistake. He grabbed a couple of sand mats and got out of the ute. Damn Alice and her soft-heartedness.

Four hours later he turned onto a single track that was so heavily corrugated he had to drive at snail's pace to avoid jolting the utility to bits and soon caught a glimpse of the homestead iron roof glinting in the winter sun.

In the yard a grader mouldered under a shade tree and he wondered why Berry hadn't bothered smoothing out the track, a day or two's work, that's all it would have taken, unless the machine was kaput. He parked next to it and peered into the adjacent workshop, an open-fronted shed constructed of rough-cut timber and tin and packed with broken machinery, empty kerosene tins, saws and hammers, fencing equipment, all, like the grader, rusting away. So Berry wasn't into maintenance – why should he be surprised!

He crossed the yard, past the donkey, a boiler converted from a forty-four-gallon drum, and a pile of mulga wood someone had collected from the bush, half of it ravaged by white ants. Next to the boiler was the laundry with a wooden sink lined with lead, a galvanised tub with a wash-dolly in it and a handful of wooden pegs on the side and, opposite, a small wooden shed with its door hanging off – the dunny.

Over to the right was a water tower and, near it, a temporary shower arrangement made from an old kerosene drum – flipping cold in winter, and not even a nod at modesty. Was that where Val washed or did she use the sink? Bit of a comedown after the two-up two-down on Bridge Street in Liverpool even with their outside lavatories.

Between the water tower and the grader the yard was strewn with cannibalised utes and lorries. An untidy heap of tyres worn down to the canvas had been dumped months ago if the dust layer was anything to go by, while other piles of wood, gradually turning to sawdust, and roll upon roll of rusting barbed wire that had been bundled up and left, littered the yard.

He picked his way through the mess to the tiny shack. No garden, or shade trees, just a disintegrating picket fence that marked the boundary between yard and house, the sandy soil dotted with empty beer bottles.

At the top of a short flight of steps an ill-fitting fly screen hung drunkenly on one good hinge. Jon mounted the steps, opened the screen and knocked on the inner door. He waited a moment, listening.

He pushed open the door, stepped into the kitchen and looked about him. The ancient cooking range was as dilapidated as the rest of the homestead. The grate was broken and ashes lay scattered on the slab of concrete upon which it stood. The assorted cupboards were in a similar state of disrepair, held together with string and bits of wire. The pine table, in the centre of the room, served as a work station and dining table, and what was left of the linoleum was covered in frayed hessian mats made from sacking. The window panes were clean, so was the kitchen, even so there was no comfort in the place.

'Anyone home?' he called, stepping further into the kitchen.

26

He heard movement from the next room, the only other room in the shack by the look of things, and watched the inner door swing open.

'That you, Berry?' he heard her say and then came a gasp when she saw him. Her hand flew to her throat, the shock writ large on her face. 'Has somethin' happened to Alice?'

He couldn't answer for his own shock at the state of her. She'd lost weight, her dress hung off her, a shapeless, creased sack of a dress. Her skin had taken on a pallid hue and her blonde hair, usually carefully arranged in cascading waves, hung limp and greasy, framing her tired face. Her eyes were sunken with dark smudges under them from lack of sleep, or crying, he couldn't tell which, and he couldn't be sure but he thought he could see the yellow tint of old bruising near her left temple.

She ran roughened hands through her hair. 'I look a right mess, don't I, hon?'

He didn't know how to answer. 'You look okay to me,' he lied tonelessly.

'It's the pregnancy, it isn't suiting me. I've bin throwin' up for a month now. Berry's fed up with seein' me. Says I'm an old hag and he's not wrong there.' Her laughter was hollow as she looked him straight in the eye, daring him to contradict her.

'It won't last forever, Val.'

'No!' She flopped down at the table. 'It just feels like it. So what brings you to this neck of the woods? Is Alice okay?'

'Yeah, she's fine, leastways, she was this morning. She's worried about you. She'd heard that you're feeling crook.'

'You could say that.'

He looked at her, at the exhaustion and despair in her face. 'Why don't you go home, Val? I'll buy you a ticket. Liverpool's got to be better than this for someone in your condition.'

She rounded on him. 'Go home! Go home! Lookin' like this? How would I hold my head up, Jon, you tell me that?'

He backed off, shocked by the vehemence in her voice, the anger in her eyes.

'You know what me mam always says – you've made your bed, my girl, now you've gorra lie in it.'

'Your mam'd be pleased to have you back.'

'Would she?' The scorn in Val's tone was shocking. 'Like hell, she would.'

They sat either side of the table not talking, the silence heavy

27

between them. 'How's Merle?' asked Val eventually.

'Fine.'

'What's that supposed to mean?'

'Fine…it's just…'

'Just what?'

'Well, she's not…she keeps mentioning the flies and the dust.' He chewed his lip. 'Anyway, she's got her final exams soon.'

'She still writes to you then?'

'What's that supposed to mean?'

'Dorothy said she was seein' someone else.'

Dot! Val's friend with the curtain of hair that hid the sly look he'd found so disconcerting. He'd never liked her. 'You mean Paul Vincent. Yeah, Merle told me, they go to the Philharmonic for the concerts sometimes. He's just a mate,' he said, 'like us.'

'Well, that's all right then, isn't it!' She lapsed into a tight-lipped silence.

'Now what's wrong?'

'Merle's not the type to rough it, Jon, she's a city girl. Do you think she'd be happy married to—'

'To what?'

'A jackaroo-cum-prospector living in the middle of the outback, in that shack of yours.'

He resisted the urge to look about him. 'You like the outback well enough.'

'Yes, but what sort of a future did I have in Liverpool?'

'The same as here,' he said nastily, not caring that his words were well below the belt. He watched the colour drain from her face and was glad his words had hit home.

'What d'you mean?'

'One fella's the same as the next if you're that way inclined,' he said bluntly, wanting to hurt her, to shut her up.

She jumped up from her seat and slapped him hard. 'I'm not like my mam and my sister, I'm not on the game, and I never will be. Now clear off.'

He glared at her and pushed back his chair. 'My pleasure!' he yelled and slammed out of the shack, muttering obscenities under his breath. He got into the ute and stopped. He could hardly tell Alice they'd argued and that he'd left her to it. Besides, it wasn't like Val. It was the pregnancy. She was overwrought. He got back out of the ute and return to the shack, tentatively knocked on the door and re-entered the kitchen.

'I shouldn't have said all that. Can we start again, Val?'

When she didn't reply he sat down opposite her. 'Shall I make us some tea?' he said presently.

'Suppose so, but you'll have to light the range, it'll need cleanin' out first though, the ash box is full.'

'No worries.' He was pleased to have something to do. 'And I'll light the donkey and get some hot water running.'

He left Val sitting at the kitchen table.

'The shovel and the ash bucket are outside the back door,' she called after him.

Over the next hour Jon got the range cleaned and relit and built a fire under the donkey. Within half an hour there was plenty of hot water and the oven was hot enough for cooking. In the laundry he found some fabric suitable for a modesty curtain and a galvanised tub big enough to bathe in. When everything was ready he returned to the shack.

'I've organised you a bath. You'll feel better once you've had a soak and washed your hair and while you're getting cleaned up I'll make us some tea.'

She opened her mouth to argue, he could see it in her eyes.

'Come on, Val. You look a mess. You need to make an effort.' He said it as kindly as he could.

Stung by his words she turned away and disappeared into the back room. For a while he thought she was going to ignore his suggestion but after a time she came back with a change of clothes, a towel and soap and, without speaking to him, crossed the yard to the laundry.

While Val was bathing he fetched in the basket Alice had given him, put the stew in the oven to heat through, the vegetables on to boil and laid the brown paper parcel on the table ready for her to open. When she returned he was reading a dog-eared newspaper, the *Pilkington Gazette*, the news a year old but interesting for all that.

'Feeling better?'

'Yes, thanks.'

She had more colour in her cheeks and her damp hair was already flying away in the light breeze, the dark blonde rapidly drying to light. The dress she wore was faded but clean and still fitted well, he'd never have guessed she was pregnant from the look of her but there and again, he supposed, most women didn't look pregnant in the first few weeks or so.

'Alice sent you the parcel.'

'What's in it?'

'Open it and see.'

'Books!' Her eyes lit up and then the pleasure faded from them when she saw the clothes and realised what the garments were.

'They were David's,' he said.

'That's nice of her.' There was no enthusiasm in her voice.

Jon looked at the baby clothes Alice had kept for years and wondered how she and Jack had coped after the death of their only child in the Gallipoli Campaign. 'Alice says they're old but still in good condition.'

'I can see that.'

'You reckon it'll be a boy or a girl?'

'Berry wants a boy.'

'And what do you want?'

She looked at him. 'I don't want to be pregnant.'

'Maybe you should have thought of that sooner.'

'Piss off,' she said, dropping the garments back onto the table.

He stared at her, his mouth open, shocked by her language. He'd never heard her swear before. 'Sorry,' he mumbled eventually.

'So you should be. You don't honestly think I went and got myself knocked up on purpose?'

'Berry's a good-looking bloke.'

'What's that gorra do with it?'

'I thought you fancied him.'

'He can be good company when he's half a mind to it, but he's not husband material if that's what you're thinking.'

'It's just a pity you didn't realise it sooner,' he said, remembering Scally was of the same opinion. 'I did warn you.'

'Hindsight's a wonderful thing,' she said bitterly.

'Look, Val,' he softened his tone, 'I'm not here to fight with you. What about having something to eat, you don't look like you've had a square meal in a while.'

'I haven't, haven't felt like eatin'.'

Glad of the distraction Jon busied himself at the stove while Val organised plates and cutlery. He served up mutton stew and vegetables and sat down opposite her.

'Alice says Berry's away working with Cadge and the boys.'

She nodded. 'He should be back at the end of the week.'

'How do you find living out here on your own?'

'Lonely.'

'That's what Alice said. What do you do all day?'

'Throw up.'

'Still?'

'No, I'm much better; I wasn't sick at all yesterday.'

'Alice thought you might like the books and...' He racked his brain for ideas. 'You could always start a vegetable patch – that would take up your time.'

She glanced at him briefly and let the suggestion pass.

He ate in silence. Perhaps it was a stupid idea. There was no garden just a yard full of junk and accumulated rubbish. There were no citrus trees like Alice had at Jarrahlong, or shade trees that made life more bearable in the heat of summer. Recalling the hard-packed earth outside he realised it wouldn't be that easy, it'd require some serious digging before she could even think of planting. And all the water would have to be lugged over from the water tank by hand. It wasn't going to happen; even he could see it was a non-starter. 'You see much of Rachel?'

Val shook her head. 'It's a long drive to Charlestown and, besides, I haven't gorra car. How's Simpson's doin'?'

'It's back to how it was before, but worse, at least Larry knew what he was about. His brother's a dead loss. According to Alice, Fred upsets the customers, no tact, that's what Alice says, which is a bit ripe coming from her.'

Val grinned. 'But her heart's in the right place.'

'Yeah, that too. Anyway, I can't see Fred staying much longer. He hasn't made any friends and isn't likely to with his attitude. Reckon before long we'll be getting all our clothes by mail order.'

'Pity,' sighed Val, 'that place could be a little gold mine if it was run right. There are no good clothes shops in Pilkington either. People have to go all the way to Kalgoorlie or Perth to get anything half decent.' She stood up. 'You finished?'

'Yeah, thanks.'

She took his plate. 'Tea?'

'Wouldn't say no.'

'Why don't you sit outside, there's a bit of a breeze, cooler than bein' in this stuffy kitchen.'

He took the hint and settled himself on one of the kitchen chairs Val and Berry used, overlooking the yard. Val handed him a mug and sat down on the other chair, propping her feet up on an empty kerosene drum.

'Alice says you should have a break, she's invited you to stay with her at Jarrahlong for a while. And I think she'd like the company too.'

Val hesitated. 'I don't know.'

'It'd do you good,' said Jon briskly.

'I don't think Berry would like it.'

'Why not for God's sake, if he's never here, and in any case when did what anyone else think stop you?'

'What's that supposed to mean?'

'Well, you've always done what you wanted. Why change the habit of a lifetime?'

She didn't answer at first, just gazed slightlessly across the yard. 'I'll think about it,' she said eventually.

'Which means you won't.'

She was about to reply when they both heard a truck approaching. Val leapt up, spilling tea down her front.

Jumpy, he thought. The tension in her was palpable as they watched Berry's battered Leyland truck drive through the yard and park next to Jon's ute.

Berry stepped down from the cab, took off his bush hat, bashed it against his thigh and flopped it back on his head.

Val waited anxiously as he crossed the yard to them.

'G'day to ya,' said Berry grimly. 'And to what do we owe the honour?'

'Alice sent over some books and some baby clothes. Isn't that nice of her,' gabbled Val.

'See y're having a bit of a tea party with yer Pommy pal.' Berry draped a heavy arm over Val's shoulder and dragged her closer to him.

'I wasn't expectin' you back today,' she said, a smile on her face.

'So I can see,' sneered Berry. 'Cadge told me to take a couple of days off. What's for tea?'

'It's on the stove. I'll go and gerrit, hon.'

'Teck it y're leavin',' said Berry pointedly, directing his words at Jon as he shoved past him into the kitchen.

Jon wiped the dislike off his face. 'Yes, I'll just get my hat.' He followed them and stood in the doorway.

Berry looked at the dirty plates. 'I see y've already eaten.'

'Alice sent it over,' said Val brightly.

Too brightly, Jon thought. What the hell was going on?

'Did she now.' Berry's tone was menacing. 'Well y'can tell yer precious Alice we're not charity cases. I can look after my own, thank ya.' He picked up the opened parcel of baby clothes and books. 'We won't want these. Tell Alice to find a more needy cause.' He thrust the parcel towards Jon's chest forcing him to grab hold of it and then he tossed Jon's hat after it. 'Close the door after ya,' he snarled.

Val had her back to them, busy dishing up Berry's tea.

'Val?' He hesitated in asking her to come back with him.

She turned briefly. 'See ya, hon.'

That bright smile again, he couldn't make her out. Earlier she'd said Berry wasn't the marrying kind, she'd sounded fed up and depressed and now she was running around after Berry like a doting wife. He just didn't understand her.

He shrugged. 'See you, Val.' He spun on his heels and left the kitchen. What did she see in the bloke? He was a bastard.

At the laundry he stepped inside and put the baby clothes and books in a basket and replaced it on a lower shelf out of sight but where Val would find it, and then he got into his ute and drove out of the yard, feeling uneasy, worrying about what would be said between the two of them the minute he'd left, wondering whether they'd end up rowing.

He gentled the ute over the corrugations, oblivious of the uncomfortable ride. What on earth had happened to Val over the last few months that she should have changed so much? What had happened to the feisty, devil-may-care girl who'd arrived in Charlestown three years back? He wouldn't have believed someone could have changed so much. Still, if she wanted to be with Berry who was he to argue?

CHAPTER 4

That September Alice was in a good mood. It had been a fair
spring clip, with high-class wool. All the bales had been stamped
with the Jarrahlong mark and were ready for shipment to the coast.
Jon still didn't agree with the decision to go for split shearing, but
that was Greg all over, keen to put his own mark on the place, and
Alice was easy-going enough to let him have his way.

Jon stood next to her watching the stockmen driving the mob
back out into the paddock whilst inside the shearing shed came the
familiar banter as the shearers cleaned their equipment.

'You staying for tea?' asked Alice. 'Maybe I can persuade you to
have a go at the bale rolling this time.'

'No, not me,' laughed Jon, remembering the last time he'd taken
part in Alice's end-of-shearing entertainment – a bale-rolling competition. 'I reckon my bale rolling days were over before they began.' He flexed his leg, feeling the tightness where Yildilla had
speared him and knew that the damaged muscle would ache for
days afterwards if he were stupid enough to let pride get in the
way. They wandered over towards the lean-to where the meals
were served. Rachel came out carrying plates and cutlery.

'Hi, Jon, long time, no see,' she called.

'How's the family?'

'Well.'

'And the baby?'

'Amy! She's doing grand. She has her granddad wrapped around
her little finger.'

Jon smiled. He knew Rachel wasn't exaggerating. He'd never
seen such a change in a bloke once Scally had taken on the mantle
of granddad with young Joe and then, when Amy was born last
July, he was smitten, love at first sight, Ty had said. 'Your dad
looking after the kids?'

'No, Val is.'

'Val?'

'Yeah, she said she'd rather stay in town.'

It was almost four months since he'd last seen her at Mike Smith's place. 'Has she married that bastard, yet?'

'Who?' asked Rachel.

'Berry.'

'No,' interrupted Alice, 'they're not married.'

The information brought him up short. After seeing them together the last time he'd have put money on it. Val would have known the gossip her pregnancy would cause, so maybe people were right, Berry wasn't the marrying type. Geoff Wheat, a rouseabout on the shearing team, had once said as much and so had Scally, and Val in an unguarded moment; they couldn't all be wrong.

He shook his head. He'd never understood her going with Berry. He'd have thought she, more than most, would have seen through his silver-tongued spiel.

He brushed off the thought. It was none of his business what Val did, except a small part of him missed her Liverpool banter, the friendly insults they exchanged and her feminine ways. After Merle, he had to admit, she was the most attractive woman he'd ever had dealings with and she had the knack of making a fella feel good about himself – that was probably why Larry Simpson had liked her and why Wes Chapman had gone out of his way to teach her to drive when she'd first arrived from England.

'Where is Berry?' asked Jon.

'He left early,' said Alice, 'said he'd got business in town.'

The drone of an aircraft interrupted them. The three of them stopped what they were doing and turned to look. Away, over on the horizon, beyond the acacia scrub, a small plane came into view.

'What's that doing here?' asked Rachel.

Greg stepped out of the shearing shed with Cadge Coles and squinted into the sun, following the others. 'That's Chips,' he said, wiping sweat from off his brow.

'Chips!' Jon felt a frisson ripple down his spine. 'Chips?'

'Yeah, Chips Carpenter, he's a Brit.'

'And what's he doing flying over my land?' asked Alice, suspicion making her voice sharp. 'Is he planning on visiting, or something?'

Greg smiled. 'No, he's searching for the plane he crashed in a canyon somewhere in the outback.'

Alice glanced at the aircraft. 'It must be a pretty special plane.'

'It's not the plane, Alice; it's the gold reef he found.'

'There're no gold reefs on Jarrahlong; anyway, how come you know so much about him?'

'Met him when I was last in town – he's staying at The Grand.'

'That's right,' said Rachel. 'And he's renting a section of Wes's shed, keeps his plane there when he's not flying.'

'If you want my opinion he's wasting his time,' said Alice, 'there are no wrecked planes around here and if there was a gold reef it'd have been found by now.'

'Stan Colley never gave up though, did he?' commented Cadge.

'And look where that got the silly old so-and-so,' snapped Alice.

'Well, Chips is convinced it's around here someplace. He says he's seen the reef with his own eyes and he's even chipped...' Cadge grinned, '...chipped a few nuggets out of it. He's offering a stake in the find for anyone willing to invest in the search.'

Alice turned her back on the plane. 'Anyone doing that is a real drongo. They'd be throwing good money after bad. They'd stand a better chance of keeping their money in the two-up ring, and that's saying something. Now then, Rachel, is tea about ready?'

'Indeed it is,' said Rachel still holding the plates and cutlery.

Cadge held out an arm for Alice to take. 'Allow me, Ma'am.'

Jon threw his swag into the back of the ute and whistled the dogs. The shearers would be in town for the monthly film show as well as for the two-up that ran as often as Les Harper could get away with it. Everyone knew Les gave Constable Nickson a backhander to keep out of the way, but the State was clamping down on gambling, reckoned too many people were losing their shirts on the throw of a couple of coins. And, according to Wes Chapman, Greg was one of them, he lost everything he earned in the ring, unluckiest bastard going, he'd once said of him.

Greg was a fool. Money was too hard earned to risk losing it on the toss of a couple of coins. Alice was right: gambling was a mug's game.

He stowed his swag, whistled for Smoky and lifted Stan's old dogs onto the passenger seat. He rarely went into town these days, he was too busy mining the gold in his spare time, but he needed to find out what Chips was doing and knowing Chips's suspicious nature that wasn't likely to be a five minute job. He resigned himself to spending the evening in the bar rather than watching a third-rate film in the town hall. Anyway, he'd probably seen it years ago, in the Gaumont, with Billy Wainwright. His thoughts shifted to Liverpool. Merle hadn't written in ages, not that she ever mentioned any of his old friends. He pushed thoughts of Liverpool, Merle, and Billy Wainwright out of his mind, it wasn't the time for reminiscing, there were more important things to think about. A sharp turn on the starting handle and the engine spluttered into life, he threw the starting handle into the back of the ute and slipped it into gear, he'd doss down on Scally's verandah if all the rooms in The Grand were taken.

Jon whistled as he drove into town. Wes would be surprised to see him. Wes was forever telling him to make more of an effort, warning him against ending up a recluse like Stan, and he wasn't far wrong; it was all too easy not to bother, to get used to your own company like Alice had before he'd arrived at Jarrahlong. She'd been living alone for years with only blacks for company and the fortnightly mail and supply drop to look forward to. He didn't want to end up like that; there was still too much living to do.

In Charlestown he went straight to The Grand. The place was empty except for Connie Andersen and a couple of stockmen leaning against the bar; they nodded a greeting and turned back to their beers.

Connie finished drying a glass. 'Hello, Jon, we haven't seen you in a while. Still searching for Stan's gold?'

'No, I've got more sense.'

She pulled him a beer, placed it on the counter and accepted payment.

'I thought you were still living out at Stan's place,' she said, handing over his change.

'I am.'

'Jarrahlong's not good enough then.' A smile softened the statement.

Jon laughed, 'Not at all, Connie; the fact is, Alice's place is a great deal more comfortable than Stan's shack, but I reckon I've got used to my own company.'

'And, I suppose, keeping out of Greg's way has its advantages.'

A faint smile creased Jon's face. 'You could say that.' He indicated the saloon behind him. 'Where is everyone?'

'Can't you guess? – two-up, out in the bush, the word is that Nickson's on the prowl. Don't think he'll manage to catch anyone, Les will have that well covered.'

'Bit warm to be out in the bush, isn't it? Can't imagine Nickson wanting to chase fugitives from the gambling laws across saltbush and spinifex, can you?'

Connie laughed out loud at the thought.

'When are they likely to be back?'

'This evening sometime. Who're you wanting? Greg?'

'No, just thought I'd take a bit of time off, be a bit more sociable.' He finished his beer. 'Looks like I've got my timing a bit out. Maybe I'll take a wander over to Wes's place.'

She shook her head. 'He'll be at the two-up.'

'Scally's then.'

'He'll be about, he isn't a gambling man, isn't Scally. I see you two are getting on just fine these days.'

'You could say that, though he's still not mad about Poms.'

'Leopards and spots,' said Connie, 'leopards and spots.'

Jon stepped out of The Grand, called the dogs and crossed over to the verandahed walkway, a cloud of flies following him, circling around the brim of his hat attracted by the sweat band, blackened and greasy with age.

Charlestown looked deserted, but then it often did at midday even on the cooler spring days. He glanced up at the cloudless sky – hot for September, around eighty degrees Fahrenheit he guessed, but not like in midsummer when the temperature could reach over a hundred degrees, when the heat sucked the moisture out of the lungs and made breathing difficult, when pacing yourself was the secret to coping with the heat.

He checked the time, come late afternoon the place would be busier. Blokes would drive in with their wives and families for the film show. Val was a film fanatic, she always insisted on calling them the flicks even when all their mates in Liverpool called them the pictures or the movies. Now she had to put up with old films, comedies and B pictures from the early forties. He guessed it would be quite a while before Charlestown could run to John Wayne's latest.

He ordered the dogs to sit and wait and hammered on Scally's fly-screen door, opened it, and entered the kitchen. Scally was sitting by the table with Amy in his arms.

Jon grinned. 'You look like you were born to it.'

'What?' growled Scally clearly irritated by the look on Jon's face.

'The doting granddad.'

'Y'don't say!'

'It suits you,' said Jon, 'takes that snarling edge off you.'

Scally looked down at his granddaughter and his face softened. 'She's just like Rachel was when she was a baby.'

Jon cocked an ear listening for movement out the back. 'Where is Rachel?'

'Out with Ty and Joe. They've gone over to one of the creeks for a swim. I said I'd look after Amy. What are you doing in town then?'

'Thought I'd come in for a bit of company, maybe see the film this evening.'

'Well, while y're here y'd better put the kettle on for a brew.'

Jon missed the film show and ending up in The Grand drinking in the bar with Greg, Chips and Maurice Cato.

Greg, in ebullient mood, clapped him on the back and bought him a beer.

Jon found Greg's jauntiness irritating but masked his impatience; he needed to find out what Chips was up to, what his plans were. At least Chips wasn't as drunk as he had been the first time he'd seen him, and he looked smarter, he'd had a haircut and his clothes were cleaner. Perhaps he was still at the stage where he wanted to impress. Maybe he had changed, slowed down on the boozing, got himself together.

Greg introduced them.

Chips nodded an acknowledgement, pulled out a packet of cigarettes, selected one, lit it and frowned. 'We've met before, haven't we?'

'That's right.' There was no point in lying about it, Chips would remember eventually anyway. 'You've extending your search then?'

Greg looked at Jon sharply. 'You didn't tell me you already knew about the gold reef,' he said in a clipped tone.

'Didn't I?'

'You know damn well you didn't, so when did you hear about it?'

'Chips told me a few months ago, when I was in Leonora.'

'What were you doing in Leonora, selling off gold from your lease?' sneered Greg.

Chips's eyes narrowed against the smoke. 'I thought you said you were a jackaroo?'

Jon ignored the arctic tone. 'I am.'

Chips indicated in Greg's direction. 'What's he on about?'

'An old prospector left him his mineral lease over at Yaringa Creek,' interrupted Greg. 'Jon's been there ever since...when he's not at Jarrahlong helping me out.'

Jon let the last part of the statement pass and took his time taking a long draught of beer, aware that Chips was watching him.

'Much gold there?' Chips asked eventually.

'Not that I've found, and Stan Colley didn't find much either, spent thirty years looking and never found a reef, only a bit of alluvial gold, enough to keep him in tinned dog and rum.'

'Why are you living out there then?'

'I see enough of Greg as it is.' Jon took another pull of beer conscious of Chips, iceberg cold and about as friendly. The bloke wasn't satisfied.

Chips leaned back in his chair and fixed gimlet eyes on him. 'Where is this mine?'

'Out on the Pilkington road a few miles beyond the Jarrahlong turn-off,' volunteered Greg. 'He spends more time there than he does doing his job.'

'Does he!'

'Yaringa's an outstation and when I'm working for Alice, I work,' said Jon, knowing Greg would rise to the bait. 'Not like some I know.'

'Are you referring to me?' snarled Greg.

'Who do you think? You spend more time in the bar and down the two-up than you do on the station.'

'It's my money.'

'Is it? As I see it you're short-changing Alice.'

Greg's chair crashed to the floor and he leaned over the table, his eyes glittering with menace. 'Take that back or I'll thrash you.'

Jon glared back, refusing to back down. 'You can try.'

Chips drew on his cigarette and then exhaled slowly. 'I see you two don't like each other.'

'Can't stand the bastard,' Greg picked up the chair and flopped onto it, 'never have.'

Satisfied, Chips turned back to his beer.

'I'd have thought you two would've got along better, being cousins,' commented Cato.

'What the hell are you talking about?' shouted Greg, bristling like a cornered boar.

Jon kept his face bland and unreadable. Trust Cato to put his bloody foot in it! He'd never liked the bank manager, he was too smarmy by half; he even looked smarmy with his Vaselined hair and sweaty hands.

Cato's voice faltered. 'You know?'

'Know what?'

'Jon is Alice's nephew.' He corrected himself, 'Great-nephew.'

Greg slammed his glass down on the table. 'Since when?'

Cato licked his lips and glanced from Jon to Greg and back to Jon again. 'Tell him, tell him you're a Macarthur.'

'He damn well isn't.' Greg's voice was ice. 'He's no bloody relation.'

Chips sat back in his seat and smiled at the fresh row that was brewing. Cato shrank back into his. Greg leaned across the table, his jaw thrust forward, challenging Jon to explain himself.

'Greg's right. Alice took me in when I ran away from Karundah orphanage. And when people asked questions she told them I was her great-nephew. Then, later, when I wanted to go back to England to find my sister I didn't have a birth certificate to get a passport so she gave me her son's, and got a mate to 'doctor' it so it looked like mine.'

'You're a liar. Alice wouldn't take in a runaway kid.' said Greg.

'You're wrong, Greg. She was short of stockmen, half the blacks had gone walkabout and she was in the middle of a drought. She needed men to move the sheep, and I turned up.'

'So!'

'She was a desperate woman. She'd have taken on the Devil himself to save her Merinos. You ever seen sheep dying, belly deep in stinking mud, their eyes pecked out by crows?'

Cato looked at him, and then at Greg, expectantly. Jon finished his beer, waiting for Greg's reply. He avoided looking at Chips and kept his hands relaxed on the table.

Greg scowled. 'I still think you're lying, I reckon you saw your chance, a gaga old woman living alone. I bet you thought you'd

41

got it made.'

Jon laughed. 'Her sheep dropping like flies, no stockmen to speak of, I was fifteen for God's sake and a runaway. And Alice isn't gaga.'

Cato looked briefly at Greg and then turned to Jon. 'What is your name if it isn't Macarthur?'

'Cadwallader.'

Chips stubbed out his cigarette. 'No plane wreckage in that valley of yours, I suppose?'

'No. I told you, I haven't come across anything like that; it's not exactly easy to miss a wrecked plane, is it?'

'He's right,' said Greg, 'and there's no wreckage on Jarrahlong Station either, I'd have found it by now if there was. And there's none on Jindalee, at least not on the Yaringa Creek side of the station.'

Jon kept his face deadpan. Greg didn't know what he was talking about, he didn't know Jarrahlong and Jindalee like he did, he didn't know the secret places like the green pool and the other hidden-away places like Galston Gorge, even so, Greg was right about the wreckage, the remains of Chips's plane wasn't on Jarrahlong, or Jindalee. 'You're welcome to check it out for yourself, any time, but there's no plane.'

'And no gold either,' Greg sneered. 'If there was he wouldn't be spending so much time at Jarrahlong under my feet...or driving a clapped-out utility.'

Jon ignored the jibes. 'What are your plans, Chips?'

'Start a proper aerial search, find the plane, mine the gold.'

'It can't be cheap keeping a plane in the air,' commented Jon.

'That's why I'm forming a company. Greg here is going to invest.' He nodded in Cato's direction, 'And Maurice...he's keen. When we find the gold we'll all be wealthy, you interested?'

Jon shook his head conscious of Greg's relief. 'No, thanks. Nice of you to ask but I don't have any spare cash, I barely have enough to keep my ute on the road.' He finished his drink. 'I think I'll call it a day. It's a long drive back to my place.'

He flapped a farewell hand in their direction and towards Connie, whistled his dogs and headed out to his truck, his mind in turmoil as he turned over the engine and felt it catch. If Cato and Greg were putting money up it meant Chips would be able to spend more time flying, which meant that sometime he was going to find Paradise Canyon with the wreckage and the gold. And while the great gash in the Ranges was only one of several in the ironstone plateau there was no guarantee that Chips wouldn't favour the right one for a thorough search. He couldn't risk it, he was going to have to go out there and do something about the plane.

He shivered at the thought of facing the demons the place held for him; this time he didn't want to go there alone. He'd ask Bindi if she would go with him just as soon as he'd back-filled the entrance to the lightning-strike cavern in No Hope Mine, just in case Chips decided to have a look around while he was away.

CHAPTER 5

A fortnight later, on a fine October morning, Jon pulled into Jar-rahlong yard and parked next to the bungalow where Alice was sitting watching his approach. A plume of red dust created by the backdraught swirled around him as he stepped from the vehicle.

'What's the tearing hurry?' Alice asked as Jon bashed fine sand off his hat. Smoky jumped down from the back of the ute while Jon lifted the two old dogs from out of the cab.

'I wondered if you'd look after the dogs for me, Alice.'

She contemplated him for a long moment. 'Anything wrong?'

'No, not really.'

'What's that supposed to mean?'

'An Abo stopped by, one of Curly's mob; he said Curly's grand-father, Jigger, wants to see me.' It was the best excuse he could think of that would satisfy Alice.

'And now you're planning on chasing across the outback after Curly's family. Are you mad?'

'It's not that, Alice.'

'Guilt?'

'I suppose.' She wasn't far wrong on that count; he still had dis-turbing dreams about his first Aboriginal friend, Curly, and his totem animal, Perentie.

'I've told you before, you need to put that business behind you. No good ever came from dwelling on what might have been.'

'I know, Alice, but—'

'But you can't let go.'

'No. I can't, Curly believed—'

'Believed what?'

'That what happened to him, his dying, was because I killed a perentie.'

44

'Did he say that?'

'No, not in as many words.'

'Well, there you go, put it out of your mind, forget about it. Now, how about a cup of tea?'

'Thanks, I wouldn't mind.'

Alice looked at him long and hard. 'You're still going, aren't you?'

Jon nodded and drew up a chair while Alice poured the tea.

'What about the Cathay Cup?'

'What about it?'

'Well, you'll miss it, the best sporting event in the Charlestown spring calendar; they reckon Bartokas is a dead cert for the owner's cup this year. Why don't you go after the meeting?'

'Can't wait that long, Alice. Besides, I might be back in time for it.'

'And, there again, you might not!'

She handed him a cup of tea, watching him speculatively again. He hated that look; he never knew what was coming next.

'I gather you met up with Greg last weekend?'

He sipped the hot tea to avoid answering. She knew!

'Greg was full of it. You know he wants to invest in the search for Chips's reef?'

'Yes, Chips offered me the same deal.'

Alice snorted her derision. 'And what did you say?'

'That I barely had enough to keep my ute on the road.'

'I wish Greg had as much sense. He's been trying to talk me into bankrolling him, says he can't lose and wants a year's wages up front, and some.'

'What did you say?'

'I told him he needed his head examining.'

Jon laughed. 'I bet that went down well.'

'You reckon Chips is telling the truth?'

'What about?'

'The gold?'

'It's possible, I suppose, but the outback's a big place and if he has no co-ordinates then he's going the same way as Lasseter.'

'Humm, that's what I think.'

Jon leaned back in his chair, funny thing gold and what it did to people. He thought about the prospectors in the early days, risking their lives working a dry stage, searching for the elusive metal. To be that obsessed was a terrible thing and then there were the kaditja

45

men – the Aboriginal lawmen who exacted vengeance for wrong-doing, the executioners – Chips must lead a charmed life! He had no idea that anyone violating the cavern would be hunted down by one of them and maimed or killed. Places didn't come any more sacred than Perentie Cavern and it had nothing to do with the gold, so how had Chips escaped retribution when he, Jon, hadn't? – unless it was killing the perentie that had brought Aboriginal vengeance down on him. Perhaps he'd never know for sure.

'Where's Bindi?'

'Last time I saw her she was heading for the vegetable patch.'

'She likes gardening, doesn't she?'

'That's right, she says it's restful and Alistair doesn't bother her there.'

Jon laughed. 'I'll take a stroll over. I won't be long, Alice.'

He skirted the stockmen's quarters and headed out past the water tower to where Alice had created a vegetable plot two decades earlier. Since Bindi had taken over responsibility for it its productivity had tripled and it now supplied all the station needs for vegetables and herbs.

'Bindi!'

She looked up from hoeing and smiled. 'Bring that basket over, will you?' she waved her golden-brown arm in the direction of the gate.

He picked it up and closed the gate behind him to keep out the chooks. 'Where's your grandfather these days?'

She stopped what she was doing and leaned on the hoe. 'Yildilla? I'm not sure.'

'Come on, Bindi, I want to know, it's important.'

'Probably over near Mullin Soak, maybe further east. Why?'

'I need to get in touch with him…fast.'

She resumed hoeing.

'I know…you'd think he'd be the last person I'd want to see, but something has come up.' His hand dropped to his scarred thigh and he briefly massaged the damaged muscle that still pulled when he walked. 'Remember that plane in Paradise Canyon?'

She nodded.

'The owner is looking for it.'

A small frown creased her brow. 'Why? There's not much of it left. It'll never fly again.'

'It's not the plane he's after, it's the gold.'

'What gold?'

He stared at her, shocked by her words. Surely she knew about the gold. Or did she? Was the ancestor cave forbidden to women? Or was it because she wasn't a full blood? He hid his surprise. Yildilla doted on Bindi, Ty said he did and yet the Aboriginal had kept the ancestor cave a secret from her. He felt the damaged muscle pull as he bent down to gather up the vegetables and fruit Bindi had picked earlier and massaged the aching thigh again. He'd come to the conclusion that Yildilla had meted out tribal punishment either because he'd killed Curly's totem animal or because Curly had shown him the sacred place; would the same thing happen to Bindi if she were to enter the cavern? Or would she escape punishment like Chips had done?

'Is this anything to do with Greg's gold?' she asked.

'Not you too!'

'What's that supposed to mean?'

'Alice has been bending my ear about him. Now, about Yildilla, any chance you could take me to him?'

'It's that urgent?'

'Yes, it's that urgent, otherwise I wouldn't ask.'

Bindi thought for a moment. 'I suppose we could drive over to the depot near Pinjupin, the constable might know something.'

'What, over by Mullin Soak?'

'That's the one.'

'If anyone asks where we're going it's to do with Curly's family.'

Bindi looked at him, a question on her lips.

'I don't want Greg to know.'

'What about Alice?'

'I'll square things with Alice, she'll be all right.'

They set off the same day, the utility loaded with a tool kit and assorted replacement parts, spare tyres, a fan belt, water, fuel and sand mats in preparation for the off-road travelling needed to get to Mullin Soak. As Jon drove he glanced at Bindi, her nose in a book. 'What're you reading?'

'Kafka's *The Trial*.'

'Heavy going?'

'Fairly.'

'What does Alistair say about it?'

'Don't know yet. He said I'm to read it and then present my con-

47

sidered opinion on the content.'

Jon grinned. 'You reckon he's read it?'

'Yeah, he's read it, right enough.' She turned back to the book, her brow furrowed as the ute jolted and bounced over the corrugated track. A few miles down the road she stopped reading again. 'What did Alice say when you told her I was going with you?'

'I didn't.'

'I thought you said you'd square things with her?'

'I will…when we get back.'

She shook her head in disbelief and turned back to her book.

For the next few hours Jon concentrated on his driving, avoiding the worst of the soft sand and thinking about the task ahead. If they couldn't find Yildilla then it would be up to them to hide the plane. He shivered at the thought of returning to Paradise Canyon, it was a beautiful and yet terrifying place that would forever hold mixed feelings for him.

They arrived at the depot in the late evening. The constable wasn't about although the wisps of camp-fire smoke told them that several families were encamped close by. As they drew up next to the lock-up stores dogs stirred and wandered over, sniffing the wheels of the utility, their feet and Jon's trousers. The Aborigines sitting around the fires looked up. Jon recognised Curly's family, the first he'd seen of them in over five years, since before Curly died. He recognised Rube, Curly's mother, first – she didn't look much different, hair a little more grizzled at the temples but otherwise the same as when they'd spent time together at Murrin Murrin and Mullin Soak.

'Hello, Rube.'

She inclined her head in his direction whilst keeping a fixed eye on Bindi.

'This is Bindi,' he said. 'We're looking for Yildilla, word is he's in the area. Have you seen him around?'

'What's he like?'

Jon held his hand up to chin level. 'About this big, thin, grey hair, scars on his legs.'

'Nope, ain't seen no Yildilla round here,' she said in a voice that implied *and don't want to either*.

Jon didn't believe she hadn't seen him; the old man put the wind up everyone, except Bindi.

Myrtle joined them, a toddler hanging on to the skirt of her dress, his fingers jammed into his mouth. Myrtle was Rube's sister,

Curly's aunt, and one of the senior women. 'He was here a few days ago...no tellin' where he is...' She let her eyes take in the land about them as if half expecting Yildilla to turn up at the mention of his name.

'How's Jigger?'

'He all right. Sleeps lot.'

'Have you seen Jimmi recently?'

'Nah, he livin' with Molly's family out Emu Plain way. You want tucker?' asked Rube. She indicated they should join them. Later she wiped out a couple of tin dishes with a grubby piece of cloth, hacked off a piece of half-roasted kangaroo and tore off a piece of damper. While he and Bindi ate, the others sat staring into the embers of the campfire, dozing in the heat, their fronts and faces baking and their backs chilled by the night air. After they'd eaten Bindi fetched their swags and they settled down for the night, safe in the company of Curly's family.

Later, while the rest of the camp slept, Jon lay back, looking up at the familiar stars traversing the night sky, the Southern Cross, the False Cross and Orion and then there were stars Curly had taught him to recognise, Vega and Altair, although they weren't the names Curly had used.

Curly would have been in his mid-twenties had he lived, maybe a family man. An image of the young Aborigine standing stark naked, poised to dive into the green pool that lay on the north side of Jarrahlong Station, sprang into his mind. Curly had been good looking, as pretty as Bindi with his copper-blond, curly hair, his white teeth, and the gap between the front two that gave his smile an irrepressible quality. Curly had been his first real friend in Australia, the first person he'd ever felt kinship with, but it had been all too brief, a few short months and Curly was dead, he'd died in his arms, in agony, his body and brain poisoned by gangrenous flesh. He'd wanted to talk to Rube of Curly and knew he couldn't, that Aborigines preferred not to speak of the dead. Instead, he'd need to find another way to honour his friend's memory, to atone for his thoughtless action in killing the infant monitor lizard, the perentie, Curly's totem animal.

Now he had an opportunity. It was up to him and Bindi to save Paradise Canyon from Chips Carpenter, even if it meant tribal punishment at the hands of Yildilla. They needed to remove the remains of the plane if they were to keep the canyon's secret hidden, and preserve it for future generations of Curly's family.

* * *

When Jon woke Jigger was standing over him with a quart pot of billy tea in his hand.

Jon rolled onto his side and smiled at the old fella who was still as thin as a lath. Jigger's straggly beard, discoloured with food, swept his chest as he chewed on the baccy that stained his remaining teeth brown.

'You want tea?' The Aborigine indicated the billy hanging from a stick over the fire.

'Don't mind if I do.'

Jigger squatted down on his haunches. 'Rube say you lookin' for Yildilla.'

'Yeah, Aborigine business.'

'Reckon 'im back next week, sometime.'

'Can't wait that long, Jigger. You tell 'im Bindi and me goin' long canyon.'

'Yildilla, 'im bit mean bugger.'

Jon smiled as he poured himself a mug of stewed tea and laced it well with sugar to disguise the tannin. Jigger wasn't wrong, but Yildilla was only keeping blackfella law, the fact that it didn't always sit easy with whitefella law was beside the point.

After breakfast Rube packed them up food for the journey, said they'd keep an eye out for the utility while they were at the depot and watched as the two of them headed out, on foot, into the outback towards Paradise Canyon.

'You know the way, Bindi?'

She smiled at him. 'As well as the pattern on a perentie.'

He grinned at her, not doubting her for a moment. He scanned the landscape before them – this time they would be approaching the high plateau from the north-east. He'd never travelled over the country they were now in and he wondered if the journey would be as onerous as the south-westerly route he'd followed before.

They left the camp and Curly's family and travelled fast, walking through the night once the moon had risen. At dawn they stopped for a quick meal and watched the sun breasting the horizon, turning the distant plateau pale blue. By midday their destination seemed to shimmer in the heat, the rocky outline fading to nothing in the bright, eye-watering light. It was then they rested, sleeping in a shady place, conserving their energy, readying themselves for the next leg of the journey.

50

Late afternoon the high plateau became a ribbon of deep purple darkening to indigo as they prepared an evening meal. Another night and day of travelling and they'd reach the canyon.

The north-eastern edge of the plateau was riven with clefts and narrow gorges barely wide enough for them to pass in single file. Twice they had to turn back when a gully petered out to nothing, but the third brought them to the rugged rock on the top of the plateau with its uninterrupted view across the vast sea of sandhills that surrounded the once great range.

Jon turned his back on Paradise Canyon and looked north. He could see dark smudges in the ironstone; other canyons that had been carved out of the softer rock by a once mighty river, the remnants of which sparkled in the gorge behind him.

He turned back to Bindi who was standing at the top of the question mark gash, looking down on the water, the zigzag of silver that disappeared into a soak over a hundred feet below. Already the light was fading and birds were settling for the night, the noise loud in the confined space, their chittering calls bouncing off the canyon walls. Flashes of brilliant plumage appeared against the darkening ground as squabbling birds tumbled out of the ghost gums or flitted from bush to bush, trying to find peace amongst the racket created by their number.

A thrill rippled down his spine. The place never ceased to move him.

Bindi pointed to a route down the rock face, a narrow path that snaked to the valley floor and they took it, anxious to reach the bottom of the canyon before the light failed.

There they set up camp beneath an overhang and scraped out the ashes of an old campfire. While Bindi made damper he went fishing for yabbies and later, replete, with pannikins of billy tea cooling, Bindi asked about the plane.

'Chips Carpenter crashed it about ten or eleven years back, ever since he's spent his time and money searching for it.'

'What's so special about it?'

'It's not the plane that's special; it's what he found in the canyon when he recovered consciousness.'

'The gold you mentioned?'

'That's right,' said Jon.

'So where is the gold? I've never seen any, not in this gorge.'

Jon hesitated. Yildilla hadn't told her, or shown her the ancestor cavern, otherwise she'd know about it.

'It's a sacred place, a man's place, isn't it?' she said simply.

'How many Aboriginal mobs use the canyon, Bindi?'

'Five, it's on five routes.'

'You ever brought Ty here?'

She shook her head. 'He's not a blackfella; besides, he doesn't work in this part, too far east.'

'Do you reckon Yildilla will come?'

'He'll come.'

'How can you be so sure?'

She shrugged. 'He'll come.'

When Jon woke, stiff and cold, Yildilla was sitting on a flat rock beyond the dying embers of the campfire, watching him. Their eyes locked briefly and Jon looked away first; he rolled out from under his blanket and threw fresh wood onto the fire as Bindi stirred.

They breakfasted on damper and tea. Jon watched Yildilla as they ate, amazed and yet uneasy at the speed with which the old man had arrived. Not for the first time he wondered about the sixth sense that he'd seen with Jimmi, the time Jimmi had rescued him from certain death after Curly died, the time the Aborigine couldn't explain how he knew that Jon was in deep trouble.

'We need to move the plane wreckage,' said Jon. 'The bloke who crashed it is out searching for likely looking canyons. Soon as he sees this one from the air he'll be back to quarter the area.'

'You can't hide a plane,' said Bindi.

'We can if we put it in a cave, out of sight.'

'It's too big.'

'A lot of it is matchwood, we can burn it.'

Yildilla didn't speak; he just drank his tea and chewed on the damper.

'He could still find it even if we hide it,' said Bindi.

'He could, but if he doesn't find the wreckage, or any sign of the wreckage, then he'll think it's the wrong canyon.' Jon wished the Aborigine would speak, say something, either for or against the idea. Instead, once Yildilla had finished his breakfast, he picked up his staff and walked off in the direction of the crash site. Jon and Bindi followed and so did the finches, their bright colours catching the light as they flitted from branch to branch.

'We need to disturb the ground as little as possible,' said Jon, 'and we mustn't damage the bushes. Bindi, if you carry what metal bits you can over to the entrance of that cleft in the rock and leave them on the ground I'll take them the rest of the way. We must clear everything away, we can't leave a scrap, no pieces of wood, canvas, leather, glass...nothing, everything, every last bit has to be removed or burnt.'

The three of them worked in silence for hours, pulling apart the remains of the plane, peeling back aluminium panels and canvas, unscrewing bolts to lift out the seat and later the engine. For two days they worked until their arms, backs and legs ached and their fingernails were broken and their fingers were bleeding. Bit by bit and piece by piece the plane was dismantled and carried into the sacred cavern by Jon and Yildilla and stacked in the dark recesses, where the gold reef disappeared into the rock, as far away from the wall painting of Perentie Man as they could place them.

When they'd finished, the place where the wreckage had been was bare, and branches that had grown around the fuselage looked straggly and misshapen. To anyone with half an eye for detail it was obvious, but that couldn't be helped.

Later, they gathered brushwood from further up the valley and swept away the marks of the plane in the sand, and their footprints, while Bindi scoured the oil-soaked rock with sand and threw more of it onto the rock to hide the stains she couldn't erase.

High up on the rock face Jon could still see the scars where the plane had nose-dived over the lip. Chips wouldn't be fooled, would he? Had they wasted their time?

Desolate, he sat by the campfire, eating roast rabbit that Bindi had caught, chewing on the near raw meat that Aborigines favoured. In the end he gave up and skewered the half-chewed meat and held it back over the embers to cook some more. While he waited, staring into the fire, Yildilla started to speak to Bindi in his own language. That it was some story was clear, the style of delivery told him that, and Bindi's rapt attention as the old man spoke.

'What was that all about?' asked Jon when Yildilla had finished.

'The Dreaming,' said Bindi. 'He was telling me how Perentie Man journeyed over this land.'

Jon leaned back against a rock and watched Yildilla sitting before the fire, staring into the flames. The Aborigine knew English, he was sure of it, but Yildilla wasn't about to talk to him in the language. Jon watched him through half-closed eyes, just so long as the old fella didn't pick up his spear and run him through with it then he could cope with the silence.

Jon shivered. Everything about the Aborigine was intimidating, from his deeply furrowed brow down to his thin, scarred legs. There was nothing soft about Yildilla, no wonder he put the wind up people. Well, he wasn't going to let the Aborigine intimidate him, he'd done more than he needed to do for Curly's people, it wasn't his fault that Chips Carpenter had stumbled on Paradise Canyon and the gold. If the old fella couldn't see that and didn't recognise his attempt to preserve the sacred site for future generations then sod him.

Jon threw a couple of hefty roots onto the fire, keepers for the night, then, wrapping his blanket around him, he left Bindi and her grandfather to yammer on in their own dialect.

When he awoke Bindi was making fresh damper and Yildilla was nowhere to be seen.

'He's gone?' he asked.

She nodded. 'First light.'

'He say anything?'

Her eyes danced with amusement. 'No.' She flung tea leaves into the boiling water. 'You don't like him, do you?'

'What do you think?'

'You know he won't do anything else to you?'

'That right! You mean, not unless I break some other tribal law.'

Bindi didn't answer and Jon knew he hadn't been far wrong.

After breakfast they packed up their gear and took one last look at the crash site. In the cold light of day it didn't look too bad, maybe it would stand a cursory glance. Perhaps that was all they'd need. He couldn't see Chips doing a fingertip search of the whole canyon; he'd be too busy looking for obvious signs of wreckage. In any case it could be months before Chips found the canyon, if he ever found it, and by then the bush would have grown a bit, the rocks weathered some more. Maybe they'd get lucky.

'Does Alice know about the gold here?' asked Bindi.

'No.'

'Does anyone?'

'No, only me...and Chips, of course.'

'Aren't you tempted?'

'What, and lose my life to that grandfather of yours, because sure as eggs is eggs if I went prospecting in this valley Yildilla would terminate the project, quick-sticks.'

She glanced in his direction, a quizzical look on her face.

'Besides, it's a sacred place, isn't it? It'd be like stealing the gold plate from a church back in Liverpool.'

'So what are you going to tell Alice?'

'I don't know, I'll think of something.'

CHAPTER 6

Jon knew he was in for a roasting the minute he saw Alice waiting for him on the verandah.

'You didn't tell me you were taking Bindi with you.' Her piercing eyes gleamed with ill-concealed anger. 'You might have had the decency to speak to me and Alistair before waltzing off with her. She is supposed to be having lessons you know and I am responsible for her while she's living here.'

Alistair sat with one hand resting lightly on the table between them, an open book on his lap. Jon noticed the briefest of smiles flicker across Alistair's face; the academic had Alice mapped, not that anyone needed a qualification in human nature to know when Alice was annoyed.

'Sorry, Alice, at the last minute it occurred to me it might be wise to take Bindi with me. It was a spur of the moment decision.'

'So *spur of the moment* you didn't have time to mention it?' She glared at him. 'So what was this *something*? What did Curly's grandfather want with you that couldn't wait?'

Jon racked his brain trying to think of a plausible excuse convincing enough to satisfy Alice. He'd been thinking about it on the journey home and hadn't come up with a good idea, at least not one good enough to placate Alice. Bindi had been no help either. 'Jigger,' he said suddenly, an idea forming even as he said the name. He crossed his fingers hoping he wasn't tempting providence.

'Jigger, who the hell's Jigger?' asked Alice.

'I told you, Curly's grandfather. It turned out he was sick and he wanted to see Curly's grave.'

'Why didn't you tell us this before?'

Jon threw up his hands in exasperation. 'I didn't know myself until we got there.'

'He's dying, is he?'

'I hope not,' said Jon in a calmer voice, 'but that's why I asked Bindi to go with me. I didn't want to find myself in trouble again, not with Yildilla around. No telling what he'd do with that spear of his a second time around.'

Alice sucked on her cheroot, held the acrid smoke in her lungs and exhaled slowly, all the while watching him, trying to pick out the truth from the lies. 'This story takes some believing. You get word that one of Curly's people wants to see you, so you just drop everything and go haring off into the desert and, not only that, you drag Bindi along too. I'm surprised she went with you.'

'She wasn't keen,' admitted Jon. 'She only agreed to go because I told her I was afraid of meeting up with Yildilla again.'

'What's wrong with this Jigger fella then, apart from old age?'

'Don't know, Alice. He perked up after Bindi gave him some Aboriginal medicine.'

He sat back in his seat amazed at how convincing he sounded. He didn't like lying to Alice but it was best she didn't know the real reason. He glanced at Alistair about to take a sip of Alice's favourite bourbon whiskey, his face inscrutable behind the bland expression he favoured when he kept his thoughts to himself. Alistair rarely gave away his feelings. If pressed he'd give a view, but in Jon's experience it was always considered and tempered with caution as if he didn't want to go upsetting the comfortable lifestyle he'd landed for himself. Not for the first time Jon wondered what had happened to make a man Alistair's age up sticks and move to the outback. He noticed Alice watching him and felt his colour rising, had his face given him away?

'Look, Alice, I couldn't say no. In a way it was my fault Curly died and I feel sort of bound to protect the family, do for them what I can.' And it was true! Okay, so Jigger wasn't sick, hadn't asked to see Curly's grave, but he was protecting their heritage, their supply of food in the desert, their insurance against drought and, at the end of the day, that was more important to an Aborigine than most things.

'What did he do when he got to Curly's grave?'

'Just sat beside it, did a bit of chanting, a bit of thinking, not a lot, I suppose.'

Alice snorted. 'And what did Bindi make of it?'

'I don't know, Alice, you'll have to ask her.'

'Don't you worry, I will.'

'Trip probably did her some good,' said Alistair, breaking the chilly atmosphere. 'People need a rest from time to time; it recharges the batteries, so to speak.'

'Don't you go letting him off the hook,' chided Alice.

'I suppose I'd better go and get cleaned up before tea,' said Jon keen to get away from the interrogation.

'At least your timing is spot on.'

'What d'you mean?'

'A call came over on the radio, two of the Kenton kids, from Harrison Station, have gone missing and they want help with the search.'

'When did they go missing?'

'Yesterday afternoon. Everyone on the station went looking but didn't find them so they sent out the call on the evening schedule. They resumed the search at first light. Greg's over there helping, flying spotter with Chips Carpenter.'

'We'll hear tonight how the search has gone.' She looked at her watch. 'Not long to wait. I'll get Belle to make us a brew.'

The evening schedule didn't bring good news. The two children were still missing and David and Joan Kenton, who managed the station, were asking for more Aboriginal trackers.

Jon looked across to Bindi. 'How're you fixed for a spot of tracking tomorrow at the Kenton's place?'

She nodded. The bush out that way had been her backyard as a kid and she was one of the best trackers he knew, she'd been taught by a master.

'Bindi and me, we'll drive over, Alice.'

'What about Adie, you want to take him too?'

'Yes, looks like the situation is desperate.'

'You're not wrong there,' said Alice quietly, 'it'll be two days tomorrow, it's a long time for kiddies to be out in the bush.'

Bindi finished her tea. 'I'll go and have a word with Adie. What time do you want to leave?'

'It's a fair hike to Harrison Station so I reckon we should get an early night and aim to leave here about half past two, they'll want to continue the search at first light.'

After the evening meal Alice, Alistair and Jon sat around the kitchen table. 'It's buggered up the chess,' commented Alice.

'You and Alistair can always have a game.'

'He always wins.'

Jon took in the scowl on Alice's face and smiled. 'And you fancied thrashing someone easy, that it?'

'Something along those lines,' conceded Alice with little enthusiasm. 'I wonder what made those kids wander off?'

'How old are they?'

'About six and seven.'

'No telling at that age,' said Alistair. 'They were probably busy doing something and before they knew it they were out of sight of the homestead.'

'Yes, I think that's about right,' agreed Alice, 'it's easy enough to get disorientated out in the bush, and for little kids it's easier still. Let's pray to God it doesn't end in tragedy like the Bryson case.'

'Never heard of that one,' said Jon.

'No, you wouldn't have. It happened soon after Jack and I moved here. Their youngest wandered off during the afternoon. They think he followed the family dog. Anyway, the family went looking when the dog came back alone. They spent hours searching every bit of the homestead and all the land about. Come nightfall and they still hadn't found him so they sent a stockman into town for help. Next day the police and everyone from miles around joined in the search, didn't do any good though, they even brought in Aboriginal trackers when all else failed. The blacks reckoned it was impossible to track him, too many people had trampled over the place, obliterating any marks the lad had left.'

'Did they find him?' asked Jon.

Alice shook her head. 'No, they never did. It turned Mrs Bryson mad. She ended up in a psychiatric hospital. Family sold up and moved out, couldn't face living there after that.'

At first light Harrison Station homestead yard was packed with police and locals who'd driven, ridden or flown in from the surrounding stations and from Pilkington and Charlestown. Many of them had slept in the stockmen's quarters overnight determined to stick it out until the boys were found.

Chips flew out with Greg in the passenger seat to resume the aerial search soon after dawn. Jon watched as the plane bounced along the rough ground, a temporary landing strip that the stock-men had cleared of scrubby saltbush, bluebush and spinifex.

The rest of the search teams left shortly after that. Jon, Bindi and Glyn, one of the Harrison Station stockmen, had been allocated part of the north-eastern quadrant while Adie joined another team searching equally difficult terrain south of the homestead.

They picked up the search from where the men had left off the night before, just before the light failed. They'd been given the high land, a barren plateau and stony plain because of Bindi's tracking skills. Jon was relieved, he didn't want to be the one to find their bodies, and most thought the boys had headed north-west where the majority of the stockmen and the police Aboriginal trackers were searching.

The three of them quartered the plateau closest to the homestead and began a careful search looking for anything that would indicate children had passed that way, scratch marks, disturbed ground, discarded clothing, toys, something out of the ordinary.

'Anything out this way that the boys could have been heading for?' asked Jon.

Glyn shook his head. 'No, just plateau.'

'No soaks beyond the plateau, or billabongs where they might have gone for a swim, or to fish?'

'No.'

Jon squinted at the rock depressed by the hopeless task. He'd once spent agonising hours on a stony plain not dissimilar to the terrain they were on, dehydrated and dying. What if the children were in the same state? What if they were already dead?

He took in the clear, cloudless sky, by mid-morning the heat would be relentless. It had been a particularly hot, dry spring, the worst sort of conditions to be lost in the outback. He couldn't bear to think about what the boys were going through, or how the Kentons would cope with losing their two youngest children. And yet the possibility was on everyone's minds, over the years people vanished in the outback, their bodies never found.

His thoughts switched back to England, to when he'd returned to Liverpool only to discover his sister had been adopted. He'd been gutted by the news. The superintendent at the children's home had refused to tell him who had adopted her, had told him that she was no longer his sister, that she had a new family. He'd spent days searching after that, visiting all the places he thought she might be or might go to. He'd examined faces, looking for a twelve-year-old girl he'd last seen as a five-year-old child.

Then, when he had found her, he hadn't recognised her. Her face had been slick with blood and rain as she lay on the wet tarmac beneath the van he'd been in when she'd dashed across the road without looking and Frank Cooper hit her.

He pulled himself up; best not to look on the dark side. He'd found his sister, they'd find the boys. He pushed thoughts of Liverpool out of his mind and renewed his efforts, scanning the ground, looking for signs, anything that would give them hope.

They reached the end of the plateau mid-afternoon and looked down on a dry creek bed with thicker bush running along its length. Searching this section would be more time consuming, they'd need to look under bushes or into clefts along the edge of the escarpment, anywhere children might shelter. Glyn chose to scout along the creek, Bindi opted for the more difficult terrain beyond the creek, while Jon searched among the rocks on the edge of the escarpment, but he wasn't hopeful of finding the boys, they were a long way out from the station and Chips had already covered the ground they'd been allocated. During the morning they'd watched the light aircraft flying along the creek bed, had the boys heard the plane they would have been out in the open, waving. Greg would have been sure to have seen them. But they hadn't seen Chips dip the plane wings, hadn't seen the plane circling one spot, indicating a find.

Two and a half days the boys had been missing and he feared the worst; the light was fading, it would be dark soon. He finished his search and met up with Glyn and Bindi.

'Any sign?' asked Jon.

Bindi shook her head.

'No, nothing,' admitted Glyn.

They headed back to the homestead, hoping the others had had better luck, wanting to see jubilant faces, but they knew instantly that the boys hadn't been found, everyone was standing round in uneasy groups, keeping a watchful eye on the family members who were doing their best to keep their despair under control.

'No luck?' asked Jon when he saw Cadge.

Cadge nodded in Nickson's direction. 'One of the Abo trackers found a pair of shorts and a shoe.'

Jon felt his heart jump, he knew better than most what that meant. 'Was he able to follow the trail?'

Cadge shook his head. 'Poor little buggers...' He dragged his hand slowly down his face as if rubbing away his frustration and despair and looked across at Jon. 'Maybe they've had the sense to sit down under a shady tree and wait to be found, let's hope so, because then we'll be dealing with bad sunburn and dehydration, if they haven't then...'

Cadge didn't need to finish the sentence, Jon knew the score. He'd experienced the delirium, the hot, dry skin, the overwhelming urge to discard clothing, a classic symptom of severe dehydration, and, if they weren't already in a coma, they'd be wandering through the bush in ragged circles oblivious of their surroundings.

And what if they were already dead? He knew the answer to that too, the meat ants would have started on them. He shuddered not wanting to think such thoughts, the boys weren't dead; there was still time to find them.

For the first time Jon fully appreciated the size of the search party, the homestead was heaving with people. It seemed to him that every adult for miles around had turned up to help find the Kenton boys. Nickson had arrived at first light with a couple of police to coordinate the search. Barnes and two more police arrived soon after. Connie had driven over from Charlestown to help organise the food along with her Chinese cook. Wes, Scally, Les and Ty were there, and men and women Jon didn't know who had driven in from Pilkington; then there was Cadge and his shearing team, and the owner of the station they'd been working on, together with his stockmen who had driven into the yard soon after the police arrived. Every available man from Jindalee and Jarrahlong was there too. All had brought their swags ready to doss down wherever they could find somewhere to lay their heads.

Old man Kenton, the boys' grandfather, had slaughtered one of the station bulls and butchered it to feed the crowd – it would have been one hell of a party had their reason for being there not been so serious.

The mood that night was subdued. Men and women ate in silence, and only later talked in small groups, anxious not to say anything that would upset Joan and David Kenton who were barely holding it together. All of them had a tale to tell of such searches that had ended in tragedy, prospectors who had got lost in the bush, kids who had wandered off, like the Bryson kid, and had never been found.

That night, before they all turned in, Nickson had a word, reminding them that anyone searching out in the bush was at risk of dehydration, he warned them to take plenty of water and to cover up.

'We don't want to have to send out rescue parties to pick up sick buggers,' he said. 'It's not a medical centre here, so take plenty of water with you, and wear a hat.'

Most of them didn't need telling, although a few of them did, those who rarely ventured out in the bush needed to be reminded of the dangers. Dehydration and twisted ankles were common on searches like these, not to mention insect bites and eye injuries from pushing through thick scrub, as well as the hassle of repairing staked tyres and holed radiators.

At first light everyone was up and ready to begin a fresh search, time was critical, the boys had been lost for three days – without water they'd be in a bad way and wouldn't survive for much longer. The Kentons knew that as well as anyone and the strain showed on their faces.

The plan was to begin the search where they'd found the clothing. A convoy of vehicles set off, pushing through the bush to the site to save time. The police and two of their trackers were in the first truck, while Glyn, Bindi, Adie, and another black tracker from Cavanagh's Creek, were in the second. Jon followed behind in his ute with Cadge and four stockmen in the back, and two more trucks followed on behind them.

They parked and left the trackers to do their business, looking for signs, however faint, a stone flipped out of place, blades of grass bent the wrong way, a broken twig or maybe branches at unnatural angles where they had been disturbed.

All morning they scoured the bush in thicket so dense walking was difficult, thorny branches snatched at their clothing, ripped off their hats and lacerated their skin, progress was agonisingly slow, their feet ached and their eyes were gritty from tiredness and dust long before the sun had reached its zenith.

Sweat trickled down Jon's legs and he felt the trouser fabric chafing, even so it was as nothing to what the boys would be suffering. He blocked his mind to the pain and discomfort and pushed on; no wonder the boys hadn't been spotted from the plane, the area was heavily overgrown with acacia, the canopy too dense to see through.

He knew the others felt the same despair, conversation had ceased hours ago, now each person concentrated on the ground in front of him, praying for a miracle, a sign that the boys were close.

In the distance he heard someone call out. Those around him stopped and listened.

Nothing!

Had they been mistaken?

'Do you reckon they've found them?' said Cadge who was closest to him. 'You found them?' he yelled as loud as he could, cupping his mouth to direct the sound.

A muffled shout came back.

'Reckon that's a yes,' said Cadge unable to keep the elation out of his voice. 'Reckon they've found them,' he yelled to the others.

Jon, Greg, Bindi and Adie arrived back at Jarrahlong in the late evening. Alice and Alistair were waiting for them having heard the good news on the evening schedule.

'Where were they?' asked Alice.

'In a patch of dense scrub, south-east of the homestead, they'd taken shelter under a big gum tree, stark naked they were, huddled together and delirious, badly dehydrated the pair of them,' said Jon.

'They're lucky to be alive,' said Greg. 'They could do with a good thrashing, wandering off like that.'

'They were in pretty bad shape, another few hours and it would have been too late,' said Jon. 'The flying doctor rehydrated them intravenously and then flew them and their mother to Kalgoorlie hospital, but it's touch and go, especially for the younger one.'

'I hope they make it,' she commented.

'So do we all, but I reckon it'll be a while before we know for sure, word is they may have suffered some organ damage.'

'Do they know why the boys wandered off?' asked Alistair.

'No, they were in too bad a shape to question,' said Jon. 'You didn't pick up anything, did you, Greg?'

'No, when we first arrived Mrs Kenton was hysterical.'

'I'm not surprised,' said Alice. 'There've been enough lost in the bush over the years.'

'Where's Belle?' Greg grabbed Alice's handbell and rang it outside the back door. 'I'm bloody starving,' he grumbled. He filled the kettle, put it on to boil and then picked up the bell and jangled it again. 'You should have a word with her, Alice, she's getting slow in her old age.'

'Belle's done all right by me. I don't plan on making any changes just at the moment.'

Greg turned his back on them, a tense look on his face as he reached for the coffee and spooned a measure into a mug.

Jon knew that Greg would make more than one or two changes if he had half a chance. He'd get rid of all the blacks on Jarrahlong straight off, even though it was increasingly difficult to get white stockmen to live in the outback miles from the nearest town. He didn't understand Greg's attitude. He hadn't come across such antipathy towards blacks in Liverpool and there were more than a few of them, not to mention the Chinamen living in the city, but Greg was from Lincolnshire. As far as he knew blacks were pretty thin on the ground there, so what had happened to make him so prejudiced?

Greg sat back down at the kitchen table, fingers drumming while he waited for the kettle to boil and for Belle to appear from around the side of the stockmen's quarters. 'You any plans for tomorrow, Jon?'

'No.'

'Do you mind driving me over to Charlestown? I need to pick up the ute. I left it at Wes's when I flew out with Chips.'

'There's no hurry,' said Alice. 'Why don't you have an easy day tomorrow? Jon'll drive you over on Monday, won't you, Jon?'

'Tomorrow would suit me better,' said Greg.

'Well, even if you don't need a break I'm sure Jon does, he and Bindi only got back the day before yesterday and then they've been over at the Kenton's place. You're all looking a bit jaded, if you ask me.'

Greg started to speak and then thought better of it; he turned away from them, his mouth a tight line. He seized the bell again, opened the door, jangled it, dumped it back on the kitchen table and then, without a word, went through to his room and returned with a towel. The door slammed behind him for a second time as he went out towards the wash block.

'What's upset him?' asked Alice.

'He's probably just tired,' observed Alistair.

Anxiety, thought Jon. Wes reckoned Greg was losing money hand over fist in the two-up ring and Sunday was two-up day. Greg's bad humour was more likely to be about his debts than tiredness.

CHAPTER 7

Jon woke with a start in the middle of yet another hot and muggy December night. Thunder rumbled overhead and lightning briefly lit up the sky as he angrily kicked off the thin over-sheet – the bloody weather! What they needed was a downpour to clear the air, although rain wasn't going to happen any time soon, he could smell that it wouldn't.

A sick, tired feeling washed over him, the clammy heat drained energy and made sleeping difficult and when sleep did come he dreamed, vivid, disturbing dreams in which he always seemed to be searching, but searching for what?

The clock dial read ten to two. What had woken him? The heat? The storm? Or something else? Above, the thunder rumbled again and rolled on westward while he drifted in a twilight world, dozily planning the day ahead, thinking about the new stock Alice needed and the replacement fencing wire to be ordered and fitted.

'Jon!'

He sat bolt upright. Someone was calling him.

Was it Curly?

He listened. Nothing! Just a dream then, it wasn't Curly's voice at all, but whose? He lay back on the bed and dredged his mind for the dream. Val! It had been Val's voice calling to him, he was sure of it.

He hadn't given much thought to her recently and then knew he was fooling himself. He couldn't help but think about her, what with Alice asking after her every time he was over at Jarrahlong, and Rachel nagging on about her when he was in Charlestown, not to mention Wes, Connie and Al's enquiries.

The last time he'd seen her was months back, he did a quick cal-

66

culation, the baby would be due soon, in two or three weeks probably, maybe that was why she'd been on his mind. Fresh sweat prickled his skin, being pregnant in the summer heat must be unbearable for her.

'Jon!'

He wasn't dreaming that time though, was he? He swung his feet over the side of the bed again and sat on the edge.

'Jon!'

Fear caught in his throat. Why was she calling him? Was she in trouble? He tried to brush away his disquiet. Berry would be with her, she'd be fine, she didn't need him. He sat with his head in his hands, listening, straining to catch what he thought he'd heard, then glanced at the clock again, quarter past two, he was sure he'd heard her voice. He tilted his head to listen.

Nothing!

Imagination then!

He swore under his breath, now that he was wide awake he'd never get back to sleep. He pulled on strides, a fresh shirt, a clean pair of socks and his boots, threw a couple of logs into the range and put the billy on to boil while he washed and shaved, but he couldn't stop listening for Val. She was like a niggling whisper in his ear, and then he remembered Jimmi, the time Jimmi had travelled out into the desert to save him from certain death because he knew that Jon needed him. He'd recalled that incident only a couple of months back, when the Kenton boys were lost in the bush, and now he'd recalled it again.

But why?

He rinsed his face and dried himself and set about cleaning his teeth. He wasn't an Aborigine; besides, no one in their right mind would believe all that telepathy stuff, there'd be a logical explanation in there somewhere. He gargled, spat out the rinse and felt better.

Bonny stirred in her box next to the dresser, she waddled over and leaned against his leg for a bit of affection as he flung a few tea leaves into the billy. Val had been with him when Stan died. She'd watched him lift Stan's dogs onto the bed so Stan could stroke his 'old gals' as he called them. Val had heard his promise to look after Bess and Bonny, heard him say that he wouldn't take them out and shoot them. She'd been there for him then when Stan's death had been a lump in his throat choking him up.

He slammed Stan's enamel mug down on the table and grabbed

the ute keys. If Berry's truck was parked in the yard he'd turn around and drive home again.

Half an hour from Berry's place he was feeling like a prize idiot. Two bloody hours it had taken and for what? A wild goose chase across the outback just because he thought he'd heard Val calling for him; he flushed at the thought of it.

The ute headlights cut a swathe through the bush as he avoided the deepest of the ruts on the old Pilkington road, while up above lightning briefly lit up the sky again. Rain, that's what they needed to wash away the oppressive heat, but it wasn't going to happen that night; there was still no smell of it in the air, just the stink of the hot engine and the red earth as the vehicle chewed its way through patches of bulldust and bounced over the corrugations.

Jon felt himself drifting, taking longer and longer blinks, wanting his bed and sleep even as he tried to concentrate on the mesmerising headlight beams jolting along the road. He slid open the side window hoping the draught would stave off the overwhelming fatigue and thought about what lay ahead. What if Berry wasn't there? What if she'd gone into labour early? He wished he wasn't alone, he could have done with Bindi, or Rachel, or Alice, even Curly would have done, anyone. He blinked again...

... 'No good wishing for me, mate,' says a familiar voice.

He glances at the passenger seat and sees Curly hanging on to the dashboard as the ute bounces over the washboard road.

'What are you doing here?' he asks.

'Kids,' says Curly, 'that's women's business. Men don't know what goes on in the birthing places.'

'What are you on about?'

'Men and women,' says Curly. 'Men do men's things, secret from women, things women not allowed to know about, and women, women's things. Women not allowed in men's sacred places and men not allowed in women's.'

He recalls what Stan had told him about the cutting ceremonies Aborigine boys had to go through, and Curly himself had referred to it, the time he had to use pituri to get through it, using the narcotic drug to numb the pain of circumcision, and the rest.

Maybe Curly was right, he was getting involved in something that wasn't his business...

...The steering wheel snatched, jolting him awake.

'You reckon I should go back?' But there was no answer. Curly had gone.

This time he stuck his head out of the ute window hoping the rushing air would keep him awake; it was no good having these hallucinations, if he wasn't careful he'd end up off the road, the bonnet crushed against a eucalyptus tree, leaving him with the mother of all headaches.

He caught sight of a white hand-painted sign, Berry's place, and turned off the graded road, easing the ute along the dog-rough track, searching for a glimpse of Berry's truck in the yard. The battered khaki-coloured Leyland was nowhere to be seen, though that didn't mean it wasn't parked up in one of the lean-tos. He switched off the engine and stepped out of the cab. On the horizon another dull flash of lightning lit up the sky momentarily and then threw everything back into darkness as he crossed the yard and checked the sheds. No truck!

No one answered when he hammered on the shack door – no surprise there – at half past four in the morning anyone half sane would be fast asleep. The fly-screen door wasn't fastened, nor the inner door so he stepped into the kitchen.

'Berry! Val! Anyone home?'

Still nothing! Had Val gone into labour? Had Berry taken her into town? He spotted a kerosene lamp when another bolt of lightning lit up the room. He found matches, lit the lantern and, carrying it aloft, pushed open the inner door.

The bedroom was as basic as the kitchen. He took in the battered wardrobe with no doors on it, the cheap chest of drawers and the bentwood chair with clothes draped over it. On the scrubbed timber flooring was a thin piece of shabby matting and pushed against the wall was a double bed covered in a mound of bedding.

So they'd gone somewhere! He turned back to the kitchen and stopped. She was on the bed. He knew she was. He stepped closer, pulled back a blanket, and saw her lying in the middle of a tussle of linen, her skin and the bedding soaked in sweat, a nightdress rucked up around her breasts, her legs and swollen belly gleaming in the lamplight.

Fear washed over him; was she dead? Another flash of lightning illuminated the room, followed by a clap of thunder that rattled the building.

'Val!' he said, dragging the chest of drawers closer to the bed for the kerosene lamp.

A spasm racked her body. She moaned and flung her arms out, feeling for the bed headboard, her knees drawn up, her whole body straining to expel the baby.

After a few moments the contractions passed and she moaned again, unaware of his presence.

He shook her arm. 'Val!'

'Jon?' she moaned, her eyes wide with fear.

'Yes, it's me.'

'You came!'

'How long have you been in labour?'

She shook her head. 'I don't know, it won't come, the baby won't come.' Tears rolled down her cheeks.

'I'll go and get a doctor, or someone.'

She struggled to sit up as more thunder rolled overhead and heavy drops of rain beat down on the iron roof like marbles.

He'd been wrong about the rain!

'Don't leave me...please don't leave...' She gasped as another wave of contractions racked her body.

What was he doing here? Curly was right, this was women's business. What did he know about delivering babies? Cold sweat prickled his forehead, and his stomach and legs felt weak. He licked dry lips wishing he were miles from the place. He couldn't help her, he didn't know how.

A despairing wail interrupted his thoughts. She needed a doctor...a midwife...someone...anyone. Pilkington was the nearest, there must be someone in Pilkington who would know what to do.

Who was he fooling? He'd never get help in time. She was worn out. If the baby wasn't born soon they'd both die. He'd seen ewes that had given up from exhaustion.

The bedding was a mess, she couldn't give birth like that, he tried to straighten the soaking linen but she clung on to it tightly.

'What you doin'?' her voice, shrill and angry above the sound of the rain, stopped him.

'Sorting you out,' he said, fighting her as she tried to stop him pulling the undersheet straight. 'You're all taffled up, for God's sake.'

'Get out,' she screamed, grabbing at the blanket as another spasm racked her body.

'Suit yourself,' he yelled, backing out of the room, ignoring the stream of invective she was hurling at him.

In the kitchen he listened to the storm moving west, taking the rain with it, leaving only the sound of her sobbing. He stood immobile, undecided. She didn't want his help.

'Jon!' her voice hysterical, 'Jon!'

Her fear scared him.

'Jon!'

Hands, he needed clean hands. The carbolic soap needled his grazed skin and he was glad of the distraction as he scrubbed himself clean.

He paused on the threshold of the room. What if she died? What if they both died? He pushed the thoughts away, knelt by her side and lifted her into a more upright position.

'Come on, Val, you can't give up, the baby's almost here.'

'I can't do it,' her words a whisper.

What the hell did he say to her now? Frustration engulfed him. She had no right to drag him into this. He grabbed her arms and shook her hard. 'You can.'

'I can't.'

'Yes, you can,' he said, more quietly, ashamed of his outburst. 'When you feel those labour pains again, you push, you hear me?' He knelt on the bed beside her and held her against him, feeling her clammy body tensing as the contractions strengthened. He watched, waiting for the baby's head to appear.

'Pant,' he ordered. 'You've got to pant.'

'Stop nagging,' she raged through clenched teeth, her fingers tightening their grip on him as the contractions built. 'It hurts,' she screamed, digging her nails deeper into his arms, her hot breath fanning his cheek as she panted against the pain.

He felt her brace against him. 'That's it, Val, now push,' he encouraged, seeing the baby's head. 'Come on, Val, keep pushing.'

She tried, he could feel the effort, hear her grinding her teeth, and then came the sobbing.

She was too exhausted and close to giving up, he could see the despair on her face. He'd have to help the baby out like he did with lambs sometimes.

Jon moved to the foot of the bed. 'Look at me, Val,' he ordered.

She shook her head, tears rolling down her cheeks.

'Damn well look at me, won't you.'

'Why?' Her blue eyes flashed at him, tired as she was.

'You're going to have this baby, you hear me?'

'It won't come,' she wailed.

'Yes, it will, it's almost here.' He waited for the next wave of contractions to engulf her. 'Push,' he shouted, 'keep pushing.'

His fingers locked round the baby's skull, guiding its head and when the contractions faded he held on so it couldn't slide back. 'Next time, Val,' he said, sweat running down his neck, 'it's nearly here.'

With the next contraction he eased out a shoulder and then the other, and after that the baby came with a rush of blood and water. Shocked by the speed of it he could only stare.

'It's a girl!' he said finally, laying the baby on Val's belly. 'You've got a girl.'

'A girl,' she whispered, stroking the baby's forehead, tears trickling down her cheeks.

Later, after he'd cleared away the afterbirth and soiled linen, organised clean bedding and made Val a mug of tea liberally sweetened with condensed milk, he leaned against the sink, overcome for a moment, staring sightlessly through the window at the scrubby paddock beyond the yard, and shivered. What the hell was he doing here? Cold sweat prickled his skin. She could have died...and the baby...out here, in the back of beyond, miles from medical help. What on earth had possessed him to want to live in such a place? And Val! It was even worse for a woman. What the hell was keeping her here? Not Berry, surely!

And now there was the baby. When he'd picked her up to give her to Val her eyes had opened and she'd looked at him, piercingly, as if searching for something, some recognition, then, after a long moment, she seemed to relax as if, somehow, he'd passed muster. A warm tingle had rippled down his spine as he'd held her in his arms, and there'd been an overwhelming urge to protect. But how could that be? She wasn't his, she was Berry's.

Movement among the saltbush caught his eye – a euro, one of the smaller kangaroos common in the area, grazing on the far side of the paddock. His stomach growled – he hadn't eaten for twelve hours. He downed the rest of his tea and went through to Val and told her not to worry when she heard a rifle shot. 'Got to get us some tucker,' he added, 'otherwise we'll starve.'

She blushed.

'It's okay, Val. I won't be long.' He crossed the yard to the ute. There'd been no food to speak of in the larder, just a couple of tins of flour, a few cans of stewing meat and some root vegetables that had seen better days. Was that how she'd been living out here, on tinned dog and damper? What the hell had happened to her?

Jon savagely kicked at the ute tyre. Bloody Berry! The bloke deserved a thrashing. He had no right to treat Val like he had, dumping her in the outback miles from anywhere.

He collected his rifle and a couple of bullets and rounded the sheds.

Two hours later a large pot of stew simmered on the range. The aroma filled the kitchen and made his stomach squelch in anticipation. He checked the meat to see if it was cooked and that the potatoes and carrots were soft, added some salt and flour to flavour and thicken the gravy and, when he was satisfied that it was ready, he filled a bowl and carried it through to Val.

'Dinner, Val.'

She opened her eyes.

'How're you feeling?'

'A bit better.'

'And the baby?'

'She seems okay.'

'You hungry?'

She nodded.

He put the bowl of stew on the chest of drawers. 'Here, pass the baby over and I'll put her in the crib while you eat.'

Val levered herself into sitting position while Jon laid the baby in the makeshift crib he'd made for her from a laundry basket while the dinner was cooking. Then he sat on the edge of the bed while Val ate.

'This is good. Better than tinned dog,' she said, a weak smile on her face.

'Where's Berry?'

At first he thought she wasn't going to answer.

'He's gone up to the Northern Territory.'

'Hasn't he got any sense?'

'What do you mean?'

'Well, his timing is—'

'He wasn't to know she'd come early,' Val said, her cheeks turning pink.

'When's he back?'

'Dunno,' she said and leaned back onto the pillow as Jon took the empty bowl from her.

'Tea?'

'That'd be nice,' she murmured. 'Thanks.'

'That's all right.'

'No, I mean it. Thank you.'

Embarrassed, he looked at her serious face.

'How did you know the baby was coming?'

'I didn't.'

'So…why?'

He hesitated; he could hardly tell her he'd heard her calling to him. She'd think he was mad.

'But you must have had a reason. Did Alice send you?'

'No.'

'You heard me, then?'

'What?'

'You must have heard me. When things were really bad I was yellin' at the top of my voice, callin' for help, for you, Berry, anyone, and swearin' at God. If Father O'Keefe had heard me I'd have been excommunicated.' She tried to laugh. 'I thought I was goin' to die at one point, hon.'

'You reckon I heard you calling me?' he asked.

'I think you must have.'

Maybe he was wrong about the telepathy thing, he decided, as he cleared away and began washing the pots. Perhaps, somehow, he'd heard her distress, heard her calling for help just like Jimmi had heard his call for help when he was dehydrated in the outback, dying under a razor-sharp thorn bush out on the stony plain.

From the kitchen he could hear her crooning to the baby. He dried his hands, crossed over to the doorway and watched them wrapped up in each other. She needed a safe place, they both did, someone to care for them. Alice! He'd take them to Alice, she'd look after them.

Val sensed his presence and looked up.

'I'm taking you to Alice tomorrow, you reckon you can manage if I drive slowly?' he asked.

She smiled and nodded and looked down at her baby again.

He saw her kiss the child's forehead. At least she wasn't going to argue with him this time, he thought, turning away.

74

CHAPTER 8

'I didn't know where else to take her.' Jon looked Alice in the eye, daring her to argue. 'I couldn't take her back to my place, folk would talk.'

'Indeed they would,' said Alice in a tone Jon didn't care for. 'The place Rachel used has been empty since she moved back into town. She can stay there. What are you going to do about Berry?'

'Nothing. Val left a note to say she'd had the baby and was staying with you.'

They both watched Val on the verandah, sitting in Alice's chair, the baby asleep on her lap.

'She doesn't look the same girl, does she? Seems to me the stuffing's been knocked out of her,' commented Alice. 'Do you reckon she'll go back to him?'

'Your guess is as good as mine. If she has any sense she'll go home.'

Alice looked at him in surprise. 'With an illegitimate baby?'

'Yeah, but she'll probably end up going back to Berry. He'll only have to crook his little finger and she'll be all over him again.'

'Sounds to me like you're jealous.'

'Jealous! Don't be daft, Alice. Val and me, we're mates, and that's all.'

They heard footsteps and looked towards the door. Val pulled the fly screen back and came into the kitchen carrying the baby.

'Jon'll take your things over to the other bungalow,' said Alice.

'It's really good of you to let me stay, Alice.'

'Oh, go on with you, what are friends for.'

'Yes, but—'

'No buts. You're welcome to stay as long as you like. Now, let's have a look at this daughter of yours.' She held out her arms and

Val handed the baby over. Alice looked down into the tiny face, at the child watching her. 'She's bright enough, and pretty for a newborn. What are you going to call her?'

'Ruby.'

'Ruby, eh? Is it a family name?'

'No, I just like it and I think she might end up with auburn hair, with me being fair and Berry dark.'

'And what does Berry think?'

'He doesn't know yet,' she caught Alice's eye. 'He was hopin' for a boy.'

'Most men want sons,' commented Alice, 'I shouldn't worry, he'll be fine as soon as he sees her, you'll see.'

'The bastard had better be,' said Jon under his breath.

Alice glanced at him, an inscrutable look on her face. He blushed and looked away. She turned her attention back to Val and the baby. 'You'll both be needing a check-up at the clinic when you're feeling up to it. Jon'll drive you over to Pilkington. Won't you, Jon?' she added, watching him squirm.

Jon didn't bother to answer. It was an order, he could tell by the tone in Alice's voice.

Berry arrived at Jarralong a month after the baby was born, according to Wes. Jon and Wes were sitting on a bench seat drinking tea and looking down the main street at the comings and goings of folk in the town.

'How do you know?' asked Jon.

'Scally told me. Seems he was over at Alice's place last week and she gave him chapter and verse. Alice said Berry took one look at the kid and reckoned there was no guarantee it was his. When Val told him the baby was his he didn't argue just said he was off up north for a spell and if she wanted to go she'd better get her gear together.'

'Then what happened?'

Wes chuckled. 'Alice said Val told him to "bugger off" – her exact words – that as far as she was concerned the baby didn't have a father and Ruby was none of his business, and Berry said that suited him just fine, he didn't want a sheila and a brat hanging off his coat tails, and that was that.' Wes took a sip of tea. 'What do you reckon she'll do now? Do you think she'll go back to Liverpool?'

'Best place for her,' said Jon, remembering an earlier conversation on the same topic. 'But she's stubborn; she'll probably stay, knowing Val. She might move to Kalgoorlie though, get herself a job there.'

'You know, it's a pity she's not managing Larry Simpson's place. That brother of his has made a right mess of running the business, not to mention upsetting half the women in the district with his manner. Word is he's about to shut up shop and return to Perth. Pity she doesn't have the cash to buy him out. I'd lend her the money myself if I had any.'

Jon looked at him in surprise.

Wes flushed scarlet. 'You needn't look at me like I've lost me marbles. We need more lasses like Val in Charlestown; the place is dying on its feet.'

'I suppose you're right, but I can't see what she sees in the place, there's nothing much here.'

'You like it right enough.'

'That's different.'

Wes gave him a sidelong glance before finishing his tea. He stood and hitched up his pants. 'Talking of upping sticks, word is that the Samuels are finally moving on. They've been talking about it for a couple of years.'

'Who told you that?'

'Scally. Jeb's looking to retire and the boys aren't keen on keeping on the station, mind you, the last seven years have been bummers for the family. Anyway, the boys want to sell up and move north. Scally reckons they want to manage a bigger outfit up in the Territory, seems they don't want the financial responsibility of their own place after all they've been through.'

'You'd think they'd want to stay, it's where they were brought up.'

'Well, yes, but it isn't exactly a family station, not like some that go back two or three generations. Jeb and Mary took it over when they were first married, a couple of years after Eli Jackson died, so it's not as if their roots go down a long way.'

While Wes got on with replacing the gasket on the ute Jon thought about what Wes had just told him. The Samuels had never recovered from the drought, and then there had been the bush fire, five years back, when the station burnt to the ground and just about wiped out all their Merinos. The few that didn't die in the inferno were so badly burnt they'd had to be shot, a nasty business at the best of times. Alice said they'd attempted to rebuild on the back of a bank loan and had restocked, but the protracted drought that had been so disastrous for the pastoralists had been good for dingoes and three years ago they too lost all their lambs, as Alice had done, including a number of their ewes. One natural disaster would have been enough to send a lesser family under, but it had taken three catastrophes to sink the Samuels if what Wes was saying was true.

'Do you think they'll go, Wes?'

'Mary's not keen despite everything, but the boys are. Reckon they'll wear her down in time. Come this time next year the place'll be on the market. Pass me that spanner, will you, the one with the red tape.'

Jon held it up for Wes to see.

'Aye, that's the one.'

He handed it to Wes and returned to the bench seat. Jindalee was about the same size as Jarrahlong, restocked with cattle now because Jeb had had a belly full of sheep after the dingoes got all his lambs.

Jon imagined running a cattle station might be easier than managing sheep if his experience with Alice's cattle was anything to go by. If he sold Stan's gold he could buy the Samuels' pastoral lease and stay in the area. He wouldn't have to make a fresh start somewhere else. The problem would be what folk thought, somehow he needed to convince everyone he'd made his fortune elsewhere that his wealth didn't come from Stan's No Hope mine.

He tossed his tea dregs into the dust. He needed to talk to Alice, perhaps it was time he went to Kalgoorlie and became a prospector in the goldfields.

CHAPTER 9

Jon coughed and sat back on his heels, his head throbbed and his throat was sore from breathing in dust. For two years now, ever since he'd discovered the gold reef, he'd spent most of his spare time down No Hope Mine, mainly working a couple of hours late at night to minimise the risk of discovery, but for the last ten weeks he'd been up against a deadline, he needed to get the rest of the gold out, or at least as much of it as possible.

The more he thought of it the more his plan to save Yaringa Creek from a gold rush made sense, and Alice had agreed with him. He'd go to Kalgoorlie, or Leonora, get a list of abandoned mines, take out a mineral lease and work it for a few months, long enough to satisfy folk he'd found his gold there. Then he'd sell most of Stan's gold in one go and buy the Samuels' pastoral lease as soon as it came on the market.

Jon selected a chipping hammer and attacked the reef again, picking out walnut-sized nuggets embedded in the seam. He glanced at the bucket full of similar sized nuggets and raw chippings from the rich gold-quartz stratum glinting in the light from Stan's battered miner's lamp. Thousands of pounds worth he'd dug out of the ground, the result of hard graft with no social life to speak of except for chess on Fridays, and the occasional visit to see a film at the monthly showing in Charlestown.

His earlier fears that someone would guess what he was doing hadn't happened because he wasn't flash with money and only spent what he earned from Alice. He still drove the old utility truck he'd bought off Les when he first returned to Australia from England in 1948, and he didn't gamble in the two-up ring like Greg did. His only luxury was a book club subscription and, like Alice, he looked forward to the monthly package of two books that arrived with the mail. Travel books were his favourite, and he also liked biographies, and Alistair kept him up to date on politics at home and abroad. He reckoned Alistair was right; the British Empire was on its last legs; Australia was the place to be with its vast mineral reserves and its sheep and cattle. There was a good life to be made in the outback for those who could stick it.

He chipped away at the last of the seam, no longer listening for the cracking signalling weakened fault lines in the rock above his head. In the early days it had been hard getting up the courage to make the journey into the mine, inching along narrow tunnels and galleries, squeezing through tight spaces, but a good slug of rum had helped, that and the knowledge that Stan had reinforced the rotten timber with sturdy mulga pit props.

Four hours later the day's gold gleamed in the bucket. The last of the reef disappeared into the rock, snaking its way deeper into the strata beyond his capability of reaching it. That was it! Finished! Backfilling could wait until tomorrow. He picked up his tools and the galvanised bucket and made his way back to the mine entrance.

It was eleven o'clock when he emerged. The moon was high in the sky, hanging like a silver orb above the sacred rock on the other side of the valley. Bess, Bonny, and Smoky rose from the old coat he'd laid on the ground for them and nuzzled his hand. It didn't matter how long he was in the mine they were always there, waiting for him.

He crossed over to the flat rock next to his coat, sat down and took out Stan's silver hip flask. 'Cheers, Stan!' He saluted Stan's grave with the flask and then took a long draught. The fiery liquid made him cough and tears pricked his eyelids. He wiped his nose and mouth on his sleeve and leaned back against the rock, letting the alcohol warm his empty stomach while the dogs lay curled up at his feet.

The midsummer night air prickled his sweaty skin, raising the short hairs on his arms, as he sat looking at the grave, at the railings casting shadows in the full moon, dark spears that pointed to the entrance to Stan's mine.

'Tomorrow, I'm backfilling the tunnel to the lightning-strike chamber, Stan. It'll look like a dead end by the time I'm finished – a No Hoper.' He smiled. 'You'd like that, wouldn't you, mate?' He turned to his right, towards the overhang where the Aboriginal paintings were. Someone had been up there during the week, touching up the ancient symbols and adding new handprints in red and yellow ochre. He hadn't seen the Aboriginal, nevertheless, he knew a blackfella had been there watching his comings and goings. What did the Aborigine think of him talking to Stan lying six foot down in the ground? Did he think he'd lost his reason?

He smiled again. 'So what, old fella. Who did you talk to? Bess? Bonny? Yourself?'

Living alone made folk do daft things. That was why he'd found himself talking to Stan and to Curly in the lonely moments. If anyone had heard him they'd have thought he was well on the road to madness. After two years he was beginning to understand how easy it was to become a recluse, although Alice's Friday chess nights had ensured it hadn't happened to him.

He turned his mind to Alice's suggestion that they let folk believe they were buying the pastoral lease together. The locals already believe I've more money than sense, she'd said, and with you spending time in the goldfields they'll never suspect where your gold really comes from, but if you suddenly appear too wealthy folk might get suspicious.

Her words had made sense and at the end of the day he didn't really care what people believed, Jindalee would be his, paid for with Stan's gold, and the valley and the Aboriginal Dreaming would be saved from another rush. Greg wouldn't like it, and no doubt there'd be recriminations, but it could be years before the true ownership became generally known, if it ever did, and a lot could happen in the meantime.

'So there it is, Stan, me and Alice, partners. What do you make of that?'

There was no reply. Stan was silent. Sometimes Jon knew what the old prospector would have said, but not that night. Stan had always been non-committal when it came to Alice, and she was the same whenever he mentioned Stan's name. He took another sip of rum, screwed down the cap and slipped the flask into his back pocket. He shook the dust off his coat and slipped it on, whistled the dogs, picked up his tools and the bucket of gold nuggets, and headed back to the shack, following the trail that Stan had trodden along the valley for the last thirty years of his life.

PART II

[February 1953 – November 1953]

CHAPTER 10

Jon stood in an open patch of heavily wooded land, under a late summer sun, looking at the mine he'd leased in the goldfields. It had been the name that clinched it, and its location. He'd spent a couple of weeks or so searching for something suitable, a mine with a lapsed lease in good auriferous country, way out in the bush, with no immediate neighbours, and the Deborah fitted the bill. According to the agent in the office, where he'd signed for the Deborah, the two mines closest to his were Fifty Mile and Boobook. Fifty Mile, the bigger outfit with a derelict engine house and five-hammer battery, was leased by Anton Kodiak, a middle-aged Pole, who lived in a tin shack built on blocks with not even a dog for company, and the other, Boobook, was leased by a pair of brothers from Ireland.

He wandered around the site taking everything in. All he'd got for his money was a hole in the ground, a mound of spoil, the rotting remains of a tin and wood shack similar to the bloke's down the track and the detritus of an abandoned mine – just as someone had left it, littered with shovels, spades, empty cans of tinned food and discarded bottles that had once contained grog.

'Well, gals, we'd better get started.' Jon opened the door of the Bedford truck he'd bought off Wes and lifted down Stan's dogs. Bonny and Bess were both older now and not likely to wander off like Smoky would have done. He hadn't wanted to leave Smoky at Jarrahlong but Alice said he'd be happier working the sheep with Adie and she'd promised to keep an eye out for him. It's only for a few months; he's not going to forget you in that time, she'd said. Jon knew she was right; even so, he'd still miss the dingo-cross that Alice had given him.

He watched Bonny squatting in the dust to pee and Bess investigating her surroundings. They were used to the mining life, they'd soon settle.

He moved the truck closer to a gimlet and parked in the shade. It took time to rig up a temporary tent from tarpaulin good enough to last until he could repair the shack. He unloaded his tools, an iron camp bed with a thin horse-hair mattress, and the lockable ironbark trunk containing Stan's gold, and stashed them against the sawn boarding and corrugated iron he'd bought in Menzies. Then he built a campfire, put the billy on to boil and leaned back against a truck tyre out of the sun. There was a lot to do before he could start mining, the shack needed work first, he wanted somewhere better than a makeshift tent to live in, and then there was the mine. He looked about him; there were plenty of suitable trees to replace the rotten props and for the new ladder needed to get down to the lower levels.

It never ceased to amaze him how quickly the land regenerated. According to Stan, at the turn of the century the whole area had been cut down to supply the woodlines, except for a few really big trees that had escaped the razor axes. The re-growth, now sizeable timber, was suitable for what he had in mind. The area he'd chosen was heavily forested with eucalypts, predominantly salmon gum, a tree that wasn't common around Jarrahlong, ribbon gum, black-butts, gimlets and snap and rattle. Underneath the bigger trees grew the mulga, the dense acacia that included varieties he couldn't always identify. In the more open patches the ground was thick with bluebush, saltbush, cotton bush and turpentines and the bristly cushions of spinifex – the hummocky, drought-resistant grass with its sharp leaf tips that pierced the skin as easily as needles if you weren't careful – and, in the sandier parts, the mallee, the low growing eucalyptus that grew just about everywhere.

Jon set off to explore and spotted a bright green kurrajong and further on still a quandong. He smiled as the remembered the first time he'd eaten a quandong fruit, the flesh was so sharp it had turned his mouth to cardboard. Curly had laughed at the expression on his face; he'd said his mouth looked as tight as a cat's bum. On higher ground were the rock strata with the all-important layer of quartz, the stratum he'd be looking for once the mine had been made safe. Where the quartz petered out was a waterhole in the rock. He broke off a branch and lowered it into the water – four feet deep – a gnamma hole, permanent by the look of things. He'd chosen his site well.

He imagined the place in the past, long before gold was found in the eighteen hundreds, before the rush when thousands of people descended on the area. He guessed this had once been a sacred site, although there was no way of telling for certain. Any Aborigines that had once lived off the land had gravitated to the town and were now living miserable lives, for the most part, on the fringes, in tin and canvas shacks, eking out a mediocre living.

He thought about what it had been like for them when white men first arrived, looking for mineral wealth, for gold, and good cattle and sheep country, and suitable routes for droving animals to market.

Curly had spoken of his ancestors, great-grandparents, Jon suspected, who had been captured by explorers desperate for water. He imagined their terror when they were tied with rope so they couldn't run off and were fed salt beef to induce a thirst that would force them to reveal their waterholes. Thieves, Curly called them for stealing his grandparents' belongings when they'd run away from their camp in terror. He'd spoken of carved ceremonial sticks, spears, woomeras, shields and coolimans that had been taken by the white men on such raids.

It was the shortage of water that was the real problem in arid land. There was enough for the Aborigines most of the time, they knew where to find it and they looked after the precious sites, but not the white man who thought nothing of using up all the available water and, when sheep and cattle were introduced, what little water existed was often polluted by the animals. No wonder the Aborigines had been driven further and further from their old ways of living. It wasn't right, but he guessed that was the nature of things in those days, and, from what he could see, not a lot had changed in the intervening years.

A week or so after he'd settled in, a young fella on a rusty bike rode into the yard, or what Jon thought of as his yard, and juddered to a stop on squealing brakes.

Jon stood with the dogs at his feet and a mug of tea in his hand while the rider dismounted and leaned the pushbike against the handiest tree.

'Whatcha, mate,' hailed the fella in a broad Irish accent, the words pure Aussie.

Jon tipped his hat for a better view of his visitor and guessed he was one of the Irish brothers the agent had mentioned. He was of a similar age to himself but shorter and more slightly built, with dark, straight hair that flopped over his forehead. The bloke had regular features that were easy to forget, but not so his eyes, they were deep set and arresting with dark grey irises that held his own for a long moment. Then, when he least expected it, the fella dusted off his hands on his trousers and extended one towards Jon.

They shook hands, eyeing each other openly.

'Don't suppose you've got a spare jack have ya, mate?'

'I haven't got a spare, but I'll lend you mine so long as you bring it back when you've finished with it, and sooner rather than later.'

The fella gave a whistle. 'Haven't heard that accent in a whiles. Where you from, Liverpool?'

Jon laughed. 'Yep, Liverpool, right enough.'

'I'm Luke Cafferty from County Clare…in Ireland,' he added after a moment.

'And I'm Jon.' A grin split his face. 'Yeah, I know where County Clare is.'

'Yeah, I suppose you do. Trouble is most Aussies don't, unless they've come from the Old Country. We've been here a whiles now and we haven't met many other Irish so far.'

'There're a fair few with Irish backgrounds hereabouts, particularly in Kal. Did you say we?'

'Yup, me and me brother, Matthew.' Luke nodded over his shoulder, 'At Boobook mine, back there a ways. We're looking to make our fortune so we can go back home and buy us a smallholding.'

'You seen any yet?'

'You mean gold?' asked Luke.

'No, boobooks.'

'Don't know what you're talking about.'

'Your mine is named after a bird. Some folk call them mopokes because of the sound they make; it's a type of brown owl. Just wondered if you'd seen any, or heard them, with you being a country boy and all.'

'Can't say I've seen any, and I wouldn't know one even if I heard it.'

'*More-pork* that's the sort of sound they make…distinctive,' said Jon, 'a bit like the cuckoo back home.'

Luke shook his head. 'No, can't say I've heard any *more-porks* around, leastways, not while we've been here.'

'Probably all been frightened off with the mining,' commented Jon. 'Wouldn't be surprised, mining's a pretty noisy business at the best of times. What was it you wanted? A jack?' He led the way over to the Bedford and found what Luke was looking for. 'Like I said, I'd appreciate it back sooner rather than later, you never know when you're going to get a puncture out here.'

Luke grinned. 'Aye, tell me about it.' He took the proffered jack. 'Tell you what, why don't you come over tonight. You can collect it and have a bite to eat with us. Nothing special mind you, just bully-beef stew. What do you say? You can listen for some of those *more-porks* of yours.'

'You're not going to let me forget that, are you?'

'What do you think, especially with them sounding like one of those English toffs ordering seconds.'

Jon laughed. 'Have it your own way.'

'See you fiveish then…all right, mate?'

'Five it is,' said Jon as Luke climbed back onto his bike.

When Jon rolled up at Boobook Mine, Luke and Matthew were waiting for him. They were sitting in the shade of a small verandah cobbled together from saplings and a tarpaulin, sipping bottled beer. When he joined them they passed him a bottle, an opener and a chair to perch on.

'I take it you're Matthew.' Jon held out his hand.

Matthew stood briefly, shook Jon's hand solemnly and returned to his seat.

'We don't look like brothers, do we? And even less like twins,' said Luke.

'Twins!'

'Yeah, twins. He's the biggest and I'm the oldest, by eight minutes, according to our mammy.'

Jon looked at the pair of them and had to agree they didn't look a bit alike. Luke was of medium height and dark, and more slightly built, whereas Matt was taller by a couple of inches and broader shouldered. He had sandy hair and deeply pitted skin from acne. His eyes were grey, like Luke's, although not as deep set. He had an open face and Jon guessed that, with Matt, what you saw was what you got, whereas with Luke there was wariness and reserve about him.

'Get your tyre fixed?'

Luke indicated the truck bought from an army surplus store parked over to the left. 'She's right. Thanks for the loan of the jack. We need to get ourselves one, didn't think to look when we bought her; it'd be a right sod if another tyre went while we were miles from anywhere and we didn't have the wherewithal to fix the so-and-so.'

'You been mining long?' asked Matt.

'About a month.'

'Find any gold yet?'

'No, still getting myself set up, replacing rotten timber, making new ladders into the mine, you know the sort of thing? What about you?'

'We're doing okay,' said Luke a shade too quickly, 'found enough to keep us looking, you might say.'

Jon sipped his beer. That was good news; he reckoned they were working the same rock strata. If they'd found gold then he'd be able to say the same even if his mine was barren. 'You been here long?'

Matt took a quick swig of beer. 'Getting on for two years now.'

'Planning on staying in Australia?'

'No, only long enough to make our fortune.'

Jon smiled. 'If I had a pound for every time someone has said that, I'd be a rich man.'

'Luke says you've been around a bit.'

'Did he?'

'Yeah, says you know about the Irish hereabouts and all about the native birds, feathered variety,' he added.

'I wouldn't say I know any Irish personally. When you're in Kal you hear the brogue now and again, and one or two own businesses in the town. I'm a newcomer to the area, but I was working on a sheep station a way west of here until a couple of months back.'

'You got fed up with looking after sheep, did you?' asked Matt.

'No, I want my own place and this is the fastest way to make the money, just so long as I get lucky and find myself a reef.'

'Luke says you're from Liverpool.'

'Yeah,' grinned Jon. 'Can't ya tell?'

Darkness descended as they talked and Luke suggested they move indoors to eat. Jon followed them into the shack and waited while they found eating irons and plates and then they tucked into the corned-beef stew, similar to the type Stan favoured. The damper Luke had made was burnt and tasted more of charcoal than

90

bread, nevertheless it soaked up the gravy well enough.

Jon left them soon after the meal having arranged to go with them to a two-up match out in the bush the next time one was on the cards. The brothers offered to pick him up in their truck on the way through – just so long as he brought his jack along with him.

CHAPTER 11

Two months later, Matt and Luke pulled into the yard.

'Don't need the jack,' yelled Luke from the cab. 'We got one, bought it off a scrappy.' He opened the passenger door and slid across to make room for Jon.

'I thought you said sometime soon,' said Jon.

Luke grinned. 'Yeah, well, you know what it's like when you're on a roll.'

He guessed Luke meant they'd found gold which was more than could be said for him. He'd almost given up at one point, and the loneliness hadn't helped, he hadn't expected it to get to him as much as it had. If it hadn't have been for Stan's dogs he'd have quit a month back.

'You got your betting money?' asked Luke.

'Yeah, but not a lot.' He jiggled the loose change in his pocket. 'It's all too easy to lose your cash in these places.'

'Reckon you're right,' said Matt, concentrating on the driving.

'Well, you two had better get in the mood for some serious gambling,' said Luke, 'it took me a lot of drinking in the bar to get us an invite off Bernie Bates. You know what these fellas are like with outsiders. They don't trust no one, they don't.'

Matt chuckled. 'You can't blame them, not with the police crawling around, listening in to conversations, trying to find out where the next game is being played.'

'Where are we heading today?' asked Jon.

'The Old Beauty Mine, right out in the bush, miles from anywhere. Bernie reckons there are plenty of routes in, the landfall screens the site from all directions, and there're a couple of good lookout spots for the cockies,' said Luke.

Jon smiled broadly. 'And, if we have to make a run for it, plenty of bush to hide in, is that it?'

'What the hell is a cockie?' asked Matt, still concentrating on the road ahead.

Luke turned to Jon and indicated in Matt's direction. 'He isn't a gambler, thinks gold's too hard won to lose it in the two-up ring. It's the lookout, Matt; it's short for cockatoo, 'cos they make a flaming racket when disturbed.'

Jon sat back and let the miles slide by. A while ago the Government had cracked down on betting. Since then two-up had become a highly organised game of cat and mouse. It was the same back in Charlestown except Constable Nickson was more lenient. He usually gave fair warning of a raid unless someone had upset him and then there was a panic on when the cockie spotted his distinctive truck trundling along the track. Cash and betting paraphernalia were gathered up quick smart, utes were gunned into life and vehicles sped off in all directions, over disused roads or straight through the bush, and some blokes even scarpered on foot.

'You'd think the police would have better things to spend their time on,' said Jon.

Matt changed down a gear and negotiated a rough patch on the road. 'It's the mine owners, I reckon, putting pressure on the Government. Too much theft going on down the mines, that's what it will be.'

Jon considered Matt's words, perhaps he was right, he'd not given much thought to the reason for the legislation.

'Wouldn't happen if they paid a decent wage,' muttered Luke.

'Yeah, but it's the amount they take, Luke. When gambling gets to a man he needs more and more money. They reckon some are stealing twenty quid's worth of gold a week.'

Jon whistled long and low, 'That much?'

'Aye, and then they're losing it all on the toss of two coins.'

'And don't forget the fights and the beatings up when one fella accuses another of double-dealing, not to mention the occasional murder,' said Luke.

'So much for a bit of fun,' commented Matt dryly. 'Don't know why we're bothering to go.'

Jon and Luke laughed.

'Because it makes a change from mining, that's why, Matt. Old Kincaid—'

'Kincaid?' queried Matt.

'Tom Kincaid, a prospector who props up the bar in Menzies,' said Luke, 'he says there'll be no police around today.'

'Why's that?' asked Jon.

'Too busy preparing for some bigwig's visit.'

'Who?'

'Reckon it'll be the Governor or some other dignitary.'

'What the hell does he want to visit Kal for?'

'Beat's me,' said Luke.

'I suppose it's on the way to someplace else,' said Matt.

Jon laughed. 'Kal ain't on the way to anywhere.'

'Anyway,' said Luke, 'the police will be too busy clamping down on the riffraff in Kal to be worried about a few gamblers playing two-up out in the bush.'

'Maybe you're right,' conceded Jon, he certainly hoped so, he didn't fancy being caught up in a raid right out in the middle of the outback.

They drove the rest of the way in silence, eyes peeled, looking for the track through the bush. They spotted another truck turning off the main road and followed it to the two-up site – just a collection of corrugated-iron sheeting thrown up for shelter and plenty of parking.

Jon recalled the last game he'd gone to in the goldfields not long after he'd arrived. He'd met up with a miner in The Exchange bar in Kal. After a skinful the fella had invited him along. He'd never seen a two-up ring like it – a patch of ground raked clear of debris in the middle of derelict mine workings. Rough benches had been brought in for seating and old buildings cannibalised for the corrugated-iron walls and roofing used to provide shade. From a distance the grey iron, most of it streaked with rust, melded with the surrounding land and was partially hidden by scrubby eucalypts. After a while he'd come to the conclusion that, even camouflaged as it was, the police were being paid to turn a blind eye. It was the only way they could have avoided a raid for so long.

The site they'd arrived at had a similar look about it. Jon hoped that Luke was right about the Governor's visit because there was nothing surer, the local police would have been well aware of its location.

Matt spun the steering wheel hard round and parked next to a ute.

'Do you reckon it's wise parking so close to the ring?' asked Jon.

'Don't fret yourself,' said Luke as the car behind dropped off three men and sped back down the track.

'Why?' asked Matt.

'If there's a raid, they'll have the truck covered.'

Matt jumped down from the cab. 'No worries. I'll keep the keys with me.'

'I've told you,' said Luke, 'there'll be no police around today; they'll all be in Kal preparing for the social event of the year.'

'If you say so, but I still think it'd be wiser to park a bit away from here, just in case,' said Jon not yet ready to give up the argument. But Luke wasn't listening; he was out of the truck and half-way across the open ground to the two-up ring.

Jon stepped out of the cab and felt the sun's bite through his shirt. It was going to be a hot one for autumn. He glanced up at the cerulean sky – almost midday. Ahead, men were buying soft drinks from the booth set up for the purpose. It was a big meet, at least forty blokes excited at the prospect of a good session.

He followed Luke and Matt and found himself a spot not too close to the front, with a reasonable view of the ring, and placed a two bob evens bet on the next toss. The tension in the ring was palpable. The young miner had started with a five-pound bet and was well on the way to making a hundred – his luck couldn't last and the crowd knew it. One bum throw on the next toss and he could lose the lot – all he'd won and the five-pound stake – a lot of money by anyone's standards.

In a brief interval the fella next to Jon nudged him in the ribs with an elbow.

'Yer new, aren't ya?'

'Yeah, don't usually have much spare cash for betting.' Jon took in the bloke who'd spoken and guessed that he was fifty if he was a day. He was slim, maybe five foot six in height and he had the lined, weather-beaten face of someone who spent most of the day out in the sun, and Jon noticed that even under his peaked cap his eyes were thin slits against the light.

'Squinty,' said the fella, extending a hand, 'Squinty Morgan.'

Jon shook it. 'Jon Cadwallader,' he said, doing his best not to smile.

'You with those Irish lads?'

'That's right.'

'I see the dark one around pretty often, he likes his game, that one.'

'Luke.'

'Is that what they call him? Well, he's handy enough with the kip but if you really want to see how it's done you need to watch

95

matey over there.' He nodded towards his right. 'He's one of the best there is. He's half Greek, his dad came over to make a pot and met up with one of the ladies on Hay Street, Christos was the result. His dad died in a mining accident when he was six, left his mother with enough money to set up a little gambling business – the dice, you know. He's pretty good at the dice but when it comes to spinning, there ain't nobody like him.'

'Which one's Christos?'

'The swarthy looking one.' Squinty indicated the direction with another quick nod of the head. 'He's always careful with his betting though. I reckon his mother taught him that.'

'What do you mean, he's one of the best?'

'He can throw eight or nine heads, real easy. On a good day he can throw thirty. Thing is, he's consistent. The trouble is he keeps on going until he's all span out. And you see that fella over there, with the red neckerchief,' he nodded across the ring, 'well, he can't do nothing right. Never met a more unlucky bastard. Don't know how he keeps smiling, I don't. They reckon his missus gives him a real hard time at home.'

The game started and first in the ring was a tail better, Mussolini, he was called, and he was known for his habit of winning enormous amounts and losing it all straight off. The story was that he was still in the goldfields because he could never keep enough money together to buy his ticket home to Italy where, it was said, he'd got a wife, three sons, and ten grandchildren.

Mussolini took things seriously, but the next fella into the ring treated it as a huge joke. The moment he stepped onto the sand the crowd groaned. He ignored them and took an exaggerated bow.

'Yer better play the game, Sparkie, no messin,' yelled a voice from the other side of the ring. 'If you bugger it up I'll kill ya, mate.'

Sparkie saluted the heckler and took his time selecting the coins. He then went through a protracted warm-up ritual, getting a feel for the kip until the crowd was yelling abuse.

When he finally tossed the coins it was like tossing pancakes, some he tossed high, others low, the crowd didn't know where they were and the suspense was winding them up so much that they were all threatening to duff him up on the road home.

The problem was that there was so much shouting going on that the cocky's warning yells were missed and before they knew it they were in the middle of a raid.

Jon had never seen a body of men move so fast; the ones the coppers hadn't nabbed were off, running through the bush as if the devil was after them, pursued by a mob of police.

Jon could see Matt and Luke ahead of him and was aware that Squinty wasn't far behind; he could hear his rasping breath as they jumped clumps of spinifex and crashed through mulga scrub. Someone else was running with them too, a portly fella who was wheezing his lungs up. They'd be calling for an undertaker if he didn't take it easy; Jon glanced behind him, glad to see he was dropping back.

After a good quarter of a mile, even Jon, fit as he was, was finding it hard to keep up with Matt and Luke. He spotted a rocky outcrop ahead just as Matt and Luke disappeared over the top of it and decided, police or no, he'd lie up with the other two until the hue and cry had died down.

He cleared the higher ground and flopped down next to them, air whistling out of his burning lungs.

'Took your time, didn't you,' said Luke, struggling to get his breath back.

Squinty joined them next, flopping at their feet on all fours like a dog. His tongue lolled out of his mouth, and his squinty eyes were tight shut as he dragged air into his starved lungs, while the other fella, the fat one, rolled down the incline and bashed into Squinty's feet, his breathing coming in equally short, shallow breaths.

'I thought you said all the police would be in Kal sorting out the riffraff,' gasped Jon.

'Sweet Mother of Christ,' Luke panted, still fighting for air, 'but they're a mean set of turds.'

After an age, Squinty rolled onto his back and looked up into the sky. 'I'm too old for this game. It's about time someone did something about those bastards.'

'And what would that be, Squinty, my lad,' said the fifth bloke who had got his breath back and was now squatting close to him.

'Hey, what d'you think you're doing, mate?' yelled Squinty as the big fella clamped handcuffs on him. The fella ignored him and fixed his eyes on them. 'Now then you lot, what're your names, your real names, I don't want no Alphonsos and Adolphs, got it?' He pulled out a notebook and licked the end of a pencil.

Luke didn't hesitate, he was off like a greyhound from the trap, Matt on his heels and Jon not far behind them. They ignored Squinty's yells for help and the constable's order to come back.

They ran as fast as they had on the way out, following the line of hills, sweeping back to the two-up ring by a circuitous route. When they were near to where they'd parked the truck they stopped and took in the lie of the land and the two police keeping guard of the vehicles. Jon looked about him. There would be others hidden in the scrub, waiting for the police to leave, except it didn't look like they were planning on going anywhere soon. It was going to be a long wait until nightfall and it was hot out in the bush.

'Good job I've got the keys,' murmured Matt. 'We'll just have to wait until it's dark.'

The afternoon dragged, and Jon wished they'd had water with them. Every now and again they'd hear shouting and a scuffle when someone tried to make their escape in one of the vehicles still under police guard. But in the end it was a fracas between the police and four blokes who had tired of waiting for them to leave that created the diversion necessary for them to retrieve their lorry and head for home.

Jon was really pleased to get back down the mine. Galloping for miles over mulga scrub in the mid-afternoon heat wasn't his idea of fun. Matt and Luke had dropped him off and after downing a much welcome mug of tea he decided to spend the next day digging out spoil just in case one of the constables came nosing round, although he didn't think it likely, in the circumstances.

Three months earlier, when he'd bought the lease, he hadn't been much bothered whether the mine was profitable or not, but he'd come to the conclusion that the previous lessee had found gold otherwise he wouldn't have spent so much time excavating the galleries as he had. And he was right, since he'd started digging he had come across low-grade ore with small amounts of gold. The discovery had lifted his spirits, mining the gold would give him something to do until he dynamited the main gallery so no one could prove his gold hadn't come from the Deborah.

Deborah Mine wasn't as claustrophobic as No Hope had been, for a start the galleries were bigger and more regular and he didn't have the oppressive feeling he'd had in Stan's mine. He often wondered who his predecessor had been; he'd found his belongings, candle stubs and a baccy tin with a bit of rough cut still in it, together with a few cigarette papers stuck together with damp. And then there'd been the Bible, a small, black, soft-bound Bible, dog-eared from much use, wedged in a cleft in the rock next to a ledge with plenty of candle grease and stubs. He'd put it in his back pocket when he'd returned to the surface and, that night, by the light of the kerosene lamp he'd read the legend inside – *For Douglas. Come home safe. Yours forever, Lucy xxx.*

He often thought about Douglas, had even asked around Menzies, but no one could tell him anything about the prospector who had worked the mine before him, that was until he'd met an old digger in the bar there while having a break from the mine. It turned out he had known Douglas, said he'd found gold but not enough to make his fortune and, in the end, he'd gone back to Perth a disappointed man.

He had asked what sort of a character Douglas was and had been told that he was quiet, that he preferred to sit by himself with a beer and that he barely said a word.

Jon had known exactly what the old digger meant. Prospecting in the outback did that to some fellas; others, driven mad with loneliness, did strange things; some walked out into the bush and kept walking, or shot themselves. He'd even heard tell of one miner who'd stuck a plug of dynamite in his mouth and lit it, blowing his head clean off.

That night Jon had finished his beer knowing that his picture of Douglas didn't fit the reality. Some made a fortune but most only made a living and a few ended up broken men. That's what the goldfields did to blokes. That night the thin blanket of fact put an end to his fanciful imaginings.

Chapter 12

It was the loneliness that surprised him. He hadn't expected it to affect him as it had, especially after the months of living in Stan's shack at Yaringa Creek. He was glad he'd thought to bring books with him for the long winter evenings when there was nothing to do except brood, write letters, or read. He'd done all three and the most satisfying was reading, especially as it took so long to receive replies to the letters he sent. Alice wrote regularly to the post office address in Leonora but Merle's letters were infrequent and his sister, Kathy, back home in England, didn't bother to write at all.

He thought of Merle, she'd be qualified by now. He'd written a while back inviting her to stay with him, to see Charlestown and Jarrahlong for herself, and he calculated it would be another two or three weeks before he got her reply if things went well.

Bonny growled and he wondered what she'd heard, a nocturnal animal out in the bush perhaps, but when he checked there'd been nothing there. Later, when he took the dogs out for their late-night stroll, nothing disturbed the quiet except the rustle of leaves caught in the winter wind. He clapped his arms about him to warm up and headed back to the shack, noting the clear star-spangled sky, it would be a cold night and he'd need extra wood in the stove if he wasn't to wake up in the morning chilled to the marrow.

All that week the days were grey and overcast with occasional rain showers. The thought of going down the mine depressed him; he'd been living like a mole for over four months, burrowing away in the bowels of the earth, chipping at a reef that wasn't giving up its gold easily. Every couple of months he sold what he'd mined along with some of Stan's gold, and word was getting round he'd found a

100

rich seam and that suited him fine, even Matt and Luke were joshing him about it.

He poured himself a second cup of coffee and peered out of the window. The day wasn't going to get any better. He considered visiting Boobook but knew the Caffertys were busy. Luke Cafferty was anxious to go home to Ireland – only the other week he'd said they'd been in the goldfields for too long, longer than they'd planned. But Matt hadn't agreed, he reckoned they were mining more gold than they ever had and it was clear the twins disagreed about when it was the right time to return. Was that how it had been for Stan in the early days, staying just another month, and then another, until he became so used to the life that he didn't want to leave? And then there was Alice. Jon wondered just how much Alice's presence had influenced Stan's decision – a great deal if Stan's comments in his dying hours were anything to go by.

After he'd finished the coffee, he rinsed out the dregs, made himself a pack-up of damper and leftover salami, slipped on an overcoat, picked up his rifle, and whistled the dogs. A walk was what he needed, something to clear his head, take his mind off the ruddy mine and maybe shoot something for the pot, he was sick of bully beef. He headed due west into the bush, marking trees as he went, keeping his direction by compass – the compass Alice had given him a couple of years back – it wouldn't do to lose his way.

The route took him through dense bush, past a couple of graves, the markers so faded it was impossible to read the inscriptions. He'd come across a number of graves in the goldfields and as he walked he remembered the story of the Siberia disaster in 1893 that the old digger had recounted to him on one of his rare trips into Menzies. According to the old fella, hundreds of men had left Coolgardie in a mad scramble to get to a rich strike north-west of the town without heeding the warnings that the seventy mile journey was a dry stage. When news got out that men were dying of thirst, the Government ordered water supplies sent out from Coolgardie and men's lives were saved, but not before many had succumbed to terrible deaths deep in the bush.

Jon shuddered as he recalled the tale. He knew better than most what it was like to be dehydrated, dying of thirst under the relentless Australian sun – the madness and hallucinations that thirst induced, when the tongue swelled and the body stopped sweating, when the urge to strip down to the skin became overwhelming, as it had for the Kenton boys. He would have died like those Siberia men had done, if it hadn't have been for Jimmi. An image of the Aboriginal as he'd last seen him slid into his mind: a man in his prime, strong and sure, a man entrusted to carry out Aboriginal retribution on Gerry Worrall, a piece of white Australian scum if ever there was one.

Gerry had killed Wally and his son, Buni, Jon was convinced of it, and, in his book, Gerry had deserved all he got. He didn't blame Jimmi for killing Gerry and he'd never regret throwing Gerry's body down Old Faithful mine shaft to protect the Aboriginal. The bloke was dead anyway, what did it matter where he was buried?

He wondered where Jimmi was, still in hiding from the law no doubt, living deep in the Australian outback, unaware that Stan had confessed to killing Gerry.

He banished the terrible memories of that day and thought about the old digger's tale of madness, death and unimaginable wealth, of how Siberia had become a profitable gold mining area and was gazetted in the late 1890s as Waverley, although everyone still called it Siberia.

Jon reflected on the weird and wonderful names of towns he'd come across in the goldfields, Leonora, Ora Banda, Broad Arrow, Kookynie and the rest; and the fancy names for mines like Boo-book, Sons of Gwalia, Niagara, and his own mine, Deborah; and of the hundreds of men buried out in the bush. Many had not even a marker to indicate their passing as they'd searched for gold-bearing rock and the lucky break that would make them rich beyond imagination in a land with too many dry stages for comfort.

The countryside opened out as he walked and he realised he was in the middle of regenerated bush. He kept an eye out for signs of the remains of the woodlines, the temporary single track railway lines constructed deep into the outback that had once supplied wood to the mines, like the Sons of Gwalia Mine near Leonora. Stan had told him of the days when tons of timber were felled for pit props to shore up the tunnelling deep underground and to fuel the huge beam engines that pumped out the water, a perennial problem especially in the deeper mines. Wood also fuelled the condensers that converted salt water into drinking water, a precious commodity in the goldfields.

According to Stan, Italians and Jugoslavs favoured wood-cutting. Many of them had settled in the area, using the big crosscut saws needed to fell the huge salmon gums, while others worked down the Sons of Gwalia Mine. Stan had once shown him the makeshift camp they'd constructed, timber-framed shacks covered in canvas, hessian and corrugated iron and painted Mediterranean shades of pink and blue – 'little Italy' some of the locals had dubbed the township that grew up close to the mine.

That was one thing about gold; it attracted folk from all over the globe, folk like the Cafferty brothers with a yearning to get rich quick. Jon smiled; the trouble was getting rich quick required hard graft unless you were a Bayley, Ford or Hannan, men who had fallen lucky in the early 1890s – unlike Stan who had taken thirty years to find his reef and by then it was too late, the old fella was dying of pneumonia, no doubt exacerbated by the dust he'd breathed in for more than half a lifetime.

At three o'clock he decided he'd had enough, there was still no sign of the sun, not even a brightening in the cloud cover, and it looked like rain, and then he briefly caught a whiff of wood smoke. He called the dogs to him and made them sit while he turned on his heels smelling the air, trying to get a fix – south-west he reckoned.

He headed in that direction, curious to know who was camping out in the bush. He picked his way through dense undergrowth, keeping the dogs close, scenting the air as he went until he came to more open ground where he disturbed a small mob of kangaroo before he had a chance at a shot. They were off as soon as they heard him, their tails undulating with each bound. It was then that he saw her, an Aboriginal woman with a spear in her hand. She shouted at him, Aboriginal words he couldn't understand, her face expressionless and then she turned away and strode off into the bush. Jon swore to himself, how long had she been there waiting for the right moment? He remembered hunting kangaroo with Curly, how tiring it had been, and then the long run after the speared animal until, when it was weakened from loss of blood, Curly had caught up with it, dispatched it and butchered it.

He followed the woman at a distance, keeping the dogs close and quiet. Half a mile he walked, the smell of wood smoke more pronounced as he neared the camp. He kept himself well hidden and watched as she approached the fire and the old man sitting hunched over the hot ashes, a piece of hessian draped over his shoulders for warmth. He heard voices, saw her gesticulate and fling her spear down onto the ground. A couple of kiddies and several mangy dogs appeared from a humpy and joined the two at the fire. To Jon's eye the camp had been there for a while; the main protection from the cold nights was afforded by strips of hessian laid across branches leaning against a couple of large rocks – the makeshift shelter from which the kiddies had emerged. Scattered around were discarded tins, old bones and piles of firewood.

Their meal would be a meagre one that night, not that he could do much about it, he'd already eaten his damper and salami, and in any case it wouldn't have been enough to feed four hungry bellies. He turned his back on the Aboriginal family and, following his trail, made his way back to the Deborah Mine.

Jon woke early. After breakfast he locked the dogs in the shack and set off with his rifle and a bag of flour. He headed back to the place where he'd seen the kangaroos determined to be there early enough to shoot one of them. He knew it would be a long day and that he would have to be in place, well hidden and downwind of the animals when they came to graze in the mid-afternoon. He half expected to see the Aboriginal woman, but didn't, and he wondered whether she'd gone looking for easier game. At three o'clock he got a clear shot and felled a half-grown male with a single bullet to the head. He gutted the animal where it fell and then hauled the carcass onto his back and set off for the Aboriginal encampment. By the time he arrived he was sweating despite the dropping air temperature.

The camp dogs pounded towards him, their hackles raised. He stood still while they circled about him, sniffing the other dog smell on his trousers and the bloody nose of the kangaroo dangling down his back. Then, when he was satisfied they weren't going to bite, he walked steadily towards the old man.

The Aborigine looked up at him, shading his eyes against the sky. Jon slid the carcass off his shoulder and eased it onto the ground between them.

'Yesterday, I spoilt it for the woman,' he indicated her children who had emerged from the shelter. 'I frightened off the kangaroo.'

The old fella nodded.

Jon hunkered down next to him. 'I didn't want your family to go hungry, it's cold at night and the kiddies need food in their bellies. There's some flour too, for damper.'

The old fella nodded again.

Jon stood up. The Aborigine hadn't understood what he'd said; either that or he was deaf. He made to leave.

The Aborigine spoke in his own tongue to the elder of the two children and waved in the direction of the shelter. The child scampered inside and returned with a battered pannikin which she passed to the old man. He filled it with stewed tea from the billy and handed it to him.

'Thank you,' Jon said, taking the tea. He squatted, sitting back on one heel like the ringers did, and sipped the bitter liquid. The old fella spoke again, gesticulating towards the bush and Jon guessed he was referring to the woman he'd seen yesterday.

Jon told the old man where he was from, told him about the mine, that he was a prospector, but how much the Aborigine understood was difficult to tell. He finished his tea and was readying to leave when the woman returned with a couple of twenty-eight parrots dangling from her hand. She dropped them on the ground next to the fire and stared at Jon.

Jon stood. 'I brought you a kangaroo. Sorry I spoilt things yesterday.'

She looked at him and then down at the kangaroo.

She didn't speak English either and he hadn't recognised any of the words he'd heard. He handed the pannikin back to the old fella. 'Be seeing you, mate.'

'Thank you,' she said as he turned to leave.

Surprised at the clarity of her voice, he hesitated. 'Look, I'm really sorry about yesterday, I didn't realise until it was too late.'

'Good job you wasn't close, there be a mean bit spear in your gut.'

He stood, shocked by her words; surely she wouldn't have killed him!

'Whole day wasted,' she said, ''cos of whitefella.' She grinned then, 'You think I kill you?'

Jon shrugged. What could he say; he didn't know what she was capable of. 'Just the four of you?'

'Yes, m'fella gone walkabout, maybe get work on station for little bit.'

'What about the rest of you?'

'Rest?'

'Yeah, your mob, aunties and uncles.'

'They's fed up with old ways, them livin' in town.' She indicated the old man, 'He don't like town livin', says it's death of him, so we live out here, till all food gone.' She indicated the kangaroo. 'That keep us goin' little bit more.'

'I hope so. Anyway, I'd better be on my way.'

'Where you livin'?'

'Deborah Mine.' He indicated the bush to the north-east.

He picked up his gun and set off for home, feeling happier about the family, pleased that they'd sleep with full bellies that night. He'd spent enough time with Curly and Curly's family to know what it was like to go to sleep hungry.

He was back at the mine by dark and let the dogs out for a run. It had been a long day and he was ravenous. He opened a tin of beans and another of bully beef and put them on to heat, and then poured himself a quart pot of tea liberally sweetened with sugar. Tomorrow he'd get back to the mine and investigate a promising seam he'd found, hopefully it would be richer than the one he'd been mining recently.

Chapter 13

October, and it was time to leave, he'd been hard at it, down the mine, preparing to dynamite the main tunnel, but he needed a break. He'd seen no one for weeks, apart from the Aboriginal family, and he fancied a natter, but the Cafferty brothers had gone into Kalgoorlie for a few days and there was no point in driving over to Anton Kodiac's place. Kodiac was a dour so-and-so, driven half mad by loneliness. According to Matt, he'd work like a navvy for weeks on end and then, after a period of frenzied activity, he'd wander around the place like a maniac, talking to himself and threatening anyone who came within range of his pickaxe.

The drive over to Menzies and the pub didn't appeal either, he'd never been a drinking man and in any case he didn't want to be drawn into talk about gold, not now he was on the point of leaving.

Over the months he'd had the occasional visitor, prospectors mostly, searching for good auriferous country, and one or two sightings of Aborigines, like the family he'd come across a couple of months back, rake thin, eking out a living in the bush, turning their backs on the meagre pickings on the edge of town.

And then there was Merle. He'd had no reply to the letter he'd sent months back inviting her to visit him as soon as she'd qualified, all expenses paid. In the letter he'd told her about Perth, said it was a bonza city and that Kalgoorlie had a theatre, and plenty of dress shops as well as two hospitals. He'd written about prospecting in the goldfields and of his plans to buy a station like Jarrahlong. Weeks he'd waited, anxiously making the monthly trip into Leonora, but there'd been nothing, not even a reply to his most recent letter where, in desperation, he'd asked her to marry him. Perhaps he should return to England soon, five years was a long time to keep a flame alive by post.

Jon poured himself a coffee and took it out to the bentwood chair on the apology of a verandah he'd built for shade. Bess and Bonny followed and flopped down at his feet. For three weeks now he'd been preparing to collapse the main gallery and tunnel but it was always a risky business, especially when the dynamite was old. He'd found the sticks in one of the tin sheds, the paper covering long degraded. He hadn't a clue what they contained and hoped it was the more stable gelignite, but he still needed fuses, which meant another trip to Leonora, and then he'd blow up the mine and sell off the rest of the gold he'd brought with him from Yaringa Creek. There'd be a few questions, but no one back home would suspect the truth that the gold hadn't come from the Deborah Mine.

Jon's stomach heaved at the thought of setting off the dynamite. Stan had told him of accidents with explosives, and deaths. His own experience was limited, only that gleaned from watching the Catholic Brothers at Karundah when they'd blasted for stone to build their damned orphanage and church, and later what he'd learned from Stan. He was sipping the last of his coffee, his mind chewing over his worries, when he heard the sound of a truck grinding its way along the track. He glanced at his watch, twenty past three, he wasn't expecting visitors, but the prospect of a good natter cheered him.

A truck he didn't recognise pulled into the yard. The driver killed the engine and stepped out of the cab.

Scally!

'Watchya cock! You made your fortune yet?' Scally swept off his cap, mopped his brow, and flipped it back on his head. 'Y'certainly took some findin', that's for sure. A miserable old goat a ways back told me where you were.'

'Anton Kodiac. Did he threaten you with an axe?'

'Nah, can't say he was exactly friendly though. Anyway, how are y'doing? Y'found any gold?'

Jon grinned. 'My word, yes, but I think the reef's about worked out.' It was close enough to the truth. 'Reckon I'll be home before too long. So, what brings you to this neck of the woods?'

'Les, sent me over to Kal to pick up some stores he wanted urgent like. When Alice heard I was heading out this way she asked me to pay y'a visit, see how you're doin' and all.'

'You got time for a coffee?'

'Aye, but I'd prefer tea if y'don't mind, and while you're putting on a brew I'll get the stuff Alice sent.'

In the shack Jon cleared the table and wiped it. He could imagine

Scally reporting back, describing the Spartan living conditions, not that that would bother Alice, she already knew how he lived at Stan's place.

Scally elbowed open the door, carried in a cardboard box and dumped it on the table. 'From Alice, she doesn't want y'to starve, and the beer and newspaper are from me, the paper's a bit tattered, picked it up from the place I stayed last night. The news is a fortnight old but I reckoned y'd like to know what's happening beyond the bush.'

Jon passed Scally a mug of tea and poured one for himself, then he opened the box and the whiff of ripe, roast mutton nearly knocked them backwards.

'Phew, she's a bit off,' commented Scally. 'I told Alice y'might have to chuck it, but she sez it'll come good if y'cut it up and boil it up in a stew.'

'What do you think?'

'Reckon she's right, boiling it up'll see off any nasties.'

'You staying for tea?'

Scally grinned. 'If y're asking. I'd sooner make an early start in the morning if y've a place I can put me swag.' He sat down on the nearest seat and stood up again. 'By the way you've got a couple of letters.' Scally fished in his back pocket. 'One from Alice and the other from yer lady friend in Liverpool.'

Jon's heart lifted at the mention of Merle's letter, he knew there'd be a good reason for the delay, that she hadn't forgotten him. Scally handed over a plain white envelope from Alice and a blue deckle one from Merle, her favourite colour; both were creased from where Scally had been sitting on them.

'Jeb Samuels has put Jindalee up for sale; Alice sez she's mentioned it in the letter.' Scally grinned. 'Y'reckon y've mined enough gold to put in an offer?'

'Place like Jindalee'd take some buying.'

'Aye, reckon it would, never mind, lad, one day.'

Jon ripped open the white envelope and scanned the double page in Alice's familiar hand. Scally wasn't wrong; Jeb, good as his word, had offered Alice first refusal, they'd agreed a fair price and arranged for a bill of sale to be drawn up by their solicitors in Kalgoorlie with a date provisionally set for the second week in November. Alice needed him to be there to sign and with the wherewithal to pay Jeb out. Two weeks, not long, but plenty of time to blow up the mine, retrieve the buried ironbark trunk full of Yaringa gold and sell it in Kal if he got a move on. He read the rest of the letter: Bindi had secured a position in a solicitor's office in Esperance; Joe, Amy and Ruby were growing up apace; Alistair was spending his spare time out in the bush, painting, and Greg had gone home to England for his brother's wedding. Jon folded the letter and returned it to its envelope. Was Greg intending to return to Jarrahlong? Or had his brother's wedding been the excuse he needed to leave Australia behind him for good?

'Ain't y'going to read the one from y'lady friend?' asked Scally.

'Later,' said Jon.

'Alice sez she's training to be a doctor. Y'reckon she'll like it out here?'

Scally sounded just like Val, she'd asked the same question once, but in those days he'd been nothing more than a jackaroo working for Alice. Things were different now, he was a wealthy man, and soon he'd own a station, Jindalee, if everything went to plan, and there'd be plenty left over to build a fine bungalow, one like the Samuels used to live in before the bush fire destroyed it. Merle would want for nothing, why shouldn't she like living in the outback? 'Rachel likes it well enough, and Val, so I don't see why not, Scal.'

'Maybe y're right, but in my experience it takes a special sort of woman to be happy in the outback, such women aren't ten a penny, that's for sure.'

Later, after Jon had shown Scally around the mine, they sat down to mutton stew, damper and beer, Stan's dogs at their feet.

After they'd eaten Scally indicated the two-week-old newspaper he'd picked up in Kal. 'What do you make of that?'

Jon looked at *'The News'*, an Adelaide daily dated 15th October 1953, with a three-quarter page photograph of a mushroom cloud and a headline about the atom bomb.

If he was honest he didn't know what he made of it. In his experience you couldn't trust the British Government about anything. Any government who shipped orphan kids to the back of beyond, just to rid themselves of the responsibility, wasn't to be trusted, but he kept his thoughts to himself. Scally was Australian through and through, and if the Prime Minister, Mr Menzies, approved the testing then it was likely that, as far as Scally was concerned, it was all right by him. Jon picked up the paper and read the detail.

'What do you think of them exploding an atomic bomb near Woomera, Scal?'

'According to the paper there'll be another atomic test carried out soon. I suppose the Government knows what it's doing, but trust the bloody Abos to get in on the act.'

'What do you mean?'

Scally tapped the photograph. 'That.'

Jon studied the image; the huge cloud looked more like the outline of an English oak tree than a human being.

'Can't y'see it? It looks like an old Abo.' Scally tapped the picture again and then, in exasperation, outlined the brow, nose, upper lip and chin of an Aboriginal in profile. 'And I'm not the only one to think that.' He indicated the print. 'See!'

Jon scanned the sub-heading, and read how the cloud surged into the sky like a giant mushroom, and then how it seemed to change shape until it looked like the profile of an Aboriginal.

Jon read on about the flash, the double explosion and the shock wave that reverberated over the plain. It must have been a sight to see, no doubt about it. 'You reckon Mr Menzies has got it right then?'

'Y'not wrong there, Australia needs to be prepared, no point in waiting until the yellow peril comes charging down through Indonesia like they did in forty-two, bombing our cities.'

Jon cast his mind back to something Wes had once mentioned, about the Japs bombing Darwin in 1942, was that what Scally was on about? 'You mean Darwin?'

'Too right, I do. Australia was ripe for the taking if the Japs had had the guts to follow through. Lucky for us the bastards chickened out.'

Jon didn't know what to say and he didn't want to argue with Scally over something that had nothing to do with him. He folded the paper and laid it to one side.

Scally yawned. 'Reckon I'm ready for me bed.'

Jon indicated a canvas cot in the corner that he'd nailed together from an old tarpaulin and a couple of saplings. 'That do you?'

Scally unrolled his swag and stripped off down to his long johns. 'By the way, I forgot to mention that Chips is smitten.'

Chips! He'd forgotten all about Chips. 'What do you mean?'

'Connie, he's got an eye for her, scrubbed himself up he has and spends his time wooing her when he's not looking for that gold reef he reckons is out in the bush some place.'

'And what does Connie have to say about it?'

Scally chuckled. 'Connie's got a good head on her; don't reckon she'll fall for his aristocratic chat. Besides, she's seen it all before, her husband—'

'Vince Andersen?'

'Aye, that's the fella, he was the same sort, one for the ladies, a bit like Berry Greenall in that respect.'

Scally flopped onto the makeshift bed and pulled the blanket over his shoulders while Jon opened Merle's letter, took in the date, 27th July, and started to read.

Dear Jon,

I'm really sorry it's taken me so long to reply to your letters...

Jon scanned what she'd written, looking for her answer to his offer of marriage and of his promise to build her a bungalow better than anything back home in Liverpool, with wide verandahs on all four elevations, an indoor bathroom, and state-of-the-art air-conditioning fans imported from Singapore – but there was no mention of his offer of marriage or the bungalow he was going to build for her. Disappointment choked him up. Had she received his last letter and the one before it, or had they both gone adrift, lost in the post?

He returned to the beginning and re-read everything more slowly this time...*but you know how it is with all the revision and final exams? Well, that's all behind me, thank God, and then, when I did have a moment to write, I couldn't find your letters with the post office address you sent me. Leon or something wasn't it? Anyway, how is the gold mining going? Have you made your fortune yet?*

How could she have been so careless with the address he'd sent to her? – But perhaps she'd had her mind on other things, her final exams that had been looming at the time, he could imagine his earlier letters getting scooped up with revision papers and mislaid, it was easily done. Just because he kept all hers safe in a lockable chest didn't mean everyone was as soft about keeping old letters as he was.

He continued reading...*I don't think I can manage the time to travel to Australia this autumn and, besides, you know the parents, they like us to celebrate the festive season as a family.*

So she had received the earlier letter! But what was she saying? He hadn't specified a time to visit, just after she'd qualified and to suit herself, so what was that all about? Was she having second thoughts?

The rest of the letter spoke of the degree ceremony and the party afterwards, and general chat about her family. Finally ...*I know Alice will forward this and in any case you'll be back at Jarrahlong before too long, won't you?*

Disappointment was a bitter taste in his mouth as he flopped back in his seat. Perhaps she was unsure of her feelings after so long apart; maybe she'd forgotten the affection they'd had for each other when he'd last held her in his arms.

His heart ached at the thought of her, the scent of her hair as it brushed against his face, the softness of her lips when he kissed her, and her smile that made his heart leap – memories so vivid they choked him. The sooner he returned to England the better. But before England he needed to buy Jindalee to prove to Merle that he'd made something of himself, that he could provide a good life for her in the outback.

CHAPTER 14

Jon was in Leonora for supplies and the extra fuses he needed to blow up the mine soon after the cyclone hit. The spring weather had started to deteriorate the day Scally left and now the wind was screaming around the town like a banshee and the rain was hammering on the tin roofing so loud he had to shout to be heard. He'd been lucky over the months he'd been working at the mine, there'd been no extremes in the weather just the usual bitterly cold winter nights followed by a near perfect spring, and now this! He could have done without it and hoped the bad weather wouldn't spoil his plans, he was ready to leave; he'd had enough of the goldfields and besides, he needed to get back to England as soon as he'd got himself settled at Jindalee.

'Send 'er down, Hughie!' hollered Ted Manson as he measured out the rice Jon had ordered.

'Who the hell is Hughie?' shouted Jon above the din.

'God, I suppose,' yelled Manson.

'Why do you call him Hughie?' asked Jon during a slight lull in the storm.

'Beats me, that's what folks say around here.'

Jon stood in the doorway looking out. 'Won't last, will it?'

'Difficult to say, some cyclones last longer and do more damage than others.'

Jon glanced up at the tin roof, listening to the battering the building was taking. 'Reckon it'll blow off?'

'I hope not,' said Manson, 'but it won't be the first building to crumple if it does. Forty odd years ago she blew down the Catholic Church in Gwalia, then, about ten years later, in 1922 or thereabouts, another cyclone destroyed the Protestant one in Leonora.'

'Can't accuse Hughie of favouritism then.'

Manson laughed, 'No, that's a fact. Reckon the worst was just over ten years ago, the bloody blow decimated the place, took out dozens of buildings, then came back for a second bite of the cherry two years later and left us cut off for weeks, no traffic in and no traffic out, including the train. The roads and the railway were under water, getting on for ten inches of rain we had in four days.'

'That bad, eh?'

'Yep, pastoral properties lost livestock as well as buildings and fences, and mines were forced to shut down because they were flooded, I tell ya it was some inundation, folks say it was like the Biblical flood.'

Jon listened as another gust of wind battered the building. 'Do you think I should leave before I get stranded in town?'

'You got far to go?'

'Out beyond Menzies.'

'Maybe, but you be careful, a lot of trees get blown down in this wind, and the road could be washed out in places.'

'I should be all right in the Bedford, pretty much keeps going through anything.'

Jon paid for his supplies and carried the box out to the lorry, wrapped it in a tarpaulin to keep it dry and lashed it down to stop it getting blown away. When he got into the cab the windows were steamed up from the dogs. 'We've got a sod of a drive ahead of us, gals. Let's hope we make it home safe,' he said as he wiped the windscreen with his sleeve and struck up the engine.

Jon ducked in his cab as pieces of timber boarding flew through the air. Sheets of corrugated iron blown loose from roofs and huge branches littered the route. Water was cascading down the road and the run-offs weren't coping, and the land on the outskirts of town was starting to flood. He was tempted to turn back and seek shelter in one of the hotels. Then he dismissed the idea, turning back wasn't his style, a fault maybe, and in any case he wanted to get home as soon as possible and lash down the shack, in this wind the lot could blow away and all his belongings with it.

The journey was a nightmare. The window wipers couldn't cope with the deluge and half the time he had to guess where the road went. Every now and again the truck slewed as a torrent of water poured over the road, catching the wheels, sweeping the vehicle along with it. It was worse than driving through bulldust.

Doggedly, Jon kept his foot down and hoped it wouldn't get any worse. At least he wasn't down the mine. He shivered. The thought of being underground with the water level rising was enough to drive a sane man mad. He remembered Stan Colley telling him about the Italian miner, Varischetti his name was, or something similar, being trapped underground at Bonnievale in 1907.

According to Stan the mine had been a big one, and well over a hundred and fifty miners escaped as it began to fill with water, whereas Varischetti, working at the end of a tunnel, was trapped. The whole community became involved, the unfolding rescue attempts reported in the press. Nine days Varischetti was down the mine, five of them in the pitch dark, it was only his tapping out the miner's code that saved him – until then everyone thought he was dead, drowned in the flood. According to Stan, they'd tried pumping the water out, but there was too much, instead they brought in equipment from Fremantle on the train and a Welsh diver – a bloke called Hughes, eventually got him out after nine long, lonely days.

Thinking of Varischetti made him shudder. He hoped the Cafferty brothers had the sense to keep out of the ground. Their mine wasn't as deep or as big, it would flood faster and if they were stupid enough to be down there in this weather there'd be no Welsh diver about to save them.

Jon was tired and jaded by the time he reached the turn-off for the Cafferty brothers' mine, all he wanted to do was get home with his dogs, get a meal inside him and sleep out the cyclone. It wasn't fit weather to be outside for neither man nor beast. But something had stopped him passing the turn-off – half an hour, that's all the time it would take to check, then his mind would be at rest.

He swung the truck tight right and followed the submerged track. It was like driving down a creek bed and the water was getting deeper. A dark, ominous feeling descended. He half expected to hear Curly's voice in his head giving him advice like he sometimes fancied he heard, but there was nothing, just the headache of rain hammering on the roof. Rain had been hammering on the van roof the day he and Frank were delivering furniture for George Henry Lee's store in Liverpool, the day Kathy ran across the road in front of them and Frank hit her. That had been a heavy downpour, but nothing like rain in a cyclone. The feeling of dread increased as he approached their shack.

The big old salmon gum had gone; when it fell it had flattened the water tank and had buried one of the store sheds in its canopy. The Cafferty's truck was parked next to the store shed and Jon could see that their shack had taken a hammering too; corrugated-iron sheeting from the roof was banging and flapping in the wind, a banshee racket audible even above the sound of his engine and the wind. Surely they weren't still inside! He parked next to the truck, checking for large trees, making sure that nothing was going to flatten the Bedford like the salmon gum had the water tank.

'Stay,' he ordered, conscious that the old dogs hadn't had a run for a couple of hours. He'd let them out in a minute or two when he'd checked on the brothers and made sure they were safe.

Across the yard the shack door flapped in the wind. They weren't in there, the door wouldn't be banging if they were, but it didn't hurt to look, they might be sick or injured.

The shack was deserted. It had to be the mine then, it was the only other place they could be. He lifted up his collar against the rain and followed the track to the shaft entrance, skirting the ramshackle collection of sheds and old, disused equipment. Halfway across the open ground a piece of sacking flapped in the rain-sodden wind.

A shiver rippled down Jon's spine and his skin prickled as he staggered forward and knelt next to it. For a long, terrible moment his eyes locked on to the horror lying in front of him.

Matt lay on his back with half of his head scythed off as if cut through with a samurai sword. One eye stared at him through the rain, a surprised expression in the already dulling iris. The nose and mouth were intact but half of the skull was gone and rain hammered the exposed brain, battering the soft tissue, scattering grey matter, splattering it onto what was left of Matt's face and also onto the ground next to him.

Jon vomited. Bile and water spewed out of him and mixed with the blood and the gore, creating rivulets of lurid colour in the flood water.

Afterwards he sat back on his heels, oblivious of the downpour battering his body, looking for the rest of Matt's head. And then he saw it, next to a piece of tin sheeting that had done the damage, the other half of the skull upturned next to it like a bowl full of porridge. He vomited again, this time retching on nothing until his stomach ached from the effort.

Shock drained his energy, he couldn't think or plan, mindlessly he watched the mess swirling around him before it joined the stream of water tumbling down the mine shaft.

Another piece of debris lashed past, a branch from a gum tree slashed his face, drawing blood. The near miss galvanised him into action, Luke must be down the mine, it was where Matt had been going.

He'd only been down Boobook once. He tried to recall the layout. He knew they were working on a big seam that bore off to the right, a seam that had been worked in the past and which they were extending. Was Luke in there, oblivious of the torrent cascading into the mine?

The deluge pounded him as he descended into the depths. At the bottom the water was knee deep and rising. He yelled for Luke, his voice bouncing along the galleries and echoing back as he slopped along the tunnel until he reached a fork. Now which way did he go, to the left or the right?

'Luke,' he yelled again, the water still rising.

Fear, churned through his guts like a paddle through butter, Varischetti, trapped in Bonnievale Mine flashed into his mind and the image of a hosepipe.

He needed a hosepipe!

He'd seen one, but where? He forced himself to think as he floundered back to the ladder and scrambled up to the surface...on the peg...it was on the peg...hanging against the shack wall.

Minutes later, with air whistling in his lungs, he hurried back to the mine again, unwinding the piping behind him. At the lip he secured the end with wire and descended into the mine, dragging the rest of it after him, an airline should they need it.

The water level was higher, he was sure of it, an inch, he guessed. There was time, but not much.

At the fork he hesitated. Left, an inner voice seemed to say, so he took the left tunnel, splashing through the darkness, hands feeling the way, calling to Luke as he went. But was he following a false lead? Would the tunnelling branch again? He couldn't remember! And how long did he stay? There was no point in them both dying.

'Luke!' he yelled, the water up to his chest, fear making his voice croaky. 'Luke!'

A faint gleam of light shone and disappeared. 'Luke!' he yelled.

The light flickered again.

'Bloody hell!' Luke called. 'That you, Matt?'

'No, it's Jon. Get a move on, can't you; we're going to be drowned.'

The light ahead bobbed up and down as if Luke had speeded up his pace, and all the while the water was rising.

'Where's Matt? What's happened?'

'A cyclone, hurry, for God's sake.'

He took the light from Luke. 'Stay close, you may need air,' he shouted above the noise of the water.

'What air?'

'From the hosepipe, the tunnel's flooding fast, we may have to swim for it.'

They waded through chin-high water their heads tilted back, facing the roof of the tunnel in order to breathe. Water lapped around their ears and splashed over their faces, but eventually, coughing and spluttering, they reached the bottom of the shaft.

Water, cascading down like a waterfall, blinded them as they felt their way up the ladder. Shaken and exhausted they both flopped onto the muddy apron of the mine as the wind bowled branches over them. Jon recovered first, mindful of the body that lay not twenty feet away. He glanced at the sack-covered mound and was glad it wasn't obvious it was Matt. Telling Luke wasn't going to be easy but at least he'd be better prepared for what he was going to see.

Luke sat up. 'This is a cyclone, you say?' he yelled above the howling wind. 'Where's our Matt?' He pushed himself to his feet. 'In bed, is he, the lazy bugger, you wait till I get my hands on him,' he shouted.

It was then that Jon told him.

Jon left Luke with the remains of his brother, weeping. He went and let the dogs out and wasn't surprised that one of them had peed on the seat. In the rain and wind he led them out into the bush to do their business and then took them back to the shack where he lashed down the flapping corrugated iron and, once the place was watertight again, put the billy on to boil for tea. An hour later he went back out to where he'd left Luke and found him, still in shock, with Matt's head in his lap. Luke had ripped his own shirt into strips and had used the makeshift bandages to bind Matt's severed skull into place, restoring, as best he could, his brother's face and head.

'Come on, mate, let's get him home.' Jon lifted Luke by his armpits, dragging him to his feet with sheer brute strength and force of will and then, together, they carried Matt's body back to the shack and laid him on his own bed.

Luke stood before the cot and Matt's body, shivering. Jon found

119

dry clothes and a towel and made him change and borrowed dry clothing for himself. He poured out a mugful of tea, added plenty of sugar and then gave it to Luke along with a large tot of rum. He watched while Luke tossed the grog back, choking on the fiery liquid, and his tears.

That night, while the rain and wind continued unabated, they held a wake. As the night drew on and the level in the grog bottle dropped Luke started to talk and once he started he couldn't stop. He spoke about their Irish childhood in County Clare, about the poverty, of living on a subsistence smallholding barely making ends meet.

'Eight of us there were, four lasses and four lads and our mammy worn out from childbirth and tilling fields.'

Jon didn't speak, he just listened.

'Our da was a hard-working man, a grafter, and his da travelled to Australia for the gold rush in the 1880s, when fellas kitted themselves out with wheelbarrows, picks and shovels and walked from Fremantle to Coolgardie to make their fortune. Da always said he wished he'd had the gumption to do something similar, to make his fortune like his da.'

'And did your granddad make a fortune?' asked Jon.

'Did he heck, he died of typhoid within six months of arriving, buried in Coolgardie cemetery, he is. Mammy told us to visit soon as we arrived.'

'You find his grave?'

He nodded. 'You been to the graveyard there?'

'No.'

Luke sat nursing his drink, staring into the bottom of the glass. 'Pretty bleak place, not a turf of grass, just the red earth, same as everywhere, not a place to be buried,' he said bitterly.

Jon didn't know what to say about that. He'd abandoned his faith, more or less; he wasn't bothered where his bones were laid to rest. He'd come across markers in the goldfields, graves where men had been buried by fellow prospectors where they'd fallen. And there'd be graves that had been lost, the simple wooden crosses consumed by white ants, the wood dust blown away on the wind.

Stan had wanted a permanent marker. Just dig a hole, bury me in it and put up a marker, he'd said. He pictured Stan's granite headstone, a headstone that would last forever, and figured Stan was right to be buried where he'd been happiest and where he had found contentment. He'd liked the idea of a marker for Stan, a gravestone with words on it that gave something more than a name and dates, that said something about what the old prospector had achieved in life. He thought of the words he and Alice had chosen for Stan: *'who found gold'* and smiled, words truer, it turned out, than had been their intended meaning.

'So why did you and Matt come here?' he asked, changing the subject.

'Well, I suppose it was Da talking about all the folk who went overseas to make their fortune, to find a better life. When our Da died Matt said: "Let's do it, let's go and get rich." Matt had met up with a bloke who'd told him about the gold rush in Yellowknife, he'd showed him a newspaper cutting about the prospecting there, and it fired him up.'

'Yellowknife, in America?'

'Canada, Northern Canada. They found gold, in the thirties.'

'Is that near the Klondike?'

'No, that's in the Yukon. Yellowknife's sort of in the middle of Canada, on the Great Slave Lake.'

'Snows a lot there, doesn't it?'

'Yeah, well, Matt was real keen, till I told him it gets to forty degrees below. Matt never was one for the cold. That's when we decided on Australia. Mind, we didn't know how hot it was going to get out here.'

'Pretty cold in the winter though. It can get pretty close to freezing, especially out in the desert.

'Aye, too right it does, but it isn't forty below, is it, even though it feels like it sometimes,' said Luke.

'What did your mother say about you two going off prospecting?'

'She wasn't happy. She didn't see the need to go halfway around the world to make our fortune, but she couldn't stop us. It was hard enough to feed everyone as it was and she couldn't argue with that. The older girls had got themselves shop jobs and my second brother, stupid bugger, got himself shot up in the war, came back a cripple. Liam, the eldest, was tilling the soil, and his wife was expecting their second, seemed to us it made a lot of sense. We planned on making enough to set ourselves up with a smallholding or a haulage business, with enough to make life more comfortable for Mammy and the little 'uns. Instead...' His voice caught. He coughed back tears. 'What about you?'

121

'The British Government sent me when I was a kid. I got shipped out from Southampton to Fremantle with a load of orphans from Liverpool and other places.'

'Both your parents are dead then.'

'Nah, just Mam. Dad ran off with a woman from the next street, skipped over the Atlantic to Canada, he did. I hope the bloody forty below has frozen his balls off.'

Luke laughed, choking on his rum. 'So you've been here ever since?'

'More or less. I did go back to Liverpool once, to find my little sister. I found out she'd been adopted and was settled and happy and I realised I missed the heat and the flies, so I came back.'

'And now you're trying to making your fortune.'

'Something like that.'

'Will you go back to Liverpool?'

'Yeah, but only for a visit, not to live.'

Satisfied, Luke turned back to the cot and stared at his brother's body on the bed. 'I'll have to tell Caitlin.'

'Who's Caitlin?'

'Matt's intended. Matt was forever talking about the place he was going to build for them when he'd found the gold, but the gold got to him in the end. He'd been bitten; it was always more he wanted, enough for a cushion against the bad times, he said.'

Luke downed another slug of rum and refilled his glass. 'We should have been back in County Clare a year ago, would have been if we'd stuck to the plan. We had enough for what we wanted. But it wasn't enough for Matt, was it, you stupid bugger,' he said bitterly, his words directed at his brother's body. 'Trouble was we'd found a good seam, not the best, but rich enough. I told Matt we could sell the lease, that there was no guarantee the gold would last, but it had got to him, the thrill of following the gold. Folk are right about one thing.'

'And what's that?'

'Gold fever, it changes men, and not for the better.'

'What are you going to do now, Luke?'

'Go home, go home to County Clare.'

Jon sat next to Luke thinking about the arrangements to be made once the cyclone had passed. They'd have to report the death to the police, arrange for Matt to be buried. Menzies was the nearest, unless Luke wanted him buried next to his grandfather in Coolgardie. He contemplated the small, painted statue of the Virgin

Mary hanging on the wall. Luke was Catholic; he'd want a proper burial for Matt. He didn't know how to broach the subject. Instead he listened to the wind howling around the building, rattling the corrugated-iron sheeting like a demonic monster trying to break in and demolish them. He'd been in a few blows over the years, but nothing this bad. He'd been told often enough to steer clear of big eucalypts when the wind was blowing a gale, 'widow-makers', folk called them, and it wasn't just in heavy wind that branches came down. The big gum trees were renowned for dropping huge boughs out of the blue and, at the end of the day, dead was dead if you were in the wrong place at the wrong time like Matt had been. There was no doubt about it, life was a bitch sometimes.

'I'm taking him with me.'

Jon regarded Luke, saw his grim profile as he sat on the hard kitchen chair, his elbows on his knees, the empty tumbler in his hands, leaning towards the cot where Matt's body lay.

'I'm taking Matt back to County Clare.'

'You can't do that; it'll take weeks to get back.' He imagined the body decomposing, the stench.

'Zinc-lined coffin, I'll have a zinc-lined coffin made. We'll go together on the train to Perth, take a boat from Fremantle.'

'But—'

'Me Mammy would want me to. She won't want him buried half a world away.'

'It won't come cheap,' said Jon quietly.

Jon saw that Luke's jaw was set. He'd never heard of anyone shipping a body anywhere – although, he supposed, if you had enough money anything was possible.

CHAPTER 15

The day after Luke left with Matt's body, Jon woke at dawn with a clouting headache and a sour taste in his mouth. He didn't feel rested, all night he'd been wrestling with ghosts, justifying his actions, setting up the detonators with Curly and Stan chewing his ear.

In the dream everything had been in slow motion: trying to do the simplest tasks had been like swimming through molasses. Bad idea, Stan kept saying. Just abandon the mine, mate, Curly had said. And Luke, standing behind Curly, had wagged a finger at him and told him to use his common sense. And then there'd been Perentie Man, his reptilian skin glistening in the lantern light, his foetid breath making him gag as he'd struggled to set up the charges in the right order. And there had been the bones, piles of them strewn on the floor of the mine, he could still feel them beneath his feet, slippery smooth, cracking and snapping when he'd walked on them, and he knew whose bones they were: Mum's, Gran's, Stan's, Curly's, Perentie Man's and Matt's. He shivered, spat out a gob of bile and walked over to the trough for a wash. The icy water cleared his brain, but the headache remained.

He didn't feel like breakfast, instead he reheated the coffee and drank the bitter liquid, shut the dogs in the cabin and made for the mine before he could change his mind.

The dank, familiar smell of sour rock, dust and old air prickled his nose. This time he carried a torch, a small chipping hammer, explosives, fuses, and matches. The site was prepared and three-quarters of the way back to the entrance he'd half sawed through all the pit props to ensure their collapse when the dynamite blew. He'd also taken care to clear the route of obstructions, it wouldn't do to trip on the way out, and he'd timed his escape, over and over, with leeway, he wanted to be well clear of the tunnel when she collapsed.

Jon made his way deep underground, avoiding all contact with the pit props, until he came to the site for the explosives. Once the dynamite was in place he connected the sticks together and wound out the remainder of the fuse back along the tunnel as far as it would allow, double checking everything as he went.

Hand shaking, he hesitated, whispered a hasty Hail Mary and lit the fuse.

On the surface he waited for the boom deep underground and the shake when it blew apart the whole shebang. He paced the ground, chewing the skin on the side of his thumb. Five minutes…ten minutes… Nothing! Had the fuse gone out? After twenty minutes he knew he'd have to go back down the mine. Sick to his belly he descended the makeshift ladder…one more attempt, if it didn't work he'd throw a couple of sticks down the shaft and collapse the entrance, it'd be better than nothing.

The fuse to the first detonator had gone out three-quarters of the way along its length. He'd been too cautious, half the length would have done and then the lot would have blown. He calculated how long he'd got once he'd relit it and knew he'd have to get out fast. He struck the match, touched the charred end and ran, stumbling over the uneven ground, torch light bouncing off the walls.

When the first explosion came it blew him over. He lay on the ground, gasping for breath, in sight of daylight from the entrance shaft. Would he be safe where he was? Behind him came a deep rumble and loud cracking similar to the time he and Stan had thrown Gerry Worrall's body down Old Faithful mine shaft. He scrabbled at the rock with his fingernails trying to pull himself upright, and then came a second blast, and a third. Timber and rock rained down on him and he heard himself screaming…

…Stan leans back against the dark rock, looking at him, 'Well, that wasn't one of your brighter ideas, was it, son?'

Stan's words penetrate the pain racking his body, the throbbing in his head. He squints, trying to pick out Stan's shape.

'Why didn't you just take the gold and sell it? Why the hell did you come to this bloody mine, for God's sake?'

'To protect the Dreaming… and your grave.'

'The what?'

125

'The Dreaming.' He looks at Stan. *'You told me about the Aborigines visiting every year, repainting the symbols at Yaringa. If I told everyone where the gold came from there'd be another rush, there'd be prospectors crawling all over the place, it'd end up a big open pit with slack and spoil and slime heaps everywhere. Anyway, I thought you wanted to protect the place?'*

'I suppose,' says Stan, *'can't say I gave it much thought.'*

An unearthly chuckle interrupts Stan's words and the hair on the back of his own neck prickles. He glances round and sees a face gleaming in the darkness. He shivers as the crazed, bloodshot eyes hold him.

'Abo-lover, was it worth it?'

Gerry? What is Gerry doing here?

Lights sparkle in his brain. Nausea sweeps over him. He's dead! The three of them are in Purgatory!

He spits out bile, he doesn't know where it hurts the most, his head, his stomach, or his back. He feels as if he's been thrown down a mineshaft like he and Stan had done with Gerry's body.

'Yeah, y'bastards, y'couldn't give a man a decent burial, could ya?' says Gerry.

'You reckon you deserved one?' asks Stan.

'Abos are animals, vermin, the sooner we wipe 'em out the better, ought to string up those sons of bitches who shack up with 'em too.'

Jon remembers everything Wes had told him. 'One was only a kid.'

'They shouldn't've been on the road, should they?' sneers Gerry. *He laughs. The sound echoes around them, wrapping them in its evil amusement. 'You should have seen the old fella's face, he knew they were done for; they were like shit-scared rabbits trapped in the headlights.'* He chuckles maniacally. *'The old Abo's head bust like a melon, brain all over the road.'*

'You mean you stopped and you didn't help the kid?'

'I gave him a fighting chance. I didn't bash his brains out and I could've done, he thought I was going to, the runt.'

'You're evil.'

'Pragmatic,' snaps Gerry. *'I'd have done it again, given the chance, 'cept that dingo speared me in the back.'*

Stan's eyes glitter in the half-light. 'No he didn't. That spear hit you fair and square in the chest; you were executed Abo style.'

'Same thing,' snarls Gerry. *'The bastard still killed me.'*

His head throbs. Jimmi should have made Gerry suffer before he killed him, a spear through the heart was too kind, a too easy death for scum.

'Scum, eh! You don't know what scum is, lad.'

The bloke sickened him. He was glad he'd hidden Gerry's body. Jimmi wouldn't have had justice and Gerry wouldn't have been punished for killing Aborigines, manslaughter would have been the charge, and he'd have got off with that too.

'What are we doing here, Stan?'

'We're not,' he thinks he hears Stan say, Stan's voice very far away...

...The pain was excruciating, something was pressing on his back, crushing his chest. A sob caught in his throat, blue and white lights flashed behind his eyes and his head throbbed.

He lay still a while, waiting for the nausea to pass, and then blinked dust and grit out of his eyes. Where were Stan and Gerry? He listened...nothing! Was he dreaming? He tried to move but white, jagged pain seared his body, he gasped and felt himself slipping...slipping...

...When he next came to, he remembered. He'd been down the mine! He looked about him, darkness...not even a glimmer of grey! Was it night? He made to get up, but the searing pain stopped him. He caught his breath, dizzy and sick with fear...he was trapped!

Terror choked him...he couldn't breathe, his chest was too tight for his pounding heart... ragged sobs of air made him light-headed. It wasn't real, he was dreaming...

... 'Stan!' he gulps. 'Stan!' – But he knows he's alone, there is no Stan. Alice's face drifts in front of him, her mouth forming words he can't hear...and Merle...what is she saying? Everything starts to spin, black crowding the edges of his vision, and Val...Val's voice whispers in his ear... 'You dozy, daft fool, hon...' Her words echo in his head, and in the space around him, 'Hon...hon...hon...'

The words fade and he seems to float, he sees himself lying in the tunnel, buried face down and chest deep in fallen rock, not moving, his cheeks ashen white, gleaming, eyelids closed, his hair matted in dust and blood, his pit helmet lying upturned, the strap ripped off.

127

This is death then, the dream a premonition. Jerky images, like faulty film, kaleidoscope before him...lads playing football in a Liverpool park...Mam smoking a cigarette...Curly skinning a kangaroo...Alice laughing...sheep kicking up red dust...Stan panning for gold...and Yildilla.

Rage wells up like viscous, roiling oil as he looks at his body buried under the rock. He isn't dead, he can't be...it's too soon! He isn't ready! He has things to do. He's damned if he'll die!...

...Panting breath sang in his ears, rock ground into his cheek, his neck ached, he still couldn't breathe and he wanted to vomit – he was back in his body!

'Stop it,' he groaned, blinking away the sweat stinging his eyes. 'You're alive; you can get out of this.'

He licked his dry lips and lay, forcing his breathing slower, blocking the paralysing fear, the pain, focussing on the helmet he'd seen just feet from his head. He needed that helmet; he needed the pituri lodged in the rim; the narcotic drug the Aborigines used would help him cope, if only he could reach it.

The muscles in his back and arms ached, shock waves of pain rolled over him when he strained against the rock. Something gave. Rock rolled and clattered past his ear, a single piece that landed close by and stopped. He held his breath and waited for the jagged lights behind his eyes to fade, afraid of further rock fall, of death, and then he started to laugh hysterically, tears rolling down his cheeks. Sawing through the pit props had been idiotic. He licked away salt tears from his lips and cursed, his hoarse voice echoing along the gallery, mocking him.

He moved his shoulder again, shutting his mind to the razor blades sawing through nerves, and tried to draw his hand up, the skin scraping against the jagged edges of stone and shattered timber. Warm stickiness trickled down his arm, slick against his fingers, its sickly scent rising with the heat from his body. He swore and bit his lip against barbed-wire agony, forcing his shoulder and arm against the rock, listening, with baited breath, as more stone clattered past him.

In time he created enough space to free an arm, then, piece by piece, he rolled away rock, freeing his upper body. Hours later, exhausted, his body screaming for rest, he closed his eyes and watched the sparkling lights behind his lids – five minutes, in five minutes he'd start again, and then he slept.

Light! His heart lifted at the sight of pale grey rock and he knew he'd slept longer than five minutes. He looked about him; only a couple of feet to the safe section. How stupid was he! The dynamite would have been enough!

He was still trapped, his legs were smashed, he was sure, and he'd suffered blood loss, the light-headed feeling told him so. He clamped his jaws, shutting out the pain and reached for his helmet, picturing the marble-sized ball of pituri dried on to the inner rim, praying that it hadn't been blown off in the blast. His outstretched fingers brushed against the strapping and, sobbing with relief, he dragged the helmet closer.

Time was meaningless, his thoughts confused, he chewed on the pituri and felt the drug slip down his throat. He'd been like this before...in Paradise Canyon...when Yildilla speared him...that had been as bad...the pain...the delirium...but pituri got him through it. He savoured the bitterness and swallowed...he'd survived before, hadn't he? He ground his teeth as bull ants bit their way along his legs, the agony of sensation returning to deadened flesh when he shifted his position. He rolled further over while chewing hard on the pituri, swallowing the drug-laden saliva as the pain peaked, holding back the barbed-wire agony as blood coursed through numb legs.

'Holy Mary, Mother of God, but I can't do this,' he hissed through clenched teeth, his eyes prickling with tears. *'Yes, you can'*, he thought he heard Stan say and hung on to the encouragement, even though he knew it wasn't real.

The potency of the drug weakened as he chewed, the images he'd been creating of happier times to take his mind off the agony, less vivid. He worked faster, oblivious of torn fingernails leaving bloody marks as he lifted the rock, bracing himself against the worst, waiting for the ear-splitting roar as the tunnel roof gave way. And then he realised he'd been lucky, one of the pit props had fallen across him and jammed, protecting him against further collapse.

Over the next two hours he shifted stone, then, when he least expected it, he was free. He flopped onto his back and levered himself away from the fallen rock, dragging his broken body clear of his tomb.

He lay for a long moment, panting, watching pinpricks of light circling above him, listening to the blood roaring in his ears.

'You'll never make it, lad', he thought he heard Gerry say.

'I damn well will,' he muttered.

His left leg was the worst; he inspected it in the thin light. Through the rent in his trousers he saw a large three-cornered tear deep in the flesh of his thigh, the skin blackened and puffy, like Curly's had been in his dying hours. Not broken then, but had he got gangrene? Was he going to die in agony like Curly had done? He buried his fear and chewed on the pituri, swallowing the weakened drug, willing it to work.

Sweat poured off him as he inched along the tunnel, dragging his battered body to the entrance shaft and the ladder.

He rested. Above him the sky was blushed with cold pink – sunrise!

After a few minutes he hauled himself upright and tested his right leg, it'd hold, it had to. He slid his arm over a rung until he had it against his armpit and pulled himself up, one rung at a time, his torn leg bashing against the ladder, knocking the breath out of him. On the surface he lay panting, his head spinning, gathering himself for the next effort.

The shack was within his sight but a good hundred yards away. The dogs were silent. Were they still alive? He shut his mind to the daunting distance ahead, shuffling along on his thigh, pushing on his good leg, inching forward over the muddy ground.

Closer to the shack he could hear scratching on the door and whimpering. One of the dogs was still alive…maybe they both were. When he reached the door he leaned against the jamb, sweat starting on his brow. He knew what would happen and steeled himself, the door would swing open and the dog would be all over him.

He howled like a baby when Bonny jumped on his damaged leg, he bashed her on the nose, heard her yelp and saw her back off and stand beside Bess. He hobbled across to the dogs' water bucket and drank the stale, dusty water, oblivious to the hairs floating on the surface and the scum that had formed. He wanted to flop on to the floor and sleep, his arms wrapped around the bucket, but he knew he couldn't, his leg was a mess and if he didn't get to hospital he'd end up an amputee. He pushed the unwelcome thought to the back of his mind, found the keys to the Bedford and a prop to walk with.

On the passenger side he opened the door and called the dogs. Bess was the first to poke her nose out of the shack door – keeping his voice light he called to her. He coaxed her over to him and half lifted, half shoved her into the truck. But Bonny wasn't to be sweet-talked, it didn't matter how many times he called her 'old gal' she just stood in the shack doorway, her head lowered.

'Good gal,' he encouraged in soft tones. He couldn't abandon her, he'd promised Stan.

'Come on, Bonny, old gal.'

She hesitated and Jon held his breath as she sidled over to him. He grabbed her by the scruff of the neck when she was close enough and rubbed her chest until she relaxed, then he helped her clamber up and join Bess on the passenger seat. 'Good old gals,' he murmured as he slammed the door on them and hobbled round to the driver's side.

'Dear Mary, Mother of God, let the motor start,' he said to himself as he turned the key, a flat battery would be the end of him. The engine chewed over a few times and coughed. He jabbed the accelerator, gentling the engine, as it spluttered into life.

He sat for a moment barely able to believe the sound and then rammed the vehicle into gear, withdrew his foot from the clutch and switched it to the accelerator. The vehicle kangarooed across the yard. When he reached the main road he swung the steering wheel hard over and headed south. All he needed now was a straight run through to Kalgoorlie.

The journey was a blur, the battering his body had taken, the pain in his legs and the loss of blood made him light-headed and nauseous. He passed the turn-off for Broad Arrow wondering if he should stop and get someone else to drive, but the thought of all the effort it would take kept him on the main road. He was managing, he hadn't blacked out, he'd make it.

He reached Kalgoorlie mid-afternoon, a busy time for traffic. Twice other drivers sounded their horns at him and shook their fists at his bad driving. He kept his eyes fixed on the road ahead, gritting his teeth against the pain and the dizziness, concentrating on the route to the hospital. He pulled up at the main doors, switched off the engine and leaned on the horn until a porter and a nurse arrived, both shushing at him to stop the racket.

It was the nurse who marched up to his open side-window first; she looked like a ship in sail in her stiff, starched uniform.

'What do you think you are doing?' she demanded in a voice that sounded Liverpudlian until he realised she was Irish.

'Sorry, nurse.'

'It's sister, Sister Lewis.'

'Sorry, sister. I've hurt my leg.'

She yanked open the cab door.

He felt his world spinning, the edges of his vision closing in. 'Mining accident,' he mumbled, his body tilting towards the open door.

The nursing sister caught him. From a long way away he heard her call the porter.

'My dogs…someone look after them… I'll pay…gold…I've got gold. I can pay.'

'Bring a trolley, quickly,' she ordered, supporting his weight against her chest.

'My dogs…'

'Don't worry about the animals,' she said. 'I'll get someone to see to them.' And then she spoke to someone else. 'Mining accident, trauma to his leg, concussion, possible chest injuries; we may need to get him to theatre.'

'Which mine? Is there anyone else down the mine?' demanded another voice, a male voice.

'The Deborah…no, only me…no one else,' he heard himself say through a fog of pain as he slipped in and out of consciousness.

He heard the rattle of a trolley, felt arms lifting him and white hot pain shooting through his body into his brain.

He forced himself to notice, saw a green room and more people, felt the sharp prick of a needle in his thigh, heard scissors snipping away his trousers, smelt the tang of anaesthetics and disinfectant, and then came the euphoria when the drug kicked in, and later came the bright lights directed onto him and the mask over his face, and finally came blessed oblivion.

When he woke it was dark. He was in a curtained-off cubicle and a nurse stood next to him, a thermometer in one hand and a hypodermic in the other.

'How are you feeling?' she asked.

'Crook.'

'I'm not surprised.' She nodded in the direction of the tented bedding over his damaged leg. 'I hope you're a patient patient, you're going to be here for a while. Lucky for you the doctor was

132

able to fix you up, although it will take time for the wound to heal.'

He felt panic rise up and engulf him. 'What about my dogs?'

'Don't worry about your dogs, I'm sure the nursing sister will get the porter to see to them. They'll be looked after until you're on your feet again.'

She took his temperature and then he felt a cold swab on his thigh and the needle. 'Morphine,' she said, 'you'll need it for a few days.' He watched her check the drip as, once again, he was bathed in a warm gentle light, a feeling of utter peacefulness washed over him and he smiled...

..Stan is sitting at the side of the bed, his white hair as spiky as ever, his ice-blue eyes, half hidden under bushy brows, considering him.

'You got a death wish or something, son?'

'No, Stan, just got a bit unlucky.'

'No, son, not unlucky, just bloody careless. What was the point of me leaving you that reef if you go and kill yourself in a clapped-out mine?'

'I already explained.'

'When?'

'When we were down the mine, when it collapsed.'

'Don't recall,' says Stan. 'You must have imagined it.'

'Am I imagining this?'

'Don't ask me, I'm not a mind reader.' Stan scratches his stubbly chin with gnarled fingers. 'Who's looking after me dogs while you're taking a holiday?'

'The porter.'

'He likes dogs does he?'

'I don't know, Stan.'

'Well, you'd better find out. I don't want my gals looked after by any Tom, Dick or Harry.'

'Likes his old dogs, doesn't he?' says Curly.

He opens his eyes and sees Curly sitting where Stan had been not a minute before – not that he could be sure about that, but it felt like a minute. Perhaps he'd dozed off.

Curly's face breaks into a wide grin. 'Thought back there you'd be joining me. You can't afford to make mistakes like that in the outback. It's an unforgiving place.'

'I know.'

Curly contemplates him, a faraway look in his dark eyes. 'Then what do you think you were doing wasting your time in that mine, mate?'...

...'Protecting the Dreaming,' murmured Jon. 'I was protecting the Dreaming.'

'Are you all right?' a voice asked.

Jon pulled himself up through the fog, licked his dry lips, and took a moment or two to recognise Sister Lewis looking down at him.

'Were you dreaming?'

'No.'

'You were talking about dreaming, something about protecting your dreams.'

'Was I?' he said, suddenly remembering the dream that wasn't a dream. 'Stan spoke to me. He's worried about his dogs.'

'Your dogs!'

'Well, yes, they're my dogs now, but they were Stan's and he doesn't want any Tom, Dick or Harry looking after them. He wants them looked after by someone who likes dogs.'

'When did Stan tell you this?'

'Just now.' He looked at her face and realised how bad it sounded, as if he were losing his mind. He forced a grin. 'It must have been a dream. How long am I going to be in here?'

'A couple of weeks or so.'

Jon frowned. Would Bess and Bonny be all right for that long? Would they pine?

'Your dogs will be fine,' she said. 'Do you think Stan would mind me looking after them for you?'

'I don't know. Do you like dogs?'

'Yes.'

'In that case, thanks. I'll pay you.'

'Not to worry. I lost my own dog a bit back; it'll be nice to have yours about the place again. Now, are you ready for your next injection?'

'That nice stuff?'

'The morphine?'

'Yeah, the morphine.'

She gave him his injection and he let it cradle him until he melded with the beautiful oblivion that took away the pain.

CHAPTER 16

Jon looked at the ward clock and sighed, it was only twenty past ten! He'd been in hospital for a week and the days were dragging, he wanted to get back to the mine, not be stuck in bed wasting valuable time. Alice would be in Kalgoorlie any day and he needed money to pay for Jindalee. He thought about the gold he'd buried in Stan's ironbark trunk and smiled grimly. Alice had offered to look after it for him, but with Greg on the scene it was too risky. Alice was fit enough all right, but she was no longer young and he hadn't wanted to chance Greg inheriting everything, besides, he needed the gold with him when he came to sell.

'Jon Cadwallader,' said Sister Lewis, approaching the bed. She turned to the doctor next to her and handed over a file, 'Mining accident, he was lucky not to lose his leg. How are you feeling today, Jon?'

'All right.' He nodded towards the cage protecting his damaged limb. 'How much longer am I going to be in here?'

'Not long now, this is Doctor Cooper.'

Jon looked at the doctor, 'Doctor Frazer sick?'

'He's on leave, I'm the locum.' He flipped through the notes Sister Lewis had given him while she rolled back the bedding and removed the cage. 'Another week I should think, sister, and then he'll need to build up the strength in that leg.' He inspected Jon's toes, asked him to waggle them and tested them for warmth, then he turned his attention to the scar tissue on the thigh of the other leg.

'An old scar,' said Sister Lewis, 'another mining accident.'

'Fell down a shaft and speared myself on a splinter,' said Jon, repeating his earlier explanation.

'Seems you're prone to bad mining accidents,' commented the

135

doctor, tartly. 'Who fixed you up?'

'No one.'

'Septicaemia, or gangrene, could have set in. Why didn't you come in to the hospital?'

He could tell by the doctor's tone of voice that he didn't believe him but he answered anyway, 'Too far, it happened out in the bush.'

'Does it affect you?'

Jon shook is head, 'Bit of a limp, that's all.'

'Last time I saw a scar like this it was on an Aborigine out in Alice Springs.'

'That right?' said Jon in a flat voice.

'A blackfella came in telling some cock and bull tale of how he'd slipped and fallen on a spear while out hunting kangaroo. Truth was he'd been messing with another fella's woman, either that or he'd got himself mixed up in some blackfella business that he didn't ought to have done.'

Jon forced a smile. 'No, mate, like I said, a mining accident, haven't come across any Abos pretty enough to fancy.'

The doctor handed the file back to Sister Lewis, a sceptical look on his face, then the pair moved on to the next patient.

Twenty minutes after the awkward conversation Bindi turned up dressed to the nines in a smart dress and smarter shoes and carrying a fancy bag. Her hair had been cut and styled and she turned the head of every fella on the ward. Jon was relieved the doctor wasn't about.

'Hello, Jon.'

'How did you know I was here?'

'Alice, she got your letter.'

'What are you doing in Kal?'

Bindi grinned. 'Visiting you while Alice is with her solicitor.'

'Alice is in Kalgoorlie?'

'At this very moment. She said she'll be over later with a document for you to sign. What are you two up to?' she asked with a broad grin on her face.

Jon pulled himself up into a sitting position and changed the subject. 'I'm surprised Sister Lewis let you in.'

'She took pity on me when I told her we'd only just heard about your accident, but she did say to keep it short, that visiting's this afternoon.'

'Did you see a doctor?'

'Thin…glasses?'

'Yeah, that's the one.'

'Yes, but he didn't speak to me, he just looked at the sister and said, "Mining accident, huh".'

'I bet he did,' muttered Jon.

She smiled at him. 'I take it you're going to survive.'

'Yeah, so long as I don't die of boredom.'

'That's what Alistair said.' She fished in the bag she had with her. 'He sent you these.' She piled up the books on the bedside cabinet.

'Who drove you?' asked Jon suspiciously, knowing full well that Alice didn't like driving distances.

'Me.'

Jon looked at her. 'I didn't know you could drive.'

'Val got Wes to teach me.'

'How is Val?'

'She's really well, she moved back to Charlestown and rented Simpson's Store from Mr Simpson's brother and Alistair made sure that she's got an option to buy the place if Fred ever decides to sell.'

'What about the baby?'

'Ruby? She's lovely; she's coming up to a year old now and running around the place. She's got a shock of red hair, all curly, and she's a chatterbox. Alice really misses them both.'

'Where are they living?'

'Above the shop.'

'It's a bit cramped up there.'

She nodded. 'Yes, that's what Val says, but she's prepared to put up with it, she says she's going to save every penny so she can buy the place, she reckons Fred Simpson will sell up before too long, he doesn't like the outback and he thinks Charlestown is a dump.' Bindi gazed at him, a speculative look in her eye. 'Why did you decide to take up prospecting over here? Doesn't Alice pay you enough?'

'It's not that…I just needed—'

'More money?' She looked at the cage protecting his damaged leg. 'Was it worth risking your life for?'

'Yeah, it was, I'll tell you all about it one day.'

She looked at him long and hard. 'Promise?'

'Promise.'

Bindi took out a parcel wrapped in greaseproof paper and placed it on the pile of books. 'Belle baked you a cake, she said she doesn't want you to starve.'

'Thanks,' said Jon without much enthusiasm. Belle was the world's worst cook when it came to cakes. She wasn't that good when it came to normal grub either.

Bindi laughed. 'I'll tell her you're looking forward to eating it.'

'How's the studying coming along?'

'Good, and I'm going to Esperance soon.'

'Alice mentioned it in her letter. When?'

'Next month. I don't know how often I'll get back home, not that often, I suppose, but it'll be worth it to qualify.'

'Qualify?'

'Yes, get my articles.'

'I thought you wanted to go to university?'

'I did, but they turned me down, Abos aren't allowed. Alistair did his best, but the answer was still no. Alistair said they were intractable, that was the word he used, anyway he suggested I get a job as a trainee solicitor.'

'I'm surprised they accepted you.'

'You mean because I'm a half-caste?'

'Yeah, so how did you do it?'

'Alice, she said that where there's a will there's a way and Alistair suggested Esperance would be a good location. By all accounts there're a fair few foreigners living there and he said I'd blend in and, besides, when I'm done up to the nines I don't look like an Aborigine. He said I'd get away with it as long as I've got the right papers.'

'Don't tell me...Ken Bates.'

Bindi grinned. 'That's right, from Cavanagh's Creek. How did you guess?'

'Because Alice had him 'doctor' David's birth certificate so I could get a passport a few years back.'

She chuckled. 'By the way, I'm a Belinda now, not Bindi.'

'Whose idea was that, Alistair's?'

'You're not wrong,' she said dryly. 'Anyway, I applied for a post, and Alistair took me for the interview. Introduced me as his great-niece, which helped, him being a Cambridge graduate and so well-spoken and all, anyway, they offered me the position.'

'What do your parents think?'

'Me ma's not keen, she's worried about me being a half-caste, she thinks they'll guess and that I'll get into trouble. Dad reckons if Alice says it's all right, then it's all right.'

'And what do you think?' asked Jon.

'I dunno, I wasn't keen on lying about my background or changing my name, but Alistair says it's a means to an end and he reckons Aborigines need sympathetic solicitors and lawyers more than most. He says I'm bright enough to cover my tracks for long enough to get my articles and that eventually it won't matter who knows I'm a half-caste.'

'He's got a point, I suppose, and why shouldn't you be a solicitor. I don't see why you can't go to university either.'

'No, neither can I. Anyway, Dad was all for it, said it was too good an opportunity to miss. He said that if it's what I want then I'm not to let anyone stop me.'

'Well I happen to think your dad's right,' he said.

'The only thing is I don't know anyone in Esperance.'

'You'll soon make friends.'

'Yes, I suppose so, and Ty's promised he'll drive over now and again. He says it will be a good opportunity for him and Rachel and the kids to see the coast and have a bit of a holiday.'

'Can't see Rachel wanting to leave her Dad behind,' said Jon.

'It'll only be for a week or so, and she's looking forward to it, says she's always wanted to travel and seeing the south coast will make a change after living in the outback all her life.' She glanced at her watch. 'The sister said I couldn't stay long, so I'll be over later with Alice.'

'Before you go, have a word with Sister Lewis and collect Stan's dogs, she's looking after them for me.'

'Yes, I'll do that, does that mean you'll be home soon?'

'Yeah, just as soon as I get out of this place.'

'Right then, I'll be off.'

'You won't forget Stan's dogs?'

She smiled at him. 'I'll find Sister Lewis right away.'

The day Jon left hospital he'd caught a glimpse of himself in a mirror and didn't recognised the peaky-looking, skinny bloke staring back at him. It would take time to get fit again; he'd lost muscle laid up in bed. He felt sick and light-headed as he drove north and was unsure of what he would find.

At the mine he parked the Bedford and took in the scene, the derelict shack, the door hanging off its hinges, and, inside, the leaves and twigs packed against the stove and deal table where the wind had driven them. He swept the place clear, lit the stove and opened a couple of rusting tins of corned beef and baked beans, eating the food straight from the tins, then, exhausted by the unaccustomed exercise, he lay down on the bed, dragged a blanket over himself and slept.

When he awoke the sun was well up. He collected his rifle, a pickaxe and a shovel, put them in the back of the Bedford and drove to the site out in the bush where he'd buried Stan's trunk, and started digging.

The pickaxe felt heavier than usual, the effort made him sweat and he realised just how weak he was from his time in hospital when all he'd had to think about was Jindalee and Merle. He swung the pickaxe again, steeling himself against the impact – the sooner he paid for Jindalee the better.

Inch by inch the hole grew deeper as he worked under the blistering sun, his wasted muscles screaming for rest. Now and again he'd stop and listen, startled by an unfamiliar noise, then, reassured by the presence of the rifle, he resumed digging.

In the early afternoon came the dull thud of metal against metal – Stan's trunk. He dragged chain from the back of the truck and bolted it to the metal handles and attached the other end to the towing hitch. Carefully he nursed the Bedford forward, anxious not to break the chain or damage the trunk, and pulled it out of the ground.

He brushed off the earth, revealing the cross-banding and the dark ironbark – there was enough gold left in the trunk to buy a station and with spare besides, not even counting the healthy bank balance he'd accumulated over the months he'd been in the goldfields. He unbolted the chain and threw it in the back of the truck. Stan's trunk had been heavy when he'd last buried it and he knew he'd have difficulty lifting it in his condition. He bent over, tentatively bracing himself against the weight, and lifted, and let go – it was heavy, heavier even than he remembered. He looked about him and studied the eucalypt spitting distance away. The big gum tree had a suitable branch, a widow-maker sure enough. If he attached block and tackle to it he could haul the trunk off the ground, drive the Bedford under it and lower the trunk, job done, so long as the branch didn't give way.

'You needa some 'elp?' enquired a voice.

Jon spun around and saw a fella standing behind him with his

140

weight on one foot as he half bent over a cigarette. Jon heard the rasp of a cigarette lighter and saw the flame flicker as the man drew on the tobacco. He pocketed the lighter and straightened, exhaling a steady stream of smoke.

'What are you doing here?' flared Jon, angry he'd been caught by surprise.

'I'm a looking for the work.' The stranger nodded in the direction of the ironbark trunk. 'I give you some 'elp, yes?'

Jon stepped closer to the Bedford and rested his hand on the rifle. 'No thanks, mate.'

'Reckon she's 'eavy, no?' The fella glanced up at the eucalyptus tree Jon had been inspecting. 'You going to need some block and tackle, I think.' When Jon didn't answer he drew on the cigarette again and exhaled slowly, his eyes fixed on Jon's face. 'You 'ave a mine back there.'

'That's right.'

'She collapses, I see,' he indicated in the direction of the mine.

Jon nodded, never taking his eyes off the bloke.

'I 'elp you clear the mine, yes?' He stepped forward, his eyes drawn to Jon's hand resting on the gun. 'Look, I 'elp you lift a the chest and if she too 'eavy I fetch a the block and tackle while you look after the chest, yes?'

Jon watched him, Italian he guessed from the accent. They were of a similar size but Jon reckoned the fella was ten years older. His arms were muscular and there didn't appear to be a spare ounce of fat on him; if it came to a fight he wouldn't stand a chance against the bloke, not in his condition.

'I'm not a going to steal from you.'

Jon could see he didn't have a gun, and, as far as he could tell, he didn't carry a knife. He slid the rifle closer. 'Thanks, if you catch hold of the handle maybe we can swing her up.'

The fella dropped the last of his cigarette and ground out the burning stub with his boot heel. He took an easy pace forward and leaned over, catching hold of a handle. Eyes fixed on the stranger, Jon did the same. Together they braced as they stood upright, holding the box between them.

'It's a 'eavy,' grunted the man.

'Ironbark,' hissed Jon through gritted teeth.

'After the three,' said the bloke, 'then lift 'er, okay?'

Jon nodded, sweat already prickling his brow.

'Two, three....lift 'er,' grunted the fella and together they lifted it onto the truck. The Italian stepped back, dusted off his hands on his trousers, took out another cigarette and offered the packet.

Jon shook his head, waiting for him to make the next move, watching as he lit up.

'Gillespie, Antonio Gillespie,' the bloke said, extending his hand. Jon ignored it.

'People call me Tony. Now, 'ow about a that job? You and me, we dig some more gold together, what you say?'

'Reckon the mine's all worked out,' said Jon.

'Then we dig a new gallery…when we find a the gold you pay me.'

'Reckon it's too big a job.'

'You dig all that, yes?' Gillespie indicated the trunk.

'Some of it,' said Jon not wanting to lie to him. He raised the tailgate and secured it. 'Look, mate—'

'Tony.'

'Tony, there's not much gold left.'

'I pay you, yes?' said the Italian, his face lifting. 'I pay you…what do you call it? – a deposit, yes?'

Jon hesitated. Maybe he should sell. He looked Gillespie in the eye. 'How much've you got?'

Gillespie shrugged, his hands open, palms upward. 'I have a saved a little bit, yes.' He pulled out a wallet from a back pocket, 'It's not a that much…but I work 'ard, I pay a the difference when I make a the money, yes!'

Gillespie looked a decent type, a bit down on his luck, and desperate, but it'd take forever to clear the rock fall and make the mine safe. 'No, mate, you can have it, but I reckon it's all worked out.'

'But I pay you, yes,' Tony insisted.

'No, mate, it's not worth your money,' said Jon. 'It's kaput, no gold left.'

'But I can 'ave a the mine, yes?'

'If you want it.'

'And what she called…the mine?'

'The Deborah,' said Jon, climbing into the cab. He struck up the engine, leaned out of the window and held out a bill of sale hastily written on the back of an old invoice. 'You'll need to register it in Kal.'

Gillespie took the note as Jon pulled out.

Jon looked in the rear-view mirror, Gillespie could have the lot, he'd seen enough of mining to last him a lifetime.

When he reached the main road he turned south for Kalgoorlie and the solicitor's office to pay the residue on Jindalee.

PART III

[December 1953 – December 1954]

CHAPTER 17

Jon leaned back in an easy chair sipping Alice's favourite bourbon whiskey. It was late, Alistair had retired for the night and they were alone.

Alice finished the last of the rye and put the empty glass on the side table. 'I take it everything ran smoothly.'

Jon nodded. 'I sold the gold and arranged a bank draft for Jindalee, Bateman reckons the paper work will come though in a few days, he said to pick up the keys from Cato.'

'Keys, what are you talking about?'

'It seems there was a spare set of keys to the old bungalow at Jindalee, Cato has them in a safe deposit box and I need to claim them.'

'But the bungalow burned to the ground, the keys are—'

'I know, Alice, but I wasn't about to argue, besides, it's sort of symbolic, isn't it?'

'I suppose, just seems a bit odd having keys to a building that no longer exists.' She topped up both glasses and changed the subject. 'It's been quiet here since Greg went back to England.'

Jon savoured the alcohol and Alice's comment. He'd never taken to Greg, had never liked his attitude. 'Didn't reckon on you missing him, Alice.'

'What do you mean?'

'Greg, he isn't exactly cut out for the outback, likes the high life too much. I'm surprised he stuck it so long.'

Alice chuckled. 'You two never did get on.'

'You're about right there.' Jon caught the gleam in Alice's eye and wondered what was coming next.

'He's due back any day.'

Jon swore under his breath. Greg hadn't left! He didn't like the bloke, but Greg was no fool, he knew where his best interests lay.

'And what about Alistair?' he asked. 'What's he going to do now Bindi's settled in Esperance?'

'Alistair's in no hurry to leave. He's been out in the bush painting for the last few weeks.' She indicated a couple of new pictures on the walls. 'Not bad for an amateur. I got Adie to knock up the frames, I quite like the rustic look, it suits the subject matter.'

Jon looked at the paintings and took in the familiar scenes. One was of Sandy Spit showing children bathing in the water and adults picnicking, and it reminded him of the time Val had organised a day at the creek soon after she'd arrived from Liverpool; the other depicted a muster, men driving a mob through the bush, drovers and animals mired in red dust. 'They're pretty good,' he agreed.

'He sent some to a gallery in Perth and sold a couple. The gallery owner wants more,' said Alice.

Neither spoke for a moment, both lost in their own thoughts. 'I've asked him to stay on,' she added after a while.

'Why?'

'Well, he's good company and he's better at chess than you are. Second, we've got youngsters growing up on the station and he's a good teacher.'

'The Aboriginal kids?'

'That's right, and then there's Ruby, and Rachel's kids.'

Jon heard the edge in her voice.

'And he likes it here. He's offered to pay his way and I've said yes.' Her tone was final.

'I still think he's hiding from something.' It wasn't that he didn't like Alistair, he did, he was good company, Alice was right on that count, even so there was something odd about an academic who wanted to bury himself in the outback.

'Why are you so suspicious of him?' asked Alice.

'He's a bit old to be making a fresh start.'

'Well, it's none of our business, and in any case, I don't think he is hiding from something as you so delicately put it. I think he wanted a change and he ended up liking it out here. You did.'

'You got me on that one, Alice,' said Jon, a wry smile on his face.

Alice got up out of her seat, selected a fresh cheroot and lit it. 'Now, tell me about your time in the goldfields. Did you learn anything aside from the dangers of blowing up a mine with old explosive?'

Jon's face broke into a broad smile. 'Too bloody right, I did.'

He spoke of the good times, and then of the bad, and his face darkened as he recalled Matt Cafferty's death. 'Me and a couple of mates got caught up in the cyclone.'

'Aye we heard about that, a chap from Kal was telling Ed. He reckoned it did a fair bit of damage in Leonora.'

'Yeah,' said Jon, 'that was the one. Me and Matt and Luke were in the middle of it. A tin sheet severed the top off Matt's skull.' He looked down into the empty glass, remembering the horror of it all.

'It doesn't do to dwell on these things,' said Alice after a moment or two, 'I don't suppose blowing yourself up down that mine was a picnic either.'

'No, you're right on that one, Alice.'

'What are your plans now? When are you thinking of moving into Jindalee?'

'Tomorrow, Alice, just as soon as I pick up the keys from Cato.'

Ed Scally leaned back in his chair, his eyes fixed on Jon. 'So then, Alice, what do y'reckon Greg'll say when he gets back from the Old Country?' The three of them were sitting in The Grand drinking coffee after a midday meal. 'Y'planning on giving him Jindalee to manage?'

Alice glanced at Jon.

Ed caught the look. 'Y're not letting Greg manage it, are ya?'

Alice shook her head. 'Greg still has a lot to learn. He hasn't got to grips with the demands of Jarrahlong yet.'

'And I suppose young Jon here has.'

'There's more to it than that, Ed.'

'Oh yeah, like what?'

'Jon's investing the money he made in the goldfields.'

Scally looked at him askance.

'I mined enough to buy a stake in the place,' said Jon.

'And the pair of ya have gone into partnership, that it? That's big of ya, Alice.' Scally took out his tobacco pouch, rolled a couple of cigarettes and handed one across to her. 'Seems to me it'll be a bit lop-sided, and that's the way Greg'll see it too.'

Alice leaned towards the flaring match, lit the cigarette, inhaled deeply and flopped back in her chair, savouring the noxious smoke.

'Greg'll not take kindly to y'handing the job over to a younger

149

fella, even if he is putting up some of the money. And there's another thing, Alice, have y'thought about what'll happen when y're dead and gone? There'll be strife once y're not around to keep an eye on things.'

Alice exhaled slowly and took another long drag on her cigarette. 'I see you think of everything, Ed.'

'Someone needs to.'

Jon didn't like to admit it, but Scally was right. Once Alice wasn't around any more there'd be a few in Charlestown who'd be in for a shock, not just Greg. He imagined the scandal when people assumed that Alice had left her share of Jindalee to him and not to her own flesh and blood. The fact that Jindalee was totally his, paid for with the gold he'd mined in old No Hope, would have to remain a secret for ever if the Dreaming at Yaringa Creek was to be preserved.

He considered Alice, apart from a touch of arthritis in her hip she was fit for her age; she'd make eighty-five. At least he hoped she would, another twenty odd years or so and he'd be part of the landscape. The only problem would be if Greg decided to demand what he saw as his inheritance early. Still, that was in the future and as Stan had often said, things have a habit of working out.

'When do y'take over the place?' asked Scally.

'Today,' said Alice.

Scally clicked his tongue at the news. 'I see you don't waste any time! I reckon this calls for something stronger than tea.' He crossed over to the bar and returned with three measures. 'Cheers to you both.' He downed his whisky in one swallow. 'Still, if you want my opinion, the place is pretty run down. There's a lot needs doing and it'll need restocking. The Samuels never had the cash to do it properly after the fire, and then there was the dingo predation and all.'

'Yes,' agreed Alice, 'we will have to restock.'

'And finish the rebuilding, Alice.' Scally's gimlet eyes raked Jon. 'That should keep y'out of trouble for a while, won't it?'

Jon ignored him, even after all this time Scally still had a dig now and again; Scally still half believed that he was Joe's father and he'd never really forgiven him for not marrying Rachel after he'd returned from England six months after Joe's birth.

'Well, lad, I can't say I'd like to be in your boots when Greg gets back. He'll be as angry as a cut snake over the whole business.' He turned to Alice. 'When does he get back?'

'Any day, Ed, and don't you worry, I'll see to Greg. Jindalee needs someone who knows what they're doing and Greg, good as he is, has one foot in the two-up ring.'

'Aye,' said Scally, 'I can't argue with you on that count.'

CHAPTER 18

On an early December afternoon, four years to the month after inheriting Stan's mineral lease and No Hope mine, Jon drove into Jindalee yard and parked his battered ute next to the neglected vegetable patch. Red, the horse Alice had given him, was already in the corral with Daisy. Adie had ridden over earlier with the horses on lead-ropes.

Smoky bounded out of the back of the utility while Bess and Bonny waited to be lifted down. Jon picked up the box of provisions he'd bought in town, opened the picket gate and walked up the crazy-paving path to the homestead door. The building was nothing like the one that had burnt down. That had been a big, beautiful, sprawling bungalow with a wide, sloping roof that took in deep verandahs on all four sides, with bougainvillea and roses growing up the support posts and shade trees all around the building. But all that was gone now; instead, a small shanty-type bungalow had replaced it on a new site away from the original. It was all the Samuels could afford after the fire.

Jon opened the fly screen and then the inner door into the kitchen. Mary had left it clean and tidy with enough equipment to get by. Apart from the few personal possessions that she'd taken with her – nothing of any value had been left after the bush fire, no books, no photographs, no paintings, no fine furniture, the lot had gone up in flames.

He placed the box on the kitchen table and looked about him. He'd already spoken to Alan Bynon about the rebuild, a bungalow like the old one with a big sitting room and a large stone fireplace, a study for his books, and the others that he would buy, three or four bedrooms and a bathroom with an inside loo and a big family kitchen, one that Merle would like.

That night Jon ate roast kangaroo with damper prepared by one of the Aboriginal women and the next morning he saddled Red, loaded up a packhorse and set off to explore the station.

It was a fine December day, perfect for riding out, hot, but not as unbearable as it could be in midsummer. He followed the high ground, alongside the creek and reached the bare dome-like hill overlooking the homestead where he took out a map of the station showing the boundaries, the fenced paddocks and all the soaks, wells and bores.

He knew that the lease he'd bought gave him grazing rights to over eight hundred thousand acres of mulga and mallee scrub, salt-bush, spinifex and wanderrie grassland. The west side of the station had the better grazing, according to the Samuels, whilst the eastern side was more arid and had fewer wells and bores.

According to Jeb the station currently carried one thousand two hundred head of cattle and a few Merino sheep that had escaped the inferno that had devastated the station in the late forties. Then there were the wild goats, feral camels, brumbies, kangaroos, emus and dingoes. According to Ty their numbers had increased since the Samuels had stopped culling the vermin.

He looked at the map again, a couple of permanent springs, a fair number of soaks and the wells and bores that had been sunk over the years: Western Well, Emu Bore, Jeb's Well, Tom's Well and Will's Bore and the rest. Jon smiled to himself – the next he'd call Cadwallader's.

In Western Paddock he spotted small mobs of cattle. While there he checked that the windmill was working, lifting the water from deep underground into the storage tanks. He inspected the water troughs, cleaned out the skeins of green algae and made sure the ballcock system was running freely, and then he tied a rope around the decaying back legs of the dead cattle and dragged their carcasses deeper into the bush away from the water.

Hours later he reached the Eastern quarter; he sat back in his saddle, looking at the landscape and shaded his eyes against the sun reflecting off the glassy surface. On this section of the station the red earth was covered with large grained ironstone, shiny black from a distance, like a coating of fine coal. The first time he'd seen it he'd dismounted his horse and had run his hand over its glossy surface, amazed by its character, convinced that, somehow, the planet had pushed the glassy black grit to the surface.

He loved this harsh land, Stan had seen it in him, and now this portion was his. He smiled as he recalled Stan stomping back to his shack after the cave-in in old No Hope. He could see Stan's tired face, blue eyes, and spiky, white hair sticking out at all angles, and the fierce look when he'd shouted back at him and made him realise what the place and the people meant to him.

England wasn't for him. *This place death* was how Curly had put it when he'd appeared to him in a dream, the time he'd returned home to find his sister. And Curly had been right. Liverpool, once an energetic, rich city had been brought to its knees, it had been ravaged by German bombing, but it wasn't just the devastation, it was what the place did to his soul, it crushed him, there was nothing he'd seen that could provide him with the sense of belonging that this place gave him. At some point he'd ceased to be a city boy and deep down he'd ceased to be a Pom. He might not have the papers to prove it, apart from the passport he'd acquired with David Macarthur's 'doctored' birth certificate, but where it mattered he was Australian now.

The sky was darkening in the west, the last of the sun setting it alight with apricot and azure, pretty colours like a summer dress. The sunsets in England were neither as vibrant nor as beautiful as they were in Australia and he wondered why that was so. What was it about the atmosphere above the outback that made the sky different to that of England? Big questions for a big land – he urged Red forward – too big for him to answer.

He looked for a suitable campsite and caught a whiff of wood smoke. He wasn't the only one out and about! He followed the scent that led him back onto higher ground, the rocky backbone that rose on the arid north-eastern border of the property and found three Aborigines camped next to a natural waterhole in the rock – men with painted faces and chests, wearing traditional clothing. They stood as he approached and it was then he saw the scrub bull with spears through its chest, flies already crazed by the smell of death.

No one moved. Three pairs of eyes awaited his reaction. He could tell by their tense muscles and the stances they had taken. In the past there had been too much killing between whites and blacks and it had been the blacks that had come off worst, massacred, in some cases, for killing sheep and cattle by pastoralists and cattlemen incensed by what they'd seen as stealing. From what Alice had told him there had been little attempt to understand what had lain behind the events.

He slowly dismounted, hitched his packhorse to a sprout of bluebush and led Red over to the dead animal. He tied a rope around the bull's back legs and attached the other end to the pommel, then he remounted and urged Red forward, dragging the carcass a good distance from the ceremonial site before riding back to the three men and dismounting.

'You speak English?' He guessed they did, he was sure he'd seen one of the men in Charlestown. They probably worked on one of the stations, not Jindalee, although he couldn't be absolutely sure of that.

When they didn't answer he held out his hand. None of them moved to take it. 'I'm Jon Cadwallader...from Jindalee.'

The smallest of the three nodded, the one he thought he'd recognised.

'Charlie,' the man said, his eyes watchful. He indicated left, 'Sandy,' and then right, 'Ned.'

Jon acknowledged the introduction. 'I didn't mean to intrude on your ceremony,' he said, remounting Red. He touched his hat, unhitched the packhorse from the bluebush and left. It was clear his presence wasn't welcome, he'd stepped onto a sacred site and some sort of Aboriginal ceremony what with them done up to the nines in paint and feathers, and besides, he couldn't hang around for long, he needed to find a suitable place to set up camp for the night.

He backtracked and once off the ridge followed a dried-up creek bed until he came to a patch with kangaroo scrapes and pitched camp. In no time he had a fire blazing, then he dug down like the kangaroos had done for water to fill his billy, and while the water boiled he made damper and put it in the camp oven to cook. He skinned and gutted the rabbit he'd killed earlier, pierced the carcass with a stick and balanced it across the fire to spit-roast while he unrolled his swag and made the billy tea.

The horses watered and hobbled for the night, Jon settled down to wait for the rabbit to cook. Curly liked his charcoal on the outside and the flesh raw and bloody, but he'd always found raw meat difficult to stomach, preferring his better done. Jon turned the spit and the juices spat and hissed on the hot ashes. He liked rabbit; it was similar to chook only better, sweeter, and more flavourful. The one animal he drew a line at was cat. He'd never acquired a taste for cat although he'd had to eat it a few times. He smiled at an old memory: Curly poking in the campfire ashes out at Mullin Soak and pulling out a well-charred back leg and handing it over. Even

155

before he knew what it was the smell had put him off, although Curly's mob had tucked into the rest of the animal with relish. No, rabbit was tasty, but cat…he'd have to be starving to want to taste that again.

He sipped his billy tea, listening for Aboriginal voices, for chanting, or music, but heard nothing. Had his arrival spoiled things or was the ceremony already over? He had no way of knowing. He pulled a blanket around his shoulders and glanced up at the night sky. Not a cloud in sight, a colder night then. He leaned back against the rock and watched the fire, mesmerised by the flames rising and falling, the white ash dropping off consumed mulga roots, and the glow when a gust of wind made the wood burn brighter. Later he ate supper, then he burned the bones and poured himself another pannikin of stewed billy tea. As he stared into the embers he became aware of a figure standing at the edge of the firelight.

'Tea?' offered Jon.

The short, stocky Aboriginal, the one called Charlie, stepped forward. 'Don't mind if I do.'

Jon threw away the dregs of his tea, wiped the pannikin, refilled it and passed it over.

Charlie squatted on the ground next to him. 'About the bull.'

'Shouldn't have been there, should it?'

Charlie shrugged.

'Forget about the bull,' said Jon.

Charlie didn't answer. He sipped the bitter tea, staring into the fire as Jon had done earlier.

Jon considered the situation. There was nothing worse than sheep or cattle for contaminating water. Paddling in it, pissing and shitting in it, fouling what they would later have to drink. No wonder the Aborigines hated them. 'What if I fence that section off and keep the cattle out?' He waited for a response and didn't get one. Problem was it would stop kangaroos and euros and the other wildlife. Maybe the solution was to sink a well. They did need more water in the eastern quarter.

Charlie threw tea dregs onto the sand and handed back the pannikin. 'Rotten tea, but thanks, mate,' and he was gone, as he'd come, like a shadow, silent as a moonless night.

'Well, what do you know!' said Jon to himself. He added more wood to the fire, drew the blanket closer to him and settled down to sleep.

In the morning the Aborigines had gone. There was nothing to show for their presence except fresh painting on the rocks next to the waterhole. Jon gave the place wide berth and spent the rest of the morning looking for a suitable site to sink a well. It was a long way to cart the wood and metal for the windmill, nonetheless it was a good place to construct one and it would provide permanent water for the cattle, even in a drought.

Two days out from the homestead he came upon Ty Henderson.

'You're one hell of a fella to track down, mate.' Ty's face split into a broad grin. The terrible, diagonal scar across his cheek pulled when he smiled, giving his face the now familiar sardonic cast. 'How're things? I gather Alice has promoted ya?'

Jon smiled. 'I suppose you could say that.'

'Given up on the mining then?'

'Yeah, it's a mug's game.'

'Aye that's what Scally thinks. Sez you were off your head going to the goldfields, then you were gone so long he reckoned you wouldn't come back. Nice to see you proved him wrong. You made a packet then?'

'Enough.'

'Enough to go into partnership with Alice, I gather. You stick with her, mate, she'll see you right.'

'Thanks for the advice, I'll bear it in mind,' said Jon.

'You know Greg's at Jindalee, waiting on your return?'

'When did he get back?'

'Yesterday.'

'Hasn't he got enough to do on Jarrahlong?'

'Reckon he wants a word. Never seen the bloke looking so grim. He looks like a fella who thought he'd caught a dingo and ended up with a goanna. If I was you I'd watch me back. You know what Poms are like, you can't trust the buggers.'

Jon grimaced. 'Yeah, I'll remember that.'

'Yeah, you see that y'do.' Ty looked up at the sun, 'You fancy camping out again, or do you want to get back to that mongrel?'

Jon laughed. 'Another night under the stars won't go amiss; it'll give Greg time to cool off. What you got for tea?'

'Tinned dog and damper do you?'

'It'll do fine,' said Jon.

'Before I forget, it's Alice's birthday next week and Val's planning a party for her, she reckons you should be there.'

'I'm a bit busy.'

'Aye, that's what I said, but Val wouldn't have it, she sent me out to find you, said you're expected, and she's not taking no for an answer.'

There was nothing he could say to that. 'Will you be going?'

Ty grinned, twisting his scarred face into a disconcerting smile. 'Wouldn't miss it for anything. Val's organising a picnic out at Sandy Spit. Rachel's looking forward to it too.'

'Alice really likes that place, doesn't she?'

'Too right, she does, according to Scally she and Jack used to go there when David was a kiddie.'

'When's it arranged for?'

'Sunday.'

'Can I tell her you'll be going?'

'Yeah, I suppose so,' conceded Jon, knowing he had no real choice in the matter.

They organised camp between them, seeing to the horses first, then collecting a heap of bone-dry mulga wood and soon they had a fire blazing and the billy on to boil. After the meal they sat back drinking tea.

'You know what, mate, it's got so I miss the company these days. In the past I was happy on me own for weeks at a time, with just the horses, but since you and me went after dingoes together, and ever since I took up with Rachel things have changed – I don't like to be away for more than two or three weeks now.'

'You've had the rough edges knocked off, is that it?'

'You could say that.'

'Talking of rough edges, how's Bindi doing these days?'

'Like a bilby in a burrow.' A grin lit up Ty's face. 'She's got herself settled in Esperance, sharing a room with another girl, a secretary with the same firm. Seems they get on well together. But you know what, I reckon Alice bringing in that tutor fella made a big difference.'

'She's a bright girl,' commented Jon.

'Yeah, but she wouldn't have got where she is without Alistair's help.'

'Maybe you're right.'

'I am right.'

They sat for a while, watching the flames, not speaking, listening to the night-time noises out in the bush.

'She ever tell you she saved my life?' said Jon presently.

'No, Bindi can be pretty closed-mouthed when she's a mind.'

'Well, she did – four years back when I was over in that canyon I told you about, I thought I was a goner. I reckon I'd never have made it out on my own, not with the leg wound going bad on me like it did. All that Abo knowledge of hers got me through.'

'She always was into Abo ways. She sez she's going to fight for Aboriginal rights once she's qualified. I told her to keep quiet about that, warned her they might kick her out if they think she's goin' to cause trouble for them later. She just smiled and told me she wasn't born yesterday.'

'She's got more sense than my sister, then.'

'What's she doing?'

'Hairdressing, she jacked in school at fifteen.' Had he known of Kathy's plans sooner, he could have offered to help financially, but she hardly ever wrote. He wished she'd seen the value of education like Merle had done. She could have done something similar, got an academic qualification.

'I thought she liked ballet,' said Ty.

'Who told you that?'

'Bindi.'

'Bindi!'

'Abo girls not supposed to know about ballet, is that it?'

'Something like that. I'll tell you one thing for nothing. I won't underestimate her again.'

'Wise,' said Ty, 'and certainly not with old man Yildilla behind her.'

'Aye! No one wants a kaditja man on their tail.'

'You what?'

Jon looked up from his tea and saw the shock on Ty's face. 'Didn't you know he's one of their lawmen, an executioner?'

'No, I didn't. How come you do and I don't?'

Jon put down his pannikin and stood up. 'I'll show you how.' He dropped his trousers and indicated the terrible scarring on his thigh. 'That's what he did to me in that canyon.' He buttoned himself up and sat down again.

'Why?'

'God knows. Bindi wasn't sure either, but whatever it was I must have fallen foul of some Aborginal law. It might have been something to do with the tjuringa Curly gave me to look after, or maybe it was the perentie I killed.'

'What perentie?'

'A monitor lizard, Curly's totem animal. Anyway when Yildilla stood in front of me with that spear of his he wasn't exactly interested in explaining the logic of Aboriginal law.'

Ty gave a long, low whistle. 'No wonder he puts the wind up Gracie. You know she can never go back to her own people, not after shacking up with Dad.'

'She violated one of their customs, did she?'

'Something like that,' said Ty quietly. 'You must hate the bloke.'

'I did, but not any more, as he saw it he was only doing his job.'

'But it's illegal, mate. Black man's law don't count. You could have had him arrested if you'd wanted to.'

'And what good would that have done?'

'I don't know, but you might have felt better. I know I would if it'd been me.'

Ty left him after breakfast and Jon continued his survey of the station, checking the bores and wells as he went.

Sightings of cattle had been sparse on the east side and Jon was beginning to wonder whether Jeb's estimate had been over generous until he came to Snap and Rattle Bore, named after the profusion of snap and rattle growing in the area. There he saw plenty of cattle gathered around the empty water troughs, some animals clearly in distress from lack of water in the stifling summer heat. A cursory check told him he couldn't fix the problem alone and he set off back to the homestead for the necessary equipment – there weren't enough cattle left on the station to risk losing more through tardiness.

CHAPTER 19

Jon reached the homestead at midday. He rode past the collection of humpies where several of the black stockmen and their women stayed and approached the station from the rear, past the burnt-out shearing shed and the stockmen's quarters. When he reached the corral he slipped off Red, tethered him, undid the girth and bridle and carried the tack into the barn. When he turned back, Greg was waiting for him, standing in the doorway with the light behind him, the dark outline of a man spoiling for a fight.

Jon walked over to the door. 'Morning, Greg. How was England?'

Greg didn't move or answer. Jon sidestepped around him, refusing to be intimidated by his hostile manner. He walked across to Red and began brushing the horse, waiting for Greg to start the harangue.

'Couldn't wait for me to go, could you?' snarled Greg. 'Minute my back's turned you're at Alice, sweet-talking her.'

Jon looked up from his task. 'You what?'

'You heard, you bastard. Well, what goes on here you discuss with me from now on. I'm the one with the say so, not Alice. You got that?'

'Is that what Alice wants?'

'To hell with Alice, she's gaga anyway.'

'If I were you I wouldn't let her hear you talking about her like that.'

'Why not, she's my relative, not yours, and at the end of the day most of this place and all of Jarrahlong will be mine.'

Jon stopped brushing Red and looked over the animal's withers at Greg's face, ugly with fury and barely concealed frustration.

'It's in her will,' Greg snarled.

'Is that what she's told you?' said Jon, knowing full well that she'd left Jarrahlong to Greg's father, Eric, having been there when the will was signed and sealed.

'Yeah,' growled Greg.

Jon supposed he wasn't far wrong; no doubt it'd eventually end up in Greg's hands.

'Well, you're wrong about Jindalee, Greg. I've got a stake in the place and Alice has left me in sole charge. If you want I'll drive back to Jarrahlong with you and we can sort this out.'

He waited for Greg to absorb his words, glad that everything was locked up legally, that he had the papers that proved Jindalee was solely his even if Alice died suddenly.

Greg kicked out at the fence, then spun on his heels and stormed over to his utility truck. He fired up the engine and leaned out of the side window, 'I'll fix you, you bastard,' he yelled, slamming the ute into gear and, tyres spinning, he roared out of the yard.

'Sod you!' Jon shouted after him as he unhitched his horse. He realised Ty had been right, he had better watch his back.

After Greg had left, Jon went to find George and the other stockmen to check how much headway they'd made with the new fencing posts he'd asked them to make. After the fire the Samuels had bought in cattle and only part of the station had suitable fencing. Everyone told them they were laying up unnecessary expense, that they should restock with sheep but it was the sheep that had survived the fire that finished Jeb Samuels for Merinos. He and his sons had searched the burnt countryside for days looking for survivors – those animals dying in agony with their flesh badly charred, their ears and noses damaged beyond recognition. It was the stench of burnt wool and living flesh, and the pitiful cries of the tortured sheep that haunted their sleep for months afterwards, that and the killing – shooting animals to put them out of their misery had been too much, it had turned their stomachs leaving half-digested food in the dust.

George Pinjuti looked up as Jon approached. He liked George, and Jeb Samuels had once said that George was the best black stockman he'd ever had. He was another Adie, a man you could rely on, a man who knew his business and, like Adie, he never went walkabout, but there the similarity ended. While Adie was small and stocky and had skin as black as bitumen George was lighter skinned and rangy looking, with a shock of dark, curly hair and his wife had a similar look about her. His kids and his dogs were all rangy looking too. He was also the only black stockman to live in the separate quarters that the Samuels had initially built for their sons.

George had asked for proper accommodation when Jeb Samuels took him on. He'd never said why he and his family had upped sticks and travelled across country to Western Australia. Jeb reckoned he was in trouble with the law and had wanted to put distance between himself and the Queensland police. Not that Jeb cared; he had too many worries of his own to be bothered about George's. He'd offered the accommodation and George had taken it.

'George, we've a problem out at Snap and Rattle Bore.'

'Blockage?'

'Reckon so. Guess we'll have to drag out the pipe and check; the horses'll be no good, better take the truck with the winch on the back.'

'Righto, boss, I'll get Timmi and Sam; they're pretty good on mechanics.'

'I'll organise the truck,' called Jon after him.

Within twenty minutes they were driving out to Snap and Rattle, Timmi and Sam leading the way in a ute while he followed behind in the truck with George. When they arrived thirsty cattle were crowded around the dry drinking troughs. Soon Sam was climbing the ladder to check that the windmill was working while George unscrewed the bore pipe and hitched the end to the back of the truck and indicated to Jon to ease her forward. In no time at all sixty foot of piping was laid out on the ground like a sleeping reptile. It took time to flush out the blockage and to lower the pipework back down into the bore. Soon the windmill was clanking away and water was filling the empty cisterns. The boys cleaned out the troughs, dragged away the carcasses of a couple of skinny cattle that hadn't coped without water for two extra days, and then they were off, back to the homestead. Jon and George waited a while, watching the cattle.

'When's the next muster, George?' asked Jon.

'Mister Jeb organised it for the end of February.'

'It's still a bit hot to be transporting cattle, isn't it?'

'Reckon Mister Jeb needed the money.'

Jon eyed the cattle still waiting to take their fill of water. 'Rangy looking, aren't they? Do you think there're enough fat bulls out there to make the muster worth our while?'

'They're a bit scrawny lookin',' admitted George. 'A spell in the fattenin' yards would help.'

'You're not wrong there,' agreed Jon. The sight of the skinny animals depressed him. He needed to get the station on its feet as soon as possible. Alice had given him the name of a stock agent he could contact through Les Harper, and Jon had already placed an order for sixty young heifers and a couple of bulls.

'Got a delivery of new breeding stock due, reckon I'll arrange it to coincide with the muster. It'll be a saving if our cattle go back to Perth on the same wagon.'

'What y'buyin' in, boss?'

'Herefords, mostly.'

'You buyin' in new bulls?'

'Yeah, I think I'll have to, the ones we've got don't look up to much.'

'Station owners in Queensland are buyin' Brahmans.'

'Brahmans?' He'd read about Brahmans in one of the stock magazines. They were imported from India; some said they were better at surviving the droughts, but to his eye they were ugly looking cattle with big humps. 'What's so special about them?'

'Well, apart from being good in heat and drought, they're tick resistant, quiet, easy to manage, and y'cows'll have no problems calving. Some fellas been keepin' the best of the half-breed bulls and usin' 'em on half-breed cows. It's reckoned they produce calves with good conformation, just right for beef – and they're docile and easier to manage than them Shorthorns and Herefords.'

'Is that so,' said Jon, trying to remember where he'd put his stock magazines when he packed.

'Yeah, reckon you'd do right to buy a Brahman bull.'

The pair of them leaned against the truck, watching the cattle, satisfied that the bore was working as it should. It was time to get back to the boys he'd left drilling holes in the new gimlet wood fence posts.

Jon slipped into the driving seat and George sat beside him for the ride back to the station.

'You interested in carrying on as head-stockman?' asked Jon.

George glanced at him.

'Jeb told me you did a pretty fair job after his sons left to take the post up north.'

'Yeah, I'm interested. Me and the wife, we like it here.'

'Good, that's fixed then.' He drove on a way. 'Who does the gardening?'

164

George looked up, confusion on his face. 'Gardenin'?'

'Yeah, looking after the vegetable plot. No veggies, no tucker. And I need someone in the house.'

'When Mrs Samuels was here May did it.'

'Well, tell your missus I'd like her back and the sooner the better. D'you think she can organise one or two of the other women with the garden and train up a youngster in the house?'

'Will she be in charge?'

'She will if she does it right and the pay'll be fair.'

A grin lit up George's face. 'Right, boss, I'll tell her.'

It was almost dark by the time they got back to the station. Jon left George to sort out the truck and store the equipment while he headed for the bungalow and the two boxes he'd brought with him full of Alice's old stock magazines. He'd got some reading up to do, on Brahmans.

CHAPTER 20

The morning of Alice's birthday Jon left George in charge at Jindalee and drove into town to pick up Val and Ruby. As the utility bounced over the corrugations he worried about meeting Val again. He'd hoped it would be at Sandy Spit, that there'd be plenty of people around to fill in the gaps in conversation but then Ty had asked him to pick them up.

'Hiya, hon,' Val said with a wide smile as soon as he drew up outside Simpson's Store. 'Long time no see. How you doin'?'

'Nice to see you, Val.' He smiled back at her. He'd forgotten how infectious her cheerfulness was.

'And this is Ruby.' She swooped the child up from the floor and held her firmly in her arms. 'Say hello to Jon, Ruby.'

The child stared at him with solemn eyes, dark grey Jon noted, and her hair was a mass of dark auburn curls. She was a beautiful child and very different in looks to her mother. She had her fingers rammed in her mouth and Jon had the distinct feeling that she was assessing him.

'Hello, Ruby, I'm your mother's friend.'

'Say hello,' ordered Val.

Ruby's eyes never left his face; she withdrew her wet fingers from her mouth, wiped them on the front of her dress and said solemnly, 'Hello.'

Val plonked Ruby on the ground. 'Now you stay there while Jon and I put all the picnic food into the truck.'

Ruby sat on the wooden steps and watched while they carried baskets, boxes and rugs out of the shop and loaded them into the back of the utility. 'Have you got your dolly?' asked Val when they'd finished loading.

Without a word Ruby tucked her doll under one arm and picked

166

up a bucket and spade with her free hand.

'Shall I put them in the truck for you?' asked Jon.

Ruby nodded and held out the bucket and spade, keeping a firm grip on the rag doll.

Soon they were on their way, Ruby sitting on Val's lap while Jon drove.

'Does your mam and Evelyn know about Ruby?' he asked once they were clear of Charlestown.

'No.' Val sat looking straight ahead wearing the defensive look he'd seen more than once.

Me and my big mouth, he thought and promised himself that he wouldn't say anything that would end in an argument, he wouldn't even mention Liverpool. Val was old enough to know what she wanted, and besides, it was none of his business. 'She's a pretty kid,' he said to ease the tension.

'Thanks.'

'Bet she keeps you busy.'

'Yes, and you're a good girl, aren't you, Ruby?' Val kissed the top of the child's head. 'How did things go over in the goldfields? Did you make your fortune?'

'You could say that, I mined enough gold to buy a share in Jindalee.'

'Alice told me, and she said you'd had a bad accident. Is that why you came home?'

The word *home* jolted him. He had come home; this place was home in a way no other had ever been since before Mam died. He glanced at her but she was still looking straight ahead, an unreadable expression on her face. 'I suppose.'

'What happened?'

'I miscalculated with a stick of dynamite.'

Val grinned. 'You mean you nearly blew yourself to kingdom come?'

Jon smiled. 'Yeah, mangled a leg pretty bad and had to get myself to the hospital in Kal…spent a couple of weeks in bed.'

'And that gave you time to think, that it? You realised Greg was the lesser of two evils and you decided to come back and be a thorn in his flesh.'

'You don't mince your words, do you?'

'You know me? Say it as it is…at least Alice is happy to have you back. She really missed you, you know.'

There wasn't anything he could say to that. He'd missed Alice, but he wasn't about to admit it. 'She's got Greg.'

'Yeah,' said Val. 'I forgot, she's got Greg right enough.'

'You don't like him, do you?'

'Well, let's just say I've met more charming rats in my day.'

'Berry?'

She laughed then, a happy, mirthful chuckle that made Ruby turn to look at her mother. Val kissed the top of her head again. 'Yeah, Berry, bless him.'

'You seen him recently?'

Val shook her head. 'No, Cadge says he's got a job in the Northern Territory that's payin' a better rate.'

'You miss him?'

'What do you think?'

Jon didn't reply, confused by her answer, besides, he didn't want to fall out with her over Berry, the bloke wasn't worth it.

They drove on without speaking after that, Jon concentrating on avoiding the bulldust and the worst of the potholes, while Val pointed out the wildlife to Ruby – a lone euro, a couple of emus and, in the distance, the dust kicked up by brumbies trotting off into the bush. 'And that's a wattle bush' she said, pointing out a flowering acacia, 'see the pretty pompom flowers, and that one with the white bark is a ghost gum. Can you remember that, Ruby?'

'Wattle,' repeated Ruby.

'And ghost gum,' said Val.

'Ghost,' said Ruby, stuffing her fingers back into her mouth.

Val turned her attention to Jon. 'By the way, I've chosen a hat for you to give to Alice.'

'A hat!'

'Yes, a hat…for her birthday, remember?'

'Alice doesn't celebrate birthdays.'

'She does this time, everyone likes birthday presents.'

'Do they?'

'When's yours?'

'Last week.'

'Does Alice know?

'No, why should she, and don't you go telling her.'

No one had asked him when his birthday was since before he arrived in Australia, when he was eight. The last birthday he remembered was when he was seven and his mother had made a birthday cake with seven candles and she'd given him a football, a real one made of leather. He smiled at the memory.

'What're you smilin' at, hon?'

'Nothing.' He didn't want to talk about those days.

They arrived at Sandy Spit at the same time as Scally, Alice and Alistair. Val and Ruby hopped out of the utility and went to help Alice get settled in the rattan chair that Scally had brought with them.

'I suppose this was your bright idea,' grumbled Alice when she saw Val.

'Too right, Alice,' said Val in broad Aussie. 'We couldn't let your birthday go by without celebratin' it, hon,' she added, reverting to her more familiar Liverpool dialect. 'And it's a perfect day for a picnic. Give Grannie Alice her present, Ruby.'

Jon stepped back to where Alistair was standing and watched, fascinated, as Ruby handed over a book-shaped parcel.

Val took Ruby's hand. 'It's not new, Alice. I found it in Perth, but it looks interestin', and I thought you might like it.'

Jon looked at the cover as Alice removed the wrapping, *Spinifex and Sand*.

'It's a first edition, its got the maps and everythin' and it's written by a fella called Carnegie who explored all the way from Kalgoorlie to Halls Creek in the 1890s. I thought you might know a few of the places he visited along the way.'

'Thank you, Val, I shall enjoy it and I'm sure Alistair would like to read it too.' She handed the book to him to look at.

Jon went back to the utility to pick up the hat just as Ty drove up with Rachel, Joe and Amy.

'Are we late?' Rachel asked as she and the kids got out of their truck.

'No, only just arrived ourselves. You got a pressie for the birthday girl?'

'Yeah.' Rachel grinned. 'Why, haven't you?'

'What do you think this is?' He picked up the parcel and waved it at her. 'Val organised it.'

'Us too. What are you giving her?'

'A hat.'

'I've made her an embroidered cushion for her chair.'

Ty lifted a couple of baskets out of the ute and joined them. 'She's been sewing for weeks, hasn't she, Joe?'

The six-year-old turned to Jon, a big grin on his face. 'Did you sew the hat?'

Jon flapped the parcel on Joe's head. 'No, I didn't, you cheeky young pup.' Trust Val to embarrass him with a flipping hat.

Joe laughed and ran off to join the others.

Jon waited for Ty and Rachel and then followed them across to where Alice and the others were sitting in the shade.

'Happy birthday, Alice!' Rachel kissed her on the cheek and gave her the cushion. 'We thought you might like something soft to sit on.' She laughed as Alice inspected the embroidery, placed the cushion carefully on the seat and settled herself on it.

'Perfect,' beamed Alice. 'I'll be able to sit in comfort all day.'

Jon handed over his gift. 'Happy birthday, Alice.'

Alice smiled at him. 'Who told you it was my birthday?'

'A little bird.'

Alice opened the parcel and took out the hat, a straw affair with a blue bow and a wide brim, smart looking, the sort of thing she could wear on Race Day.

'Lovely, Jon! I didn't know you knew about fashion.'

'It was that bird again,' mumbled Jon, too embarrassed to look Alice in the eye. He crossed over to Alistair sitting on the flat picnic rock watching the gathering.

Alistair moved over to make space for him. 'This is the first time I've ever been to a birthday party like this. It's better than Christmas; it will be something to write home about.'

'You got family in England?'

'Two sisters, both married with grown-up families and grandchildren, one lives in Kent and the other in London.'

'Don't you miss them?'

'Sometimes, but I never really saw that much of them anyway, we kept in touch by letter mainly.' He looked over his shoulder just as Jon did when they heard the horse, and saw Greg come into view.

They both nodded a greeting.

'I wondered when he was going to arrive,' commented Alistair.

Jon eased himself off the rock. 'I suppose I better get a fire lit for the billy.'

'I'll help you with the wood,' offered Alistair.

The day reminded Jon of the last picnic Val had organised and this one followed the same pattern, kiddies paddling at the edge of the creek, the braver adults swimming in the deeper section dammed especially for the purpose decades ago. Alistair got out a sketch book and did some drawing while Scally and Alice reminisced about the old days that only they remembered.

Jon was sitting near to them listening in to their conversation when Ruby stood up from where she was squatting by the water's edge and came across to him carrying her bucket and spade. She stood in front of him and held out the spade without speaking.

'Seems she wants your help,' said Alice.

Jon pushed himself to his feet. He didn't know anything about toddlers, his memory of Kathy when she'd been four or five was dim and he couldn't remember what she'd been like at Ruby's age. He went to take the spade but instead Ruby put her hand in his and dragged him after her. He followed, smiling at his ungainly gait, conscious of the warm protective feeling that washed over him the minute he took her tiny hand in his. Was it how fathers felt? He glanced down at the child's auburn curls. He'd like a family one day, he'd never mentioned it in his letters to Merle, perhaps he should, four children would be nice, two of each.

At the water's edge Ruby gave him the spade and soon they were making mud pies together for her to jump on. Before he knew it Amy and Joe had joined them and all three of them were yelling and shouting *more* every time he went to leave. He was relieved when Val called them over for their meal.

Ten minutes later he was sitting back against a large boulder, a selection of picnic food at his side, when Ruby plonked herself on his lap and helped herself from his plate.

'Looks like she's taken to you,' commented Alice. 'She won't entertain Greg, turns her back on him,' she regarded her great-nephew for a long moment, 'doesn't she, Greg?'

'Well, what do you expect,' said Val lightly, 'the girl has taste.'

Everyone laughed, except Greg who scowled and glared at Val as she gave Alice a slice of birthday cake.

After lunch everyone dozed in the shade of the eucalyptus and acacia trees growing along the edge of the creek. Talk turned to the newly established autumn race meeting designed to fill a gap in the social calendar. Jon smiled as Alice told Alistair all about the annual Cathay Cup race held in the spring, and how he'd been strung along by everyone and hadn't realised that the Cathay Cup was awarded to the fastest bullock on the racecourse.

'Pot Luck won it three times,' said Ty.

Val turned to him. 'You reckon he'll win next time?'

'Not a chance in hell. They cut him up for steak straight after the last race.'

Alice tilted back the birthday hat. 'So which horse is favourite to win the Owner's Cup this autumn?'

'Cracker,' said Scally.

'Not a chance.' Greg waved his beer bottle at them to emphasise the point. 'I'll be putting my money on Do Better.'

Ty gave Greg a long look. 'It's a clapped-out old nag, not even fit for dog food, and it's got a wall eye.'

'I don't know so much,' commented Scally. 'Batesy reckons he's got speed in the final furlong, sez that's where he'll be putting his money and Batesy don't often make a mistake when it comes to horse flesh.'

'What about Bomb Proof? Les says he's a good horse, reckons he doesn't take any notice of anything else on the track, just keeps on going,' said Val.

Alice wafted the air with her book, glad of the cooling draught. 'Talking of bombs I hear they're planning on doing more tests over in South Australia.'

Greg snorted his derision at the very idea. 'Why can't old Wilcox train his horse here?'

Alice caught Greg's eye. 'I'm talking about atomic bombs, not Bomb Proof.'

'We read about the two they did a couple of months ago, didn't we, Scal, remember?' said Jon.

'Yeah, there was a picture in the paper.'

'That's right,' said Alice, 'taken some place north-west of Woomera.'

Alistair flapped at the flies buzzing around his sweaty brow. 'The British Government sent a friend of mine to Japan soon after they dropped the bombs on Hiroshima and Nagasaki. They wanted a report on the after-effects. He told me that no decent person in their right mind would want anything to do with atomic bombs after seeing the devastation. People and property were laid waste, the cities were deserts.'

'The bloody Japs deserved it. They should have dropped a couple on Tokyo while they were at it,' said Greg.

Scally clapped Greg on the back. 'Reckon y're about right there. The bastards bombed Darwin in '42. If it hadn't been for our blokes out in Indonesia it'd have been a sight worse, I can tell ya. No, we need our own A-bomb, can't always be relying on the Yanks.'

Alistair shaded his eyes against the sun. 'There are some people who think we don't know enough about the effects of radioactive fallout from these weapons.'

'Are you saying we shouldn't have bombed the Japs?' bristled Greg. 'You a commie or something?'

'No, I'm not a communist. All I'm saying is that we should consider the long-term effects, the damage to future generations—'

'If we'd listened to the likes of you we'd have lost the bleeding war,' sneered Greg.

'What are you saying, Alistair?' asked Jon. 'You mean people could be at risk?'

'Exactly that.'

Scally gave Alistair his full attention. 'The Government wouldn't be doing it if it was dangerous.'

Jon frowned. 'What about the Aborigines?'

'What about 'em?' said Scally. 'They're only doing tests at Emu Field not bombing Abos like the Yanks did the Japs.'

Rachel sat up and dusted sand off her legs. 'Surely they'd have moved them out before they started if it was that dangerous.'

'One would hope they did,' commented Alistair, 'these nuclear weapons are pretty fearful things.'

Jon closed his eyes and settled down for a nap, bored with the conversation. It was too hot to argue; besides, Emu Field was miles away, in another State. It wasn't likely to affect any of them, and Scally was right, they'd only been testing bombs, not doing anything nasty with them.

'Emu Field is a long way from here.' Scally's tone was scathing. 'It won't affect us.'

Alistair caught Scally's eye. 'That will be contingent on climatic conditions at the time they detonated them.'

'What d'ya mean?'

'Well, it will have depended on such things as atmospheric pressure and the wind speed and direction as to how far the radioactive fallout travelled. No doubt the Government had someone in a plane tracking the mushroom cloud, taking readings.'

Greg pushed himself to his feet. 'I'm not listening to all this bullshit about radioactive fallout; they're only doing tests for Christ's sake. I'll leave you to it, Alice.'

'Are you going back to the station?'

'No, town, reckon it'll be more entertaining playing cards with Chips than listening to Alistair whittling on.'

Val watched Greg go then turned to Jon, a grin on her face. 'Do you fancy a paddle?'

He stirred himself. 'No, it's a bit too cold for me.'

'Too cold, in this heat!'

'Yeah.'

She sat beside him making patterns in the sand with a stick and he wondered what she was thinking, what the next suggestion would be. He lay back, closed his eyes and feigned sleep.

'I'm sorry about Merle, hon,' she said quietly so that only he could hear.

Her words were a dousing of cold water. 'What about Merle?' he asked, keeping his eyes firmly closed.

'Her and Paul Vincent.'

'What about them?'

'Their engagement.'

He rolled onto his belly so she couldn't see his face. Engaged? What was she talking about? He could feel his heart pounding in his chest, nausea rising up his throat. 'Who told you?' the words choking him even as he said them.

'Dorothy, I had a letter from her last week. She went to the party Pete threw for them at his new house, in August, hell of a do apparently, all the old crowd were invited.'

The blood rushed in his ears. He should have seen it coming, but he hadn't: none so blind, he thought bitterly. Merle had written to him in July, why hadn't she said? Why hadn't she told him she was going to marry someone else? And Dorothy, he imagined her revelling in it all, writing to Val with the news. He wished she'd minded her own damned business instead of passing on gossip.

'Anyway, hon, I'm really sorry. I know what she means to you.'

He couldn't answer for the lump in his throat and after a while she got up and went to paddle in the water with Ruby.

They stayed at Sandy Spit until late afternoon, watching the children playing in the water while they dozed in the shade of the big gum trees.

'Thank you; I've had a lovely time,' said Alice to all of them as they packed away the picnic paraphernalia, 'it's been the best birthday in a long time.'

'We should do these picnics more often,' said Rachel. 'It's been fun and the kiddies have enjoyed it.'

Alice turned to Jon. 'I've been meaning to visit Jindalee. I don't suppose it looks anything like it did in the old days.'

'No, it doesn't, that lovely timber bungalow burnt to the ground, there was nothing left of it but the stone foundations and the remains if the chimney stack.' He didn't mention that Alan Bynon had already started on the rebuild.

Alice turned to Val. 'Maybe, you could drive us over?'

Val coloured up. 'Oh, I don't know, it'd be a bit much all of us turning up at the same time, besides—'

'Besides nothing,' said Alice briskly. 'Jon'd be pleased to have us, wouldn't you, Jon?' She looked at him, daring him to wriggle out of it. 'And I'd like to see these Brahmans you're planning on getting.'

Jon knew he was fighting a rearguard action with Alice, but he wasn't about to give up. 'They won't be here until February, and then they'll be out in the bush, no guarantee you'll see them.'

'I'll give you notice then and you can get them down to the home paddock. I'd like to see where my money's gone.'

Jon caught the twinkle in her eye.

'I wouldn't mind seeing these Brahmans either,' said Scally. 'We could all go.'

'Yes, why not,' beamed Rachel. 'We're game for a party, aren't we, Ty?'

'That's fixed then,' said Alice. 'We'll organise a date for after Christmas.'

Jon busied himself with the packing, glad he didn't have to answer. What the hell was she thinking about? Alice wasn't interested in Brahmans, she hadn't had a good word to say about them when he told her of his plans, and Val wouldn't want to drive all the way out to Jindalee, she was too busy with her own business; besides, it was one thing Alice and Alistair visiting but something else again if everyone else turned up, there was nothing for them to do and he wasn't exactly good at small talk or at entertaining toddlers.

He turned round to load up the picnic basket and saw Ruby sitting on it, watching him, her fingers stuffed in her mouth, her doll tucked under an arm and the bucket and spade at her feet.

She held out the doll for him to take. He took it and she hopped off the basket, picked up her bucket and the spade and held them out for him to load. When he'd packed them she was still standing close to him.

'Now what do you want?' he asked.

'Dinah.'

'Dinah?'

'My dolly.'

'Oh! Right!' Jon searched in the picnic basket, found the doll and handing it to her.

She looked at him briefly. 'Thank you, Jon-Jon,' she said solemnly, then she turned and ran over to her mother who was busy folding up the picnic rugs.

'As I said earlier, she's really taken a shine to you, hasn't she?' commented Alice.

'Don't be daft, she's only a baby.'

Alice gave him an arch look. 'She's just like her mother, she knows her own mind.'

'And what's that supposed to mean?'

'You work it out for yourself.' She turned her back on him and called across to Val. 'Thanks, Val, it's been a lovely day.'

'Glad you enjoyed it, Alice. We did, didn't we Ruby? Go and give Grannie Alice a kiss goodbye.'

She watched as Ruby ran across to Alice and planted a kiss on her cheek.

Alice beamed. 'Now don't forget, I'm expecting you all for Christmas dinner.'

'Who's cooking?' asked Scally. 'Belle?'

'No,' laughed Val, 'I am. Is that all right?'

CHAPTER 21

The drive home dragged. He couldn't stop thinking about Merle. She hadn't written since the July letter that Scally had finally delivered in October. He'd known things weren't good but there'd been his accident and then he'd been preoccupied with selling off the gold and buying Jindalee, and planning for the future he'd thought they still had together despite everything, so Val's news had come as a shock. Perhaps he'd been a fool to believe Merle would feel the same way as he did after so long apart.

In the kitchen, the billy was simmering gently on the stove and on a plate was a beef sandwich covered by a kitchen cloth that Yang-dhow, the new station cook, had left for his supper. He didn't feel like eating, instead he showered and went to bed, but he couldn't sleep. At three he got up and sat on the verandah, in the moonlight, looking at the work Alan Bynon had begun on rebuilding the bungalow. He laughed harshly, the sound grating in his ears, was there any point in continuing with it?

He leaned back in his chair. Perhaps it wasn't too late. Maybe there was still time. It could be months before the wedding. Was he giving up too easily? Should he go back to England, tell her about Jindalee, about the gold? Maybe he could convince her that life out in the bush could be good.

By dawn he'd made a decision, he'd go to England; he could be there before Christmas if he went by plane. He could be in England in less than ten days if he didn't hang about.

'Have you lost your mind?' yelled Alice.

Jon took a step back shocked by the anger in her voice, in the hard, glittering eyes. Even Alistair looked up from the book he was reading, taken aback by Alice's fury.

'What the hell do you want to go to England for? I thought you said she was engaged?'

'She is, but she's not married yet.'

'How do you know?'

'I don't for sure.'

'What difference will it make?'

'What do you mean?'

'You going back to England.'

'She might change her mind.'

'What, if she sees you, you mean!'

The scorn in Alice voice stirred his anger and he snapped back. 'She's the one for me, I knew it from the minute I first saw her.'

'You're as bad as Stan.'

'And what's that supposed to mean?'

'He was a fool too, and you're another, a man who's created an image in his mind of a perfect woman, well there's no such thing. And Stan had another stupid idea – that love conquers all. Well, love doesn't conquer all, life isn't like that, it's about ups and downs, about compromise, about caring for someone more than you do for yourself, and sometimes even that's not enough. I know,' she said bitterly.

'I can't give up on her.'

'And what happens if she says she'll ditch what's-his-name and marry you but she wants to stay in England? What then? You prepared to sacrifice everything you've got here?'

'She might not say that when she knows I own a station, that I'm a rich man,' he yelled.

Jon caught Alice's glance at Alistair and saw the speculation in Alistair's eyes.

'You didn't hear that,' she snapped at Alistair.

'If you say so, Alice,' but Alistair didn't have the grace to move, he remained where he was, his book unread in his lap, listening in to the row.

'Who's going to look after Jindalee?'

'George.'

'What about the cattle?'

'The next muster isn't due till February, and if I'm not back George'll see to it and he'll check the wells and bores, ride the boundaries and see to broken fencing, he's a good bloke.'

Alice gave him an old-fashioned look. 'I don't doubt it, but Greg won't like it, not an Aborigine managing the place.'

Jon couldn't argue with that, but if Greg moved in he'd just have to sort that out upon his return. The trip to England was more important. He couldn't give up the girl he loved without at least trying to win her back.

'You haven't heard a word I've said, have you?' raged Alice. 'What does Val say?'

'What's it got to do with Val?'

'Does she think it's a good idea?'

'It doesn't matter what Val thinks, I'm going to England and that's the end of it.' Jon picked up his hat and stomped out to his utility. Everything he'd meant to talk about, to ask, had fallen by the wayside in the argument. He hadn't told her that he'd given George instructions to speak to her if he had a problem and under no circumstances to ask Greg's advice. He hadn't told her where the unsold gold from Stan's mine was hidden or where he kept the deeds to Jindalee. Maybe he should have put it all in the bank. But with Cato in sole charge and knowing how the man gambled he wasn't about to risk it.

Jon flew from Perth to Darwin where he'd boarded the Qantas Constellation for the flight to London, but he didn't really relax until they left Singapore after an overnight stay. Ahead lay refuelling stops at Calcutta and Karachi, a night stopover in Cairo before refuelling in Tripoli and then the final leg of the journey to London. He wriggled in the seat, wishing he could have worn more casual clothing instead of the new suit he'd bought specially in Perth. And his shoes felt tight. He didn't dare take them off in case he couldn't get them on again. He didn't fancy walking across the tarmac at Cairo airport in stockinged feet and besides no one else had slipped off their shoes as far as he could see.

He looked about him at the other passengers, well-heeled the lot of them if the women's clothing was anything to go by – the sort of clothes Val favoured when she wasn't on the back of a horse: nice dresses and pearls. He wondered how many of the blokes had made their money from gold, wool or beef because the flights weren't cheap, paying for it all had made his eyes water, he wasn't used to spending the sort of money the ticket had cost.

From his seat he could see the wing and one of the four piston engines keeping the whole shebang in the air. According to the bloke in the seat behind him the Constellation was a workhorse; Qantas had bought them in 1947 for their new Kangaroo Route from Sydney to London. He looked out of the cabin window again at the propellers on his side of the aircraft, he didn't care how new the plane was so long as it stayed in the air and got there fast, in the four days they'd promised. That was the only reason he'd forked out for the return ticket. He didn't want to be away from Jindalee for the three and a half months it would take for the round trip by boat.

He listened to the drone of the Lockheed engines, worrying about what lay ahead. Already he was having doubts. Maybe Alice was right and he was a fool. Dorothy's letter had been written a while back. What if Merle was already married?

And then there was everyone else in Liverpool. There'd been no time to write and let his gran's friend, Elsie Roberts, or his aunt Marg know. Elsie would be pleased to see him, she'd taken him in the time he'd gone back to Liverpool to find his sister, but he wasn't sure of Marg's reception, especially at Christmas, she'd been all too pleased to see the back of him the last time.

It was six years since he was last in England. Kathy would be rising nineteen by now. He smiled as he recalled his plan to look after her himself back then. It would never have worked, they were too different, chalk and cheese Mam would have said. At least things had worked out well and Kathy was happy with Marg and Harry Warrener.

He stepped onto the tarmac at Heathrow in a flurry of snow four days after leaving Darwin, relieved to be off the plane and amazed to hear one woman bemoaning the fact that the journey was too short! Two days would have been too long as far as he was concerned. He looked at his watch and calculated the travelling time into the city; he needed a room for the night, preferably one close to Euston Station so he could catch an early train to Liverpool. Sight-seeing would have to wait for another occasion.

He arrived in Liverpool's Lime Street Station at one o'clock in the afternoon and caught a taxi to Bridge Street. As he paid the fare he took in the changes – numbers four and six had been rebuilt, gone were the huge wooden bulwarks that had supported the walls of numbers two and eight after a German bomb had flattened the two houses, but apart from that little had altered, the pot dog still sat on the window sill of number eight, and one or two houses had fresh paint on the doors and window frames, but even so the place looked mean, closed in and depressing. He noted the scrubbed steps and the doors and windows free of town grime: people had their pride. He wondered whether Val's mother and sister still lived in number twenty. He supposed he ought to call and let them know that she was all right.

Val had been very quiet when he told her he was returning to England. She'd guessed why, and when he'd asked if she wanted him to take anything back for her family she'd shaken her head. They never answer my letters, so there's no point, she'd said. And no, she hadn't told them about Ruby. Ruby was none of their business, she'd added before he could ask.

Better if he just avoided them and then he wouldn't have to answer any awkward questions.

He crossed over to the other side of the street and stood in front of number twenty-seven with the dark green door and the polished brass knocker in the shape of a clawed foot. Elsie polished it regularly if the tell-tale white residue caught in the detailing was anything to go by. He still thought the terraced house had looked better when his gran lived there; he'd always preferred the red door with its big iron S-shaped knocker that sounded as though the visitors meant business when they used it.

He hammered on the door. No, definitely not a patch on the old one!

He heard Elsie's footsteps shuffling to the front door and the creak as she pulled it open.

'Yes?' She stood looking up at him, squinting against the light. 'If you're selling I'm not buying,' she said. 'Try next door.'

Jon laughed. 'I see you still call a spade a spade, Elsie.'

Her claw-like hand snatched at her jumper. 'Jon?' she said, her tone doubting the name.

'The same,' he said.

She took a step forward and when she was convinced it was him she held her arms out to him.

'It's good to see you, Elsie.' He bent down low to give her a hug. He couldn't believe how small and frail she'd become in the intervening years.

'Oh my word, where have you come from?'

'Australia, Elsie.'

'Why didn't you write? I'd have made you some scouse for your supper.'

'Don't worry about that. I've bought us some steak, and some potatoes.'

Elsie's eyes widened. 'All the way from Australia?'

'No, Elsie, from a butcher in town. I thought we could have steak and chips tonight.'

'How did you manage to get steak?'

'The back door, Elsie, had to pay through the nose for it though. Now, how about a cup of tea?'

'Good heavens and here's me forgetting my manners while you're freezing on the doorstep.'

'Yeah, it is a bit parky after Australia. I reckon I'll have to go and buy a few more sweaters.'

'You can have Ted's.' She looked at him again. 'Maybe not, don't think they'd fit you. Come in; come into the kitchen out of the cold.'

The kitchen was exactly as he remembered it, the rag rug Gran had made, with its red flannel border made from an old shirt, lay on the tiled floor, worn flat now and the colours muted from frequent washing and coal dust. The stone sink was still there and the old-fashioned black-leaded range with the coal fire – almost out by the look of things. Was Elsie short of money? He felt the chill even inside the house. He'd seen how much worse her arthritis was, the swollen joints, the misaligned fingers and the painfully slow walk from the front door to the back kitchen. He hadn't realised how bad things were, how the last six years had taken their toll on her.

He noticed the scrap of tinsel decorating the mantelshelf, and the Christmas cards – not much Christmas cheer! 'How are you, Elsie?'

'I'm fine, Jon, a bit more arthritis, a bit stiffer in my joints, but I keep busy. Still do a bit of cleaning.'

Shocked, he couldn't bear to look at her. 'Are you still at the factory?'

'No, they said once I got to sixty-five I should enjoy my retirement. So after that I got a little job at Tate and Leverson, the solicitors just down the road, two hours a day dusting and polishing, nothing too strenuous. They're nice people; they always give me a chicken at Christmas. It'll go nice with a bit of stuffing and bread sauce.'

He imagined the ribs of beef Val would be cooking for everyone at Jarrahlong – the mounds of roasted vegetables and the plum duff for afters, not the sort of food you wanted in the heat of midsummer, but that was the tradition. He pictured the trestle tables set out under the shade trees, nothing like Elsie's Liverpool Christmas. He chased the thought away. 'Shall I make the tea? I think I can remember where everything is.' He pulled a chair out from under the kitchen table. 'You take the weight off your feet; let me spoil you for a change. We'll have a cup of tea first and then I'll make us steak and chips. Howzabout it?'

'I like it when you speak Australian,' she said, 'makes me feel young again.'

He grinned. 'Pathé News.'

'Aye, the Pathé News, and there's no need to mock, I learnt a lot from the Pathé News.'

'You said that last time I was here, Elsie.'

'Aye, I know. I'm not doolally yet.'

'So I can tell, Elsie,' he said with a smile. 'By the way, I got our favourite for pudding.'

'Favourite?'

'Rum babas.'

'Where did you get those from?'

'A shop in London.'

'Oh, my word.'

'That's a good Aussie phrase.'

'Is it?'

'Yeah.'

'Can't see that, Da always said it, and he came from—'

'Yorkshire.'

'By gum, but you've got a good memory,' she chuckled. 'I'll make us some custard to go with the rum babas.'

'Lovely,' said Jon. 'Make it nice and thick so it sticks to my ribs.'

'Aye,' grinned Elsie. 'Nice and thick it'll be.'

After supper they were sitting in front of the fire drinking tea.

'I suppose you'll be visiting your sister tomorrow,' said Elsie.

'Yes, I'm invited for afternoon tea.'

'Posh,' said Elsie and than a few minutes later, 'I thought you said you hadn't had time to write before you left Australia?'

Jon smiled. 'I didn't. I telephoned from the hotel in London.' He

183

saw the look on Elsie's face. 'I asked the operator for the number. I reckoned Marg was the type to have a telephone and I wasn't wrong.'

'They're still living in Childwall, then?'

'Yes.'

'Knowing Marg I'd have thought they'd have been in a detached by now.'

He wondered how long it would be before she asked about Val. The Rayners hadn't been mentioned yet and Elsie wasn't one to mince her words, not when it came to that family.

'How's Val these days?'

She'd read his thoughts! 'She's running a clothing shop in Charlestown.'

'Is she now? I take it she isn't planning on coming back to Liverpool then?'

'I don't think so.'

'And what about that girlfriend of yours, Merle someone?'

'Merle McGhee.'

'Aye, that's the one.'

'Don't know, Elsie. The word is she's met another fella, a physicist. They're engaged. Anyway, I thought I better come over before—'

'Before she ups and marries him?'

'Something like that.'

He imagined Merle as he'd last seen her when they'd strolled together in Sefton Park, when they'd sat on a grassy bank listening to the band. He remembered her long, dark hair flowing down her back to her waist and her green eyes, arresting eyes, eyes that he saw in his dreams, glancing at him from time to time, and her smile that made his heart race. He badly wanted to see her again, but he'd had no contact address since she'd left university. He planned to call on her parents; maybe she'd be home for Christmas and if she wasn't he'd be able to get her new address from them.

He arrived at the Warrener's house at three and pressed the bell. He'd put his suit on again and he knew he looked the part. Marg'd be impressed. She liked suits, and expensive shoes.

Kathy opened the door. She stood a moment staring at him and he at her. She'd grown up. Her long hair was done up in a fashionable style, she wore make-up and her nails were polished. She wasn't the girl he remembered. She looked him up and down and he could tell that she was doing a Marg, assessing his worth, and he didn't like it.

'Hello, Kathy, it's nice to see you.'

She leaned forward and gave him a perfunctory kiss on the cheek. 'Come into the lounge.'

The lounge! He'd come up in the world! Last time he'd only been allowed into the kitchen.

Kathy led the way and opened the door into the sitting room decorated with paper chains and tinsel and with a Christmas tree in the bay window. Harry rose to greet him while Marg remained seated, waiting for a peck on the cheek. For the second time in as many minutes he underwent female scrutiny, and he realised he'd passed muster when Marg put on her posh voice and offered him tea.

'So, Jon,' she said, passing him a slice of her favourite Battenburg cake, 'I believe you've got your own cattle station now.'

'That's right, Jindalee.'

'Funny name for a station,' said Kathy.

'That's what it was called when I bought it.'

'Have you any photographs of the place?' asked Marg.

He wished he'd thought of that. It had never crossed his mind he'd need evidence.

'How many acres?' she asked.

'About eight hundred thousand.'

Harry whistled long and low. 'You must be worth a bob or two.'

Jon bit into the pink and yellow sponge with the sickly sweet marzipan border. He still hated the stuff, but eating it meant he could delay answering.

Kathy sat down next to him. 'We were runners-up in the area amateur ballroom competition last week. Teddy and I are dancing in the final next Friday, in Blackpool. Would you like to come and watch?'

'Yes, Jon.' Marg beamed at him. 'It would be nice for us all to go together, wouldn't it Harry?'

'Yes,' agreed Harry, although Jon thought he detected a distinct lack of enthusiasm.

'You should see my dress,' rattled on Kathy, 'Mum and I sewed the sequins on by hand. It's pink and it looks divine.'

'He let the *mum* word pass. Kathy was adopted; he supposed Marg had a right to the title. But pink! He couldn't quite see how

185

pink would look against her reddish hair; he'd have thought green or blue would have been better.

Marg patted the skirt of her dress smooth. 'Are you staying at the Adelphi, Jon?'

He hid a smile. 'No, I called in to see Elsie and she offered me a bed.'

Disappointment was written on her face. 'I suppose you didn't want to hurt her feelings. Of course you can always stay here. We'd be delighted to have you and we've got a very nice guest bedroom.'

'Yes,' echoed Kathy, 'and then I can take you out to meet all my friends...you could come to rehearsals on Monday night, and after we could—'

'Thanks for the invitation,' he said, 'unfortunately, I can't. I've things to do while I'm in Liverpool, but I'll come and see you dance in the final, if that's all right?'

'Of course it is,' beamed Marg. 'We'll pick you up from Elsie's at seven o'clock next Friday morning. There's always a lot of preparation as I'm sure you'll appreciate.'

'It'll be nice to have some company for a change,' remarked Harry.

The afternoon dragged, he heard all about Harry's promotion to manager and about the new house they were looking at, a detached with an en suite bathroom off the master bedroom, and mature gardens. He heard about their holidays to Bournemouth and the Isle of Wight and plans to holiday on Jersey in the summer. He listened and made polite conversation, admired the new curtains and the new car and when he couldn't take any more he made his excuses and left, leaving them all standing on the front step, waving him off like royalty.

Friday was going to be a long day, he decided, as he stepped into the taxi Marg had called for him. He noted the time on the dashboard, five o'clock, perhaps Merle was at home. The thought cheered him.

CHAPTER 22

Sunday morning Jon stood looking down a sweeping drive to the large Victorian house standing well back from the road, not quite a mansion like the big black and white timber-framed Tudor Hall at Speke that Pete always talked about, but getting there. He wondered where Pete had made his money. Was he still a spiv? Merle always said her twin would be a millionaire by the time he was thirty, and from the look of it he was well on the way.

Jon strode down the drive and past the dark green Bentley parked in front of the main entrance. When he rang the bell he could hear it chime somewhere in the back of the building and then came the sound of footsteps, and a maid, traditionally dressed in black with a white apron, opened the door. She listened to his request and ushered him into a large office with a mahogany partner desk in the bay window, and invited him to sit on the silk-covered settee pushed against the far wall.

He took a deep breath. Soon he'd know where Merle was living, she might even be staying with Pete, the place was big enough, certainly she'd visit sometime over Christmas, he'd put money on it. While he waited he imagined the conversation. Jon who? Did he say what he wanted? He mentioned Merle, et cetera, et cetera. Then came measured steps and the door opened.

Pete stood in the doorway.

Jon rose to his feet and hesitated when he saw the surprise on Pete's face. Jon knew he'd changed in the six years he'd been away, but not that much; he was broader and taller, just short of six foot three in his stockinged feet, and he weighed fifteen stone and none of it fat. His hair was blonder, bleached by the Australian sun and he was tanned, but underneath it all he was still the same person he'd been when they'd last met. Pete though, with the dark, pencil moustache, slicked-back hair, snazzy suit and patent leather shoes had changed, he was every inch a spiv and his once open, honest face had that watchful look of a man with an eye out for the main chance.

'Whatcha cock?' Pete found a smile as he clapped him on the back. 'When did you get back?' He didn't wait for an answer. 'Come through to the conservatory. Come and meet the wife.' He led the way through the house and into a lovely Victorian conservatory decked out with potted palms and rattan chairs that wouldn't have shamed Raffles, and enough Christmas decorations to have opened a shop.

'Daphne, this is Jon, me old mucker from school days.'

Daphne stood and held out her hand.

Jon shook it and noticed the limp handshake, the elegant dress, the make-up and, when she spoke, a Liverpudlian accent broader than Val's had been when he first met her.

'How did you find me? Merle tell you?'

'No, I called on your parents.'

'They're in Llandudno.'

'Yeah, the neighbours said, and they gave me your address.'

'They're stayin' at the George Hotel for Christmas, Pete's payin' for them,' said Daphne. 'He—'

'I take it you're looking for Merle?' interrupted Pete. 'Are you a station owner yet?'

What were Pete's parents doing in a hotel? Merle always went on about Christmas being family time; it was one of the things he'd always envied about the McGhees. He hesitated, confused by the information, so Merle had received his letter telling her of his plans to buy Jindalee. 'Part owner.' He didn't know why he did it, but the lie just slipped out.

'On a big mortgage, I suppose.'

'That's right,' lied Jon again.

'Still, you're doing well enough to dress smart,' Pete observed and Jon sensed he'd lost interest.

'How is Merle?'

'Didn't she tell you? She's married now, to Paul Vincent.'

'It was a lovely weddin',' gushed Daphne, rising from her seat. She walked over to a small side table and picked up a silver-framed photograph. 'She looked dead smart in her weddin' gear, didn't she, Pete?'

Jon felt the floor shift and begin to spin. He should have known;

188

he'd left it too long, but until he owned a station he knew he had nothing to offer her. He thought of the rebuilding Alan Bynon was doing on the new bungalow even as he'd boarded the plane for England. He'd been a fool. He should have returned to Liverpool sooner, when her letters became increasingly infrequent. He'd been wrong to believe someone like Merle would wait indefinitely. He couldn't blame her for giving up on him.

Daphne returned with the photograph and handed it to him.

He didn't want to look but couldn't help himself. There she was, in white, as beautiful as ever, her dark hair cascading onto her shoulders, and a huge bouquet of dark red roses and fern. Blood rushed in his ears and he felt sick. He wanted to smash his fist into the frame, to obliterate the bloke standing next to her. Instead he swallowed the sour taste in his mouth and handed the photograph back to Daphne.

'You knew she was married?' said Pete, watching him closely.

'I knew she was engaged.'

'Yeah, well, it was all a bit of a rush.'

'What do you mean, rush?'

'Paul got a posting, and had to take it immediately, it didn't leave much time for anything.'

'You can say that again,' said Daphne, 'what with the weddin' and all. An' then we had to take her to London, didn't we, Pete, and get her kitted out for the tropics: lightweight suits, hats with veils, suitcases, and a trunk – it cost Pete a fortune,' she gabbled on, 'I thought we'd never get her on the boat.'

Stunned, Jon couldn't take it in, she wasn't even in England, she was somewhere in the tropics, it had all been a wasted journey.

'What's your poison?' Pete indicated the trolley laden with bottles.

'Beer,' said Jon, not caring what he drank.

'Take a seat.' Pete opened a bottle and handed Jon a pale ale and Daphne a gin and tonic.

'So where are they?' asked Jon, wishing he hadn't asked the minute the words were out of his mouth.

'They're in Australia,' said Daphne.

Australia! Jon flopped down on the nearest chair, spilling his drink on the tiled flooring, Daphne's words a kick to the stomach. 'Australia!'

'Yes, didn't she tell you? Paul's got a government research post at Woomera Rocket Range for three years,' said Pete, his eyes fixed on Jon's face.

Woomera wasn't in the tropics; it was in South Australia, so why had Daphne been talking about the tropics? And what was Merle doing out in the South Australian desert, at Woomera, after everything she'd written? According to Scally it was a crook place to live, far worse than anything at Jarrahlong and Jindalee.

'I suppose you heard about the atomic tests they did over there a couple of months back? It was in all the papers, but most of the stuff's very hush-hush; Paul had to sign the official secrets act and all that.'

'But what about her career?'

'On hold, married woman and all that, you know how it is; besides, no doubt she'll be having a family before too long.' Pete took a long draught of beer and licked his top lip. 'I take it you were expecting to see her?'

'Well, yes…just…just for old times' sake,' said Jon, stumbling over his words, his mind in turmoil. 'I knew she'd qualified but I…I didn't know whether she'd got a job…or not.'

'Blooming awful at keeping in touch, she is, she warned us before she left not to expect regular letters.'

'And I wanted to catch up with you and all my old mates.' Jon could feel the colour rising in his cheeks. He felt a fool and he was sure Pete had sensed his unease. He looked about him, at the elegant conservatory they were sitting in, desperately wanting to change the subject. 'It's a fine place you've got here…you've done well for yourself, Pete. You've come a long way from selling rabbits on the black market.'

'I was a kid then,' said Pete, an edge to his voice.

'Back then we all were. Things were tough in those days. But it's nice to see a mate doing well.'

Daphne leaned against Pete. 'Paid cash for it, didn't you, darlin'.' She turned to Jon. 'Pete did real well out of the deal, Mr Thomas was bankrupt and Pete helped him out.'

Jon caught Pete's glare, and watched him surreptitiously disengage Daphne's arm. 'Shouldn't you be checking things in the kitchen, dear?'

'There's no need, darlin', Mrs Owen's got everything under control.' Daphne topped up her gin and tonic, oblivious of the tight smile on Pete's face.

Pete looked pointedly at the clock. 'We've friends coming over.'

'Why don't you stay for a bite?' offered Daphne. 'We can easily

190

lay an extra place.'

'It's very nice of you, Daphne, but I won't, if you don't mind. I'm not over in England for long and I want to catch up with Billy Wainwright and the others.'

'You could have lunch with us and leave straight after, Mrs Owen's a crackin' cook.'

'If Jon wants to go we shouldn't detain him.' Pete leaned over and took Jon's empty glass. 'I'll come with you to the door.'

As they walked together across the tiled hallway Pete took out his wallet and pulled out a wad of notes. 'You all right for cash?'

'Thanks, mate, but I'm fine.'

'Well, if you run short give me a bell.' He took out a business card and a pen. 'It's my office address and business number.' He wrote another number on the back. 'And that's my home telephone.'

'What is your business these days?'

'Real Estate, as the Yanks say, but to you, property. I buy and sell property. And as you've probably noticed there're a lot of buildings being demolished and rebuilt. Where there's muck—'

'There's brass,' laughed Jon. 'It's been good seeing you again.' He held out his hand and Pete took it. 'Give Merle my regards when you're next in touch.'

'I will, be seeing you, mate.' Pete stood on the step as Jon set off down the drive.

Jon sucked in the cold winter air, glad of the chill after the stifling heat in the conservatory. He turned back to wave a final goodbye, but the door was already closed. He smiled bitterly – he'd lost Merle, she'd married someone else and the old, easy camaraderie between him and Pete had gone too, not that it was anyone's fault. Pete was a decent sort, not many would have offered money like that. Perhaps he should have told Pete the truth, but what was said, was said, it was too late to go back now.

He set off towards the gates, the empty feeling in his belly as raw as the December day. He blew on his hands to warm them and reached the gates as a chauffeur-driven Rolls-Royce pulled in off the road. It purred along the drive, a well-dressed couple in the back. Pete had moved up in the world, well good luck to him!

Jon's stomach ached, and he felt the gassy beer rising in his throat, seconds later he vomited on the grass verge.

* * *

By the time he got to Billy's place it was getting on for half past one and he guessed that the family would have finished Sunday dinner, but he was wrong, They were about to sit down to eat.

'Come in,' said Mrs Wainwright, 'this is a real surprise; Billy will be right pleased to see you.'

She wouldn't take no for an answer, she took his coat, ushered him through into the kitchen and ordered Kenny, Billy's kid brother, to fetch another chair.

'Hi ya,' said Billy, 'long time no see, mate.'

'And you,' said Jon while he waited for a chair.

It was a squash but eventually the five of them were sitting round the table watching Mr Wainwright senior carve the boiled brisket while Billy's mother served up Yorkshire pudding from a large pan, the sides risen up and crispy, the middle soggy from the meat juices, just like his gran used to make.

'You back for good?' asked Billy.

'No, just visiting. I fly back in a fortnight.'

'No banana boat for you then?'

Jon grinned. 'That's right.' He wondered where Billy's dad was but didn't like to ask, instead he enquired about the sister. 'How's Maureen these days? Is she married?'

'Yes,' said Billy's mum, 'to Tom Sharp and they've got a kiddie now, Simon, lovely little chap he is, and they live in the Dingle, nice terrace. Tom's doing it up right smart and Billy here's done all the plumbing for them, haven't you, love?'

'So you're a plumber.'

'Yeah,' grinned Billy, 'time served and all, just got me papers. You want any plumbing done, I'm your man.'

'You got your own business yet?'

'Not yet, I work for Sid Green. One day I'd like me own business, but I need to save up a bit first, you know how it is.'

'What about you, Kenny?'

'Trainee electrician, working for a building firm over Speke way,' said Kenny, shovelling food into his mouth as fast as he could.

'Slow down, son,' ordered his granddad. 'You'll choke.'

'I'm late.'

'You'll do as your granddad says, Kenny, or you won't be going anywhere,' ordered his mam.

'Me dad died four years back,' volunteered Billy.

'Out of the blue,' Mrs Wainwright added, 'heart attack it was, dead the minute he hit the pavement the doctor said.'

'Bit of a shock for the family,' said Billy's granddad, 'but if you ask me, it's the only way to go, here one minute, gone the next.'

They all continued eating in silence. Jon wondered if Mr Wainwright senior was right or whether a bit of warning would be preferable. He imagined the mess he'd leave behind if he died suddenly. There was the rest of the gold he'd buried and he hadn't written a will, so who would Jindalee go to? His sister? His dad? – God forbid! Maybe he should sort things out before too long, get himself a solicitor.

Kenny's knife and fork clattered onto his plate. 'Is it okay if I go, Ma? Or I'll be late.'

'What about puddin'?'

'I'll tek it with me.'

'It's rice puddin'.'

'Can't I have it when I get back?'

'Oh, go on with you.'

'Thanks, Ma.' Kenny gave her a quick kiss on the cheek, took his coat off the peg in the hallway and was gone.

A cold draught blasted their legs.

Mrs Wainwright doled out the rice pudding. 'It's about time you got that back boiler organised and them radiators, our Billy. It's like an icebox in here at times and I'm not gerrin' any younger.'

'I'll get on to it first thing, Ma. It's what the rich folk are having,' he added, addressing Jon.

'What's that?' asked Jon.

'Central heating. I put in a new heating system for Pete McGhee last autumn. You know he's married now, hooked up with O'Shaunessey's daughter.'

'The builder?'

'Yeah, Patrick O'Shaunessey's come up in the world since the war, describes himself as managing director of O'Shaunessey Construction. He's worth a packet now.'

Jon smiled to himself. He'd wondered about Pete and Daphne, somehow they hadn't convinced as a couple. Was that what the initial attraction had been – the business contacts?

'Yeah, I called round at Pete's place this morning to say hello. It's a nice house he's got.'

'Yeah,' said Billy in a flat voice. 'He drives a hard bargain, does Pete.'

'Do you think you could have a look at Elsie's place on Bridge

Street, see about putting in extra heating there? That house is as cold as charity.'

'Could put in a new back boiler, it'd run two or three radiators, only problem is it's rented, isn't it?'

Jon hadn't thought about that. 'Does that mean we'd have to get permission?'

'Should think so. Anyway, what about you? What have you been doing with yourself?'

'I went gold mining, didn't I,' said Jon, 'and got enough to buy myself a part share in a cattle station.' He hated telling Billy and his family a half-truth but having lied to Pete he couldn't risk them swapping notes after he'd gone. Why had he lied in the first place? It was a stupid thing to do. Maybe he'd speak to Billy later and tell him the truth, ask him not to say anything.

Billy dropped the spoon back into his empty pudding dish. 'You know Merle McGhee got married a while back?'

'Yeah, Peter told me.'

'I thought you were sweet on her?'

'I was, but she didn't fancy living in the outback.'

Billy laughed. 'That's women for you.'

'We'll have less of that, if you don't mind,' said Mrs Wainwright her arms up to her elbows in suds. 'Here!' She flung a tea towel in Billy's direction. 'You can dry and after you can take your grand-dad a cuppa.' She turned to Jon. 'He always takes a nap in the par-lour after his Sunday dinner.'

'I'll dry while you make the tea,' offered Jon, taking the tea towel off Billy.

Monday morning Jon caught the bus down to the solicitors' office where Elsie worked and asked to speak to the senior partner. He was directed to an easy chair next to a potted plant that had seen better days. On the side table were a couple of magazines, one for solicitors, and the other a magazine called *Town and Country*. He opened the latter and was flipping through it when the secretary called him.

Mr Tate of Tate and Leverson was middle-aged with prematurely thinning hair which he combed across his bald patch. He didn't inspire confidence, being rather mousy looking, even so, he'd em-ployed Elsie and was, no doubt, the one who'd organised the Christmas chicken.

'Gerald Tate,' he said, 'and how may I help you?'

Jon offered his hand. 'Jon Cadwallader.'

Tate ignored it.

'I'm a friend of Elsie.' Jon had met characters like Tate before. He took a seat, pre-empting the solicitor. 'She's the woman who does your cleaning in the evenings.'

Tate's brow furrowed and then cleared. He sat down. 'You mean Mrs Roberts. Yes, and what about her?'

'She's a friend of mine and as I live in Australia I want to make arrangements with you to pay some of her bills on my behalf.'

'Yes, that can be arranged. What sort of bills were you thinking of?'

'Plumbing bills and fuel, you know...coal, electric, rates, that sort of thing. When I contact the companies concerned I want to be able to give them your name and address so they can send you the invoices.'

He recalled Elsie's reaction when he'd told her about Merle's marriage. She'd made fresh tea, liberally sweetened with sugar, and patted him on the back in a sympathetic gesture that had brought tears to his eyes. There'd been no I-told-you-sos, no meaningless platitudes, just quiet sympathy. That was Elsie all over; her affection was always freely given. She was one of the most generous people he'd ever met and now he could do something for her. After all, he thought bitterly, he'd got no one else to spend his money on, not now Merle had married Paul bloody Vincent.

'And how are you planning on paying these bills and our fees for the service?' asked Tate.

'Bank draft, if that's all right.'

'Absolutely, no problem at all, Mr Cadwallader. However, I shall need some proof...' Tate's voice trailed off and he looked just a shade uneasy.

'Proof that I can pay!' said Jon. 'What about if I open an account with you now and write a cheque into that account?'

'Perfect,' purred Tate. 'I can see that we are on the same wave length.'

Jon took out a cheque book, wrote a cheque and handed it across. 'Will that do for starters?'

Tate looked at the amount in surprise. 'More than satisfactory. Kalgoorlie, I see. I'm sure I've heard of Kalgoorlie.' His brow creased again.

'Gold mining town,' said Jon, 'in Australia.'

'Oh, of course,' beamed Tate.

'And this is my address,' Jon handed over a piece of paper.

'You own a station?'

'That's right.'

'Excellent!' Tate's beam was broader still. 'I'll get things organised for you immediately. Would you be able to call in at the end of the week to sign the papers? Shall we say, Thursday, ten o'clock?'

'There's one other thing,' said Jon. 'How would I go about buying a property on Bridge Street?'

'Is it for sale?'

'No, it's tenanted.'

'It will depend on who owns it.'

'Will you find out for me and also whether they'd be prepared to sell it with a sitting tenant?'

'Certainly, Mr Cadwallader. What number?'

'Twenty-seven.'

'And how much are you prepared to pay?'

'I want the house, Mr Tate, and as soon as possible. Just buy it for the best price you can.'

'Will you need a mortgage?'

'No, I don't, let me have a rough idea of what it will cost and I'll arrange to send the money to my account as soon as I get back to Australia.'

'Do you want us to arrange for rent collection?'

'No, Elsie will be living there rent free and you're to pay the rates and water charges from my account as well as the fuel bills, and I want a monthly allowance paid directly to her. Will you set that up?'

'Indeed we will, I'll see to it personally.' Tate stood and held out his hand. 'I'll see you on Thursday, then, ten o'clock.'

'Thursday,' said Jon, ignoring Tate's extended hand, two could play that game!

On the way home he stopped off at the coal merchant Elsie used, ordered a delivery, paid for it and made arrangements for regular deliveries in the future and for the bills to be sent to Tate and Leverson. Then he called in at the plumber's, told Sid Green that Billy Wainwright had drummed up custom for him and prepared him to expect instruction from Tate and Leverson regarding a heating system. Satisfied that he'd done all he could for the moment he headed back to Bridge Street and invited Elsie out to lunch.

'Lunch?' she said. 'Where are we going?'

'The Adelphi. I've booked us a table.'

'The Adelpi,' she squeaked. 'It's too expensive.'

Jon smiled at the shock on her face. 'It's my treat, Elsie, go and put on your best bib and tucker, the taxi is coming for us in half an hour.'

CHAPTER 23

Jon flew out of London with Qantas a fortnight after Christmas, emptiness a huge pit in his stomach, not wanting to think about what might have been. He supposed his time hadn't been wasted, even though it felt as if it had.

He stared sightlessly out of the cabin window and then recalled the blasted ballroom dancing he'd gone to with Kathy, Marg and Harry. He'd hated every minute of it. All those girls in floaty dresses in pastel chiffon covered in sequins, their hair done up and lacquered stiff, their doll-like painted faces, and the fixed smiles as they waltzed around the floor on the arms of equally coiffured boys wearing dark suits and patent leather shoes. And then there was the 'darling this' and the 'darling that', the tears when couples came second, the bitchy comments when rivals took to the dance floor, and the pushy mothers chatting up the judges in the intervals. He shivered. He never ever wanted to be involved with anything like that ever again.

On his last night with the Warreners he'd taken them to the Adelphi for a meal. Marg had been in her element, done up like a dog's dinner, and he'd met Kathy's boyfriend and dancing partner again, Teddy Rawlinson, a young fella who, in his estimation, was about as shallow as Kathy.

It had all been a game with everyone on their best behaviour even though he knew that deep down Marg still didn't like him. He smiled wryly to himself; he and Kathy had absolutely nothing in common any more, but who was he to judge, she was content enough and at the end of the day that was all that mattered, wasn't it? She was certainly in a better place than he was when it came to happiness.

He closed his eyes and blotted out the sound of the Lockheed engines chewing up the miles. The time he'd spent with Elsie had been as different again, comfortable as a pair of carpet slippers. Tate had come up trumps over Elsie's house and had used some of the money Jon had given him for the deposit. There was still much to be done before it was all official, and Tate promised to keep the deeds for him and write and let him know after completion. He'd also wisely suggested that Elsie pay a peppercorn rent of one penny a year and drew up a contract that allowed her to live in the house, or derive an income from it, until her death. Just in case you should die, Tate had said, and your relatives decide they want her out of the property.

He pictured Elsie's face when he told her what he'd done. She'd cried at first, said he didn't need to. He'd told her he wanted to, that she'd been the only person who had cared about him when he'd last visited Liverpool, and still cared about him. And he told her he was rich, that he could afford it and that if she preferred he'd buy her a ticket and she could live with him in Australia.

He smiled as he recalled the look on her face. Excitement initially and then reason stepped in. If I were ten years younger, I'd jump at it, she'd said, but I don't think I'd like all that heat, and the dust, and the flies. You just make sure you keep writing me the letters, she'd added, and bless you, Jon; you're the son I never had.

He was pleased Elsie was settled and happy. Glad that her last years would be lived in warmth and comfort, it was the least he could do after all she had done for him. The world was a better place with people like Elsie and the Wainwrights. They too had made him welcome. He and Billy had had a couple of good nights together over Christmas, and he'd met up with the others he'd known as a kid, Alan Smith, Graham Eastham and Bob Robertson.

And then there was Frank Cooper. He shouldn't have been surprised that Frank had handed in his notice at George Henry Lee's and emigrated to Australia. He'd taken the government sponsorship and become a ten-pound Pom. Adelaide, he'd gone to and Jon remembered how Frank had once said that Doris fancied Adelaide. So two people he knew were living in South Australia, maybe he'd take a trip over there one day and say hello, but he knew he never would.

After the overnight stop in Singapore they took off for the final leg of the journey. Three and a half days he'd been en route and all that time his mind had been chewing over the events of the past

199

three weeks, sifting through the highs and the lows.

An image of Merle as he'd last seen her drifted into his mind. Merle, the gentlest, kindest, nicest girl he'd ever met and now she was living in South Australia. Strange how life pans out, he thought, that's what Stan would have said. He pictured Merle as they'd walked together in Sefton Park, how they'd sat together listening to the band playing popular tunes on the bandstand, and his heart ached. Was she happy? Of course she was happy, she was newly married, wasn't she? But had she settled? Did she like Australia? He didn't know anything about Woomera apart from what Scally had told him, that it was a pretty remote desert region, even more remote than Jindalee. He wondered how she'd found the summer months, the hottest of the year; had it been as bad as she'd imagined? And how had she felt about giving up medicine to be a wife? It seemed to him a pretty crook thing to happen to a person who'd spent over five years training, especially when there was a crying need for doctors in the outback.

He looked out of the cabin window, down at the Australian coastline as the plane flew to Darwin. They'd be landing soon, another couple of days and he'd be home, and then he needed to begin the rest of his life. He was thankful he'd got Jindalee; there would always be plenty to occupy his mind, he'd be back well in time for the muster and then he'd be busy building up the stock and sinking new wells and bores – he wouldn't have time to think about Merle. As the plane touched down he wondered who he was kidding.

The dogs were pleased to see him when he drove into the yard. Bonny was sitting on the verandah waiting for him and he guessed her keen ears had picked up the sound of his ute as she always did. Smoky bounded out from the barn with George strolling after him, while Bess limped out from the shade, her tongue lolling, the stiffness in her legs worse than it had ever been.

Alan Bynon had been busy with the rebuilding; he had completed the shell of the new bungalow and was busy on the second fit.

'Looks good, don't it?' said George. 'Alan's been working all hours, says he wants the bonus you promised.'

Jon liked the wide verandahs, fifteen feet deep on all four elevations, with fancy cast-ironwork supporting the huge roof that swept down from the ventilation turret at the apex.

'He's gone into town for more wiring,' said George, 'he didn't realise he'd need so much.'

'I ordered some fruit trees while I was in Perth,' said Jon. 'They'll be delivered in the autumn.'

The Samuels had always had fruit trees until the fire destroyed them. He looked at the blackened trunk of the old eucalyptus that had somehow survived the inferno, new shoots had sprouted soon after the fire and already the old tree was providing shade again. He'd plant more native trees too, desert kurrajongs, their brilliant green foliage always looked lush even in the worst of droughts, and their flowers were pretty, pale purple, flecked with green and bell-like. Yes, he'd definitely plant kurrajongs, and acacia for the silver leaves and yellow pompom flowers, and a jacaranda tree, just because he liked the name of it, and lemon and orange trees, like Alice had. And he'd try and buy in some jarrah saplings; it would be nice to have a jarrah or two. He'd frequently admired the stately gums at Alice's place, and had often wondered who had planted them. Jeb reckoned it was Eli Jackson, the botanist fella who had once owned Jindalee. According to Jeb he was the man who had planted the coolabah tree on the Jarrahlong and Jindalee boundary not far from the green pool, but if it wasn't him then someone else had because jarrahs and coolibahs weren't local to the area.

While he unpacked he thought about all the other things he needed to do, a new barn to build, more stock fencing to replace the old, new wells and bores, there was so much to occupy him, plenty to take his mind off Merle. He dumped his washing in the basket for May to see to and after a quick wash and brush up he crossed over to the cookhouse to eat with the stockmen.

The next day he set off on Red, leading a packhorse to ride the boundaries, and check on all the wells and bores. He didn't want to see anyone, and boundary riding would keep him away from the homestead and the morning and evening radio schedules until they began the muster in two weeks' time. He didn't want to talk about his trip to England, everyone would know where he'd been by now, and they'd want chapter and verse about the Old Country: that's how it was out in the bush.

* * *

He was away for a fortnight and when he rode into the yard George was already well on with preparations for the muster, the stockmen were busy loading gear onto the wagons for a protracted stay out in the bush.

'We've got an early start in the morning, George,' Jon said, watching the stockmen. 'Is everything organised for tomorrow? I want everything ready for first light.'

'No worries,' said George, a grin on his face. 'Everything's loaded except for the grub and there're plenty of stockhorses in the paddock.' He took Jon's horses and led them into the corral. 'Reckon there's one or two fat bulls out there ready for muster.'

'I hope you're right, George, seems to me most of them are pretty lean.'

Satisfied that George would see to Red and the packhorse for him Jon headed over to the lean-to next to the cookhouse. Yang-dhow spotted him and was on the verandah, hands clasped in front of him, awaiting instructions.

'Everything ok, boss? You like Yang's food? Plenty nice, yes?' Yang handed him a mug of black coffee.

'You drive a wagon and horses, Yang?'

'Me, I do everything.'

'Good,' said Jon, a smile on his face. 'We're going on a muster and I want good tucker. Come with me.' He put his mug down on the verandah railing, crossed over to the lock-up stores and opened up. 'Sort out what we need for a month.'

The store contained all the dry goods they needed: flour, sugar, rice, dried peas, cooking fat, tinned meat, tinned vegetables and potatoes. Once a week basic foodstuff was doled out to the black families working on the station, but the Aborigines often supplemented station cooking with kangaroo, and bungarra, the larger lizards prevalent in the area. When they slaughtered a bullock each family was given a share.

'Four weeks, seven of us, got it Yang?'

'Okay, boss, Yang got it.'

'Lock up after and bring me the key.'

He liked Yang; the young Chinese fella had turned up at the station a week before he'd left for England. You want cook? he'd asked. I good cook. Han Sing, my uncle, he teach me well. You want cook?

Jon had already tasted the delights of Agnes's cooking – meat that was charcoal on the outside and so bloody in the middle that if you blinked, the animal it came from would have been off at a gallop.

Month's trial, he'd said not expecting to be away over Christmas – we'll see how it goes. And, as far as he could tell, it had gone well. On the days he'd been eating Yang-dhow's food he hadn't had indigestion once, the bloke was a good cook, better even than his uncle, Han Sing, and Jon intended hanging on to him, even if he had to pay over the odds.

The next morning they rode out early with plenty of stockhorses and a couple of wagons loaded with equipment and enough food to last them a month. At two o'clock they left Yang to set up camp close to the yards in the eastern quarter, twenty-five miles from the station, while Jon and three of the stockmen repaired the yard fences and races they would be using later. George and a young black stockman called Billy set off to ride the mile-square paddock, it wouldn't do to lose the stock they'd rounded up for sale through a hole in the fencing. That night they turned in early ready for a dawn start.

Jon knew from working Alice's mob that rounding up cattle wasn't so very different from rounding up sheep; they spread out in the bush in small groups and in ones and twos, much like the sheep. But it was harder work in the thicker bush, they were more difficult to spot and the older cattle, used to round-ups, would be hiding in the shade of the larger trees or lying doggo in the scrub, especially in the heat of the day. It was impossible to get them all, and the cannier animals could go for years without ever seeing the inside of a race. The trick was to range out wide, starting far out in the bush, an hour's ride from the yards, but within hailing distance of each other, and then work their way back, collecting cattle, driving them ahead of them, fast enough to keep them moving but slow enough not to spook the animals. It was skilled work and Jeb Samuels always said his stockmen were the best and Jon was glad they'd agreed to stay on when he bought the lease on Jindalee.

Once they'd gathered a sizeable mob together they drove them forward, fanning out behind them, keeping the animals moving at walking pace, back to the holding paddock next to the yards. A quick brew and a bite to eat and they were out again, covering miles of bush, looking for more mobs.

Jon liked this side of the work, riding over vast tracts of land, and he learned a lot about the station he'd bought. He memorised the lie of the land and the permanent water, and the soaks, making a mental note of unusual rock formations, trees, the nature of the different types of bush and grassland and their relationship to each other, like the Aborigines did. He looked out for the wildlife, scanning for emu, camel and brumbies as well as for small mobs of wild goats on the higher, rockier ground that they seemed to favour. And, as he travelled, he spotted human tracks crossing his land, leading into the arid desert region over to the east, one of the ancient routes used by Aborigines over thousands of years.

It had been Curly who had told him about the old tracks created in the Dreamtime, how an Aborigine could travel from one side of Australia to the other using the ancient tribal routes of his own and other mobs. Ya can't get lost, mate, if you sing the words, he'd said once.

He hadn't fully understood what Curly had meant until long after Curly was dead, until the time Alice had sent him off with Adie to see one of the old sacred sites way out in the desert beyond Pilkington. They'd travelled by utility truck with Adie leaning out of the window directing him across seemingly featureless semi-desert with the Aboriginal chanting words at a furious pace, gabbling them so fast a stranger would have thought the old fella was demented.

When they'd arrived a few hours later Jon had been disappointed. The sacred site was a mean collection of boulders sitting in the middle of a vast expanse of sparse, desiccated bush.

So what's the Dreaming here? he'd asked.

Biting insects, Adie had said. The ancestor tricked them into a hole in the ground then buried them to stop 'em worrying the mob with their stinging tails.

And that's it? he had asked.

Yeah, that's it, Adie had said.

I suppose I'll have to listen to your manic chanting all the way back, he'd said.

Adie had grinned then. Nah, we just foller the tyre tracks.

I suppose you were singing the line, he'd commented as they'd driven home, their eyes fixed on the fresh tracks. Curly sang the line when we went walkabout, but he didn't gabble like you, he'd told Adie after a while.

Adie had turned to him and had given him a long, contemplative look. Don't reckon he was in a ute.

He'd wondered what Adie had been talking about. And then he'd come to the conclusion that the song had in some way conveyed the idea of distance as well as direction.

Jon pulled up his horse and looked to the horizon at the wispy smoke rising far to the east. It looked like a mob, most probably the Cripps Crossing mob, on the move, gone walkabout most like, firing the country in the traditional way – controlled burning that encouraged new growth for the wildlife. Curly's family did the same thing out Mullin Soak way.

Sometimes he'd wondered whether the Aboriginals had a better way of managing the land, a way of ensuring that the quality of the herbage was maintained. He'd learnt from Alice the importance of adjusting stock levels during a drought, selling off animals at critical times when there wasn't enough feed to sustain the numbers. It took thirty acres to support one sheep and three hundred to support a cow and that was in a good year when they'd had eight inches of rain. In dry years when the rainfall was only four inches or less then stock had to be sold or casualty rates increased, and that didn't do anyone any good.

He realised he had a lot to be thankful for, the spring rainfall had been higher than usual, and the summer rains had been pleasing; it would be a good muster with plenty of fat bulls to send to the yards near Perth. He wiped the sweat off his brow, wishing Jeb had organised the muster for later in the year when the temperature wasn't so hot. He geed on his horse and resumed the search for cattle, thinking about the life in the outback that he'd chosen for himself and wondering if he was mad to love the harsh and arid land around him.

Day after day they collected together the cattle that had dispersed over vast tracks of bush, quartering and re-quartering the section of the station ear-marked for muster.

Once the round-up was complete the cattle were driven into a collecting yard in batches and driven through the races where each animal was checked, and, where necessary, ear-clipped, vaccinated, treated for lice and ticks and separated out. Breeding cows and heifers were set free back into the bush; calves were branded and the male calves castrated while the cattle going for sale were released into the vast holding paddock.

A month after they'd started the muster they squatted around a campfire, drinking tea, awaiting the arrival of the cattle wagon. They saw the dust before they heard the vehicle rumbling along the graded track.

The driver, a bloke called Ken Southall, jumped down from the cab of an old military truck towing a couple of self-tracking semi-trailers. He had a sheaf of papers in his hand. 'You the manager?'

'That's me,' said Jon.

'Hope you've got plenty of water and feed for these animals. It's been a long trip.'

'Will that do them?' Jon indicated the full water troughs and the baled hay in the paddock where they planned to keep the cattle for a few days to recover from the journey.

'Better get them off the wagon quick, reckon we might have lost one or two, often do on these long trips.'

Ken fitted the ramp to the first of the trailers with Jon's help and swung open a side door. An animal stood at the brink, reluctant to leave the safety of the wagon. Agile as a monkey, Ken hauled himself onto the top of the trailer and started prodding the animal blocking the ramp. After a few minutes and a lot of cursing and swearing the animal, with its legs braced, gave a half leap forward and high-tailed it over to the far side of the open ground where she spun round, puffing and blowing, to watch what was happening. The others followed in a rush, scrambling down the boards and heading for the water. Meanwhile, Ken was fitting the ramp to the second trailer and more cattle were released. Three animals hadn't survived the journey. Two were dead and the third was pretty close to it. Jon fetched his rifle from the ute and dispatched her with a bullet to the brain and slit her throat to allow the blood to drain.

'Plenty of tucker this week,' commented the driver as they hauled the carcass over to the thirty-hundredweight truck, loaded it onto the back and covered it with a tarpaulin to keep off the flies.

The two that had died in transit they dragged deep into the bush and left.

Jon stopped for a moment and looked at the animals, fifty-seven prime young Hereford heifers and two Brahman bulls.

'What made you go for those ugly buggers?' asked Ken, nodding in the direction of the bulls.

'Supposed to be good in drought conditions,' said Jon.

Ken looked about him. 'The land don't look too bad.'

'Not at the moment, rains have been pretty good this last year but when it's dry, my word it's dry.' Jon signed for the animals, including the three dead ones, and then, after smoko, they began loading up the cattle bound for the stockyards near Perth – harder, dustier work than unloading.

'Fingers crossed they all make it,' said Jon to George a couple of hours later as they watched the wagon disappear down the track in a cloud of red dust.

'Might not,' admitted George, 'one or two looked pretty stressed to me.'

'Yeah,' said Jon, 'as I said, fingers crossed.' He turned back to look at the new cattle, their heads down eating the hay he'd bought in. 'I hope you're right about these Brahmans.'

'I'm not wrong, boss. They've had 'em in Queensland since the turn of the century.'

'Well, we'll have to see, those two cost me double a couple of Herefords.'

'Y'won't be sorry,' said George.

'I hope not,' said Jon as they headed for home.

CHAPTER 24

That evening Jon spoke to Alice on the radio when people chatted after the serious business of the day was finished. Their conversation had been perfunctory, Jon knowing that every station in the area would be listening in. Yes, he'd enjoyed seeing his family, yes, they were all fine and, yes, he was pleased to be back.

When Alice told him she wanted to visit the following weekend, he said the bungalow wasn't finished and that they'd only just finished a muster and were dog-tired. Poppycock, she'd said, anyone would think you're my age. We're having a picnic and that's the end of it, and I'm bringing Alistair with me. Make sure that cook of yours prepares plenty of tucker, and I want to see one of those Brahmans you've been on about.

He swore as he switched off the transceiver, why couldn't she wait a bit? That meant he'd have to bring one of the new bulls down to the home paddock so she could inspect it, well she could whistle, the Brahmans could stay were they were. And a picnic! Where they hell were they going to picnic? The only suitable place was near to the creek. It was nice down there, where it ran along the sandstone ridge, just before it entered the small gorge. The bush had regenerated after the fire and there were grassy patches nearer to the water's edge, he reckoned that would do.

Saturday came all too soon; his stomach churned at the thought of the interrogation Alice would give him. She'd want to know everything; what the flight had been like, whether Marg had made him welcome, what Kathy had said or hadn't said, and then there'd be the barrage of questions about Merle. Jon swore at the thought of what lay ahead, especially when Alice learned that Merle had upped and married and moved to South Australia. She wouldn't be able to avoid the I-told-you-sos.

Jon batted at a mob of flies, at least Yang had excelled himself on the culinary front. There'd be no complaints about the food. Picnic, he'd repeated when Jon told him what he'd wanted. So Yang prepared won tons – little stuffed dumplings, spring rolls, and other Chinese delicacies for them to eat and promised a pretty fine roast if Alice wanted to stay for tea.

Jon paced about the yard waiting for them to arrive. Soon as he saw the plume of dust he felt better, it'd be over soon and then he realised there were two vehicles approaching.

He watched in horror as Alice's utility truck stopped and out stepped Alistair, followed by Val with Ruby in her arms.

'Surprise, surprise, hon! Long time no see,' Val called as Alistair helped Alice out of the cab.

Behind, in the saloon, was Scally with Ty and Rachel and Joe and Amy.

'I thought it was time we had a proper party,' said Alice. She turned to the bungalow. 'You didn't say you were going to build a mansion? Looking nice though, I like the wide verandahs.'

Val put Ruby down and the child immediately made a beeline for Jon and stood next to him, her thumb in her mouth. Jon took her hand in his and together they followed Alice across to the new building.

'Nice place,' said Alice.

'Yes, Alan Bynon's doing a good job.'

'I can see he's been busy. How did you manage to get so much work out of him?'

'A bonus if he finishes on time.'

Alice laughed. 'When's she coming then?'

Jon shook his head. 'She isn't. She got married a while ago, and you'll never believe it but—'

'At my age you'd believe anything.'

'Her husband is working for the British Government over at Woomera,' said Jon bitterly.

'I thought Merle told you she didn't want to live in Australia. I thought she said it was too hot and all.'

'She did, but it seems she's changed her mind.'

'Bit of a back of beyond sort of a place,' said Alice.

'What is?' asked Val, joining them.

'Woomera,' said Alice, 'where they're doing the atomic testing.'

'Who's at Woomera?' asked Rachel.

'Merle,' said Alice dryly, 'her husband's got a job there.'

Jon avoided Val's eyes; he didn't want to see the sympathy there.

'Rather her than me,' said Rachel, lifting a basket out of the boot. 'Come on you lot, who's going to help me with the tucker we've brought?'

'Did you see my mother and our Evelyn while you were in Liverpool?' asked Val later, while they were unpacking the food Rachel had prepared.

'Yes,' Jon said, still feeling ill at ease. What the hell was he going to say to her?

'How are they?'

'Oh, you know, the same, Evelyn's got a new man, a wealthy fella, drives a Jag.'

'And what does he do for a living?'

'He owns a scrapyard. Anyway, according to your mother, Evelyn's going to marry him.'

'Did you tell them about Ruby?'

'No.'

'Why not?'

'Because you said I wasn't to and in any case it isn't my place to tell them. You should. By the way, your mam said she'd write.'

Val laughed. 'You never spoke to them, did you?'

Jon felt his skin heating up. 'Yes, I did,' he said, suddenly embarrassed. He was a lying bastard; if she saw his eyes she'd know it too. All he'd done was repeated what Elsie had told him, and he'd added the last bit for good measure.

'My mother has never written to me, she's never answered any of my letters, and I've only ever had one from our Evelyn and that didn't run to one sheet of paper. Elsie told you, didn't she?'

'Has anyone found the tablecloth yet?' called Rachel.

Glad of the distraction he searched through the remaining box. 'It's here,' he said, escaping Val's questions.

George's two kids came over while they were organising the food. They stood a way off, watching, hands clasped behind their backs. Ruby left Jon's side and trotted over to them and Amy followed. George's younger child, a son, squatted down in the dust and Ruby joined him while his daughter and Amy continued to watch the preparations. By the time everything was ready the four of them had their clothes off and were splashing around in the shallow water at the edge of the creek, squealing with delight as they played some silly game with sticks, while Joe was busy on his own, damming the creek with stones.

'Food,' yelled Val to all the children. 'Come here you lot, let's dry you off.' She reached for a towel and dried each of them in turn. 'Right, you four, sit here.' She picked up Amy, then Ruby and sat them at the trestle table Jon had found in one of the sheds. 'And you two sit next to them,' she lifted up the boy and placed him next to Ruby, while the girl scrambled up on her own and sat next to Amy. 'What's your name?' she asked the girl.

'Daisy,' said Daisy, 'and he's—'

'I'm Tom,' said Tom.

'Well, Daisy and Tom, take a plate and have some of these. Joe, you sit next to Tom and keep an eye on him.' She handed round the pastry rolls and sandwiches, and turned back to the others. 'It's always easier to get the kids settled first. Now, Alice, what can I get for you?'

'I'll have a bit of everything, especially those won ton things.'

Before Jon knew it Val and Rachel had everything organised and soon conversation ceased while people ate.

Jon, sitting slightly apart from the others, watched the scene before him. It had been a good choice for a picnic. The creek meandered lazily along this section of the station and, according to Jeb, it rarely ran completely dry, and when it looked dry it didn't take long to dig down to water. He was lucky, Jindalee was less marginal than Jarrahlong, apart from the eastern quarter, and a few more bores would soon put that right.

'Mine!' shouted Ruby, grabbing a piece of chicken that Tom had taken.

'Ruby!' said Val, the tone a warning.

He hadn't stopped to consider just how many children there were. Five of them with George's two – they made quite a crowd. Maybe he should think about making more of the place, a piece of rope tied to the tree branch over the creek would make a good swing into the water for Joe and for the others when they were older. And if he completed the task Joe had started he could make a pool deep enough to swim in like Alice's husband, Jack, had done at Sandy Spit.

'What're you thinking?' asked Alice.

Her words pulled him out of his reverie, 'Nothing, Alice, just enjoying the moment.'

'You could do with damming the creek,' said Scally, 'make a bit of a pool for paddling.'

'That'd be a good idea,' said Val. 'This place is easier to get to than Sandy Spit especially with all the kids' stuff we need.'

After the meal had been tidied away and while the adults were taking tea, and dozing off the effects of too much food, Jon wandered off alone. As he picked his way through the scrub alongside the creek he could hear the children behind him, playing in the water, their high-pitched squeals carrying in the dry air. He often preferred his own company, just the sound of his own feet, and the bush noises, and besides, he'd never explored this stretch of the creek on foot, he'd only ever ridden along the high ground on the way to checking one of the wells.

He entered the small gorge, keeping in the shade, following the creek as it meandered through the chasm. In places the creek had dried up only to reappear further along creating small stretches of water surrounded by rushes and gum trees that had regenerated after the fire. Some of the rocks still bore scorch marks, but the smaller bushes, saltbush, wanderrie grasses and small acacias grew profusely once again in the sheltered spot.

Jon sat on a rock close to the water's edge, watching dragonflies hunting prey amidst a cloud of butterflies that were feeding on the nectar-bearing flowers around him, and counted his blessings. He liked the solitude, liked watching the zebra finches and other birds that came to drink. As he waited small lizards came to the water's edge after flies, and a bigger one, a bungarra, its large body waddling along, one out-turned foot after the other, followed. It stopped momentarily and tasted the air before continuing on its journey. The gorge was as beautiful in its own way as the one with the green pool. If only Merle had seen it she would have fallen in love with it. How could anyone not love such a wild and splendid Eden?

He lost all sense of time, maybe twenty minutes passed, a half hour, and then he spotted the mulga snake, a long, brown snake like the king brown that had killed Curly. He hadn't seen one for ages and he watched, fascinated, at it slithered its way towards the pool for water. He didn't like snakes, especially venomous ones like the mulga, but he had to admit they were perfectly adapted to the land. It never ceased to amaze him how fast they could travel, the way the muscles moved rhythmically, pushing across the ground, leaving distinctive marks in the sand. No wonder the Aborigines venerated the Rainbow Serpent who, they believed, created the mountain ranges and the deep channels that became the watercourses as she slithered across the land in the Dreamtime.

The creature tasted the water and then raised its head as if listening, except it wasn't, it had picked up vibrations: another creature coming to the pool to drink, but it wasn't an animal, it was Ruby!

Horrified, Jon watched as the child stepped out on to the sandy patch, blocking the easy escape for the reptile. She saw the snake at almost the same time and stopped as it positioned itself to strike. He'd expected Ruby to freeze, scream or run, all the usual reactions, instead she'd squatted down, cooing at the snake, and held out her hand.

He pushed himself to his feet and knew he was going to have to act fast. Options flashed through his mind, throwing a stick at it could make the situation worse, calling to Ruby would made her turn to him and the movement would encourage the snake to strike, his movement could have the same effect. He felt sick, his head felt light, she didn't have a stitch on her, no clothing to protect against a bite, what the hell was he going to do?

The snake twitched as he moved closer to the child, it had picked up his movement, had felt the vibrations; he sensed its nervousness, its awareness of two victims. Did snakes have brains, or did they just work on instinct, instinct he hoped, but would it flee or fight? He inched closer to Ruby, the damn thing was going to fight; he could see the coils tightening, ready to strike.

He crossed the sand and scooped up the child even as the snake struck. He felt the creature's head brush against his trouser leg. He ran and didn't stop until he stood knee deep in the water.

Ruby laughed and twisted round until she had an arm tight around his neck. Her tiny frame felt smooth and warm as he held her close while his own body shook with relief as the adrenaline rush receded. He stepped out of the water, the snake long gone, and, keeping tight hold of the child, leaned over and checked his leg.

Ruby giggled in his ear.

'RU...B...Y,' yelled a voice, Val's voice.

'RUBE,' yelled Scally.

'RU...B...Y,' called Val again, the panic clear in the tone.

'Here,' shouted Jon. 'She's with me.' He held Ruby close as he walked rapidly alongside the creek, back to the picnic spot. She sat on his arm, one hand resting on the nape of his neck, the fingers of her other hand stuffed in her mouth, watching where they were going.

'Where are you?' yelled Val, her voice breathless and jerky from running.

'We're here,' he called back and then he saw her and the panic in her pale face.

'Ruby,' she gasped, stumbling forward.

He held Ruby out to her and watched as she gathered the child to her breast, hugging her until the child squirmed, kissing her curls over and over, tears pouring down her face. 'I thought she was lost,' she whispered, the fear still in her voice. 'I thought she was lost.'

'She must have followed me.' Jon didn't mention the snake.

Rachel hurried to join them. 'Everything all right?'

'Yes,' said Scally. 'Jon found her.'

They all returned to the picnic spot, Rachel and Scally leading the way, Val with Ruby in her arms, the child looking backwards over her shoulder at him as he followed on behind.

What was it about the child that she wanted to be with him? Was it some memory from when she was born?

Jon recalled the feeling of her little body pressed against his, her arm around his neck. He couldn't explain it, he felt protective towards her in a way he never had with his sister or with Rachel's children. Was it because Ruby didn't have a father to care for her, or was there some deeper reason, some reason he hadn't yet fathomed?

CHAPTER 25

Few people called at Jindalee in the lead up to Easter, apart from
Scally with the regular supplies and the mail, and Ken Southall
delivering more breeding stock. Every day Jon was out with the
stockmen repairing fences, constructing new ones and building a
new well. When he occasionally visited Alice she told him he was
a miserable so-and-so for cutting himself off from his friends. He
didn't listen, there was too much to do and besides he didn't feel
like attending the social gatherings in town with all the chit-chat it
entailed, he hadn't even bothered to attend the autumn race meeting but had spent the weekend boundary riding instead.

He'd taken on new stockmen, including Charlie, the blackfella
he'd met out on the eastern boundary near one of the old gnamma
holes, and Alan Bynon had completed the second fit on the bungalow. All that was needed was the kitchen and a bathroom and then
it would be down to the paintwork, furniture and furnishings.

The Easter weekend had been quiet except for Sunday lunch
when Alice insisted he join her and Alistair, Scally, Rachel, Ty,
Val and the children at Jarrahlong. Greg had left straight after the
meal; he'd ended up in town with Chips Carpenter and Maurice
Cato, playing two-up, and when he'd returned he'd been in one
hell of a mood according to Scally, like a dingo with a sore paw.

At the beginning of May Adie rode into the yard at Jindalee saying
Alice wanted to see him urgently.

'Why has she sent you?' asked Jon.

Adie shrugged and looked at his feet. The fella knew what was
wrong but he wasn't saying.

'Alice all right?'

'Yeah.'

'What about Alistair?'

'He's fine, still paintin'. He's in Perth sellin' 'em, that's why Missus Macarthur wants you.'

'Greg?'

Adie avoided his eyes and shoved a stone about in the dust with his foot.

So Greg was the problem. 'Give me a minute or two and I'll get my horse saddled.'

'No, Missus Macarthur says you to come in truck…today.'

Jon heard the anxiety in Adie's voice. What the hell was going on at Jarrahlong? 'All right, Adie. Do you want to leave your horse and come back with me?'

'Nah, I'll ride him home.' He turned back to where he'd tied the horse to the railing and mounted up. 'You come to Jarrahlong to-day?'

Jon nodded. 'I'll be there long before you.'

He saw Adie leave and hurried into the bungalow to change out of his working clothes and into clean khaki drills and a fresh shirt. He told George where he was going and arranged for Yang-dhow to feed the dogs, and he was off, on the drive to Jarrahlong, wondering what the problem was that couldn't wait.

It was mid-afternoon when he arrived and the place looked deserted. Alice heard the utility and she met him on the verandah steps.

'Thanks for coming, Jon.' She indicated a chair and sat down on the other. Her formality put him on his guard.

Jon took off his hat and dropped it on the table between them. 'That's all right, Alice. What's wrong?'

'It's Jimmi.'

'Jimmi?'

'You know, Curly's uncle.'

Jimmi! Surely he wouldn't risk coming back to Jarrahlong, not after killing Gerry Worrall. Jimmi didn't know that he and Stan had dumped Gerry's body down Old Faithful mine shaft.

The memory of that afternoon was seared into his brain, the weight of Gerry's body, Stan's rasping breath as they'd lifted him and tossed him down the shaft, the sounds as the rotten timbers collapsed under the impact and the creaking, sighing rumble deep underground as old lumber, rusting metal and rock collapsed in on itself; and then the stench, the foetid, sour air belching upwards carrying a plume of dust and rust particles. No, Jimmi wouldn't have returned to Jarrahlong, not without good reason.

'He's brought his family with him. They're over in one of the humpies. Greg says they can't stay.'

He looked at Alice; he couldn't see her being worried about what Greg thought.

'You just tell him it's your place, Alice, that you decide who stays and who doesn't.'

'I know, but I'm not as fit as I was and I can't always be around to see what goes on.'

Jon frowned. It wasn't like Alice; she had never been the sort to listen to anyone except her own conscience.

'His wife's sick, and his kids don't look too good, bad skin rashes, all of them. Greg says they've got some pox or something and that it'll spread, that we'll all go down with it. Even Belle doesn't want anything to do with them.'

'What do you want me to do about it?'

'Go and speak to Jimmi, try and find out what's going on.'

'He'll probably tell you himself, if you leave them alone for a bit.'

'No, I want you to find out for me. You two always got on well.'

'You mean I owe him?'

'Well, that too.'

Jon picked up his bush hat and headed out to the humpies along from the stockmen's quarters, past where Adie and Belle lived.

As he approached he could see Mick's family sitting around their fire. Beyond, in the humpy furthest from the homestead, another fire burned, the smoke twisting up into the still air. Jimmi was huddled over it, he recognised him, even at a distance, but the man had changed, he'd lost weight, and his skin was greyer and blotchy looking, and his hair was more grizzled. He looked up as Jon approached and his face broke into the familiar gappy smile of the old days, before Gerry's killing.

'I was beginnin' to wonder when you'd turn up?' he said, rising to his feet. 'Nice to see ya again, Jon. You've growed a bit.'

Jon grinned. 'And put on a bit of muscle.'

'Yeah, mate, y'have.'

'Alice says you're in trouble.'

'Yeah, who's that Greg fella?'

'Alice's nephew.' He didn't bother going into the great-nephew details.

'He's a bit of a mongrel.'

Jon smiled. Ty had used the same word and it fitted.

'He told me to shove off, and to take me family with me. I told him Missus Macarthur'd let us stay 'cept he wouldn't listen. The dingo,' he said half to himself.

'Alice says you're all sick.'

'Not me, mate, but me missus is, lost a baby a few months back, born dead it was and she ain't been right since, and the little 'uns haven't got no energy, always sleepin' and complainin' they feel crook. Reckon they picked up something.'

Jon looked into the mouth of the humpy and saw a heap of bodies lying under blankets.

'Thought I'd better get me a regular job, no good us livin' Abo-style while Molly's like she is.'

Jon squatted next to Jimmi and accepted a pannikin of billy tea. 'Where have you been since I last saw you?'

'With the missus's mob over by Coober Pedy.' He waved a hand in an easterly direction. 'Thought it was time I got away for a bit.'

'You mean after Gerry?'

Jimmi didn't answer; he continued to stare into the embers of the fire.

'I didn't know you were a kaditja man?'

'It had to be done, the elders decided.' Jimmi looked up from the flames. 'I'm not kaditja now.'

'You're not?'

'No. What happened when they found his body?'

'They didn't, I did...I guessed it was you when I saw the spear, so me and Stan Colley took Gerry's body and dropped it down a disused mine shaft.'

'Thanks mate, I'll take a ride over to Stan's place and—'

'Stan's dead, but before he died he wrote a note to the constable to say he'd killed Gerry and buried him down Old Faithful. No one wanted to take a look, the whole shaft was too unstable. Reckon you got away with it.'

Jimmi didn't speak for a while and when he did his voice was quiet. 'That was the trouble – Gerry got away with it. Buny and Wally wasn't the first Abos he killed. The elders ordered him dead, reckoned he'd keep on killin' till he was stopped.'

Jon sat back on his haunches and handed back the pannikin. Was Jimmi telling the truth? Had Gerry been killing Aborigines at every opportunity? Gerry travelled about a fair bit, and no one gave a black stockman who'd gone walkabout a second thought. Maybe they hadn't all gone walkabout after all; maybe some of them were dead, their bones bleaching in the bush.

He got to his feet. 'Thanks for the tea. Be seeing you, mate.' He peered into the humpy, but no one moved.

'Reckon there isn't too much wrong with them, Jimmi's missus lost a baby, born dead it was, kids are a bit peaky, most likely they've picked up something, maybe poor diet,' said Jon when he got back to Alice.

Greg was sitting in Alistair's chair; he was still covered in dust from the muster. His eyes narrowed. 'I don't care what you think. I don't want them here. We've got enough stockmen, and sickly, scabby, snotty kids running about the place doesn't do anyone any good.'

'Jimmi's a hard worker,' said Alice.

'Maybe once,' sneered Greg. 'He doesn't look up to much now; he's too old for the job, if you ask me.'

Jon bristled. 'He's not that old.'

'Why don't you employ him then?' Greg hauled himself to his feet. 'I'm off to get cleaned up. I'm telling you, Alice, we don't need another stockman, we've got too many blacks as it is.'

Neither of them spoke as they watched Greg saunter over to the wash block.

Alice sat back in her chair, her lips a thin, tight line. 'He's got a thing about blackfellas. He's got no time for Adie, or Belle, come to that, and I'm getting too old to fight everyone's corner.'

'Do you want me to take Jimmi and his family back with me?'

'Would you, Jon? Only I can't take much more of this. Greg hasn't let the subject drop since Jimmi got here.'

'No, I don't mind. Besides, as you said, I owe him. I'll go over and see Jimmi later, tell him to be packed and ready first thing.'

Jon sat down in the seat Greg had vacated and gave the problem some thought. Where would he put them? George and his family occupied the only separate accommodation, and the stockmen's quarters wouldn't do, not with a sick woman and kids in there all the time. That just left his place, which meant he'd have to move into the new bungalow whether it was finished or not. Bugger Greg!

* * *

219

George's wife, May, and her kids, Daisy and Tom, helped him to carry his stuff over to the new place, and then she asked Yangdhow to prepare some tucker for Jimmi and his family.

Over the next few days Jimmi joined the other stockmen digging a well and mending fences, but Jon noticed he tired easily. He saw that Jimmi was as sick as the rest of his family even though he tried to hide it. He told George to keep an eye on him and not to give him too much to do.

A week later with Jimmi and his family still crook Jon realised he needed medical advice and he decided to take Jimmi and his family to the next clinic in Pilkington. He drove them there in his ute and was with them when they saw the doctor.

The doctor, an old fella with no bedside manner, took their temperatures, looked into their eyes, down their throats, felt their tummies and said he didn't know what was wrong; he suggested it might be something they'd eaten in the bush. He prescribed a tonic which he said he'd get the pharmacist to make up. And that was it! God help us if any of us get really sick, Jon thought and wished Bindi was about. She'd probably have done them more good with Aboriginal medicine. The family's ill health gave Jon pause for thought, what if there was a real emergency? What if the doctor had to come to them?

The next afternoon he took George with him and searched out a suitable piece of land for an airstrip for the flying doctor. He got the stockmen to cut down the bigger trees, dig up the roots and chop down all the scrubby bush and mulga that grew like twitch. They kept the timber for fencing and burnt the brush and then, when the worst had been removed, he struck up the grader and cleared a runway, basing its width and length on the one at Charlestown. Now, if they needed a doctor, the plane could land, it wouldn't mean a long drive into Charlestown or Pilkington.

A month passed and still Jimmi and his family were sick. Jon drove over to Jarrahlong to talk to Alice and was pleased to see that Alistair was back from Perth.

'They're still crook,' he said bluntly. 'The tonic the doctor prescribed hasn't done any good.'

'Quack medicine never did,' said Alistair. 'What is wrong with them?'

'They're tired all the time, and have rashes that come and go, and diarrhoea, and Molly is sick, vomiting, I mean. She lost a baby a while back now, stillborn.'

'Did you ask whether they'd eaten anything different when they were out in the bush?'

'Jimmi reckons they were eating the usual stuff, goannas, and snakes when they could get them, rabbits, lots of rabbit, and berries and roots, things that they've always eaten.'

'And where were they living?'

'Don't know for sure, somewhere near Coober Pedy, with his wife's family.'

'I haven't any medical training, but I'll come over and take a look at them, if you would like me to.'

'If you wouldn't mind, Alistair, because I, sure as hell, don't know what's wrong with them, and the doctor doesn't.' He hesitated. 'By the way, Alice, I've built a landing strip.'

'What do you want a landing strip for?'

'In case of an emergency – all this business with Jimmi and his family got me thinking. You want to get Greg to make one out beyond the shearing shed, it won't take him long, there're no big trees need clearing, just a couple of sweeps with the grader to clear away the scrub and it'll be ready.'

'Never needed a doctor out here before.'

'There's always a first time, and in any case you and Alistair aren't getting any younger, what happens if you have a heart attack or something?'

'I either get better or I die.'

'You're as bad as Stan, that's the sort of thing he'd have said,' remarked Jon.

The three of them, Alistair, Jimmi and Jon, sat on the wide verandah, drinking tea.

'Tell us in more detail what you were doing just before Molly lost the baby and you all became sick,' said Alistair.

'We was with some of Molly's mob.'

'Where exactly?'

'On their land, west of Coober Pedy, I already told Jon.'

'I know, but we don't know the area, can you name any places we might have heard of?'

Jimmi frowned. 'I only know the Abo words.'

'Well, were you near Ayers Rock, or the Olgas?'

'No, south of them places.'

'How much further south?'

'Nine, ten, eleven days, walk, maybe more. I don't know, we don't always go in a straight line, we folla the water, pretty dry area out Emu Plain way, so we headed east.'

'Emu Plain!' Alistair's voice was sharply. 'Are you sure?'

'Yeah, but we wasn't at Emu Plain, we was a bit away from there, that place desert and claypan.'

'What about the other people?'

'What people?'

'Other members of your wife's family.'

'Nah, didn't see any others when we was out there, just a few, old Sammy and his gin and their mob, reckon most of them was at Twelve Mile Camp, or some place.'

'Did you see anything unusual?'

Jimmi's brow puckered. 'There was the black mist that came rollin' in from the desert, leavin' everythin' sticky.'

'When you say 'mist' do you mean smoke from a fire?'

'Nah, it was black and sticky, like dust, and it covered everything, us, the rocks, everything, and after we got sick, spewing and stuff, and bad skin, and we got red eyes, couldn't open them, they was glued shut. Molly's grandfather, he got sore eyes real bad, couldn't see for long time.' Jimmi sat, staring into the distance. 'Then there was the birds.'

'Birds?' asked Alistair.

'Yeah, there wasn't none. No calls from the butcher birds and cockatoos…there wasn't no finches, only the kite.'

'Kite?'

'Yeah, one, high up, circling.'

'Why didn't you leave?' asked Alistair.

'Everyone too sick; besides the black mist stuff had gone and there was plenty of blind rabbits—'

Jon pricked up his ears. 'D'you think that's what's wrong, they're sick from eating myxie rabbits?'

'Myxomatosis? I suppose it's a remote possibility,' conceded Alistair.

'Nah,' said Jimmi, 'them rabbits not got that myxie disease, I sure of that. Reckon it was that black mist that gave us sore eyes that blinded 'em.'

'What do you think, Alistair?' asked Jon.

Alistair shrugged. 'What about water?'

Jimmi gave it some thought. 'We camped at the soak…stayed there a couple of weeks, until the rabbits was gone.'

'Then what did you do?'

'Went walkabout some more.'

'Did you meet any other black fellows?'

'No, but we met some whitefellas, they was pretty het up about us being there, told us to get off the place, said it was Government land.'

Alistair looked at Jon and shook his head. 'So did you?'

'Did we what?'

'Did you leave?'

'Nah, reckon the land is blackfella land long before whitefellas, we just nodded at 'em and set off in a different direction and then after they'd gone we turned round and went back where we was going in the first place.' Jimmi finished his tea. 'Then Molly got sicker and the baby came early, she said it didn't look right when it was born. She bury it quick. And we moved on 'cept it didn't do no good, she just got sicker, and the kids and the old man, they got sicker, so I thought I'd better do as whitefellas say and get off Government land.'

'So you came back to Jarrahlong,' finished Jon.

'Yeah, wasn't no place else for us to go, the old fella died and we couldn't find the rest of the mob, reckon they gone walkabout, keepin' outa way of Government.'

After Jimmi had returned to his family Alistair looked at Jon. 'Are you thinking what I'm thinking?'

'Well, if it's not from eating myxie rabbits, what is it? You don't really think it's something to do with the Government testing over at Woomera, do you?'

'It's a distinct possibility. Where is this Emu Field place, do you know? Is it north-west of Woomera? – because according to the paper that's where they did the tests, and their symptoms fit the description my friend gave of the people affected in Hiroshima and Nagasaki after they dropped the atomic bombs there.'

Jon fetched a map and they examined it for a minute or two.

'Bloody hell!' said Jon. 'The Government wouldn't explode bombs with people still in the area, would they?'

'Maybe they didn't know they were there. What if Aborigines like Jimmi and his family came in by the back door, arriving after they'd done a sweep of the country? According to the map Emu Field is a pretty big area. Do you think the authorities could have cleared it of all the Aborigines?'

'Unlikely.'

'Yes, that's what I think, and then there's the fallout.'

'Fallout?'

'The radioactive element released when the atomic bombs were detonated. No telling where that ended up, it would have depended on the wind speed and direction. Have you any brandy? I could do with a drink.'

'Rum, do you?'

'Anything, so long as it's alcohol. I need to think.'

Jon went rummaging through the boxes to find the half bottle that he knew he'd got somewhere. He picked up two glasses and returned to the verandah. 'What do you reckon we should do now?' he asked, pouring out two generous slugs of rum.

'You know someone working there, don't you? Alice mentioned it.'

'Yeah, what about it?'

'Do you think they'd come and have a look at these people if we told them what we suspect?'

'I don't know.'

Alistair took a sip of rum. 'They're bound to be measuring the levels of radioactivity. If we told them we've got a family that seem to be suffering from radiation sickness I'd imagine they'd be keen to have a look.'

'What do you suggest, that we write them a letter?'

'No, I think we should go there in person.'

Jon choked on his rum. 'In person?'

'Yes, tell them what we know and bring someone back to assess Jimmi and his family. We can't take them there, Molly's too sick to travel, and the children aren't in much better shape. The only difficulty will be in getting to see someone. They're not likely to let civilians onto the place.'

'It's a hell of a long way to Woomera,' muttered Jon, but it wasn't the distance that was worrying him, it was seeing Merle again, and her new husband. He downed the rest of the rum in one swallow. He wasn't sure it was such a good idea.

CHAPTER 26

The journey took longer than expected. Where they could they stayed in roadhouses on the Eyre Highway, where they couldn't they pulled off the road and slept rough, as they did when they were out in the bush.

Alistair studied the road map. 'When we reach Port Augusta we need to take the Stuart Highway north. There's bound to be a roadhouse we can stop at and someone will be able to tell us the way to the Government site.'

'How much further is it?' Jon stretched as he drove, easing the cramp in his back and thighs.

Alistair measured the map with his thumb. 'I'd say another four hours, provided it's a good road.'

'It's still a bloody long way,' murmured Jon, 'everywhere is a bloody long way in Australia.'

They arrived at a roadhouse on the Stuart Highway too late for the evening meal. The woman behind the bar offered to make them sandwiches, and they accepted. After they'd eaten and had a beer or two, they made their way to their cabin – the last available. Jon looked around the dingy room with its twin beds, tacky wardrobes and the aluminium ceiling fan stirring the soupy air. He didn't fancy sharing the stuffy little room with Alistair, but he was dead beat from all the driving and was asleep as soon as his head touched the pillow.

The trucks woke him early, Scammells, driven by army personnel. Maybe he could get a driver to take a letter to Merle? He dressed quickly and left Alistair asleep. The roadhouse was busy catering for blokes having breakfast. He found a spare seat and put in his order.

'You going to Woomera?' asked Jon of the man at the next table.

'Yeah, mate. Why do you want to know?'

'Heading there myself.'

'Hope you've got a pass, otherwise you don't stand a chance of getting anywhere near the place.'

'That so?'

'Yeah, Government property.'

'Do you know a woman called Merle Vincent, she's a doctor?'

'At Woomera?'

'Yeah, she came out from England a few months back.'

The bloke shook his head. 'Never heard of no Merle Vincent, but that doesn't mean anything, there're a lot of folk out there.' He turned back to his coffee and the bloke he was with, leaving Jon to take in the news.

Jon sipped his tea and reflected on the information; getting to see Merle wasn't going to be simple, maybe he should have written to her, made proper arrangements.

He was halfway through breakfast when Alistair turned up still bleary-eyed from lack of sleep.

'I don't think I could face a fry-up,' observed Alistair. He sat nursing a mug of tea while Jon told him what he'd learnt. Alistair gave the information due consideration. 'What do you suggest we do now?'

'Keep heading north until we get to Woomera, and then ask for this Vincent fella, I suppose.'

A corporal on the next table gave a low whistle and his mate turned and looked towards the door. 'Take a squiz at that,' Jon heard him say in an appreciative tone.

Jon saw the interest in Alistair's eyes. 'What is it?'

'Not what, but who,' said Alistair.

Jon swivelled in his seat and saw an attractive woman, her long dark hair done up in a chignon, placing an order. From the back she looked stunning, slim build and elegantly dressed, not the sort of clobber the women usually wore in the outback. She turned to find a table and Jon gasped.

'Merle!'

She glanced in his direction.

He saw her hesitate, unsure, as he stood to greet her. He covered the short distance between them. 'It's me…Jon.'

He watched mesmerised as her eyes raked over him. He hadn't changed that much had he? She hadn't, thinner in the face maybe, but more beautiful than ever. He watched the smile start and reach her eyes as she recognised him and his heart seemed to twist in his chest as she leaned towards him and brushed her lips against his cheek.

'What a lovely surprise!' She looked over his shoulder at Alistair, and then back to him.

He felt himself colour up and was suddenly aware that everyone in the place was watching them, including the old man behind the counter. 'Come and sit with us.' He took her arm and felt a shock surge through him. His feelings hadn't changed, he always knew they hadn't. He picked up a spare chair and placed it at their table. 'This is Alistair Farlane. He works for Alice Macarthur.' He heard the corporal mutter, 'Some blokes have all the luck,' and ignored it.

She smiled at them both. 'What are you doing here?'

'Looking for you.'

A tiny smile creased her cheeks. 'For me?'

'Yes, Pete told me that you'd married and you'd come out here to work.'

'You saw Pete?'

'Yes, I went back to Liverpool, to see Kathy.' He ignored the surprise on Alistair's face. 'I looked up a few old mates. Pete and Daphne have a nice place.'

Merle laughed and everyone glanced in her direction. 'Yes, not quite Speke Hall yet, but on the way.' She checked out where her order had got to, and then turned back to Jon. 'I meant to write, but things happened so fast...I...'

He felt awkward, did she think he'd come to make her change her mind? 'Alistair and I have a problem and we thought you'd be able to advise us.'

'Steak and eggs,' said the old man, venturing out from behind the counter to slap a full plate on the table.

'They always serve such huge portions, I've asked for smaller but they don't seem to do small out here,' she joked and then picked up her knife and fork. 'What sort of advice?'

'About radiation sickness,' said Alistair. 'We need advice about how to look after someone with radiation sickness.'

'I'm afraid I'm not going to be of much help on that front.'

'What about your husband?'

'What are you doing here?' interrupted Jon. 'Why aren't you with him?'

Merle smiled. 'It's a long story. Paul thought he'd be able to swing me working with him in the labs with us being married and

227

everything, especially as he had a contact, an uncle high up in atomic research. Anyway, the long and the short of it is women aren't allowed, apparently it causes too much disruption amongst the men.'

She wasn't wrong there, thought Jon. Every bloke in the place was conscious of her; he'd noticed the glances from the men having breakfast, and by the look of things nearly all of them were from Woomera if their uniforms were anything to go by.

'It seems someone saw my name and assumed I was a bloke which is why we didn't know there was going to be a problem until we got here.'

Jon grinned. 'Can't blame them, can you, it's not exactly a common name.'

'Merle Oberon,' said Alistair.

'That's right.' Merle smiled. 'The film star. My mother liked the name.'

'Where are you living? Here?' asked Jon.

'No, in Port Augusta. I drive up most weekends to spend Sundays with Paul, and he gets a long weekend off once a month.'

'It's not what you expected then?'

'No, it isn't. Have you ever been to Woomera?'

Jon shook his head.

'It an awful place. I couldn't do with living in the outback. Port Augusta's a lot cooler, much more pleasant, and there's more to do, and nice shops.'

'Your husband is coming here, is he?' asked Alistair.

'Yes, he usually finishes at midday on a Saturday; he'll probably get a lift with one of the drivers, or borrow a utility wagon.'

'And you stay here?'

'Yes, we have a room.'

While she ate her breakfast the roadhouse cleared. Outside in the yard drivers struck up their Scammells and headed for Woomera or towards Port Augusta and the railway line.

'What exactly does Paul do?' asked Jon.

'I don't know for sure. It's secret; he's not allowed to talk about it.'

That didn't sound hopeful! Jon looked at Alistair and noted the almost imperceptible rise of an eyebrow. Already he could hear the official voice behind Merle's words, the sort of voice he'd come across in the children's home when he'd tried to find Kathy, the first time he'd gone back to England.

228

'I suppose we ought to see if we can get a room for tonight,' said Alistair. 'Shall I organise it?' He stood up without waiting for a reply and sauntered over to the bar.

'So, you like Port Augusta,' said Jon.

'The word "like" is a bit strong. It's not too bad; at least it's not the outback.' She looked about her. 'It's not like this place. There's nothing to do here except read, the heat is exhausting, the rooms are dismal and they don't approve of women in the bar. I'm tolerated at meal times and then only because I'm a guest.' She laughed. 'Not exactly the Adelphi, is it?'

'How are you coping with the flies?'

She smiled and her eyes sparkled with amusement. 'How do you think?'

'You're looking really well, Merle.'

'Thank you, and how's Val?'

'She's all right,' said Jon, surprised by the question. 'She's got a little girl, Ruby, and she's running a clothing store in Charlestown.'

'Who's the lucky man?'

Jon frowned at the mocking tone. 'She's not married.'

'Now, why should I be surprised?'

'I thought you liked her well enough?'

'Whatever made you think that?'

'You were with Val and Dorothy when I first met you in Sefton Park.'

'I was only there because of Pete, if I'd have known their sort were going to be there I wouldn't have gone.'

He remembered an earlier conversation, the time they went to New Brighton together. 'You were in the same class at school, weren't you?'

'I don't see what that has to do with it. If you must know, she was a bit of a tart even then.'

Jon was shocked; he'd never heard her talk like that before. He didn't know what to say. 'Val's not like her sister,' he said finally.

Merle looked him straight in the eye. 'If you say so.' She finished what she could of the meal and stood up to leave. 'We'll see you later then.'

Jon stood as she left. He was unsettled by her sudden cool manner. Had he annoyed her?

* * *

'She's a handsome young woman,' said Alistair later as they sat in the bar drinking beer. 'I can see why you fell for her. Do you think she'll help us?'

'Your guess is as good as mine. I think a lot will depend on her husband.'

'Have you met him?'

Jon shook his head. 'Merle met him at university when he was studying for a doctorate in physics.'

'Well, he should know what the symptoms of radiation sickness are working at Woomera; the only problem is whether or not he'll be prepared to consider there may be a problem. In my experience governments tend to refuse to admit liability for everything.'

Paul Vincent wasn't anything like the image Jon had seen in the wedding photograph, he was smaller than he'd imagined him to be, five foot nine or ten, slightly built and was short-sighted if the glasses were anything to go by. He sported dark, curly hair clipped close and was good-looking, and Jon had to admit they made a striking couple as they walked into the dining room that evening.

Merle made the introductions and Jon ordered the beers while they waited for the meal to arrive – roast mutton, and the usual vegetables followed by a sponge pudding that would have sunk a battleship.

'Merle says you're a boffin, that you're involved in the research they're doing out here. A friend of mine was out in Hiroshima and Nagasaki picking over the debris, examining the victims. Is that what you're doing?' asked Alistair towards the end of the meal.

'I'm just a researcher.' Paul didn't elaborate further.

'Were you here for the atomic tests last October?'

'No, the last one was before we arrived.'

It was like pulling teeth, Paul wasn't saying anything; he had that closed look about him. 'The point is,' said Jon, 'we've got this Aboriginal family and, as far as we can gather, they were living in the Emu Field area about the time the Government was doing the tests.'

Paul looked for a napkin then wiped his mouth before answering. 'That's not possible. As far as I am aware they cleared the desert of natives and had men patrolling it to make sure it stayed clear.'

'It's a pretty big place to patrol.'

'Any Aborigines found are moved on; they're not allowed on

230

Government land. The only natives are in the camps miles from where the test site is and they're no more likely to be contaminated than we are.'

'So the problems they have are nothing to do with the tests?' persisted Jon.

'No.'

'Even though they were living in the area where the tests were carried out?'

'I'm telling you, according to my information, there were no natives living in the area where the tests were done. And besides, any Aborigines passing through the area would be no worse off than the personnel who were present at the detonations.'

'I thought you said you didn't see the testing?'

'I didn't,' said Paul abruptly, 'but I've worked with a lot of the men who did.'

'What did they say?' asked Alistair, his calm tone taking the heat out to the situation.

'Just that they were allowed to witness the effect of the blasts.'

'Did they say what it looked like?'

'They said it was like a huge black, mushroom-shaped cloud surging high into the sky, about a minute later came a loud double explosion and then they saw the shock wave bending the trees and bushes, sweeping over the ground like a tide.'

'And these men are all right?'

'Yes, perfectly all right, why wouldn't they be?'

Jon realised they weren't getting anywhere with Paul Vincent, he'd closed his mind, taking the Government line, just as they'd thought he would. Merle sat sipping her tea, not joining in with the argument although he was very conscious of her presence, the warmth of her leg close to his, her attentiveness whenever he spoke. He shifted in his seat putting more space between them. She was a married woman.

'What, exactly, is wrong with these people?' asked Paul.

Jon gathered his thoughts; it wouldn't do to mess up on the description. 'Well, first of all the whole family developed blisters and nasty skin rashes and suffered from sickness and diarrhoea straight after a sticky, black mist rolled in over them. They all had red, gluey eyes and couldn't see for a while. Then, not long after that Jimmi's wife had a stillborn baby, she said it didn't look right. She was so upset she took it away and buried it far out in the bush.'

'Bush? What do you mean *bush*?'

Jon looked at Paul in amazement. Surely he knew what the bush was; he'd been in Australia long enough. 'The countryside in the outback, Paul. Anyway, the grandfather never recovered his sight; he went downhill fast and died. It's getting on for seven months now and all of them are tired all the time and they've lost weight.They're pretty crook.'

'Crook?'

'Ill,' said Jon.

'It could be anything, something they've eaten, bad diet, anything,' said Paul.

'It could be,' agreed Alistair, 'but my friend, the one who was out in Hiroshima and Nagasaki, described people with similar symptoms and that was radiation sickness.'

Jon caught Paul's eye and held it. 'We just want you to come and have a look at them, see what you think.'

'Where are these people?' asked Paul in a resigned tone.

'They're staying with me on my station.'

Merle's hand briefly rested on his. 'So you finally got your own place.'

Jon stared at her, shocked. He'd told her of his plans to buy a station in his last letter. Hadn't she believed him? Did she think it was just talk? 'Yes, I did.' He felt the warmth from her leg again.

'And how far is it to this station of yours?' asked Paul.

'A long way,' said Alistair, 'it's in Western Australia, beyond Kalgoorlie.'

'Kalgoorlie,' laughed Paul. 'Are you both mad! There's no possibility at all that they could have been affected.'

Merle leaned closer still and Jon felt her breath waft over his cheek. 'Is it a big station?'

Jon tried to put Merle out of his mind as he answered Paul's scathing comment. 'They came to us because they were sick after living in the desert east of Emu Field, at the time the Government did the atomic tests, I told you.'

'Well, I can't travel all the way to Western Australia just to look at some natives who might, or might not, have been in the vicinity of the test site. It's just not possible.'

'What if I went back with Jon and Alistair and examined them?' suggested Merle.

All three stopped arguing and looked at her.

Paul recovered first. 'Don't be silly. You don't know anything about radiation sickness.'

'You could tell me what to look for.' Merle's words were clipped and tight. 'I *am* a qualified doctor.'

'And then what? There isn't any treatment.'

'So you agree, it's possible that is what they're suffering from?' pressed Jon, ignoring the sarcasm.

'I'm not agreeing with anything.' Paul pushed his chair back sharply. 'I think I'm going to call it a night. Are you coming, Merle?'

For a moment Jon thought she was going to refuse, but then she gathered her things together and the two of them left.

'That went well,' commented Alistair. 'Paul didn't like being caught on the back foot, did he? What do you think they will decide to do?'

'Your guess is as good as mine,' said Jon.

'The point is that if what Paul says is true then there is nothing that can be done for Jimmi and his family, no medication, nothing. All we can do is look after them as best we can and hope they'll recover.'

'It was a waste of time coming, wasn't it?'

Alistair nodded. 'It looks that way...but you never know. Now, would you like another beer?'

'I would, anything to take the nasty taste out of my mouth,' said Jon.

At breakfast the next morning Merle joined them in the dining room.

'Where's Paul?' asked Jon.

'He's gone back to Woomera.'

Jon looked at her in surprise. 'You two had words?'

'No.'

She'd answered too fast. He wondered exactly what had been said after they'd left last night.

She avoided his eyes. 'Paul says it's not radiation sickness. But he suggests I have a look at these people to put your minds at rest.'

'You're coming back with us, then!' said Jon, unable to contain his relief.

'That's the idea.' She smiled at them both. 'I'd only be hanging about in Port Augusta until next weekend, so I might as well.'

CHAPTER 27

It was Alistair who suggested that Merle stay at Jarrahlong rather than at The Grand in town. Jon wondered what Alice's reaction would be when she finally met Merle – Merle was nothing like Val who'd taken to the outback from the first.

Jon glanced at her as she stared straight ahead, ignoring the changing countryside as they left Charlestown. The drive back from Port Augusta had been long and tiring, all three of them were sick of being cooped up in the utility day after day and conversation had ceased miles back.

Merle gasped as she caught her first glimpse of the homestead gleaming in the winter sun as they drove along the track to Jarrahlong. She turned to him. 'It's not what I expected.'

Jon looked at the great jarrah trees growing alongside the creek and at Alice's new bungalow with its white, sweeping roof and wide verandahs, the panes of glass winking in the evening light. He'd described the buildings and the beautiful setting often enough in his letters.

Tight-lipped, he pulled up and parked next to the fencing, leaving Alistair to help Merle out of the ute while he dealt with the luggage. When he turned round Alistair was already halfway to the bungalow and Merle was struggling out of the ute on her own. He waited for her while she straightened her dress and then led the way over to Alice.

'Alice, this is Merle, Merle this is Alice.' The introductions complete, Jon put the suitcase and bag down on the verandah next to Alice's rocking chair.

Merle stepped forward and formally shook Alice's hand. 'It's nice of you to put me up for a few days, Mrs Macarthur.'

'It's Alice, call me Alice,' said Alice from the comfort of her chair. 'Pleased to meet you at last, Jon often talks about his friends in the Old Country.' Alice smiled when she saw him colour up.

He ignored her and waited as Merle took a seat next to Alistair.

'Long drive,' commented Alice.

'Yes.' Alistair's tone was unusually clipped.

Alice turned to Merle. 'You'll need a few days rest and recuperation before you travel over to Jon's place.'

'That would be nice, Alice, I'm still not used to the distances.' She brushed a strand of hair off her face. 'It's such a beautiful place you have here with all the shade trees.'

'Belle,' yelled Alice. 'Where's that tea?' She turned her attention back to Merle. 'A friend of yours will be over this Sunday – Val, Val Rayner.' She caught Jon's eye. 'It'll be a pleasant surprise for Val, and there'll be plenty of time for Merle to see Jimmi and his family next week. A couple of days won't make much difference either way, will it?'

Jon didn't say a word. He couldn't trust himself to speak; if he did he'd probably say something he'd later regret. Damn Alice and her plans for the weekend!

'Put Merle's case in the room next to Greg's. She'll be more comfortable staying with me than in the manager's place.'

'Manager's place?' queried Jon.

'Yes, the bungalow Rachel used.'

'I didn't realise it was for a manager, Alice, does Greg know?' He picked up the suitcases and took them inside, not bothering to wait for her tart reply.

When he returned to the verandah they were taking tea. Belle handed him a mugful, he took it and drank it down fast. 'If you don't mind, Alice. I won't stop. I want to get back to Jindalee.'

Merle frowned and placed a hand on his arm. 'Can't you stay?'

'Afraid not, Merle, I've things to do at Jindalee, the place won't run on its own.'

Merle withdrew her hand and the silence stretched between them. 'I suppose I'd better go and unpack,' she said when no one else spoke.

Alice watched her leave and then she glanced at Alistair, and then Jon, a speculative expression on her face. 'What about a meal before you go?'

'Yang will cook something for me when I get home, I won't starve.' He picked up his hat and headed for the ute, before Merle returned, conscious of Alice's eyes boring into his back.

* * *

It was dark when he drove into the yard. He was pleased to be back at his own place, and on his own. Being cooped up in the ute with Alistair and Merle had been difficult – Merle sitting close to him on the long journey, feeling her hot breath on his cheek whenever she spoke, her perfume scenting the air, and the unbidden thoughts of what might have been choking him. He'd had to remind himself more than once that she was a married woman that he had no claim on her, and he'd wondered, fleetingly, if that was how Stan had felt whenever he saw Alice.

Conversation had dried up early on the road home. By the third day even Alistair who could talk for England had struggled with Merle's monosyllabic answers as the interminable journey, and the dust and the heat, took its toll on her, and he'd wondered how she would have managed had they been travelling in midsummer instead of the cooler winter months.

Jon didn't know why it still mattered to him that Merle liked Australia, but even though she'd married someone else, it did, he wanted her to love the land as he did and it was clear she didn't.

He threw off the dark mood and felt ashamed of his ambivalent attitude to Alice's suggestion that Merle rest over for a few days. He was torn between wanting to be with her, knowing she'd never be his, and wanting the situation over with so he could forget about her and get on with his life.

He knew he was being selfish. The last few months couldn't have been easy for Merle. She had no friends or family in Port Augusta, and the roadhouse she stayed at some weekends wasn't exactly salubrious for a girl brought up in an English city. Perhaps a few days with Alice would make a difference; perhaps Merle would begin to see a different side to the country. Maybe she'd remember what he'd written in his letters and begin to see the outback as he did, a wild Eden. He still loved her and he wanted her to be happy.

In the morning he went looking for Jimmi and found the family cooking damper over a campfire in the backyard. He squatted next to the Aboriginal. 'I've got a doctor for you. She might know why you're all crook.

'A woman?'

Jon swore under his breath, he hadn't thought about her being female. Maybe they would refuse to have her examine them.

'She's qualified. I fetched her from over Port Augusta way. I thought she might have seen other people who are sick like you. She's staying at Alice's place for a few days, but I'll bring her over

236

next week.'

Jimmi didn't bother to answer and turned back to the campfire, his interest gone.

Jon left him to it and strolled over to the barn and George who was waiting for him.

'He's been pretty crook this last week,' commented George. 'You find that doctor?'

'She'll be over in a day or two.'

'She?'

'Yeah, reckon they'll go walkabout?'

'Dunno.' George tilted back his bush hat and scratched his forehead. 'Y'got time to take a ride over the west side?'

'Why?'

'Kennilworth, again.'

'What's the problem?'

'More damaged fencin' next to the creek on the Kennilworth property. The cattle have been helpin' themselves to his water.'

Jon swore, most of the cattle were branded, but the poddies weren't, they were going to have to go over to Reef Hill Station and speak to old man Kennilworth. Not a pleasant prospect! Kit Kennilworth wasn't particularly likeable, and having to broach the subject of stray animals was never easy, especially if he decided not to cooperate.

'Have you seen Kit?'

'Yeah, he saw me down by the fence, he reckons it's Abos doin' it.'

'What do you think?'

'It's not Abos.'

'So who took down the fence?'

'Kennilworth,' said George, 'same as last time, but we can't prove it.'

Jon smiled, George was the most direct Aboriginal he'd ever met, he didn't beat about the bush, just said it as it was, whereas with most other blackfellas conversation was usually more circuitous. 'What do we do if he cuts up rough, says the poddies are his?'

'Reckon we shouldn't bother askin' this time, just drive 'em back onto our property and mark 'em quick,' said George.

'I wonder if the Samuels had the same problem.'

'What, with Kennilworth?'

'Yeah. Alice says he wasn't that pleased when Jeb restocked with cattle after a bad bush fire wiped out his Merinos in 1947. Kennilworth reckoned too many people going into beef brought the prices down.'

'Wouldn't know anything about that, Jeb never said anything to me.'

'No, me neither,' said Jon as he helped George gather together the gear they needed to repair the fencing.

They loaded up the packhorses, collected tucker from Yang and were on their way by eight o'clock. When they reached the damaged fencing, they could see cattle in the distance on Kennilworth land.

'Y'reckon they're ours?' asked George.

'Only one way to find out.'

Together they rode over to the nearest mob and looked for the Jindalee mark.

'They're ours all right,' said George. 'Let's just drive 'em back and say nothin'.'

Jon looked at his cattle, the younger poddies were keeping close to their mothers.

'What d'ya want to do, boss?'

'Round them up, double quick,' said Jon, 'like you said.'

By mid-afternoon they'd collected most of the strays except for a few of the older poddies that stubbornly stayed behind on Kennilworth land, close to the water, refusing to go with the mob.

'What about the others?'

'Leave them, we'll put it down to experience, it's more important we get this fencing fixed.'

'We got time for a brew?'

'Yeah,' said Jon, 'we've got time for a brew.'

In no time at all they were sitting with their backs against tree trunks, elbows on their knees, sipping hot tea.

'How soon do you reckon we can get out here to sink that well?' asked Jon.

'Soon as y'like.' George nodded in the direction of the creek over on the Kennilworth land. 'We shouldn't have to go down too deep, not with water so close to the surface. We could do it before the next muster if y'want.'

'Pity we can't do a deal with Kennilworth, put a dog-leg in the fencing up this end and use his creek water.' Even as he said it he knew it was never going to happen. Jeb Samuels had tried to do a deal in the drought, but Kennilworth wouldn't entertain the idea, said he wouldn't have enough water for his own needs, and maybe he had a point: when there was water, there was enough for everyone, when there was drought that's when fights started and the accusations of unfair usage flew about. No, their own well was the better bet.

'Y'hear that?' said George.

They listened – horses and more than one by the sound of it. Jon rolled to his feet, keeping tight hold of his enamel mug as Kennilworth and one of his stockmen came into view.

'G'day, Mister Kennilworth. What can we do for you?' said Jon pleasantly.

'Just wondered what you boys were doing on my property?' Kennilworth nodded in the direction of the cattle they'd rounded up. 'Are they mine?'

Jon ignored the insult. 'No, they've all got the Jindalee brand. Seems the fence here got damaged, a few crossed over to the creek, reckoned you wouldn't mind us fetching them back.'

'They all marked?'

'All except the youngsters.'

'How do I know them poddies aren't mine then?'

'Because they're following their mothers,' said Jon equably. 'Can I get you fellas a tea?'

Kennilworth eased himself in the saddle. 'No thanks, this isn't a social call. Next time you clear it with me first, then me and my boys can make sure all's fair and square.' Kennilworth wheeled his horse around. 'What're you doing about the fencing?'

'She'll be right before we go.'

'Make sure it is, lad. It don't do to go upsetting the neighbours around here.' He slapped his horse on the rump and was off, his stockman following on.

'Nice fella!' said George. 'I've met his sort before. It'll pay us to get them poddies marked up quick, then there's no argument.'

Jon watched the pair ride off. Will Samuels had once said something similar about Kit Kennilworth, that he was an uncooperative bastard, quick to have his say and his share, slow to offer support when support was needed. After the bush fire he was the only one of Jeb's neighbours not to help with the burnt sheep. Killing dying and injured animals was never a pleasant task at the best of times, but that's what neighbours did, they turned out and assisted, but

not Kennilworth even though his station had escaped the confla-
gration.

Jon missed the Sunday social gathering at Jarrahlong, repairing the
fencing had taken longer than expected and then after they'd finished they had ridden the whole of the boundary fence between
Jindalee and Reef Hill Station repairing weakened sections as they
went. By the time they'd finished the weekend was long gone.

'Where have you been?' asked Alice as soon as he arrived at
Jarrahlong. 'Merle's been waiting on your coming.'

'Sorry, about that, had a problem with the boundary fence, had to
fix it otherwise old Kennilworth would have snaffled more of my
poddies than he already has.'

'What's a poddy?' asked Merle.

'An unmarked calf,' said Alice.

Jon smiled at Merle. 'Did you have a good weekend?'

'Rachel brought her kids,' interrupted Alice, 'they came with Val
and Ruby. It was quite a gathering. Made a nice change, didn't it,
Merle?'

'Yes, Rachel's very pleasant.'

Jon heard the edge in Merle's voice and looked Alice full in the
eye.

She shrugged almost imperceptibly as Alistair tapped his pipe out
on the arm of the chair he was sitting in and studiously proceeded
to refill the bowl.

Even Jon picked up on the strained atmosphere. What the hell
had gone on on Sunday? Something, clearly – the day hadn't been
a success – that was obvious.

'Well, are we ready to go, Jon, Alistair? I've got everything.'
Merle indicated the medical bag at her feet. Alistair laid his pipe
down in the ashtray.

Jon picked up the medical bag. 'We'll be back tonight, Alice, in
time for tea.'

They arrived at Jindalee by midday. Merle had barely spoken on
the journey and when she did her answers were clipped. Something
had upset her but Jon couldn't fathom out what, and even Alistair
had nothing to say for himself. He opened the cab door for Merle
to alight and then led the way over to the Samuels' old bungalow

where Jimmi and his family lived.

'If you just wait here a minute, I'll see if they're ready for us,' said Jon, not wanting to barge in on the family unannounced.

Merle's brow furrowed as Jon disappeared inside. Half a minute later he returned and ushered them into the kitchen. Merle glanced at the family briefly as Alistair followed her into the room.

'Jimmi, Molly – this is Doctor Vincent, the doctor I was telling you about,' then he indicated Alistair, 'and you've already met Alistair.'

Jimmi inclined his head in Merle's direction but it was Alistair who responded first, raising his hat in greeting to the couple.

'You were all in a bad state when you arrived at Jarrahlong, weren't you Jimmi?' said Alistair as Merle placed her medical bag on the table.

'So why were they brought here, Jon?' she asked.

'Greg wasn't keen on having them on the station. He thought Jimmi and his family could have contracted something contagious.'

'I suppose that's understandable.' She cast an eye over the family standing before her and then took out a stethoscope and placed it around her neck.

Jon watched as she rummaged through the bag and found a thermometer. 'Do you think it could be radiation sickness?'

'No. It's not radiation sickness.'

'How can you be so sure?'

'Paul said it isn't possible.'

'Well, he's not here looking at them, you are, what do you think?'

'I don't think they've got radiation sickness either.'

'Have you seen many cases?' asked Alistair.

'No, but I've read up on it in a paper Paul gave me.'

'May I read it?'

Merle coloured up. 'Sorry, I didn't bring it with me.'

'Aren't you going to ask them questions about what happened to them out in the desert?' asked Jon.

'Do they speak much English?'

Jon stared at her, shocked. 'Of course they do.'

'Sorry. It's just some of them don't, I believe.'

'They can hear as well,' said Jon, suddenly irritated by her attitude. He could detect Paul's tone in her voice. Couldn't she think for herself?

241

She turned to Alistair. 'Why do you think they've got radiation sickness?'

'As Jon explained before, the rashes, the nausea, the fatigue, then there was the stillbirth and the grandfather's death, and since then they've been picking up every sniffle going around the place.'

Jimmi's youngest leaned forward fascinated by the stethoscope around Merle's neck.

Merle briskly brushed the boy's hand away, 'It's not a toy.' She took hold of the child's chin firmly, inspecting the rash on his face, first on the left side and then the right as the boy squirmed in her grip.

Jimmi caught Jon's eye, and Jon looked away embarrassed as Merle felt the glands in each of their necks, pulled down their lower eyelids and looked into their eyes, looked down their throats and asked them to say 'Aaah', sounded their chests, and finally picked up the stethoscope and listened to their breathing.

When she'd finished taking their temperatures she sat back on a chair and looked directly at Jon. 'The little ones have bubbly chests, probably a common cold with a mild chest infection, all their glands are up which suggests a low-grade infection, their eyes are a bit yellow, but that might be normal or it might not, it's difficult to tell, and the lethargy you've described is likely to be the result of the low-grade infection I just mentioned. In my view none of these people are seriously ill; they've probably picked up something while out in the bush that we can't identify. I'd suggest you feed them regular meals, give them clean water to drink and if they haven't recovered in a couple of months maybe you should consider the possibility that they are malingering.'

'And that is it?' Jon stared at her open-mouthed, stunned by her matter-of-fact delivery and the suggestion that Jimmi and his family were bludgers.

'That's it, you asked my opinion as a doctor and I've given it to you.' She leaned forward, replaced the stethoscope into her medical bag and stood up.

Alistair rose too and so did Jon. Alistair nodded in Jimmi's direction and followed Merle out of the bungalow and across to the ute.

Jon placed a hand on the Aborigine's shoulder. 'Sorry, Jimmi. I'll come over and have a word later, yeah?'

Jimmi inclined his head and looked away. Jon screwed up his hat, unsure of what to say, then bashed the hat back into shape, smiled uneasily at Molly and joined the other two near the ute.

'Tea and sandwiches do for lunch?' he said in a tight voice.

'That would be very welcome, Jon.' Alistair indicated the bungalow. 'I take it we are over there.'

'Is that where you live?' Merle asked with interest, looking towards the new building as she put her medical bag on the front seat.

Confused by the change in her tone, Jon nodded.

'It's beautiful.' She slammed the ute door shut. 'May I have a look around?'

Jon led the way across the yard and opened the door for them. The building was finished but unfurnished, apart from the kitchen and the main bedroom with its temporary put-you-up bed and a bentwood chair.

'It's really nice.' She enthusiastically inspected every room and ending up in the empty sitting room, taking in the polished wooden flooring, the fine stone fireplace and chimney breast. 'It will be lovely when it's furnished, with proper rugs and sofas. Pete would be impressed.' She stepped out of the double doors onto the wide verandah. 'It's much bigger than Alice's. Are you having it built or was it already here?'

'The Samuels had already started the rebuild, I'm just finishing it,' said Jon, ignoring Alistair's bemused look.

'I didn't know they had places like this in the outback.' She sat down on the swing seat Jon had rigged up to take advantage of the view.

I did tell you, he wanted to say, but didn't, still irritated and confused by her lack of interest in Jimmi and his family and her attitude towards them. He removed the cloth covering the sandwiches Yang-dhow had prepared and offered them, then poured out the tea.

They ate in chilly silence, except for the creaking swing seat and the rustle of paper as Alistair riffled through a magazine. As soon as he decently could, Jon made to leave. 'I suppose we ought to be getting back; Alice is expecting us for tea later.'

Merle dragged herself away from the shady swing seat and followed him across the yard to the ute. 'Alice is not what I imagined from your letters.'

'What do you mean?'

'Well, I wasn't expecting her to be so...so...'

'So, what?'

'Prickly,' she said finally. 'She's very brusque.'

243

Jon smiled, 'She's all right once you get to know her, isn't she, Alistair?'

'Yes, she's a shrewd judge of character, and she doesn't suffer fools lightly,' observed Alistair.

'What's amiss with them then?' asked Alice when the three of them arrived back at Jarrahlong.

'Yes, I'd like to know too, contagious is it?' asked Greg.

'Nothing serious, probably a virus they've picked up, the natives don't always have the same immunity to European diseases.'

Jon stared at her in amazement; he couldn't believe what he was hearing. 'You didn't mention that earlier.'

'Didn't I? Well, it's a possibility.'

Alice leaned back in her chair and gave Merle a contemplative look. 'So there's nothing you can do for them?'

'No, I think they'll get better on their own.'

'And it's not radiation sickness?' persisted Alice.

Greg snorted his derision. 'Radiation sickness? Who's the idiot who thought it was that?'

'Me,' said Jon to spare Alistair.

'What made you think that?'

'The fact that they've been living out at Emu Field not far from the Woomera test site, and because of their symptoms.'

'You a doctor now?'

'No, that's why Merle's here.'

'Good job someone's got some sense,' muttered Greg. 'If you ask me too many people round here mollycoddle Abos. They're lazy buggers, the lot of them, always on the take.'

Merle caught Jon's eye, an I-told-you-so look on her face. He ignored it, shocked by her reaction. She wasn't as he remembered.

'What did you think to Jindalee?' asked Alice.

'It's impressive.'

'And the bungalow?'

'Beautiful, but it's huge, Jon's going to rattle around in it.'

'He'll be married before long, soon as he finds the right woman,' said Alice pointedly. 'He's a good catch.'

'That's enough, Alice, I've no plans in that direction.'

Greg laughed. 'He hasn't much to choose from. Rachel's married and Val, well, who'd want to marry that gobby female?'

Merle chuckled. 'You'll have to go to the city, Jon. You should be able to find yourself a nice girl in Perth,' she teased.

'I thought I had one, but she married someone else,' he said stung by her amusement and was pleased to see she had the grace to blush.

'I think it's about time we had tea.' Alice held out a hand for Alistair to help her out of her seat.

Conversation flagged during the meal, only Greg was in ebullient mood, chatting away to Merle, asking her about Port Augusta.

'When do you want me to take you back?' asked Jon when there was a suitable lull in the conversation. 'Tomorrow?'

'No, next week, if that's all right with you and Alice. Rachel has invited me to go to the film show next Saturday, and the ute race. And she says she'll ask Chips to take us up for a spin in his plane. It would be nice to have a look at the outback from the air. I've never been in an aeroplane.'

'You're welcome to stay,' said Alice flatly. 'But there's not a lot to do around here except read, or help Belle with the vegetable patch.'

'You ever been on a horse?' asked Greg.

'No, never.' Merle laughed, watching Jon from under her lashes.

'I'll teach you then, we can ride down to the creek at Sandy Spit for a swim.'

'I'd like that, thanks, Greg. What about you, Jon, will you come with us?'

'No, I've got to get back to Jindalee.'

'What about Saturday, will you be at the film show?'

'Of course he will,' snapped Alice. 'We all will.'

After the meal Jon took his leave of them, Alice followed him out onto the verandah. 'We'll see you Saturday, then.'

'Yes, I'll be there. I won't forget,' he added, an edge of sarcasm in his voice.

'Good!' Alice watched him as he clattered down the steps. 'Reckon you had a lucky escape.'

He turned back to her, 'What was that, Alice?'

'You heard me. See you Saturday.'

Jon racked his brain, trying to make sense of the half heard words, but it was no good, and there was no way she was going to repeat them. He got in his truck and struck up the engine, glad to see the back of the place, including Alice.

CHAPTER 28

The one and only race of the day started at eleven o'clock. Everyone was out at the track early, inspecting the vehicles and placing bets. Never had Jon seen such a collection of battered utes. His own wasn't in good condition, but it was pristine compared to the six before him. They had doors missing, bumpers and running boards hanging off, no passenger seats, and, in one, not even a driver's seat only a wooden box nailed to the floor. The noise was horrendous; he was convinced there wasn't an intact exhaust pipe between the six of them.

'Who's going to win?' asked Merle, her hands over her ears.

'The Bartokas lad.' Jon had to shout to make himself heard. 'The one over there standing on the running board. Wes says that kid can reverse a Scammell truck with a trailer attached, says he's been able to do it since he was nine.'

'Are you ready?' yelled Wes through the megaphone and down went the green flag.

'How far do they have to race?' yelled Merle above the racket.

'Five circuits of the track,' Rachel yelled back before he could answer. 'Who do you think will win?'

'Jon says the one who's out in front.' Merle batted away the dust from her face. She laid a hand on Jon's arm and leaned closer to him so she didn't have to shout. 'How much money have you put on him?'

He could smell her perfume and felt her warm breath on his face when she pressed against him. Desire flooded through him and she smiled. She knew! He felt his face flush. She was a married woman; he had no claim on her now.

'A fiver,' he said, confused and embarrassed. He turned away from her, putting space between them and spotted Val and Ruby standing further along the fence. 'Come and join us,' he called to

246

Val, glad of the distraction.

Ruby ran towards him, laughing, her arms raised ready for him to pick her up. He leaned down, swung her round and sat her on the railing, holding her so she couldn't slip. He waited impatiently while Val gathered her things together. 'Where's Alice?' he asked when she joined them conscious of the pique on Merle's face.

'Over there.' Val indicated behind her and when Jon looked he saw Alice and Alistair watching them. He swore under his breath, Alice would have plenty to say later, that was for sure. She didn't like Merle and had made no secret of the fact.

The race was 'no contest', the Bartokas lad won easily by a length and a half. Everyone cheered while he did a lap of honour and drove over to the makeshift podium for the presentation – a crate of beer.

For once Jon was pleased to see Greg, as he led Chips and Rachel over towards them.

'Did you lay a bet, Jon?' asked Chips, running an appreciative eye over Merle even as he spoke.

'A fiver,' said Jon.

Greg scowled. 'Well, I lost the lot.'

Rachel patted him on the back. 'Never mind, Greg, better luck next time.' She smiled at Merle. 'They don't do ute racing in England, do they?'

'No, they don't.' She smiled at Chips. 'Cars, motorbikes, greyhounds and horses, but no utes, at least, not to my knowledge.'

Greg turned to Chips. 'Merle's husband's works for the Government on this atomic stuff over at Woomera.'

'Is that so,' said Chips, his eyes never leaving Merle's face, 'and what does a beautiful woman like you think of Australia?'

She hesitated. 'I wasn't expecting it to be so....so...flat and so...red.'

'It's not quite what you were expecting, is that it?'

'No, it isn't. I don't think Australia's for me.'

Val shot a look in her direction. 'Why not? There's plenty of opportunity.'

'So I've noticed,' said Merle tartly, her eyes resting on Ruby for a moment or two.

Val blushed.

'Everywhere looks the same in Australia,' said Merle, 'the red

247

earth and the scrubby bush.' She batted away some flies. 'And then there are the insects, how do you put up with them?'

Val gritted her teeth. 'You get used to them.'

'You haven't seen the ranges then?' said Chips.

'What ranges?'

'How about you take us up in your plane, Chips; Merle'd like to see the outback from the air,' Rachel wheedled.

'Only space for one, she's a twin seater.' Chips finished his cigarette and ground out the stub. 'You fancy a quick spin, Merle?'

'I could squeeze into the dickie seat,' said Rachel. 'I'll keep still; you won't know I'm there.'

Chips looked at Rachel and then at Merle. 'What do you weigh?'

Merle laughed. 'What a thing to ask a lady.' She looked at him from under lowered lashes. 'Under nine stone.'

'And I'm only eight and a half,' said Rachel.

Chips did a quick calculation 'Reckon we could get away with it.'

'You're not going, Rachel,' said Ty the minute he heard the plans. 'I've got a bad feeling about it.'

'Don't be daft, Chips knows what he's doing, he's an experienced pilot,' argued Rachel.

'I don't care how experienced he is,' growled Ty.

'But I've said I will now.'

'Well, tell him you've changed your mind.'

'What about Merle?'

'If she wants to go that's her business,' said Ty, spitting his words out.

Merle saw the stubborn look plastered on Ty's face and laughed. 'Don't worry, Rachel. I wouldn't want you to upset your husband.'

Rachel turned scarlet, and no one spoke, the atmosphere suddenly tense.

Merle eventually broke the silence. 'Val'll go instead, won't you, Val?'

Shocked, Val looked at her.

'It's not as if it's going to take long, is it? – only half an hour or so.'

'But—'

'You don't have to go if you don't want to, Val,' said Jon, his voice clipped, irritated by Merle's dismissive tone. What the hell was she up to embarrassing everyone?

Merle watched Val's discomfort as the plane taxied into view and parked up. 'As I recall you were always up for anything, not like me,' her tone mocking. 'It'll be an experience for you, Val.' She glanced down at Ruby. 'You'll stay with Jon while your mummy goes up in an aeroplane, won't you, Ruby?'

Ruby nodded solemnly.

'That's sorted then. Hurry up, Chips is ready.'

Val shrugged, resignation on her face. She picked up Ruby and kissed her. 'You stay with Jon, sweetheart. I won't be long.'

'Right, girls, who's in the passenger seat and who's in the dickie?' called Chips.

'Val'll go in the dickie,' said Merle, standing aside to let her go first.

'Okay, Val, step on this when you get in.' Chips patted the section he wanted her to stand on. 'I don't want your feet to go through the wing,' he said, laughing.

'I wish I was going,' whinged Rachel, glaring at Ty.

Val strapped herself in and looked down at Jon who had lifted Ruby up for a better view. 'Look after her,' she mouthed.

'Have you filed a flight plan?' shouted Wes.

'Don't panic, we're only going up for a spin, just across there.' Chips waved his hand in a north-easterly direction. 'Over Jarrahlong way, we'll be back before you've finished your beer.' He gave Merle a hand up and showed her how to strap herself in before settling himself into the pilot's seat

Everyone moved back while Wes stepped forward and spun the propeller a couple of times, then Chips fired up the engine and soon the plane was taxiing down the strip. At the far end Chips manoeuvred it to face the runway.

For a moment the plane didn't seem to move and then they heard the engine revving up and saw the aircraft rolling forward, gathering speed, when it drew level the nose cone lifted and it was airborne. Jon caught a glimpse of Merle in the passenger seat looking straight ahead. No one spoke as the plane pulled away from them, gaining height, soon there was only a faint drone from the engine and then even that was gone.

Jon set Ruby down and took her hand, 'Come on, let's go and find Granny Alice.'

* * *

By four o'clock Jon was worried. Chips, Merle and Val had been gone for two hours. He left Ruby with Alice and walked over to Wes's garage.

'How much fuel did they have, Wes?'

'Plenty, a full tank. And Chips carries spare. He's not a fool. He knows what he's doing.'

'Does he?' said Jon unable to keep the worry out of his voice. 'You know he went down with a plane a few years back?'

'Yeah, he told me. Look, put the kettle on, it'll take your mind off things.'

Jon wandered onto the forecourt and looked out over the mulga in the direction they'd flown. Two hours – they could be anywhere in that time and the idiot hadn't left details of his intended route. Where the hell did they start to look if they didn't come home?

'I'm going down to The Grand, Wes, I'll see you later.' He didn't wait for a reply. As he walked down the main street he listened – nothing – except the drone of the ruddy flies in the unseasonal weather.

He glanced down the intersection to Scally's place and saw Joe playing in the garden. Damn Rachel and her bright idea! If she'd kept her mouth shut they'd all be safe. He chided himself, he mustn't think like that. They'd probably landed somewhere, put down on a road, maybe even landed at a station. Connie would hear on the evening schedule, and they'd all be laughing about it.

Alice was in The Grand with Ruby and Alistair, drinking tea.

'Are they back then?' she asked, concerned by the look on Jon's face.

He shook his head and looked at his watch – two and a half hours! What the hell did Chips think he was doing? Ruby crawled onto his lap and started sucking her thumb.

'She's missing her mother,' said Alice, 'and she could do with a nap, but she won't settle.'

'Scally and the others—'

'Went home,' interrupted Alice. 'The atmosphere was a bit tense. Rachel was miffed about missing out on the flight.'

'I shouldn't worry,' said Alistair, 'Chips is an experienced pilot, they'll be all right.'

Ruby started to cry.

'It's not all right though, is it?' Jon shushed Ruby and carried her over to the window. 'Something's wrong. I know it is.' He peered through the glass, looking over the roofline towards the landing strip as he cradled the fractious toddler in his arms, trying to comfort her.

'What are you looking at?' asked Alice.

'It's dark over to the east.'

Alice followed his sight line.

'Just a winter storm, it won't last, not at this time of year. It'll blow over before you know it; you know what they're like.'

On the evening schedule Connie reported the plane missing. Constable Nickson arrived two hours later to coordinate the search, while Anton Giggs from Pilkington offered to do an aerial search at first light and so did Dougie Phelps, the manager from Barwaddi Station. Every station owner and manager listening on the evening schedule offered to conduct a ground search of their land within two hundred and fifty miles of Charlestown, concentrating on the north-eastern quarter, or they offered to send men over to Charlestown to help the police.

Jon arranged for a message to be sent to Paul Vincent at Woomera and then, leaving Alice and Alistair at The Grand with Ruby, he prepared to return to Jindalee.

'Mind if I come with you?' said Greg, settling himself on the passenger seat as Jon struck up the ute.

Surprised, Jon said nothing puzzled by the anxiety on Greg's face.

'My radiator's sprung a leak; it'll never make it back to Jarrahlong.'

'No worries,' said Jon, slipping the ute into gear.

At Jindalee Jon gave George instructions to organise the stockmen and begin a search of the land to the north-east of the station, and then he headed for Jarrahlong while Greg sat silently beside him anxiously chewing his nails as they drove through the night.

At Jarrahlong, despite the hour, Jon hammered on Adie's door.

Adie appeared a few moments later, looking dishevelled. 'What's wrong, boss?'

'Chips's plane is missing we need to start a search at first light, warn the others will you? They'll need their swags, and we'll need the packhorses. Where's Belle?'

'Belle!' called Adie before he set off for the stockmen's quarters.

'Missus, all right?' asked Belle, rubbing sleep out of her eyes.

'Yes, she's fine. We think Chips has put his plane down some-

251

where. Val and Merle are with him. We have to leave early, Belle, I want tucker for the boys by four o'clock. And dig out some tinned meat, flour, and tea; we'll be gone a few days.'

By four all the stockmen were up and breakfasted, the packhorses ready and the horses saddled.

'What about the stock?' asked John Sandy.

'The stock go on hold till we find Chips and the others,' said Greg, finally pulling himself together.

'What if we don't find them?'

'We'll find them,' Greg looked at Jon, 'won't we?'

'Yeah,' agreed Jon, 'and let's just hope it's sooner rather than later.'

'I hope you're right, by God, I hope you're right,' said Greg as he mounted his horse. 'I'll string the scumbag up by his bootstraps when we catch up with him, causing all this worry.'

Jon stopped what he was doing and turned to look at Greg, expecting a sarcastic look on his face, but there was no sarcasm there, only fear.

Jon hid his astonishment. He'd never taken Greg for the caring type. Greg never put anyone first except himself, but now he was anxious to get on with the search, backing him up instead of being obstructive. The man never ceased to amaze him!

Chapter 29

Ten days passed and the search was scaled down, another twenty days passed and most people agreed further search was pointless. Alice and Alistair returned to Jarrahlong with Ruby. Rachel stayed at home and cried. Scally swore at everyone and everything, while Ty went back to his work, glad to get away from the atmosphere in town, and the day after that Paul Vincent returned to Woomera.

Numb from exhaustion, Jon set off back to Jindalee, refusing to believe they were dead. Chips had survived a plane crash once, he could have done so a second time. He was an experienced pilot. He could have put the plane down in the desert; it could just be damaged, unable to fly. Merle's medical training would stand them in good stead if any of them had been injured, and Val was capable. Besides, it wasn't as if it was midsummer, the temperatures were nowhere near as high in the winter months, although it could get pretty cold at night, below freezing out in the desert. No, it just didn't stack up, they were still out there, he knew they were, he didn't have that sick feeling in the pit of his stomach that he'd had when Curly died; he was damned if he was going to give up on them.

As soon as he arrived home he went to see Jimmi. 'How do I get in touch with Yildilla?'

'Dunno, haven't seen him in months.'

'It's important, Jimmi. Can you sing him up for me?'

'Might not work.'

'I know, but will you try?'

Jimmi nodded.

Jon patted him on the back. 'Good bloke.' He then went over to George's place and hammered on his door.

May answered.

'George in?'

She nodded and opened the door wider for him to pass into the kitchen where they were sitting.

'I'm off at first light, George; I want you to look after things for me. See Alice if there's a problem. And, May, will you make sure Jimmi and his folks get the tucker they need? They're still looking crook. I don't want them dying on me.'

'Where y'goin'?' asked George.

'Into the desert, I believe Chips saw something when they were up there and flew further than we think.'

'You sayin' they're still out there, that they're still alive?'

'Yeah.'

'How you travellin'?'

'Horse, and I'll take one on a lead-rope.'

Jon packed up his swag and filled saddlebags with food, slung water bags round the necks of the horses and secured more canvas containers of water to the packhorse. As soon as he was ready he rode out under a full moon heading for the edge of the station and the desert.

As Jon rode he thought of Yildilla, he tried to summons him, to communicate telepathically like Bindi did, but it just made his head ache. He didn't know whether he was doing the right thing taking the horses, they were a liability in the arid conditions that lay ahead even though it was winter, but he could travel faster by horse; he'd just have to pray that he could find enough water when his supplies ran out.

He headed for the range, towards Paradise Canyon, he didn't know why, but he had a gut feeling that that was where Chips would have been heading. As he rode he thought about the view from the air. He'd often imagined what the land looked like from above and knew that it must look impressive with the straight lines of the stock fencing criss-crossed by the tracks that geologists cut when searching for auriferous country, then there were the ranges, the plateaus, and the sand ridges that stretched mile on mile.

He shivered, some of those ridges were a hundred feet high and their parallel nature meant that he could pass within yards of a downed aircraft and miss it completely. Val, Chips and Merle could be there, desperate for assistance, and he could ride straight past them, unaware of their existence.

Bitter saliva flooded his mouth, he leaned forward and spat it out, he mustn't think that way, he must trust to his instincts, such as they were. He was older now, more experienced, he'd travelled this way six times already and on three of them he'd been accompanied by an expert on desert-living, but Curly was long dead and Bindi was miles away in Esperance.

Late morning he noticed the finches, dozens of them, clustering in the bushes, noisily arguing amongst themselves. Water, they were never far from water. He eased back in the saddle and watched, urging the horses forward, following the birds' erratic flight from bush to bush. And then he found it, hidden from view, a soak, and with shade trees. He dismounted and led the animals to the water and let them drink – plenty of grazing too, he noticed. Afterwards, he hobbled the horses and, when he was sure they wouldn't be able to wander far, he lit a fire and made himself tea. He squinted at the sun, high in the sky, beating down relentlessly even in July, it made sense to rest awhile, he hadn't slept for two days and it was increasingly difficult to keep awake. While he ate he watched the finches and the budgerigars that came to drink, and the euros that picked their way through the scrub to water.

Had the others found water? Or were they already dead? He banished the thought, they were alive...they had to be...for Ruby's sake. He knew what it was like to lose a mother and he'd been eight, old enough to cope, but Ruby wasn't.

He closed his eyes against the light, conscious of the red behind his lids, thinking of Curly and his ancestors living in the outback, anything to take his mind off the others. He wondered what the land had been like when the first white men explored it. Not that much different, he supposed, but what about the Aborigines, were they more numerous then than now? Would there have been larger families on the move, camping, living off the land, back burning the scrub to encourage the new growth necessary to bring in the animals they relied on for food, unlike the family he'd met in the bush over Menzies way, half starved, barely eking out a living in the bush?...

... 'Too right they would,' says Curly. 'In the old days plenty black-fella living here before them thieving whitefellas came.'

'I know, you told me before.'

''Bout how they chase my great-great-granddaddy up a tree?'

'Yes, how he fought back, hit them with sticks, stamped on their heads'.

Curly grins. 'You got a pretty good memory for a whitefella.' His

255

face darkens suddenly. 'Them fellas didn't like what they see –
dirty old fella, with scars on his chest and a bone through his nose
– they think he's stupid.'

He glances at Curly sitting next to him, his arms clasped around
his knees, his shock of dark, red-blond curls just as he remembered
them. He'd forgotten how pretty Curly was for a blackfella.

Curly turns to him and smiles showing his white teeth and the
gap between the front two.

'Used up a lot of water, they did, them and the fellas that came
after them with their sheep and their cattle, contaminating the
soaks. In the end not enough for us Abos, then came the big dry I
told you about. The people were starving and there was food at the
depots. Things never the same since. Not many of us live in the old
way now.'

Curly flops down next to him, looking up at the sky through the
gidgee tree they are lying beneath. He doesn't speak, just watches
the finches passing through the canopy, listening to the slight rus-
tling sound as the thin branches move beneath their weight.

Are Val, Chips and Merle in a shady place? Have they found a
soak? Has Curly's people found them and cared for them?

'No, mate, they still out there.'

'Where?'

Curly shrugs where he lies, looking up at the sky. 'Don't know;
reckon one of them is dead.'

'How do you know?'

'I don't know, I just know.'

'Which one?'

Curly rolls over onto one elbow and looks at him. 'I'm not a
bloody witch doctor, mate. Just got a feeling...you know?'

Instantly he has an image of a plane, a broken spar, its nose in
the dust, the propeller bent, he looks for Val and Merle and Chips,
frantic and sick with fear. No one!

Background! He concentrates. What sort of background can he
see...sand dunes...plateau...scrub? It'll give him a clue. But the
scene fades...

...Jon rolled onto his side, towards Curly, 'We've got to go east...'
But Curly wasn't there.

Jon sat up, his mouth dry as sandpaper and his eyes as gritty.
He'd slept, none of what he'd seen was real, or was it?

He made tea, ate some of the damper and meat from his saddlebag, watered the horses, refilled the water carriers and then set off east, across the sandhills, towards the stony plain. He hadn't seen any sandhills in the image, the terrain had been flat enough to land the plane and rough enough to break a spar.

All night he rode, and when he reached a ridge top he thought he saw fire, like Will o' the Wisp, or fireflies, winking in the distance. The light drew him on; it was in the right direction.

The next day brought thick cloud cover, increasing the humidity. Sweat poured off him and his shirt clung to his back as he headed in the direction of the stony plain and the ranges beyond. That night he left the sandhills under an oppressive sky. He hadn't found water, so he used what he had for the horses, conserving as much as he dared, and decided to rest up for a few hours. That night, wrapped in his blanket, he watched the sky flare with lightning. Sometimes the glow was like a white sheet low on the horizon and it reminded him of the night Ruby was born.

What would happen to Ruby if he didn't find Val? Jon pictured the child's solemn face and dark grey eyes, he recalled the way she'd slipped her tiny hand into his, how she had pressed herself against his chest when he'd swept her to safety even as she'd reached out to the venomous mulga snake. He shivered at the memory. Did he take her back to England, to her grandmother? – But he already knew the answer. He'd look after her himself. He'd adopt her. Val wouldn't want her back in England with her mother and sister – that would be the last thing she'd want.

'Don't think that way,' he said out loud. 'She's not dead, none of them are.' He pulled the blanket closer and closed his eyes.

In the morning he saw smoke rising to the north-east. Aborigines – probably out on walkabout. He hadn't planned to go in that direction, even so it was worth a detour to catch up with them. He could ask them to keep an eye out for the plane, for Val, Merle and Chips. They'd know where water was too. He didn't bother with breakfast; instead, he tracked down the hobbled horses, saddled up and set off in the direction of the smoke curling straight up in the still air.

The land was open scrub, nothing like the stony plain he'd seen briefly in his dream. He avoided the denser spinifex growth, and the low-growing spiny bushes, not wanting to damage the horses' legs, but even travelling fast it took all day to cover the distance.

By mid-afternoon the smoke was thinner, mere wisps, and he worried that the group had moved on. He kicked the horses on, desperate to make contact, but he was too late, by the time he arrived at the camp the fire was nothing but ashes.

He dismounted and lifted the water bag from off his horse and shook it. Not enough for two horses and himself, barely enough for himself even. Behind him a flock of top-knot pigeons flew out of the grasses, disturbed by the packhorse, Jon spun round at the muttering, whirring sound of their wingbeats. Water! The birds had been drinking. And there it was, not five yards away, hidden by the long grasses – a soak.

He didn't think of himself as a praying man but, even so, he said a quick Hail Mary and refilled all the water containers before allowing the horses to drink. Later he shot a couple of pigeons that came to water and that night he feasted on roast meat and fresh damper while the horses filled their bellies with the hay-like grass growing around the soak.

The sky had cleared during the day signalling a cold night; he collected plenty of wood and stacked it near to the fire, planning an early start. But shortly before midnight Curly had tapped him on the shoulder and woken him. *'Y'need to be on your way, mate,'* he'd heard him say. But when he looked there'd been no one there. Dreaming again! It must be anxiety disturbing his sleep, he thought as he rolled out of his blanket.

He set the billy on to boil and saw firelight this time, bobbing up and down in the far distance, as if from a fire-stick someone was swinging by their side. Was it the Aborigine family on the move again? He hesitated, it wasn't long past midnight. He didn't know what to do, whether to go back to sleep, or follow them. To follow them made sense, they were travelling eastward again, the way he wanted to go. Following them yesterday had brought him to water in a desert he didn't know, to travel on alone would be foolhardy, he couldn't afford the risk, not with people's lives at stake.

The horses were sleeping and didn't like being disturbed, it took longer to reload the packhorse and saddle the other one. Then, when everything was ready, he kicked sand onto the fire and, after checking that everything was safe, he set off after the fire-stick, swinging in the distance like a beacon. All night he rode, following the twinkling light, and in the morning a plain stretched before him, similar to the one he'd seen in the dream. He hesitated and then continued, unsure of the direction to take and then back came the smoke, the thin wisp spiralling upwards like a beacon again, away to the east.

He sat back in his saddle. Was he following a mirage, had he got it wrong? He wondered what Curly would have said.

Folla the smoke, he thought he heard Curly say, *folla the smoke.* Jon turned in his saddle, scanning the horizon and saw nothing but mile upon mile of stony plain and ahead, in the distance, a wisp of smoke, beckoning.

The next day he rode with only a short break to water the horses. He sat slumped in the saddle desperate for sleep, unable to rest for worry. Hour after long hour he journeyed onwards, crossing the plain, and then came a vast claypan. Did he go round or take a short cut?

He looked at the smoke, fading again, and decided to take the shorter route. The ground was heavy going, the horses' hooves sinking a few inches with each step and then, a third of the way across the pan, his horse floundered up to its knees in mud, its legs flailing, trying to find firm footing. He leapt off the horse and urged the animal round, leading it back the way they'd come. The packhorse panicked as it started to sink and Jon thought he'd have to jettison the load in order to save the animal. He yelled at the pair of them, pulling on the reins, dragging his own feet out of the sticky mud that was sucking them down. Back they floundered, yard by yard, the animals struggling against the sucking clay that threatened to exhaust them and claim them as its own.

In the end he had to leave them and return to firm ground for brushwood. There, he snapped off the leafier branches and, when he'd gathered as many as he could carry, he ran back to the horses, throwing the branches onto the sticky clay, praying it would be enough to give them extra purchase. His horse responded first, unencumbered by a heavy pack she struggled out of the mire, and Jon let her go while he did his best for the pack animal.

This time it was harder, the horse was tired, exhausted by the earlier struggles. In desperation he twisted its tail and shoved its rear end, yelling and hitting it with the brushwood until its fear of him was greater than its terror of the clay.

When he reached the bank he flopped on the ground, panting, sucking in great gulps of air while the horses just stood, their noses an inch from the ground, their laboured breath creating swirls in the dust. He lay looking up at the sky, cursing his stupidity: only a fool would have attempted to cross the pan with horses. Had he learned nothing? Eventually he looked over to the far side of the claypan, half a mile away, at the thin wisp of smoke. He wasn't going to reach the Aboriginal camp that night.

He lit a fire and let the horses rest up, giving them half of the precious water. He thought of the prospectors over Kalgoorlie way carrying condensers on their pack animals. Water shortage was a perennial problem in the outback. In the goldfields water had often been more valuable than gold until they laid the pipeline from Mundaring Weir to Kalgoorlie at the turn of the century.

He'd never used a condenser, but Stan had once shown him how they worked. It had been a long and laborious job, the boiler required constant attention, and as potable water trickled out from the cooling tray it had to be collected and stored. Stan reckoned he could only search for gold in his spare time when prospecting a dry stage, it was no wonder that he'd stayed put at Yaringa Creek where he didn't have to worry about the water supply.

At midnight he looked for the fire-stick again, and there it was, away in the distance. He couldn't make it out. It was almost as if the Aborigine family was waiting for him. He dismissed the idea – the heat and the loneliness were addling his brain – whoever carried the fire-stick had no interest in him. Was he wasting his time trying to catch up with them?

Nevertheless, he watched, mesmerised, as the fire-stick swung in an arc, back and forth, back and forth. Why would anyone do that in the middle of the night, it didn't make sense!

He tried to sleep and couldn't; when he was sleeping he was wasting the time he should have been searching. Finally, he rolled out of his blanket, loaded up the packhorse, saddled up the other and searched for the fire-stick – still there, and still swinging in a long, sweeping arc.

This time he circled the claypan, keeping to the hard ground, his eyes fixed on the winking light ahead that kept the same distance, always within sight. Was he a fool to follow the light? Was it only a Will-o'-the-Wisp?

The night was quiet, just the clop of the horses' hooves and the rattle of their tack as the moon dropped lower in the sky and the stars followed their nightly trajectory. It would be dawn soon; already the sky was brighter in the east, peach and turquoise – morning colours.

He looked for the fire, closer now and reined in the horses. The fire-bearer had stopped; he was standing at the top of a small hill some distance away, but the outline was familiar, thin legs, a wiry body, an old Aboriginal holding a staff in one hand and the fire-stick in the other.

Yildilla! It was Yildilla!

Jon stood up in his stirrups for a better view as the sun beaded the horizon beyond the raised ground where Yildilla stood. The katjita man was haloed in light. Lit from behind the Aboriginal's body seemed to shimmer until Jon realised his eyes were filmed with tears. What was the bastard up to? Why had he done this to him?

The old man bent down and laid the fire-stick on the ground, slowly he stood up to his full height and raised his staff, swinging it in a great arc, until his body appeared side on, as if he were looking over his shoulder. Then he turned back to Jon and with his free hand he saluted him.

The men looked at each other, neither moving as the morning blush faded, and then Yildilla spun on his heels and, following the ridge, walked away without looking back.

Jon sank onto his saddle shaken by what he had seen. His horse shifted its position, wanting to move on.

Why had Yildilla left the fire-stick? He didn't understand.

He slipped off the horse and ran up the slope to the ridge top. He followed its line, looking for the Aboriginal, but he'd gone, as he'd come, like a wraith.

Wispy smoke filled his nostrils and he sneezed. When he opened his eyes the plain below him was bathed in weak light, the low morning sun throwing long shadows across the flat expanse and there, not half a mile away, was the plane.

CHAPTER 30

The half mile ride across the rough ground took forever, Jon's heart was pounding in his chest and he couldn't see properly for the sun in his eyes. Four nights ago, in his dream, Curly had said one was dead, was he too late? Had the others died too?

His eyes ached from scanning the plain, looking for signs of life, but there was nothing, no movement, only the sun winking on glass.

He dismounted and tied the horses to the intact strut. He half circled the plane and it was then he found the grave, a shallow affair with rocks piled on top to keep out the dingoes.

Which one of them lay beneath him in the ground? He hoped it was Chips, but if it was then Val and Merle had been out in the desert alone. He shaded his eyes and scanned the horizon. Were they still alive? At least Val had plenty of common sense and Merle was a doctor, she'd know better than most what to do to survive extreme conditions, even if she wasn't used to the outback.

A short distance from the grave he found an arrow made of stones pointing north-west and a ragged trail, two people, one half carried if the marks were anything to go by, and other tracks, single ones, back to the plane and away again. One of them had returned, but for what? – Stuff from the plane? – He couldn't tell. He checked inside the aircraft and found it empty, so too the storage areas, any water that had been there had gone.

He unhitched the horses and remounted. They'd had water to start with so why had they left the plane? Surely they knew the rule – never leave the vehicle, it was always easier to spot than a human. It was clear that they'd stayed with the plane a while, the ground was well scuffed and stones had been cleared where they'd been sitting or sleeping in the shade, so how long was it before they'd given up hope and left? He studied the area again, they

262

hadn't lit a fire; in any case there was nothing to burn except the plane and its contents.

The aerial search hadn't found them, hadn't even come close. If they had seen a search plane they would have started a fire, there was still aviation fuel in the spare canister and there would have been matches in the emergency kit.

They'd been missing for over six weeks, if they hadn't been found by Aborigines they'd be dead. He kept his eyes fixed on the ground, trying to assess how old the tracks were, old, older than he'd initially thought. Dead then! It would be bodies he'd be taking back to Charlestown.

The tracks led across the stony desert to the sandstone ridge on the horizon. As he approached the raised ground the land changed to thin scrubby mulga bush – the acacia, and the mallee – the small eucalypts that grew almost everywhere in the outback, and there were animal tracks too, and now and again birds' tracks. There was food here. Had they been able to catch it? Was he wrong? Were they still alive?

The land narrowed between the ridges and he followed the route and the tracks. They had rested often, marks on the ground showed where a body had lain in the dust and feet had scuffed the sandy soil in the effort to lift the dead weight.

They must be close, they wouldn't have gone on and on – surely they would have stayed within sight of the aircraft. He stood up in the saddle, looking back to the plane. It was still there, a faint outline in the shimmering morning heat.

He sat back down and urged the horses forward, and it was then that he saw her, thin and ghost-like, a small goanna dangling from her hand. She didn't move or speak, and at first he thought he was dreaming, as when Curly appeared to him.

He eased himself out of the saddle, hardly daring to breathe, terrified that the image would vanish the minute he blinked. He held out his hand, saw her shoulders slump and then begin to shake, he saw tears slide down her cheeks and onto her breasts. He moved towards her. The urge to hold her close, to crush her to his chest was overwhelming. She was alive!

She fell into his arms, sobbing. 'I thought no one would come. I thought we'd been forgotten.'

She was thistledown in his arms. He stroked her hair. 'I knew I'd find you, Val. I just didn't know whether—'

'We'd still be alive!' She pulled away from him. 'How's Ruby?

Is she all right?'

'She's fine, she's with Alice.'

She looked at him then, keeping distance between them. 'I've kept her safe, Jon. She's all right, but she's injured.'

For a second or two he wondered who she meant. 'Merle?'

'Yes, she's back there.' She pointed behind her.

Val turned away from him, but not before he saw fresh tears in her eyes. She led him to a shelter she'd built of brushwood. 'It isn't much, but it's shade. She sleeps a lot. She'll be all right now you're here.' She squatted down and shook Merle's shoulder.

'Go away,' snapped Merle peevishly.

'Merle, Jon's here.'

Merle's eyes flashed open and she glared at Val balefully. 'Is this some sort of jo—'

'No, it's no joke. I told you he would come.'

Merle squinted against the morning light, shading her eyes.

He hunkered down so she could see him.

'You took your time!' She dragged herself into sitting position. 'I could have died in this God forsaken country…you never said you could freeze out here.'

The verbal lashing took him aback. 'I know, but everyone's been searching for you, we've had planes out and men on the ground for over a month, but we didn't know where to look, the outback's a big place.'

'Well, you're here now, I suppose. You'll need to organise a stretcher. I can't walk.'

How did he tell her there was only him? That getting her the medical treatment she needed would take time.

'What the hell is that?' said Merle, aghast at the goanna lying at Val's feet.

'Breakfast, Merle.'

'Rabbit I can tolerate, pigeon I can tolerate, but I'm not eating reptile, not now, not ever.'

'You've had it before.'

'When?'

'The stews I've made,' said Val in a tired voice. 'They're easier to catch in the mornin'.'

'I've got tucker in my saddlebag, Val. Have you any water?'

'Yes, there's a gnamma hole along the ridge…about quarter of a mile away. We wouldn't have made it otherwise; the water we had ran out pretty early on.'

'How did you find it?'

'I followed the birds, the little brown ones with black and white markings. Bindi told me they're never far from water.'

'Zebra finches.'

'That's the name,' she rubbed her forehead. 'Couldn't remember the name.'

She threw wood on the fire from a stockpile and waited for it to flare up. 'We haven't got a billycan, just an old tray and a pan I found in the plane, they make everything taste of aviation fuel though.'

'It's all right; I've got a billycan.' He went back to where he'd tied the horses, unpacked and carried the makings for breakfast back to the campfire, soon he had damper and a stew of tinned meat cooking, He made tea in his pannikin and handed it to Val. 'Here, drink this, you look as if you need it.'

'Is that tea, I can smell?' asked Merle.

'Yes, I'll make you some in a minute, just as soon as Val's finished hers.'

While the damper cooked Jon asked them what had happened.

'Chips was drunk,' said Merle flatly. 'We should never have gone up with him.'

Val finished the last of her tea and handed the pannikin back to Jon. 'Merle's right. He had a hip flask. It was enough to top him up.'

Jon glanced from Val to Merle and back to Val again while refilling the pannikin. 'Why didn't you tell him to turn back?'

'I did,' said Val, 'but then he saw a range of hills; he said he recognised them, that he wanted to check them out.'

'He was excited,' said Merle, 'he said there was a gold reef down there, that he'd spent years looking for it.'

'Then he wasn't sure.' Val smiled briefly. 'Then he was, so we looped round and he decided it was further along the range. He just wouldn't listen. I told him we'd get lost. And he told me not to be an idiot.'

Merle eased herself up on one elbow and accepted the tea Jon offered. 'And then we flew into the storm.'

'An electric storm,' added Val. 'We were hit by lightnin' and it blew out his instruments and we were being buffeted about. Chips was convinced they didn't happen in winter, but this one did.'

'I thought we were going to crash,' said Merle.

'So what happened to Chips?'

'The engine was coughin' and splutterin',' said Val. 'I don't know whether the lightnin' had damaged the engine or what, anyway, Chips said he'd got to put the plane down so we had to fly on until we could find a suitable landin' place.'

'And.'

'And he landed safely, 'cept the plane hit a big rock and one of the wheel struts broke.'

'I've never heard anyone swear like he swore,' finished Merle.

'Anyway, we were in the middle of an electric storm, thunder directly overhead, lightnin' forking down all around us and he decided to climb up to inspect the wing, he suspected that the spar was damaged.'

'He took a direct hit, died instantly,' said Merle. 'He wouldn't have felt a thing. Anyway, the plane's no good so how are you going to get us out of here?'

'We'll have to ride out.' He wasn't happy at the prospect, it was a long way and they'd need to take plenty of water, and neither of the horses was up to carrying two.

'How far is it?'

'Waratah Station is the closest, I think. Five days, maybe more.'

Merle stared at him in horror. 'You can't expect me to ride!' She indicated the splint on her leg. 'I've got a compound fracture. I could end up a cripple.'

'Looks like you'll have to go and get help,' murmured Val.

'But—'

'How long will it take travellin' alone?'

'I don't know, Val, three days I should think, if I don't stop.' Then he'd have to contact the flying doctor and allow for delays. 'I can get help back here in about four days, maybe five.' He looked at Val. She'd hardly eaten any of the food he'd prepared; he couldn't believe how thin she was. Had she been giving Merle the lion's share?

He started to unpack the last of his supplies, keeping just enough back to see him through, then he watered the animals and refilled the water bags. 'I'll take both horses, Val, it'll be quicker, but first I need to prepare an airstrip. And I want you to listen out; when you hear a plane light some aviation fuel, use that tray you've been cooking in, the smoke will give the pilot some idea of the wind direction and speed.'

'I'll give you a hand.'

'No, you're too weak.' He rounded on her. 'You're an idiot Val,

266

you should have eaten more.'

'Merle needed it,' she said flatly.

Jon shook his head. 'What about Ruby? She needs a mother.'

She flinched. 'The sooner we clear the airstrip the sooner the plane can land,' she said, a stubborn look on her face.

There was no point in wasting time arguing. Back on the plain he measured out an area he thought would do and started walking the route, picking up the bigger stones as he went and dumping them in a line along the edge of the designated landing strip. It was back-breaking work in the midday heat and he felt sick and dizzy from the effort. He looked across at Val, doggedly doing the same, and wondered how she drummed up the energy. He'd never come across a more mulish woman in his life.

They stuck at it without speaking until late afternoon, until he was sure it was safe to land a plane, and then they returned to camp.

After a bite to eat he saddled his horse. 'What about water?'

'We've got enough. Tomorra I can take the spare water bag to the gnamma hole, it'll be easier carryin' that. We'll be all right. I think it's permanent water.'

Merle started to cry.

Val patted her shoulder. 'A few days, that's all, in less than a week we'll be on our way to Charlestown.' She left Merle snivelling and walked with Jon and the horses to the edge of the escarpment.

He turned to her and took her by the shoulders. 'Promise me you'll eat.' When she didn't answer, he shook her. 'Promise! There's enough to last you ten days if you're careful and I'll be back in four so eat, damn it, otherwise Ruby won't have a mother,' he said savagely.

'I'll eat,' she promised, but there was no guarantee in her voice.

He mounted the horse and looked down into her gaunt face and smiled. 'Hang on in there, our kid.' He wanted to say more, but the bleak look on her face stopped him. Instead he slapped the horse on the rump and headed south-west for Waratah Station, three days ride away.

He rode hard and long and he had plenty of time for thinking. All his preconceived views had been turned upside down. It was Yildilla who had led him to them. Somehow the old Aborigine had known. He'd been there when Jon needed him most. Jon thought of the moment when Yildilla had raised his staff and swung it in a sweeping arc. They're here, he was saying, although he hadn't realised it at the time. And the salute – what had that meant? Was that an acknowledgement that his debt had been paid? That he had, in some way, atoned for killing Curly's totem animal?

Not once had they exchanged words, never had he heard Yildilla speak English, and yet he had a strange bond with the man that felt unbreakable.

And then there was the turmoil in his belly when he saw the plane, the grave, and the tracks across the desert – and Val. How had she learned outback lore? Was it Bindi who had taught her? There'd been no one else because he'd never bothered. To him she'd always been an irritation, his second thought, someone from his past who was forever a reminder of what he couldn't have.

And yet Val had saved Merle's life. She'd carried Merle across the plain, she'd found water and food and they'd survived, and they could have survived indefinitely if she'd eaten her fair share instead of putting Merle first...*I saved her for you.* What the hell did Val mean? How could she do that when she had a daughter to care for, a young child dependent on her?

And Merle! What about Merle, the woman he loved, who hated the outback with a passion? He recalled seeing her beautiful, sleeping face, saw Val kneeling at her side, waking her, telling her they were saved...then there was the petulance in Merle's voice. He brushed the thoughts aside. He didn't want to think about what he'd seen and heard, or the past, they were both safe and, provided he didn't do anything stupid, they'd be back with their loved ones soon enough.

At dawn, three days later, Jon rode into the yard at Waratah Station. The cook was up and about preparing breakfast and organising supplies for a month in the bush mustering the cattle. The cook gave him a coffee and went to fetch the manager, Bob Coates, and his missus, Delphine, who had run the station for eight years. And then there was time to kill until the listening watch when they could call the flying doctor on the station wireless set. It helped that the station had its own airstrip, a mile away, out in the bush.

Bob drove Jon out to the strip after arranging for one of his men to ride out to the stony plain with horses to bring him back to

Waratah while the plane flew Val and Merle direct to the base in Kalgoorlie and the hospital there.

Alice would have heard the news, everyone would, no one liked to miss the schedules, it was a way of keeping in touch and knowing when a neighbour needed help. Jon also knew that someone would contact Paul Vincent at Woomera to tell him his wife had been found alive. Paul would probably be in Kalgoorlie before he was back at Jindalee.

The De Havilland touched down at eleven o'clock and thirty minutes later they were refuelled and back in the air.

Flying over the arid scrubland reinforced Jon's respect for Val. Somehow she'd survived in semi-desert, territory that contained no stations between Waratah to the south-west and the pastoral lands in the Northern Territory. Below him he saw geological survey lines cutting through the desert, a reference grid created by surveyors looking for gold and other minerals for their mining companies – and he thanked God Val hadn't stumbled on one of them. Others who'd been lost had followed similar lines thinking they were roads – only to be led deeper into the desert and nowhere. As one old digger in the goldfields had once said to him: death is only a short step from anywhere in the outback. He shivered as he remembered the words.

'Pretty grim place to be stranded,' comment Mary Wood as they flew in a north-easterly direction. 'How on earth did you manage to find them?'

'Pure luck,' said Jon, not wanting to explain something that wouldn't be believed anyway.

'Three Brits, I believe.'

'What?'

'In the plane.'

'Yeah, I suppose so.' He hadn't thought about that, but they were.

'That's the trouble with Poms; they have no idea what the outback is like.'

'Chips should have known,' said Jon. 'He's been flying over the terrain for twelve years and more, looking for gold.'

They flew over the ranges and below him Jon saw the stony plain and Chips's aircraft stranded in the middle. Almost simultaneously he saw smoke, a billowing cloud of it caught by the breeze and dragged east, and the landing strip, clearly marked with a band of stones either side. He shook his head; Val had continued to extend the runway to ensure a safe landing.

'At least someone's cleared us a landing strip and there're no bulls,' said Mary.

'Yeah, Val's a stubborn woman.'

Mary looked briefly in his direction, puzzlement on her face.

Jon pulled himself back. 'You're right, there're no cattle this far out.'

She chuckled. 'Not that long ago we had to do an evacuation from a station and they had a landing strip right enough, good and flat, the manager said, and pretty. And he wasn't wrong, it was all pink and white everlastings, like a carpet, and there in the middle of it were half of the station bulls grazing on the flowers.'

'What did you do?'

'Glen had to do a few low passes over the strip to scare them off before we could land. I'm telling you it was a bit hairy at one point, one old bull was all set to charge us, anyway he lost his nerve at the last minute, thank goodness.'

Glen circled the landing strip and then pushed the nose down and soon they were on the ground, taxiing to a stop. At the last minute he swung the plane around ready for take-off.

Val met them, her face flushed from the effort of lighting the landing flare. 'It's nice to see everyone. Merle's this way.' She didn't wait just headed back towards the escarpment.

Jon turned to Mary. 'It's a good quarter of a mile, do you want to wait here while Glen and I fetch her?'

'No, all part of the service, it won't be the first time we've had a long walk.'

After a quick examination, Glen and Mary strapped Merle to a stretcher and then Jon and Glen carried her across the plain to the aircraft. Once Merle was secured Val climbed in unaided. To Jon's eye she was in a worse state than Merle, and he called to Mary to look after her even as the door was closing on him.

He stood back as the aircraft rolled forwards, smooth as a possum's pelt, over the stone-free ground for take-off. Soon the plane was a mere speck in the sky. He turned his back on it and returned to Val's campsite to wait for Bob Coates's stockman.

CHAPTER 31

Bob and Delphine Coates insisted Jon stay with them at Waratah for a couple of days to recover from his ordeal and then they loaded up his horses in a trailer and drove him home. That evening, when he got back to Jindalee, he spoke to Alice on the galah session when anyone who wanted to could have a natter after the important business was done. She sounded pleased to hear from him, but underlying her words was an edge, as if she was worried about something.

'Is Ruby, all right?' he asked, concerned that perhaps the little girl wasn't well.

'Yes, she's right as rain. And Val will be back from hospital soon.'

'Is Val okay?'

'Yes, but they're keeping her in for observation for a few days: apparently they need to build her up a bit.'

'She was very thin; she'd been looking after Merle and not herself.'

'Aye, that's Val for you.'

'So, there's nothing wrong over there?'

'No, anyway I'll see you soon enough, you'll be over before too long, won't you?'

'Yes,' said Jon, 'just as soon as the muster is over.' And that had been that! There was something worrying Alice, but she wasn't going to talk about it on the evening schedule, too many other ears listening.

It was a while before he was able to catch up on all the local news. Ken Southall came for the bulls and took them away to the fattening yards over near Perth, and then Scally turned up with the

271

monthly stores delivery and the post.

'Nice to see ya, Jon! Rachel told me to tell y'she's sorry.'

'For what?'

'For making Chips take Merle and Val on that flight. She feels bad about it, especially as Chips died, and all.'

'They didn't have to go.'

'I told her that, it doesn't make any difference though, she still feels responsible.'

They were taking a smoko, sitting on the verandah, looking out to the west, drinking Yang-dhow's coffee.

Scally rolled one of his cigarettes; he tamped the end on the back of his hand to firm the tobacco and then lit it. He drew on the noxious weed and exhaled slowly, squinting through the pungent smoke. 'Something else odd happened while y'were life savin'.'

'And what was that?'

'Cato did a bunk; word is he's been embezzling money.'

Jon shook his head. 'No, reckon you've got that all wrong, Cato likes his two-up but he's straight as they come.'

'Yeah, well, I would've said the same a few months back, but now I'm not so sure.'

'What makes you think that?'

'Well, Cato hasn't been seen or heard of for fifteen days now and last week a new fella arrived at the bank from head office in Perth. Word is he's been going through the books. Then there've been trips out to stations hereabouts. Alice had a visit from him.'

So that was why Alice sounded strained! Something had been going on at the bank. 'Are you saying Cato's done a runner with everyone's money?'

'Either that or he's gambled it away.'

Jon whistled long and low.

'Y'know how much time him and Chips were spending at the two-up, wouldn't be a bit surprised if he's got himself into debt and tried to gamble his way out of it. It wouldn't be the first time someone's done that.'

'What about Greg? He was always thick with Chips and Cato.'

Scally shook his head, 'Haven't heard anything about Greg. Far as I'm aware he's still at Jarrahlong. Alice didn't say anything when I was last over, but that doesn't mean anything, they don't come any closer than Alice when she's a mind.'

Jon sat staring into the outback with unseeing eyes. Had Alice lost a lot of money? She'd never let on how much she had stashed away in the bank, and he'd never asked – it was none of his business, but she wouldn't go under, he'd see that she didn't.

'And Val's back,' said Scally.

'How is she?'

'Thin. Connie's making her go over to The Grand for her tea, says she needs fattening up and she won't take no for an answer.'

'Can't see Val agreeing to that.'

'Aye, I'd have said the same but she is – no argument. I don't know what went on out there when that plane went down, but whatever it was, it's changed her. She's not the same woman; the life's gone right out of her, Connie says it's only Ruby keeping her going. And y'know what?'

'What?'

'I wouldn't be surprised if she upped sticks and went back to Liverpool, reckon that experience has finished her.'

After Scally left Jon couldn't settle. Val, leaving! Surely not!

Later the same day he went out boundary riding on the north side of the station with George and spent time checking the wells and bores in that area, but his mind wasn't on the job. He couldn't stop thinking about Scally's words. If Scally was right he'd never see Val or Ruby again! Chips's plane crash and the aftermath had changed everything.

So much had happened since Jimmi and his family turned up at Jarrahlong four months back. He'd met Merle again and all the old feelings, and some new, had been stirred up, disconcerting ones, ones that he didn't want to think about. And now there was this mess with Cato going missing, and Alice worried. His jaw tightened at the thought of the bank manager gambling away people's hard earned money. It was probably a good thing he'd done a runner.

'Do y'want me to finish this, boss?' asked George.

Jon looked up. 'Why?'

'Well, y're not exactly all here, are ya?' George grinned. 'Too many other things on y'mind.'

'That bad, eh?'

'Yeah, well, as I see it y'have to get your priorities sorted out. Maybe y'need to be someplace else.'

George was right; his mind wasn't on station business. 'In that case, I'll go back home. I could do with seeing Alice.' He swung his horse round, whistled Smoky and set off, leaving George to finish the boundary riding.

273

As he approached the homestead he saw Greg's ute parked in the yard. 'Now what?' muttered Jon. He didn't particularly want to see Greg and he certainly wasn't going to discuss his worries about Alice with him.

'About time,' snarled Greg. 'I was beginning to think I was going to have to doss down in the stockmen's quarters.'

'And to what do I owe the pleasure?' asked Jon as he dismounted from his horse.

'What do you think? – Business.'

Jon led his horse into the corral and unsaddled him.

Greg followed him into the barn and watched while he hung the saddle up on its peg. 'Alice is in trouble.'

'Oh?'

'Cato, he's been helping himself.'

'So I heard, but what's it to do with me?' asked Jon.

'We're putting Jindalee on the market.'

Jon turned to face him.

'It's the only way to save Jarrahlong, otherwise the bank will foreclose.'

'Alice sent you?'

'Not exactly.'

'What's that supposed to mean?'

Greg laughed. 'You don't need me to tell you that she's getting on, not as on-the-ball as she used to be. Someone's got to look out for her interests.'

'And that's you?'

Greg nodded, his eyes watchful, waiting for a reaction.

'And if I say no?'

'Then we'll force you to sell,' said Greg, unable to keep the contempt out of his voice, 'unless you can buy her out.'

Jon gave Greg a long, thoughtful look. 'I'm not doing anything, apart from going to Jarrahlong to see Alice.'

'I'm the boss now.'

'Is that what you think?'

Greg's fists clenched and without warning he took a swing, catching Jon a glancing blow to the temple. 'You're nothing but a bludger,' he rasped, his eyes wild with fury.

Jon didn't bother to reply, his fist was faster than Greg's had been and he caught him fair and square on the chin, snapping his head back and sending him sprawling into the dust. 'Get off my place, Greg. I don't want to see you on Jindalee land again.'

He didn't wait for a reply but strode over to the bungalow and slammed the fly screen door after him. When he came out again Greg had gone.

CHAPTER 32

Jon arrived at Jarrahlong mid-afternoon the next day. Greg's ute was in the yard and, apart from Alice and Alistair, no one else was about. He parked under the silver gum and crossed over to the verandah.

Alice smiled as he approached. 'Nice to see you, Jon. It's been a while.'

'How're you keeping, Alice?'

'Not too bad. I take it you've heard about Cato?'

'Yeah.'

'I never did take to the man, too much Vaseline in his hair for my liking,' said Alistair.

'Would you like a beer?' asked Alice.

'Thanks, Alice, do you two want one while I'm on my feet?'

Alice squinted at the sun. 'Why not, reckon it's about time for a sundowner.'

The three of them sat on the west side enjoying the late afternoon breeze and a beer.

'You sell many paintings in Perth, Alistair?'

Alistair nodded. 'A few, enough to keep me stocked up in canvas and oils.'

'Any chance of you painting one or two local scenes for me?'

'Be my pleasure. Large or small?'

Jon laughed. 'Large, I want one of Sandy Spit. And I'd like you to paint Jindalee homestead for me sometime.'

'Is that your reason for coming over?' asked Alice.

'Yeah, that and to offer you a loan to see you through a bad patch.'

'That's very generous of you, Jon, but I think things will work out without that. But what makes you think I need money?'

'Greg, he was over yesterday saying you wanted to sell your half of Jindalee, that the bank was about to foreclose on you.'

'Is that so?' He caught the frown and the pursed lips.

'Did Cato embezzle much of your money?'

'It could have been worse. At least he had the decency to take a bit from everyone. According to the auditor the bank will reimburse what he took.'

'Well, that's good news.'

'Yes, if that were all of it.' She batted away a mob of flies. 'Have you seen Val since she got back from hospital?'

'No, Scally says Connie's feeding her up, insists she goes to The Grand for her meals and she won't take no for an answer.'

'Have you heard from Merle?'

'No, why?'

'Just wondered.'

'Come on, Alice, what are you getting at?'

'Nothing.'

He'd seen that closed-mouthed look before; he stood more chance of getting a bilby out of a burrow.

'Will you stay over tonight?'

'Yes, if you want me to.'

'I do. There are one or two things that need straightening out, and I want you here when I do it.'

Greg arrived back about five, he barely acknowledged Jon as he collected a towel and disappeared over to the wash block where the stockmen cleaned up before the evening meal. Conversation at dinner ranged over the price of wool, the latest rates for prime beef cattle and the muster of Alice's Herefords that was due the following month. Over coffee Alice announced that Greg was returning to England.

Greg's face turned ashen. 'News to me, Alice! Why would I want to go back home?'

'Because I can't afford you any more.'

Greg slammed down his mug on the table and the coffee slopped over, splashing Alistair. 'What do you mean? I work bleeding hard.'

'This is why.' She tossed a thick manila envelope in his direction.

Greg stared at Alice's name and address hand-written in black ink.

'Aren't you going to open it, Greg?'

Greg didn't move.

'The reason Greg was at your place yesterday, Jon, telling you that the bank was about to foreclose on me was because of that,' she nodded towards the envelope. 'Are you going to tell him, Greg, or shall I?'

Pure hatred suffused Greg's face as he glared at Alice.

'He's borrowed money against Jarrahlong. And he got away with it because he and Cato were up to their necks in gambling debts and yet they still went ahead and bankrolled Chips's hunt for his mythical gold reef with other people's money. That's right, isn't it, Greg?'

'How much for?' demanded Jon.

Greg didn't answer.

'Let's say a substantial amount,' said Alice.

Greg scowled. 'It'll all be mine one day; in any case the stations are earning enough to pay it off.'

'Two maybe, but not one,' said Alice.

'What are you saying?'

'Jindalee belongs to Jon.'

Greg spun round. 'You're a bloody scoundrel, taking advantage of a defenceless old—'

'It never was mine,' interrupted Alice, holding up a restraining hand towards Jon who was half out of his seat.

Greg's face was ashen. 'But you said—'

'I know what I said, and I had my reasons.'

'But—'

'What are you going to do, Alice?' asked Jon.

'Nothing, except send him home with a flea in his ear. I can hardly have my own great-nephew arrested for fraud, can I?'

'I don't see why not,' said Alistair.

'You keep your nose out of it,' snarled Greg, 'and stop talking about me as if I wasn't here.'

Alistair ignored the fury on Greg's face and turned to Alice. 'Are you all right?'

'I will be, just as soon as this is sorted out.'

Greg lightened his voice. 'I'll pay you back, Alice, every last penny.'

'And how are you going to do that?'

'Work. I'll work hard for you, Alice. You know I will.'

'I did consider it, Greg, and then I decided no, I'm rather sick of your attitude.'

Greg's face turned ugly with rage. 'What attitude?'

'Your lack of respect,' said Alice. 'I don't like the way you speak to me and Alistair as if we are silly old duffers without a brain cell between us. You think you know everything. Well, you don't. I've forgotten more about sheep than you'll ever learn because, deep down, you're not interested. Anyway, I've already made up my mind, I want you on that train to Perth tomorrow. Jon will take you to Southern Cross; you can pick it up there.'

Greg sat staring at Alice as if she'd gone gaga in the space of five minutes. 'And how will you manage this place without me?' He started to laugh. 'You don't think Alistair is up to the job, do you? And if you think any of the blacks can run the place then you're more stupid than I thought.'

'Don't you worry about Jarrahlong, it was fine before you came and it'll be fine after you've gone.'

Greg's chair squealed across the wooden floor as he shoved it back with his whole weight on it. 'Stuff your bloody job, Alice. I'll soon find another, you just see if I don't.'

No one spoke as he slammed out of the room.

'That went well, Alice,' commented Alistair.

'That's only because you two are here, it might have become very unpleasant otherwise.' Alice sighed. 'Underneath he's basically decent, but there's a nasty, selfish streak there, spoilt by his mother, that's his problem.'

Jon sat back in his chair. It was a hell of a long drive to Southern Cross and the thought of having an irate, bitter passenger sitting beside him for hours appalled him, anything could happen. 'He's not going to want me driving him to the railway station, Alice. Can't you ask Scally?'

'No, I'd rather no one else knew about this business. Besides he'll be no trouble, I'll threaten him with a letter to his mother if he puts a foot out of line.'

Jon doubted that would make a difference. Greg had taken a swing at him before and he was even angrier now. There was no telling what Greg would do on the trip to Southern Cross. He decided there and then to put a heavy spanner under the driver's seat, just to be on the safe side. 'Do you think he'll go back to England?'

279

'Probably not, knowing Greg, he'll have got used to being free of his mother's apron strings and he's not going to want to tell them why I've kicked him out. If he's any sense he'll go north and get himself a job with one of the big outfits. You never know, it might be the making of him.'

'If he can keep out of the two-up ring,' murmured Alistair.

'How did you find out what he'd done, Alice?' asked Jon.

'The bank auditor: the bank held the deeds as surety against the loan and when Cato scarpered the auditor was called in and he went through everything, the loans, the overdrafts, the lot. Greg had forged my signature. I suppose he thought that once Chips located the gold reef he'd be able to pay off the loan and redeem the deeds. It seems Chips's big scheme dropped them all in it and Chips is the only one not facing the music, as they say.'

'What are you going to do about Jarrahlong?' asked Jon.

'Well, I can either employ a manager—'

'Can you afford it?'

'Not really, not with having to pay off the debt Greg has racked up...or you could manage Jarrahlong for me, alongside your own place.'

Jon thought about it. He'd got George; George had done a pretty good job of looking after Jindalee while he'd been away. If there was someone like George at Jarrahlong then maybe it was possible. 'That'd be difficult, Alice, but if you trained up someone to look after things this end, when I'm over at Jindalee, then it's a goer.'

'Adie's not interested, I've offered him the job before.'

'What about Dave Sandy, he's a hard worker, he doesn't go walkabout and he's bright enough.'

'What do you think, Alistair?'

'I think Jon's right, Dave Sandy's keen to do well and he stayed around even with Greg running the place.'

'If you both think he could do the job then that's good enough for me,' said Alice.

CHAPTER 33

Jon parked his ute outside Simpson's Store and went inside. After the bright sun he couldn't see much at first until his eyes became accustomed to the gloom. Val was sitting at the far counter doing the accounts while Ruby was playing at her feet, rounding up toy animals into tiny wooden corrals. As soon as Ruby saw him she jumped to her feet and held out her arms to him.

He leaned over, lifted her up, swung her round and lowered her to the ground.

'More, more, Jon-Jon,' squealed Ruby.

'Play with your toys, Ruby, Jon's busy,' said Val.

Ruby flung herself onto the floor and beamed up at him as if to say, *you'd rather play with me wouldn't you?*

Jon laughed. 'She's a handful, isn't she?'

Val smiled. 'She sure is,' she said, but the smile didn't reach her eyes. 'What are you doin' in town?'

'I'm on my way back from Southern Cross.'

She looked at him, a question on her lips.

'Putting Greg on the train to Perth.'

'Fancies the bright lights, does he?' she commented flatly.

'No, Alice thinks he should broaden his experience, get a job on a bigger station up north.'

'She's finally seen the light, then?'

'What do you mean, Val?'

'Greg, he's a nasty piece of work if you ask me. She's well shot of him.'

Jon grinned at her. 'He's not exactly overkeen on you. What did you do, give him the brush off?'

Val ignored the question and shut the ledgers.

'So, what can I do for you this afternoon? You lookin' for some

281

new khaki pants?'

'No, I called in to see you, to ask how you're doing. Word is that you're not yourself.'

'There's nothin' wrong with me, I'm fine.' She picked up the ledgers, carried them over to the storeroom and stowed them away.

Making conversation was hard going and he felt uncomfortable, not like he usually did when he was with her. Somewhere along the line the easy relationship had gone.

'Have you heard from Merle?' she asked.

'No, why should I?'

'Paul came over and stayed for a couple of weeks while she was in traction with that broken leg of hers.'

'How did she take to being a patient?'

'Not well, she didn't like being laid up for so long.'

'No, I don't suppose she did. Being laid up is pretty miserable, I can tell you.'

I know,' said Val. 'Merle was asking after you – from that Irish nursing sister.'

'Liz Lewis?'

'That's the one.'

'She's a nice woman, did she tell you she looked after my dogs?'

'Yes, and she said you'd make someone a good catch. She said you were a wealthy fella, and nice with it.'

'She did!'

'I told her she didn't know you as well as I did and that you were no great shakes, just an ordinary bloke with the usual obsessions.'

'What's that supposed to mean?'

'It means you're a bloke, just like any other bloke.'

'Thanks!'

'You're welcome. And for what it's worth, I think Merle's marriage is on the rocks. When Paul arrived there were more than a few terse words exchanged; she didn't seem to me to be as much in love as a newly-wed should be. I think that if you bide your time she'll be foot-loose and fancy-free before too long.'

He kept his face expressionless. He didn't intend to tell her about the letter he'd received from Merle written while she was in hospital. He already knew she was planning to leave Paul Vincent.

'She really liked Jindalee, did she tell you?'

'Not in so many words.'

'Well, she did, she couldn't stop talking about the place.'

'You're exaggerating.'

'Well, maybe...just a bit, but I don't think she would take much persuadin' to stay. If you play your cards right you can have everything, a cattle station, and the woman you've set your heart on.'

He watched her sharpen a pencil and then push a strand of hair behind her ear to stop it flopping over her face as she updated a stocklist.

'The trouble is, Val, life has a way of turning out differently to how you planned.'

'Tell me about it,' she said bitterly. She looked up and smiled. 'Now, how about a couple of new shirts, it'll help to keep me in business.'

'I thought the place was on the up?'

'I suppose you're right. I'll never make a fortune, not in Charlestown. I might have to think about movin' to Perth, or perhaps Kalgoorlie.'

He didn't know what to say, she was so prickly, he knew there was no point in telling her how his feelings had changed, she wouldn't believe him and he couldn't blame her, he'd been a bastard from the first, before he'd finally realised what a fool he'd been. 'You can't do that, Val, we'll all miss you.'

'Oh yeah!'

'Yes.' He looked at her with no smile on his lips. 'I'll miss you.' When she didn't reply he leaned forward and ruffled Ruby's curls. 'Are you going to shut up shop, Val? I'll shout you and Ruby your tea over in The Grand, you look as if you could do with a square meal inside you – you're still too thin.'

'I thought you liked slim women.'

'Yeah, but not skinny ones, and you're not eating enough.'

'Stomach shrunk out in the bush.'

'Yes, well, you need to get used to eating regular meals again; you've got Ruby to look after.' He hunkered down. 'Come on buggerlugs I'll shout you some squash.'

'I'm not a buggerlugs, I'm a Ruby.'

Jon grinned. 'I know, you're a little gem, just like your mam.'

Jon had plenty of time to think on the drive back to Jindalee. First there'd been the bombshell about Greg, then the vitriol he'd had to put up with on the drive to the railway station at Southern Cross. He'd been glad to see the back of Greg and all his baggage, and then in Charlestown there'd been the stilted conversation with Val.

There'd been none of the usual banter and fun. Scally was right about her – it was as if a light had gone out. He recalled what she'd been like the first time he'd seen her, after she'd arrived at Jarrah-long, the fashionable dress and the white suede shoes coated in red dust and her trying to clean them with a sweaty hand that only made them worse. He smiled at the memory. Then there was the way she organised hair cuts and manicures, encouraging Alice to take more care of herself. She'd been a live-wire in those days – he missed that about her.

He'd make more of an effort in future and try and cheer her up, jolt her out of the depression she'd fallen into. He supposed it wasn't surprising, thinking about it, it had taken him some time to get over his bad experiences in the outback. Val probably thought she was going to die out there in the desert, and it would have changed her, just as it had changed him, and she'd got Ruby to think about, at least he'd have been leaving no dependents behind.

Then there was Merle's letter. It was the last thing he'd expected. He hadn't recognised the envelope or the handwriting; it wasn't her favourite blue deckle paper, or the usual script. He supposed lying flat out with her leg in traction made writing difficult.

It was a strange letter, disjointed, and longer than she usually wrote. She'd written about Jindalee and the bungalow. She'd said how much she'd liked the homestead, how impressed she was with what he'd achieved, that she hadn't realised how well he'd done for himself in the goldfields. And she'd referred to the possibility of a job in the hospital, she'd said that Sister Lewis had mentioned a vacant post in the offing, and that she might apply for the position and stay in Australia for a while.

Jon frowned. That was odd in itself, he'd told her about the hospitals in Kalgoorlie and Merredin months ago, when he still thought she was his girl, and then she hadn't wanted to know. She'd written back mentioning the loneliness, the problems of making a new life in Australia, and of missing family and friends in Liverpool. So what had changed?

He was momentarily distracted when he caught a glimpse of a big boomer bounding away from the road, covering the ground at speed. The kangaroo stopped way over on the plain, watching him drive along the graded road with a plume of red dust following on like the tail of a comet. He smiled at the sight of the animal. Kangaroos were strange looking creatures if you stopped to think about it. There was a lot that was strange about Australia besides the animals – the vast landscape so unlike anything in England, the unique flora, and the people, real characters for the most part, people like Alice, Scally and Yildilla, people it wasn't always easy to like or get to know. Was it these aspects of the place that had put Merle off?

He pulled his thoughts back to her letter. She'd said she'd like to see him again, that she'd made a mistake in marrying Paul, and that divorce was on the cards. The letter had sort of petered out after that, just a mention of going back to England if things didn't work out in Australia.

What was she playing at? He thought of all the times he'd suggested she come for a visit to see for herself, that there were pluses to living in the outback, and every time she wouldn't entertain the idea. What was it Stan once said? – Life can be a bitch at times.

A month later, on a lovely September afternoon, Alice and Alistair drove over to Jindalee for dinner. Yang had had instructions to do a full beef roast with all the trimmings and a fruit pie for dessert and he was to serve it in the new dining room.

Alistair brought two large oil paintings with him, one of a picnic at Sandy Spit and the other of Jarrahlong showing the creek and the great jarrah trees which bounded the homestead. 'I hope you like them,' he said.

'*Jarrahlong* is a housewarming gift from me,' said Alice, 'I asked Alistair to do it for you to go with the one he's painting of Jindalee.'

Jon held the painting at arm's length. 'Thanks, both of you. I'll hang this in the dining room.'

'Dining room, eh! That sounds very grand for an outback station,' said Alice.

'You've got one.'

'True,' she agreed, 'but only since rebuilding Jarrahlong. Now what do you think of the *Sandy Spit* painting?'

Jon looked at it closely. Alistair had painted him in the foreground next to Val and Ruby; in the background was Alice, sitting in her rattan chair, a serene expression on her face as she watched them.

'What do you think?' asked Alice. 'It's a good likeness of us all, don't you agree?'

Embarrassed, he didn't know how to answer. It looked like a

family outing: the child gazing at him with laughter in her eyes, and Val looking radiant with the sun highlighting her blonde hair, while Alice was the dowager grandmother, sitting in her chair, surveying her domain.

'What about the others who were there?'

'Artistic licence,' said Alistair. 'Alice suggested that too many people would spoil it and I think she's right. If you don't like it I can always paint the scene again and Alice can have this one. She says it's my best to date.'

'Where are you going to hang it?' asked Alice. 'I think it should go above the fireplace in the sitting room.'

Jon studied the painting again. It was beautifully executed. They looked like the family he'd always wanted, but above the fireplace in the sitting room, where everyone could see it! What would Val say if she heard about it? She might not like the idea of a painting of her and Ruby hanging there.

He swallowed the lump in his throat. 'It's really lovely, thank you both. Now, how about a drink?'

'Whiskey for me,' said Alice.

'And I'll have the same,' said Alistair.

Jon poured them both a measure of Alice's favourite American bourbon whiskey, and one for himself, and carried them out to the verandah where they could catch the breeze. He handed Alice her glass. 'How's Bindi these days? Have you heard from her recently?'

'Had a letter just this last week. She's having a rare old time in Esperance. Seems she's taken to the job like a croc to water. And she's got herself a beau.'

Jon laughed at the old-fashioned term. 'A beau, eh? She told you that?'

'Not exactly,' said Alistair, 'she's mentioned him twice and you know Alice, she says she can tell these things.'

'You've missed your vocation, Alice.'

'And what's that?'

'Matchmaker.'

'Can't say I've had that much luck in the matchmaking department.'

'Will Bindi be home this holiday?'

'Don't think so, she's had an invitation to go to Albany.'

'The beau?'

Alice shook her head. 'A girlfriend, I think. How're Jimmi and his family getting on?'

'Better, the youngsters seem to be recovering fastest, they're running around the place with George's kids. Molly is still tired a lot of the time and Jimmi looks grey in the face, but they are improving.'

'The big problems will come later,' said Alistair. 'My friend says there are reports of the Japanese survivors developing cancers, and there have been a number of deformed and dead babies born.'

'Well, we'll just have to deal with that when or if it happens.'

'Are you going to keep them on?' asked Alice.

Jon nodded. 'I've told Jimmi they can stay as long as they like. And while you are here there's something else I'd like to run past you, Alistair. There'll soon be six youngsters on the station, Jimmi's three, George's two and one of the other stockmen's wives is expecting. They'll need educating, you know, reading, writing and arithmetic, any chance of you coming and living at Jindalee?'

'No, there isn't,' said Alice abruptly.

Alistair looked up at Alice's sharp tone.

'Sorry,' mumbled Alice. 'Only I'd miss you bumbling about, and the chess.'

'I don't bumble.'

'Yes you do, besides you like painting, don't you?' She didn't wait for a reply and turned to Jon. 'Advertise for a teacher, you can afford it.'

'I thought that now Bindi was off your hands—'

'What about Val?' interrupted Alistair. 'She could do it.'

Jon didn't speak for several minutes surprised by Alistair's suggestion. He looked out over the landscape watching the play of light as clouds scudded by on the warm breeze. He didn't want Val working for him, he wanted her as his wife – and in any case he knew Val well enough to know what she'd tell him to do with his damned job.

'She's got the shop,' said Jon finally. 'Besides, she wouldn't want to come out here.'

'It's ready, Misser Jon,' called Yang from the dining room.

Relieved, Jon held out his arm for Alice, led her into dinner and pulled out a chair for her to sit on.

'This looks very grand,' she said as she took in the mahogany table, crystal glasses, the china plates, the candlesticks and the damask napkins. 'You are coming up in the world. I didn't know

287

you knew about such things.'

'I'm a fast learner, Alice.'

'What did Merle think of all this?'

'She didn't see any of it; it only arrived last week.'

'Where did you get it from, Perth?'

'No, Liverpool.'

'Liverpool, indeed!' She helped herself to roast beef.

'I stopped by at Merle's brother's new place. Pretty swank, it was, with nice furnishings, fine furniture, paintings, you know the sort of thing, and it got me thinking. Then there were the dinners we had at the Adelphi, fine china, cut glass, napkins, nice cutlery, so, afterwards, I went along to George Henry Lee's and had a look around. Anyway, once this place was finished I placed an order and had them ship the lot out. The consignment arrived last week. I've also ordered some rattan furniture for the veranda from Singapore – that should be arriving any day.'

'You'll have the whole of Charlestown talking.'

'Doubt it, Alice, they're still reeling from the Chips and Cato scandal.'

'Well,' said Alice dryly, 'Merle will certainly be impressed when she sees all this.'

'What are you talking about, Alice?'

'According to Val, Merle's written to her and told her she's dumped what's-his-name.'

'Paul Vincent,' said Alistair.

'Aye, that's the one, seems she's invited herself to stay with Val.'

'News to me,' said Jon. 'It'll be a bit cramped for the three of them in that room of hers.'

'I still think Val could do a good job of teaching the children,' said Alistair. 'She's a clever girl. She writes beautifully and she's also excellent at figures. If I came over from time at time and gave her advice on what to teach, she'd soon get the hang of it – and she could educate Ruby as well. That little girl is as bright as the proverbial button, and she's not too young to learn either.'

'I don't think Jon wants to be thinking about that right at this minute,' said Alice, 'he's too many other things on his mind.'

'Like what, Alice?'

'Merle.'

CHAPTER 34

The fire flared as George threw on more wood. Jon caught hold of the camp oven just in time to stop it, and the billycan, tipping over.

'It's goin' to be a cold one,' said George, looking up at the first stars appearing in the evening sky.

'Yeah,' said Jon, 'it can be in spring, so have a care how you throw on that wood, otherwise we'll have empty bellies to see us through the night.'

George grinned. 'I will, mate, especially knowin' how much y'like your tucker.'

'What's that suppose to mean?' asked Jon. 'You saying I'm getting fat?'

'Nah, just well covered.'

Jon stood and hitched up his pants. George was having him on; it was a running joke between them. He'd come to the conclusion that George had a tapeworm he was that skinny; he was as thin as a lath, just like Yildilla. 'Pass your plate.'

George handed him the aluminium pan and waited while Jon doled out the stew he'd been cooking for the last half an hour, and accepted a hunk of damper. He settled himself down, sitting next to one of the boulders close to the fire. Soon all that could be heard was the crackle of flames consuming the wood and the sound of metal against metal as both men ate their evening meal.

George belched. 'Big do at the weekend then?'

Jon winced. 'Don't remind me.'

George grinned. 'Y'been railroaded into it?'

'Yeah, something like that.'

It was all Alice's fault. She'd decided he should have a house-warming and invite everyone over for a get-together. He'd resisted for as long as he could, and then he'd realised he was beaten when

Alistair told him he'd be better off giving in than turning a deaf ear, that Alice wasn't the sort to be put off. So a party it was to be; everyone in Charlestown had been invited. They'd slaughtered a prime bull, and butchered it, and Yang-dhow was under instructions to make sure there was enough food for everyone, for the guests and the Jindalee staff and any Jarrahlong stockmen who felt inclined to ride over. George had sorted out the old trestle tables from the shearing shed, charred from the fire but good enough if sheets were thrown over them, and for entertainment there was cricket. He'd ordered in a new set and cleared a suitable patch of ground behind the bungalow that could be viewed from the verandah for those who preferred to watch. The only problem was Merle.

'Which one y'goin' to marry?' asked George.

'What are you talking about?'

George looked sheepish, his skin darkening a shade. 'Just something one of the stockmen said.'

'And what was that?'

'That y've got two women interested in ya.'

Jon laughed. 'There was only the one, and she gave up a couple of years back.' He remembered the hard time he'd given Val when she'd first arrived at Jarrahlong, four hours in the saddle when she'd said she wanted to learn to ride. He'd been an unfeeling bastard then, when all he could think about was Merle.

He shifted his position and poured himself another pannikin of billy tea, remembering Merle and her last visit to Jindalee. He could see her now, standing over Jimmi's eldest child, listening to his chest with her stethoscope, and then she'd looped it round her neck, had turned back to him and had spoken as if Jimmi and his family weren't in the room. That was when the scales had finally dropped from his eyes, and that was when he realised what a fool he'd been hankering after a woman who didn't care about him or anything he held dear. And now she was back.

'You runnin' away?'

Jon looked at George, surprised. 'What do you mean?'

'Seems to me y're running away from somethin'.'

Jon laughed. 'I could say the same about you. Why did you up sticks and leave Queenland? You must have had a good job on a station over there.' He watched George's reaction and knew he'd got him. The stockman got to his feet and started to throw more wood onto the fire, and then he refilled his pannikin and wandered off a way, staring out into the bush. 'So what was it?' asked Jon loud enough for George to hear. 'You run off with another fella's wife?'

George turned back to the fire, his face catching the light from the dancing flames. 'Nah, nothin' like that.'

'So what did you do, kill a man or something?'

'Beat him senseless.'

'Another blackfella?'

'Nah, a whitefella.'

Neither of them spoke for a minute or two and Jon wasn't sure he wanted to know the details.

George crossed the ground between them and hunkered down, staring into the fire. 'He was messin' with May's sister.'

Jon wondered at the tension in George's face. It wasn't uncommon for white fellas to fancy Aboriginal women. Ty's father was living with Gracie and he knew of other blokes who lived with blacks, it was no big deal.

'She was only thirteen, still a kid, and a bit slow, you know what I mean?'

Jon did know, some men were brutes, particularly when it came to women. 'Where is she now?'

'We took her to the Aboriginal place, a Government reservation, left her with the family. Told them to keep her safe. We had to leave, the bastard called the police.'

'Who was he?'

'An agent. He was always at the station, lookin' at the cattle, full of himself, said he could have any woman he fancied, includin' the manager's wife. A nasty piece of work, he was. Don't reckon I was the first to take a swing at him.'

'Is that why you're here?'

'Yeah, that's why I'm here. What about you?'

'What about me?'

'What's wrong with this Liverpool place that makes you all want to live in Australia?'

Jon laughed. 'It seems that way, doesn't it?'

George nodded.

'I was sent out when I was a youngster. The British Government decided it needed to populate the Empire and it sent kids like me, who no one wanted, to places like Australia, Canada, New Zealand, and Rhodesia. I ended up in Australia, in an orphanage between here and Perth.'

'How old were you?'

'Eight.'

'Not much older than my lad.'

'That's right, and there were some on the boat as young as four or five. Imagine a government sending kiddies that age halfway around the world.'

He stared into the flames as the old hatred swept over him when he remembered the hardship and suffering that he and boys like him had been subjected to at Karundah. Young kids working in the quarry in the blistering heat to build an orphanage and O'Leary's bloody church. He thought of Freddie Fitzpatrick and the altar stone that had slipped off the trailer and crushed him to death, and of Freddie buried in the red earth half a world away from England and his family.

'You never wanted to go home to England?' asked George.

'Not to stay. I've been back twice since and there's nothing there for me, not any more, and besides, this is my home now.'

'What about the other two?'

Jon didn't need to ask who he was referring to. 'I thought I was going to marry one once, when I was still wet behind the ears.'

'The one with the kid?'

'No, the other one, the doctor, but she married someone else.'

'And what about the other one?'

'Well, I dare say she was looking for adventure and didn't find any in Liverpool.'

George grinned. 'Well, she sure found it here, didn't she, what with the plane crash, and all.'

'Yeah,' said Jon, 'and all.'

CHAPTER 35

Jimmi and Yang-dhow had been busy while Jon and George had been away boundary riding and checking the wells and bores. Yang had hung up Chinese lanterns along the verandahs and in the shade trees. Trestle tables had been set up ready, and chairs – enough for everyone – grouped around smaller tables. Jon hadn't realised they'd got so much furniture on the place, until he discovered that Yang had borrowed some from Connie. Scally had brought them out on his truck along with the beer and soft drinks he'd ordered.

'You're late,' said Alice. 'I was beginning to think you were never coming back.'

'You thought I'd gone walkabout did you?'

'Wouldn't put it past you. I thought there'd be no one here to greet your guests.'

'There's you, and Alistair.'

'It's not the same.'

'Jon-Jon,' yelled Ruby the minute she spotted him. She ran across the yard from where she'd been playing and flung herself at him.

'Don't see why not, Alice, you're the closest I've got to family.' He bent down, picked Ruby up, whirled her round on the spot until he felt slightly giddy and then he gently dropped her back on her feet, catching Alice's eye as he did so. He could see she was pleased but momentarily lost for words by the admission. 'Have I got time to wash up?'

'More, Jon-Jon, more,' squealed Ruby, her cheeks flushed with pleasure.

'Well, you can hardly greet your guests looking like that,' Alice said, taking hold of Ruby's hand. 'You come with me, Ruby, let's go and see what your mother is doing.'

Jon grinned and left Alice fussing over the details. When he rejoined them again half of Charlestown had arrived and were admiring the new bungalow.

'I see you don't hang around, Jon,' said Wes Chapman, taking in the wide verandahs, wrought iron and the fancy woodwork. 'I didn't know there was so much money in beef.'

'Beef! Not yet, but we're getting there, no, this lot just about cost me my life.'

'And how did you manage that?' laughed Merle, joining them. She laid an elegant hand on Jon's shoulder even as she spoke.

'Blew himself up down a stupid gold mine,' said Val tartly as they headed indoors.

'So that's where you made your money.' Merle looked around the dining room and through into the sitting room. 'It's beautifully furnished...lovely table.' She ran her hand over the polished mahogany surface and then crossed over to the fireplace and stood looking up at the oil painting. 'That's Jarrahlong, isn't it?'

'Yes, Alice gave it to me, Alistair painted it.'

Alice came and stood between them. 'It's lovely, isn't it? And there's an even nicer one. Where have you hung—'

'Shall we go outside and join the others?' said Jon, steering Merle out toward the French windows. He gave Alice a sharp look as he passed by and nodded towards Alistair to look after her.

'Oh, cricket, I do love cricket, Pete was always in the first team,' said Merle. 'Are you going to play, Jon?'

'Of course he is,' said Val. 'We all are.'

Merle ignored Val's comment. 'I'll watch from the verandah. It's too hot to be running about isn't it, Alice?' She settled herself in a chair and accepted the cold drink Rachel offered her.

The cricket continued at a leisurely pace in the spring sunshine. Scally, Wes, Rachel, Ty, and Connie on one team with Jon, Les, Val, Alistair and George on the other. Jindalee stockmen and their women watched the game with interest while their kids, together with Joe, Ruby and Amy, played cricket with a miniature set closer to the bungalow.

Ty turned out to be a good fast bowler and soon had all of Jon's side out for twenty-five runs. Once the opposing side reached thirty runs they decided to call it a day and eat.

Later in the afternoon Jon saw Merle heading towards him, smiling. 'It's a wonderful party, Jon; Pete and Daphne would have loved it.'

'You think so?'

'Humm,' she nodded. 'I didn't know that living out here could be so...so...'

'Civilised,' he supplied.

'Exactly.' She smiled again. 'Did you get my letter?'

'Yes.'

'You didn't reply.'

'You're a married woman, Merle. I didn't see the point.'

'I told you, we're getting divorced. Paul agrees: our marriage was a mistake.'

He couldn't look at her. He didn't know what to say.

'Do you remember that time when we walked in Sefton Park, around the lake, and the crocuses were out and we listened to the band?'

'And you said you preferred the yellow crocuses but the birds always ate them. – Of course I remember.'

'Do you think we could go back to how it was between us then and try again?'

'That was a long time ago, Merle. We've both changed a lot since those days.'

'I know but...' She leaned closer; he could feel her warm breath on his skin and smell her delicate perfume. Her green eyes held his, 'I didn't know what I wanted then,' her lips brushed his cheek, 'but I do now.'

'Jon-Jon!'

Ruby's voice pierced the air as she ran, full tilt, towards him.

He grabbed her under the arms and spun her round. 'Hello, Buggerlugs, what have you been doing?'

'I'm not Buggerlugs—'

'I'm Ruby,' mimicked Jon.

Ruby looked at him and chuckled. 'I'm Ruby, your name's Jon-Jon.'

'Not just a pretty face, are you?' Jon lowered her to the ground.

'And Mummy's pretty too.'

'Yes, she is,' said Merle stiffly. 'Now, off you go and play, Ruby.'

'See you later alligator,' called Ruby.

'In a while...' said Jon, leaving the ending free.

'Crocodile,' sang Ruby and off she ran to join the other children.

Merle flopped onto the nearest rattan chair and wafted the air with her hat to cool herself. 'She's always under your feet, isn't she? I don't know how Val puts up with it.' She patted the chair next to her. 'Why don't you join me?'

He sat not wanting to be rude and was pleased to see Alice heading in their direction.

'Lovely party, Jon.'

'Thanks, Alice.' He stood and offered his seat but she waved him to sit down again. 'We'll be leaving shortly.'

'So soon?'

'I'm not as young as I was and I need my beauty sleep.'

Jon laughed. 'You'll make old bones, Alice. I'll put money on it.'

Merle sighed. 'Have my chair, Alice, I need to go and powder my nose. Where's the bathroom, Jon?'

'Past the dining room, along the corridor, second door on the right.'

Alice watched her leave and sat down in the vacated chair. 'She's a good-looking woman.'

'Yes, she is, now what do you really want?'

'Exactly what I said. Alistair and I are leaving shortly. We've had a lovely time.' She smiled at Alistair who was talking to Wes Chapman. 'By the way, I'm going to make an honest man of him.'

'You're what?'

'We're getting married.'

'He's six years younger than you!'

'What's that got to do with it?'

Jon bit his lip, and grinned. 'Who else have you told?'

'No one, so don't go telling anyone just yet.'

'What did Alistair say when you asked him?'

'I haven't asked him yet. I'm waiting for the right moment. And I want you to come over a month from now, for a meal, when Bindi is back from Esperance. Will you do that?'

'Yes, I'll do that, Alice, and I won't say a word to anyone.'

'I'm inviting Val and Ruby and Ed and his family as well.'

'What are you two scheming about now?' asked Alistair, joining them. 'Planning on buying up another station?'

Alice smiled at him. 'No, no more stations, I'm looking to taking a bit more time off and maybe travel a bit. I fancy going to Esperance, I'd like to visit Bindi.'

'Have you been to Esperance before, Alice?' asked Jon.

'Once, with Jack.'

Jon stood back while Alistair offered Alice his arm and then he followed them out through the house to the utility truck.

'Remember, Jon,' said Alice, getting into the ute, 'not a word.'

Alistair struck up the engine and let it idle. 'What is she talking about, Jon?'

Alice chuckled. 'It's a surprise, Alistair. I'll tell you when we get home.'

Jon grinned as the ute pulled out of the yard. He wondered what Alistair would say when Alice popped the question. He returned to the bungalow, a smile on his face, and saw Merle stepping from his bedroom.

'Wrong room,' she said in a flustered voice. 'I was looking for the bathroom.'

'Second door on the right' he said, pointing along the corridor. He picked up a beer from the kitchen and made his way over to Scally, Al and Wes standing under the shade trees at the far end of the garden.

Al saw Jon first and stepped aside to make room for him. 'We were just talking about Cato, he's been arrested, have you heard? The bank took a dim view of his activities and they're pressing charges. Nickson reckons he'll do time in Fremantle jail.'

Wes took a slow sip of beer. 'Can't see Maurice Cato surviving jail, they'll eat him alive in there; they say it's a grim place.'

'If you ask me,' said Scally, 'it was Chips who was the baddie. The man was obsessed.'

Wes wiped his mouth with the back of his hand. 'That's what happens when a bloke gets gold fever.'

Scally considered Wes's comment. 'Do you reckon he found a reef, or was he mistaken?'

'What do you think, Jon?' asked Al.

'Maybe he did and maybe he didn't, I don't suppose we'll ever know the answer to that. The outback's a pretty big place and Chips had been looking for eleven years and more.'

'That's what I think,' said Scally. 'If he did find a reef it wasn't around here.'

'What are you lot talking about?' asked Val, joining them. 'You're all looking pretty intense about something.'

'Chips and Cato,' said Scally.

'Just add Greg and you've mentioned my three least favourite people.' She laughed. 'I should have had more sense than to go up in that wretched plane, the trip nearly killed me.'

'It did kill Chips,' said Wes.

'Serves the bugger right,' said Scally.

'We shouldn't speak ill of the dead, Scal.' Wes hitched up his britches. 'He had his faults, but there and again, we all do.'

'True,' agreed Val. 'Chips was always nice to Ruby.'

Scally frowned and nodded towards the bungalow, 'What's wrong with her, she lookin' a bit crook if you ask me?'

Val turned to see who he was talking about. Jon also turned and saw Merle approaching, her hand rubbing her brow. The smile she'd worn all afternoon had gone; her face looked strained and white.

'I'm not feeling well, Val. Do you mind if we leave early?'

'What's the matter?'

'I've got a migraine.'

'Why don't you lie down for a bit? Jon's got a couple of spare bedrooms. He won't mind you using one.'

Merle flapped her hand dismissing the suggestion. 'No, thanks, I'll be fine, I just need to rest; it usually goes after a few hours, but I would prefer to go back to Charlestown.' She glanced at each of them in turn suddenly aware of the atmosphere she had created. 'Sorry...I'm spoiling the party, aren't I?'

No one spoke for a moment or two, embarrassed by the conversation.

'It's still very early, Merle. Why don't I get you some aspirin?' offered Jon.

Merle didn't answer and massaged her brow.

Irritation briefly flickered over Val's face. 'I suppose we can leave now, if you think it's absolutely necessary.' When Merle ignored the query Val scanned the grounds and spotted Ruby playing with George's children. 'Ru...by!' she yelled, walking towards her daughter.

Jon followed her. 'What are you doing, Val? She's playing. Merle will be all right.'

Val spun round, her face tight. 'She's asked to go, Jon, she says she's not well.'

'She doesn't look that bad to me. How long has she had it?'

'I don't know; she seemed all right half an hour ago, then she went to the bathroom and suddenly developed a headache.' A fleeting smile crossed her face. 'What the hell have you got in your bathroom?'

He ignored the levity. 'Why can't she go and lie down somewhere quiet?'

Val stared at him, a questioning look in her eyes.

'Now what?' asked Jon.

'Nothing!'

'Yes there is, you've got that look on your face.'

'What look?'

'That look, and you know exactly what I mean. And what about Ruby, she's enjoying herself?'

'Tough,' said Val, 'she'll have to learn soon enough that she can't always have what she wants in life.'

'She's only a kid for God's sake. What the hell has got into you?'

Val sighed. 'Nothing, I'm just in a bad mood.'

'There's no need to take it out on Ruby.'

'I'm not.' She turned away from him. 'Are you ready, Merle? I'll get Ruby and I'll see you over by the ute.'

Merle rubbed her forehead, distractedly. 'I'm really sorry, Jon. I get migraines from time to time.'

'Don't worry about it.' He had difficulty keeping his voice civil. Didn't she know that social events were precious in the outback?

'Pass on my regards to Alice. Thank her for her hospitality.'

'Why, where are you going?'

'Back to England.'

'Oh!'

She stood at his side watching him. 'If you want me to stay, I will.' She waited and when he didn't reply she shrugged. 'I'm sorry things didn't work out, Jon.'

He didn't know what to say.

'I don't want to go,' screamed Ruby from over the far side of the makeshift cricket pitch. 'I won't,' she yelled, stamping her feet.

Val swept Ruby up in her arms and carried the screaming, struggling child over to them. 'Stop it, Ruby. We're going home and that's final. Say goodbye to Jon.'

'Noooo!' yelled the child, still struggling to get free. She spotted Jon and held out a hand, beseeching him to help her.

'Come on, Ruby, stop being difficult,' said Val.

'Stop it,' screamed Merle. 'You're making my head ache.'

Ruby stopped as if slapped and stuffed her fingers in her mouth, her wide eyes fixed on Merle.

'You'd better go, before she starts up again,' said Jon.

'We're just going,' snarled Val, her face rigid. 'You coming, Merle?' Val strode out to the yard, yanked open the passenger door of the ute and unceremoniously dumped Ruby on the front seat, leaving the door open for Merle while she walked round to the driver's side.

Merle and Jon followed, neither of them speaking. When Val gunned the engine into life Merle leaned against Jon and gave him a lingering kiss on the cheek. 'I've had a lovely time…'

Val scowled as Jon held the passenger door open.

'I'll write,' Merle promised. 'Bye, Jon.'

Jon saw Ruby's face pressed against the rear window as the ute pulled out of the yard, the backdraught creating a plume of dust that soon blocked his view of the receding truck.

CHAPTER 36

Jon chuckled to himself as he drove over to Jarrahlong, picturing Alistair's face as Alice asked for his hand in marriage. He wondered, not for the first time, what it was that Alistair had that Stan hadn't, and knew the answer, that there was no accounting for taste when it came to love – and, for Alice, Stan hadn't had the vital element, just as he hadn't had it for Merle. The trouble was he'd spent so long hankering after a woman who wasn't right for him that he hadn't seen the one in front of him who was. And now she was moving to Perth, Connie had told him; she'd said Val intended opening a dress shop and hoped to meet a nice fella prepared to take on a woman with an illegitimate child.

It was the reference to Ruby that had hurt him the most, that and Connie's terse comment that a pretty woman like Val was bound to be snapped up in quick-sticks. He didn't want Val to leave, and it wasn't just her he'd miss but Ruby as well. He'd come to love the child with her solemn little face and her piercing grey eyes, he didn't care that he wasn't her father; he couldn't bear the thought of someone else bringing her up, of not seeing her again, or her mother.

He patted his trouser pocket conscious of the small blue leather box digging into his thigh. Was Stan laughing at him, telling him it was about time he'd come to his senses? The problem was going to be convincing Val after all this time that it was her he truly loved and not Merle; that she wasn't second best, someone he wanted to marry on the rebound. He remembered the hollow feeling in the pit of his stomach when he thought he'd never see her again, when Chips's plane didn't return. Then there were his feelings on the interminable journey across the outback, not knowing what he was going to find. But it was when he saw her standing holding the goanna she'd caught for breakfast that he'd finally known the truth of it, that she was the one he wanted to spend the rest of his life with, that she was the woman he loved.

He rehearsed the words again; the words he was planning to say when he asked her to marry him. But would she listen? Would she believe him and give him a second chance?

When he pulled up in Jarrahlong yard he saw he was the last to arrive. He parked next to Val's ute and stepped out of his cab. He could hear music coming from the far side of the bungalow and guessed they were all sitting under the shade trees in Alice's garden. He hitched up his pants and stuffed the blue box deeper into his pocket. It wouldn't do to lose it now.

'Jon!'

He spun round at the familiar voice and saw Bindi running down the verandah steps towards him.

She flung her arms round him and kissed him. 'You've grown.'

He chuckled. 'You're imagining it.'

'No, I'm not, I'd say you're an inch taller and you've bulked out.'

'It's all the hard graft. How's Esperance?'

'Wonderful…and I've met a fella.'

'Alice said. I gather he's a doctor.'

'Yes, he's an Italian immigrant, and he's really nice, and he's all right about my mother being an Aboriginal.'

'What's your mother got to do with it?'

'My parentage, you galah!'

Jon was taken aback, he rarely thought of her as half-caste, besides, she was his friend, her colour didn't come into it. 'Why shouldn't he be? You're beautiful and intelligent, he's a lucky man.'

She blushed and grabbed his arm. 'You've seen Yildilla, haven't you?'

'How did you know that, telepathy?'

She laughed. 'No, not this time, Alice told me.'

Jon smiled. 'Yes, I saw the old fella, but we didn't speak. He turned up when I really needed some help, I'd never have found Val and Merle without him.'

'So, have you forgiven him?'

'For what?'

She indicated his leg.

Jon grinned. 'I'd be a bit of a bastard if I still held a grudge, wouldn't I?'

'No, I wouldn't say that. Anyway, come on, let's go and join the others, you've heard Alice's news?'

'About the forthcoming nuptials?'

'Is that what they call them in England?'

'What did the others say?'

'Scally said, "Good on yer, mate", and Rachel said...I can't remember what Rachel said exactly, she squealed, I remember that, and she jumped up and kissed Alice, and then Alistair. Val's offered to make Alice a wedding dress, and won't take no for an answer...and Alice said it'd be nice if Ruby and Amy were baptised at the same time, make it worth the minister's time. So I think that's what is going to happen. Come on, we're all waiting for you.' She took his hand and led the way. 'Look who I found loitering in the yard,' she called to everyone as they rounded the corner of the bungalow.

He saw Val standing in deep shade talking to Alice and Alistair and his heart lifted at the sight of her, but it was Ruby who looked his way first. She ran across to him, holding out her arms to be picked up. He bent down and swung her up and, holding her against his chest, crossed over to Alice, gave her a quick kiss on the cheek and then shook Alistair's hand. 'I gather congratulations are in order?'

'That's right,' beamed Alistair. 'Who would have thought a confirmed bachelor like me would be getting married, at my age!'

'Couldn't happen to a nicer bloke,' said Jon.

'I'm getting christened,' said Ruby. 'And Amy's getting christened.'

'So a little bird told me,' said Jon.

'What little bird?' asked Ruby.

Jon laughed. 'A little bird called Bindi.'

'Shall we sit down?' Alice indicated the trestle table laid for dinner. 'Jon, if you sit here next to me, and then Val, and then Alistair. Ed, would you like to sit on my left with Rachel next to you, and then Ty, and the children can sit at the end and enjoy each other's company.'

'I'll look after Joe,' volunteered Ruby.

Everyone laughed. 'She'd really taken a shine to him, hasn't she?' said Alistair.

'Pity Joe doesn't see it the same way,' said Ty drily.

'C'est la vie,' said Val.

'Is that French?' asked Jon.

'Indeed it is,' said Alistair.

'And what does it mean?'

'Such is life.'

'Really,' said Jon, glancing in Val's direction, but she ignored him as she passed a dish of potatoes across to Ty.

Later, after the plates had been cleared away and coffee served, Jon turned to Val. 'Are you avoiding me?'

'Whatever gave you that idea?'

'You've hardly spoken.'

'Nothin' to say.'

'That's not like us, Val, we've always got something to talk about.'

'Have we?'

He looked at her askance. He'd never seen her so off-hand before and was momentarily lost for words. He tried a different tack. 'Ruby says she's getting christened.'

'That's right.'

'Who have you chosen for godparents?'

'I haven't decided yet.'

'Well, if it's all right with you I'd like to be her godfather.'

She looked at him sharply. 'If you want to,' she said after a long moment.

'Would you rather I wasn't?'

'I didn't say that.'

'She needs someone to look out for her.'

'And I suppose you think you're ideally suited!'

He looked at her, saw the irritation on her face. It was all going wrong. He'd not intended to sound so condescending, hadn't wanted to imply she wasn't a good mother. 'I'm fond of her,' he added lamely. 'I'd like to be her godfather, if you'll have me.'

'I suppose you'll do,' she added sarcastically.

'One bloke's as good as another, is that what you mean?' He swallowed his annoyance. How did she do it? – wrong-footing him all the time.

'Somethin' like that,' she murmured.

'Flipping heck, Val! What's got into you today?'

'Nothing.'

'Talking to you is like skinning an old buck rabbit.'

'Well, you won't have to put up with me for much longer.'

'What do you mean, Val?'

'We're leaving.'

'So you've really made up your mind?'

She nodded.

'Connie said you're thinking of going to Perth.'

'Or Sydney.'

Her answer shocked him. Sydney was a continent away while Perth was practically down the road. 'You can't do that.'

'Why not? I haven't any ties here.'

He could feel the panic rising in his chest and didn't know what to say for the best, how to make her think again. 'Yes, you have, Val, you belong here.'

'Don't be daft,' she muttered. 'I'm a bloody Pom, no one gives a brass farthing whether I stay or not.'

'Alice and Alistair do,' he said in desperation.

'Perhaps, but it's not as if I'm a relative or anything.'

He didn't like the edge in her voice and knew he needed to choose his words carefully. 'You know they care about you...and what about Ruby?'

'What about her?'

'Well, just look at her.'

They both watched Ruby for a moment or two. She was sitting between Joe and Amy; the three of them were engrossed in a game that Alistair had given them to play with.

'She's going to miss everyone, particularly Alice and Alistair, and you know how fond they are of her...they're practically grandparents, for God's sake.'

'Yeah, well they're not, are they?' said Val tersely.

'And Rachel will miss you.'

Val turned to him, a scornful look on her face. 'It's not that long ago that you offered to buy me my ticket back to Liverpool, remember! I don't recall you pleading on their behalf then.'

He felt the colour rise in his cheeks as he recalled the earlier conversation, but things had changed. He couldn't let her go, not now.

'What about the shop?'

'What about it? Someone will run it; you never know Rachel might take it on.'

He leaned towards her, laying his hand on her arm and felt a frisson ripple over him, an overwhelming surge of emotion unlike any he'd experienced before, even when he thought he was in love with Merle.

She snatched her arm away, the colour fading from her cheeks.

She'd felt it too, he knew she had, the look on her face was confirmation enough and it gave him hope. 'What about me?' he asked.

'What about you, Jon?'

'I don't want you to go, Val. I'll miss you.' He saw the disdain on her face, and the disbelief. She didn't believe him! Panic surged through him. 'I'll miss Ruby and...and...you,' he took a deep breath, '...and...I...I...lov—'

She laughed harshly. 'I never thought you'd sink so low.'

Hurt by her reaction he snapped back at her. 'What's that supposed to mean?'

'You think the world revolves around you, don't you?'

'That's not fair.'

'Excuse me, will you.' Val picked up her cup of coffee in one hand and her chair in the other and carried them round to the other side of the table, to Rachel and Ty.

'What did you say to her?' asked Alice in his ear.

'I told her I didn't want her to go that I'd miss her, that I'd miss Ruby and that I—'

'That you loved her, and she didn't believe you, did she?'

'No.'

'Well, there's a surprise!'

'Why do—'

'Don't look so shocked,' said Alice, her tone scathing. 'You've mooned over Merle for years and then she turns up and practically throws herself at you.'

'She's married.'

'Yes, and getting a divorce. Val thinks that once Merle is free you'll be after her again, so why should she believe you when you say it's her you love, especially after what Merle said to her while they were stranded in the outback.'

'What are you talking about, Alice?'

'Merle and that poisonous tongue of hers.'

Jon felt the colour drain from his face. What on earth had Merle said? Then he recalled Val's words: I've saved her for you. 'What's Val said, Alice?'

'She wouldn't say anything at first, it took some getting out of her and I've still not heard the whole story, but it seems your lady

306

friend said some pretty nasty things to Val while they were together out in the bush.'

'Like what, Alice?' He remembered how flat Val had sounded and had put it down to exhaustion at the time.

'That you thought she was a joke, chasing after you all the way from England, throwing herself at your feet.'

'I've never thought that.'

'And Merle told her that no decent bloke in his right mind would consider marrying a woman with her background, her mother and sister being on the game and all, and her with an illegitimate child to boot.'

Jon's hands were fists as he struggled with his emotions. 'Val's got more sense than to believe that I'd think that way. Besides she's nothing like her mother and sister.'

'Yes, I agree, but then Merle told her that you two had...' Alice buttoned her lips and looked away.

'She told her what?'

'You know?'

'No, I don't know, Alice.' He frowned. What the hell could Merle have said that would have upset Val so?

Alice wouldn't look at him. 'What do you think? Use your imagination for God's sake.'

Jon felt himself flushing. 'She's a liar. We damn well haven't.'

Alice disregarded his embarrassment. 'And that all she's got to do is crook her little finger and you'll come running, and that's exactly what she intends doing apparently, just as soon as she's ditched what-his-name, so no wonder Val doesn't believe you.'

'Merle's going back to England. You know that.'

'Better men to choose from back home in Blighty, that it?' commented Alice sarcastically.

'No, she'd have stayed if I'd asked her, but I didn't. I don't love her, I don't even like her for God's sake, she's not the woman I thought she was, and she's not a patch on Val.'

'Well, I'm glad you've finally come to your senses on that score, but ask yourself, why should Val believe you love her after all she's seen and heard?'

'Because I do.' But he knew his words were inadequate, Val was more than justified in her wariness of his motives. If he'd been her he wouldn't have been as forgiving as he wanted her to be now that he'd finally come to his senses and seen what Stan had seen five years back.

'Then you'll have to find some way of convincing her, won't you?'

He laughed bitterly. 'And how the hell do I do that, Alice?'

'God knows, but you'd better come up with something fast because she's leaving straight after the wedding.'

'When's that?'

'A month's time, when the minister is next in town.'

He looked over towards Val who was chatting to Bindi. He thought of all the times she'd been there for him, particularly when Stan died. And there was the companionship, talking to her was so easy – or it had been until Merle appeared on the scene. They had so much in common, and more importantly, she loved the life in the outback as much as he did, he knew she did, it wasn't just his presence that had kept her in Charlestown. So how did he go about persuading her to stay?

CHAPTER 37

The problem niggled away over the next three weeks. Every weekend he went into town, but no matter what he did, or said, Val kept
her distance, always pleasant and polite and very guarded. He sank
another fence post into the ground and hammered the earth around
the base to secure it.

'What's got into ya?' asked George. 'Y're like a camel with a
sore head.'

'Know much about camels, do you?'

'Enough. So what is it?'

'Nothing.'

George ignored the terse reply and got on with the job.

Jon moved to the next post and picked up the auger. He should
have bought one to go on the back of the truck. Doing the job by
hand was flaming hard work and gave everyone who used the
damn thing blisters. He looked at his palms, raw they were and
starting to bleed. He savoured the pain; at least it took his mind off
Val. Two more weeks and she'd be gone and to date he'd made no
progress.

For the next three hours the two of them worked in silence for the
most part, only speaking the absolute minimum to each other. Jon
mulled over his problem, while George kept out of the way of his
sharp tongue. At midday Jon's mouth was parched and George
looked as if he was ready for a break. Without a word Jon threw
his tools in the back of the truck and went into the bush to collect
firewood. Soon the billy was boiling and tempers had improved
after a drink and a bite to eat.

'What's wrong?' asked George again.

'Woman trouble,' said Jon, unable to keep the terseness out of
his voice.

'That Merle woman?'

'No, that Val one.'

'Thank God for that,' said George.

'What's that supposed to mean?'

'That Merle woman's no good for out here.'

'But she's a doctor.'

'I don't care what she is; she ain't no good for the outback.'

'Yeah, I reckon you're right, pity it took me so long to see it.' He raised an eyebrow. 'I thought Abos didn't believe in God?'

'I'm a Christian. Me mother was converted by a missionary, got us all baptised, didn't she? She didn't like the idea of us all goin' to hell fire and damnation.' He grinned at Jon. 'Anyway what's that got to do with it?'

Jon nursed the last of his tea, staring vacantly out over the scrubby plain, at the mob browsing in the distance.

'That Val's a good un.'

'I know that,' said Jon, 'but I've buggered it all up.'

'Tell her y'love her, women like that.'

'I have done.'

'And it didn't work!'

Jon shook his head.

George tutted. 'She's pretty mad at y'then.' He sipped his tea, sharing Jon's view of the bush. 'Reckon y're goin' to have to come up with somethin' special.'

George wasn't wrong there but special was limited in the out-back. He'd tried everything he could think of.

'Tell her somethin' y'haven't told anyone else.'

'What the heck are you talking about?'

'What I say, tell her somethin', or maybe show her somethin' no one else knows about,' suggested George.

'Like what?'

'I don't know, do I?'

Jon finished his tea and tossed out the dregs, what sort of advice was that? 'Come on, let's get this ruddy fence finished.'

Two more days they were at it and by the end their hands were in shreds and they were bone weary.

'Camp out, boss?' suggested George, looking at the sky and see-ing the sun rapidly sinking in the west.

'Could do,' said Jon. There was no urgency to get back to the homestead, a good night's sleep and an early start wouldn't hurt.

That night, long after George had nodded off, Jon lay looking up at the stars, wondering what he could do about Val. When he finally fell asleep he was no closer to a solution.

Patchy cloud had rolled in during the night and the chilly morning air woke Jon early. He restored the fire with dry wood and set the billy on to boil. It was going to be one of those chequered December days, hot with cooler periods, depending on the shifting pattern of the clouds, and the landscape would mirror it like a patchwork quilt – all light and shade.

After breakfast they loaded up the truck and set off back to the homestead, chatting about the stock, planning the coming month's work. By ten o'clock they were on the ridge overlooking the homestead and there below them, sun winking on the windscreen, was Val's ute.

'Seems she couldn't live without you after all,' commented George.

Jon ignored him; he had as much chance of that happening as seeing a platypus at the green pool. Curious, he slipped the truck into gear and eased it down the incline, anxious to get home before she left.

They drove into the yard just as Val clattered down the verandah steps in her best high heels.

'I offer tea, but Missus in hurry,' called Yang who was hovering on the verandah with a worried look on his face.

Jon got out of the cab. 'Nice to see you, Val. Ruby with you?'

'No, I've left her with Alice. I only come over because Alistair wanted me to deliver a letter.' She half turned and indicated the kitchen behind her. 'It's on the table.'

'You'll stay for a cup of tea?'

'No, I'd better be goin'…Ruby—'

'I might need to write a reply, can't you wait until I've read the letter?' asked Jon.

Val hesitated, indecision on her face.

'Surely you can wait long enough for that, Val? Yang, tea please.'

'I'll go and catch up with May, she'll be chewin' my ear off otherwise,' said George tactfully, 'and I'll see to unloadin' the truck.'

'Thanks, George,' he walked up to Val and took her arm. 'We'll go through to the verandah at the back, it's pleasanter there.'

He didn't give her a chance to argue, he took her elbow and half steered her through the door into the kitchen, picked up Alistair's letter and then led the way through the sitting room to the verandah on the far side of the bungalow.

Val sat while Jon fetched a small table for the tea, then he joined her and opened Alistair's letter.

The crisp, white paper crackled as he unfolded the single sheet. Red dust from his fingers smudged the pristine paper. He ran his hands down his trousers and picked up the page again.

Dear Jon,

I'm sure you don't need me to remind you that Val leaves Charlestown immediately after the wedding. However, it is clear that if she leaves she will never return. I have had the devil's own job getting her to agree to deliver this letter so I suggest, most strongly, that you take this opportunity to speak to her as you may not get another chance.

I suggest you tell her that I've written to ask you to be best man at my wedding.

Alistair.

Val watched as he folded the single sheet of paper. 'What was so urgent that Alistair couldn't wait until the weddin' then?'

'He wants me to be his best man.' He held out the letter to her, praying she wouldn't take it, and breathed a sigh of relief when she waved it away.

'He's left it a bit late, hasn't he?'

'Just a bit.' He was pleased he hadn't mentioned the honour to her weeks ago when Alistair first asked him.

'And are you?'

'Yes, of course.'

'You'd better write a reply then and I'll deliver it for you.'

'Tea,' announced Yang-dhow as he put the tray on the side table.

'I'll write it in a minute,' said Jon.

Val picked up the teapot and poured. Jon looked at her slim hand grasping the handle, and watched as the dark liquid filled his cup and then hers.

'Val?'

'Yes.' She handed him his tea.

Jon winced; the tone was so clipped and cold. 'Will you spare me half a day?'

'For what?'

312

'There's something I want to show you.'

She frowned.

He hesitated. She'd accused him of being selfish and self-centred, he badly needed to get the wording right. 'There's a place, quite a ride from here, on the Jindalee-Jarrahlong boundary that I'd like you to see before you leave Charlestown.'

'I can't today. I have to get back. I've left Ruby with Alice and Alistair.'

'Please, Val.' He knew he was begging and he hoped he didn't sound as desperate as he was. 'Ruby will be fine and you know how much Alice enjoys having her to stay.'

'I don't know, I've got things planned, and...'

He picked up the indecision, the wary tone, and mentally crossed his fingers.

'How long will it take?'

'We can be back here by about four o'clock.'

She hesitated.

'Please, Val. It would mean a lot to me.'

She looked at him through narrowed eyes, as if weighing up the request, and he thought she was going to refuse. He fixed his eyes on hers and waited.

'I haven't any britches with me.'

'Is that a yes?'

'I suppose, so long as you've got a spare pair I can use, and an old pair of riding boots.'

'Good...I'll get Yang to make us a pack-up.'

'Pack-up?'

'Something to eat.'

While Val changed Jon saddled up Red and a horse for Val, strapped a billycan to the saddle and a couple of pannikins and collected the sandwiches that he'd asked Yang to make. He waited outside, pacing the yard, knowing just how much rested on the next few hours. Could he persuade Val to think again? Would she believe him when he told her that she was the one he loved, not brittle, shallow Merle? He heard the fly screen slap to, turned, and saw Val wearing strides that were too big and an old check shirt tucked into the belt she'd borrowed to hold up the trousers. She'd lost weight! His heart went out to her.

'Not very elegant,' she said when she saw him staring.

He badly wanted to tell her that, to him, she looked beautiful, instead he said, 'You'll do.'

'Thanks,' she said drily. 'It's nice to be appreciated. Is that my horse?'

'Indeed she is; she's the best mare on the station.'

'What's she called?'

'Belle.'

'Belle? Does Belle know she's got a horse named after her?'

'No, and don't you go telling her, otherwise she'll go spitting in my beer.'

'What on earth are you talking about?' Val asked, mounting the horse.

'When I first knew Belle I caught her spitting into Gerry Worrall's bottle of beer.'

'Who's Gerry Worrall?'

'Was, he was a nasty piece of work, he hated blacks, reckoned they should be shot like rabbits, and Belle overheard him. Anyway, he came to a sticky end and is buried down Old Faithful mine shaft at Yaringa Creek.'

'Stan's old place?'

'The one and the same.'

'Who dumped him down the shaft?'

He remembered George's advice. 'Stan and me.'

'Do the police know?'

'Yes, sort of, Stan wrote a letter just before he died confessing to killing Gerry and to dumping his body down Old Faithful.'

'Stan killed Gerry!'

'No, he didn't, an Aborigine killed him, tribal punishment for running over a couple of Aboriginals with his truck.'

'Did Yildilla do it?'

'I don't think so.' He looked at Val, surprise etched onto his face. 'Why do you think it was him?'

'Well, he was the one who speared you in the leg, that was tribal punishment, wasn't it?'

'How do you know about that?'

'Bindi told me. I got it out of her.' She laughed then, a deep chuckle. 'Took me all afternoon, and I suffered for it, I've never liked gardening since.'

He smiled, imagining Bindi and Val in Alice's vegetable patch, hoeing and weeding, it was a big patch and it would have taken some doing.

'Why did he spear you?'

'I'm not sure; it may have been because he blamed me for

314

Curly's death.'

'Curly was your friend, wasn't he?'

'Yes, and I killed his totem animal, a perentie, and after that things were never the same between us; and then Curly got bitten by a king brown, or maybe it was a mulga snake; anyway, he busted his leg falling over a cliff getting away from it. He died in agony and—'

'You've never forgiven yourself.'

'Something like that.' Talking about his feelings was hard, and even now the memory of those days still brought him out in a cold sweat, especially when a rogue memory caught him unawares.

Val reined her horse in, allowing him to lead the way through a gully.

He geed his horse on and then fell back in beside her when the route widened out again, his leg brushing hers when the horses briefly jostled together. A surge of emotion swept through him – the urge to lean across and kiss her and hold her close to him was stronger than ever. How could he have been so blind? And now he couldn't bear the thought of losing her. George was right. He had to open up to her. Somehow he had to convince her that she was the one he loved, not Merle.

'Or it could have been because Curly showed me a sacred place in Paradise Canyon.'

'What sort of sacred place?'

'A cave with paintings, Perentie Man, maps of the land where Perentie travelled in the Dreamtime and hand prints, lots of hand prints and...' Did he tell her about the gold?

He glanced at her. She was sitting on the mare as if she'd been in a saddle all her life, one hand lightly holding the reins, the other by her side, the hat she was wearing half shading her face. Suddenly she turned to him.

'And gold, there's gold in that canyon, isn't there?' Her blue eyes looked directly into his. 'You don't have to answer,' she said after too long a moment.

'Yes, Val, you're right, there's gold there, scads of it, more than in the Bank of England.'

She reined in her horse again. 'It's the gold Chips found, isn't it?'

He pulled up Red and nodded.

'So you found his plane?'

'Yes, and then we moved it...when we knew Chips was search-

315

ing in the ranges.'

'Who's we?'

'Bindi, Yildilla and me.'

'Yildilla!'

'Yes, Yildilla is Bindi's grandfather. Anyway, I've come to the conclusion he's finally forgiven me. It was Yildilla who led me to you after the crash.'

'When Merle and me were stranded in the stony desert?'

'Yes, I wouldn't have found you without his help.'

'I won't say anythin',' said Val simply.

He looked at her.

'About the gold,' she said, 'I won't say anythin'.'

'I know you won't, Val. I know you won't.'

The landscape changed as they travelled, the scrubby bush gave way to better country and they had to weave their way around thick acacia interspersed with desert kurrajong, the bright green leaves so different from the grey-green of the wattle and eucalypt. It was a pretty part of the station; in between stands of trees were expanses of grass, brown and hay-like in the spring but already greening over after the early summer rains.

'It's beautiful here,' Val commented.

'It's good grazing country.'

'I can see that. What's that small tree...over there?'

'Which one?'

'That one, the one with the long, spiky leaves and the pretty red flowers.'

Jon laughed. 'It's an emu tree.'

'A eucalypt?'

'No, I don't think so, and its leaves are nowhere near as spiky as a water bush; and those over there,' he pointed to a stand of eucalypts next to the emu tree, 'they're called snap and rattle because if you snap off a branch and shake it you can hear if termites have been at it from the rattle it makes.'

'Do you know the names of all the plants?'

'A lot, not all.'

When they reached the Jarrahlong boundary they crossed over onto Alice's land. Jon led the way to the bore with the windmill he'd first seen by moonlight when he was fifteen and Alice's sheep were dying in the drought. This time he dismounted near to the old eucalyptus tree and offered a hand to Val. They unsaddled the horses, watered them and, after hobbling them, set them to browse. While the billy boiled they sat back in the shade to eat their sandwiches.

'Is this a gum tree?' asked Val, looking up into the canopy of the biggest tree in the vicinity.

'Yeah, it's a coolabah according to Jeb.'

'Like in the song?'

'What song?'

'Waltzing Matilda.'

Jon grinned. 'I suppose. The thing is it's not local to this area, you find them in the north of the State.'

'Are you saying someone imported it, like they did with the kookaburras?'

'Yeah, except the kookaburras came from New South Wales, Victoria, that side of the country.'

'How do you know all this?'

'About what?'

'The coolabah.'

'Jeb told me about it after I bought Jindalee. By all accounts the previous owner, a bloke called Eli Jackson, was a bit of a botanist, he'd go travelling all over Western Australia in the 1880s looking for interesting plants and trees and every now and again he'd bring back a few saplings, plant them and then clear off again, leaving his manager to look after the place. Most of the saplings died but this was one that survived.'

'But I thought we were on Alice's land here.'

'We are.' Jon laughed. 'It seems Jackson didn't know where the Jindalee boundary was. Anyway, he found this spot and thought it would do for one of his saplings. And here it is. According to Jeb only a couple survived. The other's over on Jindalee, at Kangaroo Soak. He also said that it was Jackson who was responsible for planting Alice's jarrahs. They're not local to the area either; maybe he thought that was the ideal spot for them.'

'Is this it?' asked Val.

'Is this what?'

'What you wanted to show me, the coolabah tree.'

'No, we're going to have to leave the horses here and walk the last bit. Are you up for it?'

'I'm here, aren't I, hon?'

'It was like old times, she hadn't called him *hon* in a long while,

317

not since before Merle had been on the scene again. He made her tea, black, sweetened with sugar, and sat beside her, looking across the dried-up creek to the old windmill clanking lazily in the slight breeze.

'Val, there's something I—'

She jumped to her feet and held out a hand to pull him up. 'Come on then, show me this place. It'd better be good after bringin' me all this way.'

He bit his lip, she didn't want to listen. 'Come on then, I hope you're fit, it's quite a climb.'

'Who do you think you're talkin' to? I'm not a stupid blonde you know, I've gorra mind of my own. If I say I'm up for it, then I'm up for it.'

'You don't say, our kid, then folla me and shut yer gob.'

She laughed at the familiar turns of phrase and his Liverpool accent. 'You're losing it, ain't ya?'

'What?'

'Yer Liverpooowl accent,' she said, deliberately slipping back into broad dialect. 'It's all Aussie now.'

He didn't reply and set off at a fast pace. She reckoned she was up for it! He'd teach her! Then he remembered the last time he'd thought that, when she'd first arrived at Jarrahlong, a lifetime ago, when he'd taken her out on Daisy because she wanted to learn to ride. Hours she was in the saddle and she never once complained. Somehow, he knew she wouldn't complain now, no matter what he threw at her. He slowed down and turned to give her a helping hand over a rough patch of ground.

'Thanks, hon,' she said, breathing hard. Soon neither of them were talking – they were too busy concentrating on the ascent in the early summer heat. Jon calculated it was well over ninety degrees Fahrenheit and rising, with not even a hint of breeze to dry their sweat. What the hell was he thinking of bringing her out to the green pool on a day like this? But he knew the answer – he was desperate.

It took an hour to clamber over the quartz and sandstone outcrop – the strata layered like birthday cake – that formed the small ranges on this part of the station. Finally, they reached the top and Val turned back to face the way they'd come.

'It's a…nice…view, …hon,' she said, her words ragged as she fought for breath, 'but I'm not sure it was worth the…climb though…or the journey.' She swung round and pointed to the east.

318

'Is…Jarrahlong over…in that direction?'

'Yes,' he said, his breath equally ragged, 'but I didn't bring you up here to show you that.' He turned away from her and crossed the rugged ground to the other side of the ridge they were standing on. 'This is what I wanted you to see.'

She joined him and stood at his side, looking down into the small gorge, at the still pool of cool, green water that Curly had once shown him.

He heard her catch her breath as she took in the scene that had changed his view of the outback forever. The weeping gums still grew out of the rock and their delicate fronds still trailed in the water making beautiful grey-green patterns against the darker ground. Acacia was flowering and clouds of yellow enhanced the view, and the delicate fragrance of another blossom he couldn't identify scented the air. He took her hand and led the way, slowly this time, not the mad helter-skelter dash down the old trail that he and Curly had done. As they walked the heat from the rock warmed their faces, and the sun, high in the sky, created deep purple shadows under the overhangs. White corellas rested in the taller trees, and a flock of bronze-wings flew in for water, dipping their delicate beaks at the water's edge.

'How did you find this place?' she asked as they stepped onto the rocky outcrop above the pool.

'My friend, Curly, showed me.'

'I bet Alice loves this place.'

'You know, I'm not sure she knows about it.'

Val looked at him. 'She must do, it's on her land.'

Jon shook his head. 'I don't think so. She's never mentioned it even when we've talked about the beautiful places. It could be that she and Jack never had reason to come up here, and when you ride around the range it just looks like a thin backbone of rock, you'd never guess this little gorge was here.'

'Surely they'd see the birds flyin' in.'

'Not necessarily. From below, on the plain, it would look as if they were flying over the outcrop, so no, I'm sure she doesn't know about it. But Bindi does.'

'Did you bring her here?' asked Val.

He smiled. 'No, she already knew about the place, I was swimming here once and she saw me.'

'Why are you smilin'?'

'I was stark naked, floating on my back in the water, I reckon she

319

got an eyeful.'

'Is the water very cold?'

'Freezing.'

She grinned. 'Then I wouldn't worry about it, hon, maybe she didn't get as much of an eyeful as you imagine. Race you.'

Before he could think of a smart reply she was down to her underwear; he caught a glimpse of honey skin and heard a loud gasp as she dived into the water. When she surfaced she turned on her back and feathered the water, floating, shivering. 'Come on in, the water's lovely,' she said through chattering teeth.

'Liar,' he called. 'It freezes your balls off.'

'Good job I haven't got any then.'

He chuckled and stripped off down to his jocks and joined her. The water was every bit as cold as he remembered, and just as green. It took his breath away. He surfaced and shook the freezing water from his hair, spraying her in crystal droplets.

She slapped the water with her hand, sending a spray back, and laughed. She rolled onto her belly and began to swim, long powerful strokes to the edge and then slower, lazier ones back. 'It's too cold to stay in for long,' she said as she swam to the ledge and hauled herself out of the water.

While she sat, her arms around her knees, watching him, he circled the pool as he always did when he visited the place, his body getting used to the chill. And then he joined her on the rock, lying back as she was doing, shading his eyes with his arm, looking up at the sky.

'Cerulean,' she said.

And it was that lovely blue he'd come to associate with the outback, now dotted with fluffy clouds drifting high above them. After a while he sat up and switched his attention to the corellas in the eucalypts, dozing the afternoon away, and caught a glimpse of honeyeaters in among the flowering acacia.

'Look, Val, over there, in the wattle blossom.'

'Honeyeaters,' she said, propping herself up on an elbow.

He looked down at her. 'How did you know that?'

She sat up too. 'I borrowed Alistair's book on native birds, why?'

If he told her the truth she'd snap at him but the fact was she never ceased to amaze him. 'Just surprised.'

'Why, because I've learnt a few birds' names?' She picked up his old shirt and started to dress. 'We'd better be goin'. What time is it?'

He glanced at his watch and swore.

'What's the matter?'

'I forgot to take my watch off.'

She looked at his wristwatch, saw the foggy glass and giggled. She dressed first and stood with her back to him, taking in the beauty of the place, while he stripped off his wet clothes. 'I'm glad you brought me here, Jon.'

He buttoned his trousers and buckled his belt. 'Good, I'm glad you like it, it's my favourite place.'

She appraised him then, a strange look in her eyes that he couldn't read.

'Val—'

She turned away. Her erratic behaviour confused him, she'd been laughing a moment ago and now he didn't know what to think, or what to say any more. Maybe keeping it low key was best. 'Come on then, our kid, let's be getting back.'

He led the way and she followed as they took the path winding upwards to the top of the gorge.

She was avoiding him, she wasn't going to give him a chance; every time he attempted to broach the subject he most wanted to talk about she stopped him with a look, or lightened the conversation with jest. He felt the small blue box pressing against his thigh as they walked, single file, along the narrow route to the top.

They reached the summit and took a breather. 'Now will you stop and listen for a moment?'

'To what?' asked Val, refusing to look at him, bracing herself for the long walk ahead.

'Will you—'

'Lead the way? Certainly, hon,' she said, slipping round him and heading off down the rocks to where they'd left the horses.

He was losing her – he'd told her more about himself than anyone else, he'd brought her to a place that he'd shared with no other person since Curly; he'd already asked her more than once to stay in Charlestown, so had she guessed he wanted to marry her? Was she trying to spare him a rejection?

When they got back to the coolabah tree he lit a fire on the old ashes, put the billy on to boil and went looking for the horses. He found them grazing further along the creek on a patch of lush grass. He untied the hobbles and put on the bridles, and stood looking back towards the campfire, at Val staring into the flames. What was she thinking?

She stirred herself, looked in his direction and smiled. 'Tea's ready,' she called.

They drank their tea standing next to the horses already saddled ready for the ride back to Jindalee.

'How long will it take to get back to the station?'

'A couple of hours or so.'

'We'd better be going then.'

He doused the fire and gave her a leg up into the saddle. Then together, and alone, they rode off Jarrahlong and on to Jindalee land.

'How many acres have you leased, Jon?'

'About eight hundred thousand or thereabouts.'

'Alice says she's leavin' Jarrahlong to you. She says you'll look after the place, not like that mongrel, Greg.'

Val's news shocked him. Alice must have rewritten her will. He wondered what Greg's family would think when the time came, and then dismissed the thought, Alice had years in her, anything could happen. 'She called him a mongrel?'

'No, but he is. He never treated Alice right, Ed couldn't stand him.'

'That's nothing new; Scally couldn't stand me when I first arrived at Jarrahlong.'

'So what changed?'

'I don't know for sure.'

'He still half believes you're Joe's father.'

'Who told you that?'

'Wes. So who is Joe's father?'

A hot wave flushed through him. He pictured Ruby, the way she followed Joe about, remembered the comment Alistair made about the pair of them, and he'd not given it a thought because he'd been too preoccupied with her mother.

'It's okay, hon, you don't have to tell me, it's not my business anyway, it's Rachel's.'

He reined in his horse and she did too. 'There's something you need to know, Val. And you've got to believe me, I didn't even think about it until now.'

'What?'

He could hear the alarm in her voice.

'What, Jon?'

'Berry.'

'What about Berry?'

322

'He's Joe's father.'

She gasped. 'Are you sure?'

'Not a hundred percent, but as near as damn it. The only one who knows for definite is Rachel. Has she ever said anything to you?'

'No, apart from warnin' me about Berry, but then everyone did, I didn't think anythin' of it.'

Blast, thought Jon. Why hadn't Rachel said anything to Val? Had she buried it that deep? Well, someone was going to have to speak to her, himself or Val, it didn't matter who. He wondered, not for the first time, if Ty knew.

'I'm glad you've told me, Jon. Ruby's very fond of Joe, and you know what she's like, single-track mind, and, young as she is, she knows what she wants and she usually gets it. Perhaps it's a good thing we're leavin'.'

Val pulled her horse's head around, kicked it in the flanks and rode ahead. Jon followed. Everything was going wrong; the whole situation was a mess. Was Val thinking the same thing? He should have thought about it sooner, should have told her, and he should have talked to Rachel, people would need to know that Ruby and Joe were half-brother and sister.

They rode on for half an hour without talking, Jon taking the lead on his horse. After a time he turned in the saddle and looked at her, 'I suppose what I've just told you settles it? You're definitely leaving?'

'Yes.'

'Don't you think Ruby should grow up knowing her half-brother?'

'It'll be less complicated if we go.'

He couldn't argue with that, he could imagine the gossip once word was out, but that would pass, once everyone knew that would be the end of it. Val wasn't stupid, so what was it that had led to her decision to leave Charlestown?

'You know, Val, I'd have thought you'd have given up on this place within a few months of arriving here, but you didn't, so why have you decided to call it a day now?'

Val gee-uped her horse and drew alongside. 'What are you getting at?' she asked warily.

'Well, everyone says you've settled in like a native, and it's clear you like the outback—'

'Everyone?'

'Alice and Wes for starters, and Stan said the same, so if you like it out here, and you're settled, why are you leaving? No one wants you to go, especially me.'

He looked at her, at her blue eyes with golden flecks reflecting the highlights in her blonde hair. Why had he ever thought her ordinary? She was beautiful. Not in the way Merle was beautiful, but in her own way, in an English sort of way, like a pale pink rose with a dash of gold dust.

'Have you met someone you fancy recently, is that it?'

'What do you mean?'

'On one of your buying trips to Perth, have you met someone, another fella?'

'Yeah, one or two,' she said lightly, a slight blush creeping up her cheeks, 'but blokes in the rag trade aren't exactly my type.'

He realised then he had a chance. 'Only one or two?' He smiled. They were dancing around each other like a pair of courting weasels he'd once seen playing on a tussock on the banks of the Mersey, light years ago. 'So, you're in Australia for the duration?'

'You could say that,' she said, her words suddenly terse and clipped. 'Where's this goin', Jon? What are you getting at? Because if you think your constant dripping is going to drive me back to England then you're mistaken. Ruby and me, we're movin' on, makin' a fresh start whether you like it or not.'

'You can't be persuaded to change your mind?'

'What's the point, there's nothin' for me here.'

'You're wrong, you know. I've been trying to ask you something all day?'

She sighed. 'You want me to teach the Aboriginal kids, that it?'

Shocked, he sat back in his saddle. 'Whatever gave you that idea?'

'Alistair said you're lookin' to employ a teacher.'

So that was why she'd been avoiding him! She couldn't see, or wouldn't believe, that his feelings had changed. 'No, I wasn't going to ask you to do that.'

'Well, go on then, spit it out. It'd better be good.'

The irritation in her tone disconcerted him. He chewed his lip; he couldn't afford to get the next words wrong. He pulled Red round and reined in next to her, slipped off his horse and stood next to her, looking up into her face. 'I...I...was going to say...I was going to ask...' He took a deep breath. 'Do you reckon you and me...do you reckon we could make a go of it, Val?'

'Make a go of what?' asked Val suspiciously.

Jon held his horse steady and took out the small, blue leather box he'd been carrying with him all day. He flipped the lid. Three diamonds caught the Australian sun, glints of cerulean and vermilion sparkled, capturing the outback colours deep in the heart of the stones. 'Well, hon,' he said in broad Liverpudlian, keeping his voice light, afraid she'd reject him, 'will you marry us?'

'I thought you wanted to marry Merle?'

He'd lost her. She'd never accept. Could he blame her? 'I did...once...when I was still a kid,' he said, no banter in his voice. 'But not any more, Val. Not any more.'

She sat on her horse looking down at him. 'When did you buy the ring?'

'I didn't, Val. Stan gave it to me just before he died. He said it was for you...for when I married you.'

'You mean Merle.'

'No, that's what I said to him at the time and he said, no, it was for you. He could see what I couldn't.'

'I always liked Stan, he was a nice fella.' Val's voice was barely louder than a whisper.

'Yes, so did I; he was one of the best friends I've ever had.'

'What was Stan doing with a diamond ring like that?'

'He bought it for Alice, after Jack died, but she wouldn't have him.' He held the box steady. 'Marry me, Val.'

Val leaned forward in the saddle, her index finger ready to caress the stones.

He snapped the box shut.

Val jerked back and laughed.

He smiled at her. 'You've got to say yes first, Val,' He took her hand in his. 'Will you marry me?' He could hear the strain in his voice and knew he sounded desperate.

'Well...let me see,' her eyes sparkled mischievously. 'What have you got to offer a girl like me besides a diamond ring?'

'A cattle station, hard graft, an equal partnership, like Alice and Jack had, an old clapped-out gold mine that isn't as clapped out as everyone thinks...and me. What more could a girl want?' he said lightly, terrified she'd reject him. He watched her take in his words, and saw a smile playing on her lips, and added, 'What say us Liverpool Poms beat these Aussies at their own game and raise prime beef?'

'You really want to marry me?'

'Yes, more than anything, Val, and I want to be Ruby's father.'

He held her hand tighter and when she didn't pull away he eased her out of the saddle, held her in his arms and looked down at her beautiful face. 'Say yes, Val.' When she didn't say no he kissed her on the lips and felt her surrender, kissing him back. She seemed to melt against him and fire flared in his belly, suffusing his body with desire as he held her close. 'I love you,' he murmured after long moments.

'I love you too,' she whispered.

'Will you marry me?'

She smiled at him and nodded.

Overwhelmed, he crushed her to him, hardly daring to believe she was his, and then he took the diamond ring and slipped it on her finger.

She leaned against him and held her hand at arm's length, admiring the sparkling ring. 'It fits perfectly.'

'That's Alice for you, she told me the size.'

'Does she know the ring was bought for her?'

'Yes.'

'What did she say?'

'She said it was about time I got things right for a change and that it couldn't go to a person better suited to me or the outback.'

'That's nice,' she said, looking at the diamonds. 'You know, it's a very beautiful ring.'

'Not as beautiful as the woman wearing it,' he said and kissed her again. Then he let her go and they set off for Jindalee, riding in companionable silence. Suddenly Val pulled up her horse and turned to him. 'Tell me...what happened back there the other week?'

'Back where?'

'Jindalee, at the party. Why did Merle leave in such a hurry?'

'She saw a painting.'

'What painting?'

'One Alistair painted for me.'

Val looked at him quizzically. 'And that made her decide to leave?'

Jon smiled. 'I think so.'

'Do you mean the one Alice and Alistair gave you of Jarrahlong?'

'No, another one.'

She frowned. 'What other one?'

'The one in my bedroom.'

She looked at him for a long moment. 'It must be some painting!'

They rode on a few more yards and then Val leaned over and caught hold of Red's bridle. 'What was Merle doin' in your bedroom, hon?'

He smiled at the suspicious tone in her voice. 'She must have taken a wrong turning.'

'She didn't like it then, the painting?'

'I don't think she did,' said Jon, 'but I think you will. Come on, let's get you back to Jarrahlong, or Alice and Alistair will be wondering where you've got to.'

She let go of his horse and together they made their way back to the station. On the horizon the sun was a huge vermilion orb in a darkening sky, while around them the grey-green bush had deepened to purple in the dying light.

'It's beautiful, this place,' said Jon, 'particularly the sunsets. We've got it right, living out here, haven't we?'

Val smiled at him. 'Looking at that,' she said, indicating the vibrant, changing colours in the evening sky, 'do you doubt it?'

'No,' he said, 'how could I?'

* * * * *

The Kookaburra Bird, published December 2011.

The Kookaburra Bird.

S. E. Jenkins

In 1946 Jon Cadwallader escapes from a Western Australian or-phanage following a traumatic death. He returns to England to find the little sister he left behind in Liverpool, but much has changed and an unexpected setback ultimately affects his life in ways he does not foresee. He returns to Australia without his sister, but his new beginning is complicated and riven by lies, deception and death. Then, when he least expects it, a stroke of good fortune pro-vides him with an opportunity that has the power to transform his life forever and confirms in him a growing conviction: Australia belongs to him as much as he belongs to Australia.

* * *

Lightning Source UK Ltd.
Milton Keynes UK
UKOW052043250113

205358UK00001B/1/P